D1795747

Published 2007 by arima publishing

www.arimapublishing.com

ISBN: 978 1 84549 189 5

Printed and bound in the United Kingdom

Typeset in Garamond 10.5/14

Swirl is an imprint of arima publishing.

arima publishing
ASK House, Northgate Avenue
Bury St Edmunds, Suffolk IP32 6BB
t: (+44) 01284 700321

www.arimapublishing.com

Author's Profile

Roy Thorogood – writing as Roy Sterling.

Roy Thorogood was born in London during the mid 1930's, and began his education at Davies Lane School, Leytonstone, located at the end road where Roy lived. On passing a scholarship he continued his education at the Sir George Monoux Grammar School in Walthamstow. On leaving school he pursued a long career in Outdoor Advertising. At the tender age of 12, he learned to ride his Father's Motorcycle, and that started his keen interest in all forms of Motor Sport.

From 1952 to 1954 he was called up for National Service in the R.A.O.C. Following this his career in world of Commercial Advertising continued for almost 40 years.

His other interests are Jazz Music, Photography and Travel. In 1973 he married Ann, a widow with two lovely sons, Adrian and Simon. In 1977, their third son Justin was born. In 1985 Roy had the chance to work in Cyprus, so with his wife Ann and young son Justin they emigrated. It was here in 1989, with his interest in Motor Sport, Modern History and Spying, that he was inspired to write what are now three books under the collective title of *"Driven to the Limit"*.

These three novels are Roy's first published work.

Roy says: "We all feel *Driven to the Limit* at times, hence the title of my books."

Roy and Ann retired to Spain's Costa Blanca in April 2001 and lived in Calpe until October 2006. It was then they decided to return to England and live in Essex to be closer to their children and grandchildren. Their three sons all have high-powered careers in the U.K.

Before this book entered its final form Roy's computer skills had to be honed-up under Justin's watchful eye. Now when Roy asks his advice on a computer problem Justin says: "Read the Handbook."

Chapter 1

For Alain Clement it all began in that hot July of 1894. Young Alain was enjoying his summer holiday from school; he lived with his parents Pierre and Marie on a small farm just outside Rouen. That year, the Family Business of Coach Building had been very good indeed. Alain's great grandfather had started the business, building up a dazzling array of Clients from the local landed gentry, and Pierre's father, Auguste, had expanded this Client base.

However, Auguste Clement had died because of injuries he had received in a fall from a horse during a foxhunt. Pierre continued to carry on the high standard of work, which had established the Clements as the finest Coachbuilders in the Rouen district. Pierre had met his future wife Marie, at a local village country fair. He had fallen for her stunning beauty, and her wonderful temperament. She had long blonde hair and a figure that would have made her a fashion model. They fell in love and married within a year. Alain was an only child; his father always thought that he would carry on the Family Business. Alain was interested in anything mechanical. One day he asked his father if he could have a bicycle. Pierre told him that if his School Reports were good enough, he would take him into Rouen and buy him a bicycle. The day that his school report arrived, Alain could not wait to find out if he had got good enough marks to qualify for his prize. Pierre opened the envelope slowly; pulling out the piece of paper that held the answer to Alain's prayer. Pierre scanned the report without any expression, then passed it Alain's mother Marie. She read through the report as well, turning to her husband.
"Well," she asked, "what do you think my love, does Alain deserve a bicycle?"
Pierre's face turned to a smile.
"My son," he replied, "your report is very good indeed, the bicycle is yours. We will go into Rouen on Saturday and you my son can choose the one that you really want. Well done."

That weekend Marie, Pierre, and Alain set out for Rouen in the family pony and trap. Marie thought of doing some shopping, but Alain was impatient to get his bicycle. They came to the Cycle shop, Alain was amazed at the different types of bicycle that the store had in stock. Finally he chose one in bright sky blue. It was the greatest thing he had ever owned he could not wait to get home to learn to ride it. Marie, however, was in a local dress shop trying on several gowns when her two men caught up with her. She chose just one dress; she asked Pierre what he thought of it. He said, she looked as pretty as a picture. The assistant folded up the gown and soon they were on their way home. Alain could not wait to get home to get on with learning to ride his new machine. During that afternoon Alain took his first lesson on how to ride a bicycle, with Pierre holding him up. Soon he was riding solo and of course falling off, with the usual dose of grazed knees. He persisted; soon he was riding around the Farmyard as if he had been riding all his life. Alain asked his father if he could go into the nearby village. Pierre told him to be very careful, and to ride much slower than he had been doing in the Farmyard.

Alain promised that he would take great care. The next day, Alain set out on his very first solo ride. It was an adventure; at last, he was free to roam.

Cycling along the lane, he watched the Horses grazing in the fields, the sheep and goats just getting on with the lives. Although, Alain thought that one or two sheep stared at him as he passed along. Alain was really happy; the sun was shining down from a cloudless blue sky. Soon he arrived at the village store, laid his bicycle down on the ground and walked inside. Mrs. Dupont, the storeowner, looked at Alain dressed in long shorts and a blue and white striped shirt.

"What," she asked, "can I get you Monsieur?"

Alain thought for a moment.

"I would like one of those apples please Madam Dupont."

She strolled over to a large crate and handed him a rosy red apple.

"There you are young man."

"How much is that Madame Dupont?" asked Alain.

She thought for a moment.

"As you have come to my shop on your new bicycle," she replied, "I will not charge you."

Alain polished the skin of the shiny fruit on the leg of his shorts, and bit deeply into it.

"Au revoir Madam," he called out as he peddled furiously back up the road towards his home.

Approaching the farm, he noticed that the doors to his father's vast workshop were open, so he cycled over and leant his bicycle against the wall. He strolled in, and noticed that his Father and several of his artisans were putting the finishing touches to a wonderful carriage. It was being made especially for the Count Guy de Longchamps, who lived, with his lovely wife, the Countess Claudine in the nearby Chateau. He had ordered carriages from Pierre every two years, each carriage being more splendid than the previous one. Pierre often wondered what the Count did with his old carriages. Then he thought, as long as I am paid, should I really wonder why. At 8 years old, Alain was admiring the latest creation from the Clement workshop. Pierre was putting the Coat of Arms on the doors whilst one of the other craftsmen was polishing the shafts. Alain stood there just watching in amazement. He looked inside to see the finest leather padding on the seats, both the doors and covering the interior of this splendid vehicle. The seats would give the occupants the most comfortable ride possible. Pierre had designed special springing to give a better ride and roadholding, reduce swaying and pitching on the rough roads of Northern France.

Pierre looked up at Alain.

"Hello, Son. Did you enjoy your ride into the village?"

"Father, it was great. A real adventure," Alain replied.

Then without taking breath Alain continued talking.

"What a magnificent coach father. When will it be ready for the Count?"

"I'm glad you are back safe and sound," Pierre replied, "as for the coach it will be ready for the Count tomorrow, and though I say so myself, I must agree it is rather magnificent, now that you mention it my son."

Pierre stood back and admired the coach.

"By the way," continued Pierre turning back to Alain, "I know that you are always interested in new mechanical contraptions. When you and I were in Rouen, I picked up a magazine. It is in the Lounge. Why not take a look at it? It mentions that new invention called The Horseless Carriage."

That was the signal for Alain to leave the workshop and return to the Farmhouse. Alain asked his mother where the Magazine that his father brought home was located. Marie said it must be in the Lounge. Alain eagerly looked around and eventually found it. He thumbed through the pages until he found the article. It was entitled: THE HORSELESS CARRIAGE - IS THE HORSE FINISHED?

The article gave a brief history of The Horseless Carriage, plus some technical details about the vehicles being produced, and their cost. Alain was interested, but did not realize the cost of these things. He was still reading when his Mother called him for the evening meal.

The Farm, on which the Clement family lived, covered about 200 acres upon which they had raised Cattle and Pigs. Over the years, the Family Coachbuilding business had become so profitable, that the Stable block had now become a Workshop. Pierre's Great-grandfather had built the House in the Mid-18th Century of stone with a tiled roof; the original large open fire in the spacious Kitchen was always burning, for this was where all the cooking was done. When Pierre and Marie had got married in September 1884, they moved into Pierre's home. Pierre was already getting known for his Coachbuilding skills; Marie added a woman's touch to their new home. Since his wife had died in childbirth, Auguste, Pierre's father had given the house a masculine flavour. Now Marie wanted to make it more like a home. Pierre and Marie wanted children and, when their son, Alain was born on the 9th April 1886, they were the happiest couple alive. The baby weighed in at 4 kilos, and was born at home. Pierre was assisting the midwife for he was eager to see his first born, and to cradle him in his arms. Alain soon grew up, and was always asking questions, usually asking the next question before he had received the answer to the previous one. Now he had his bicycle, Pierre thought that the tirade of questions would start again. He was not wrong. Alain made his way from the Garden into the Kitchen.

He sat down at the large kitchen table; Marie was busy putting the final touches to the meal.

"Will father be long, mother? I have lots of questions to ask him."

"I am sure you have young man, he should not be long" replied Marie. She could see that her son was simply bursting at the seams, to ask many questions probably about the article he had just read. For Alain thought that his father knew everything about everything.

When Pierre eventually came home, Alain started asking questions, about the article of course; Pierre did his best to answer them. However, Alain did not seem convinced that he had the right answers. Pierre looked at his son and thought he needed more facts.

"Alain, next time I'm in the village I will try to get you more information on those machines. You can read then about them for yourself and then you can tell me all about them. Is that fair enough?"

"That would be excellent," Alain replied.

"That is enough questions for now young man," said Marie, "now can we sit down and have our meal please?"

The conversation ended until the meal was finished. Then Alain asked his father about his day and repeated he was proud that he had produced such a wonderful carriage.

"Father could you make a Horseless Carriage?"

Pierre gave his son a very old fashioned look.

"I might look like a genius Alain, but seriously I do not know enough about engines. I have not got a clue how to even start about making one. It is not that simple you know. You need lots of tools and really special skills. I would need a much larger workshop, more staff and it would cost a great deal of money."

Alain sat down in one of the large armchairs and picked up that Magazine again. Pierre turned to his son and tried to change the subject.

"Alain, what are you doing tomorrow, apart from riding around on your bicycle?"

"Nothing really father," Alain replied.

"Then son, why not come with me to deliver the Count's Carriage. You would enjoy that I am sure."

"That would be marvellous father, just tell me what time we are going and I will be ready."

Alain was now really excited his chance to ride in one of the Count's carriages; he could not wait for the morning to come. The sun was setting casting its golden rays across the landscape, which was dotted with clumps of trees and large fields. It was this time of the day that Pierre liked best, he had finished his latest project, and he could settle down in his favourite chair in his Study.

Alain called it "The Inner Sanctum"; you only went that room by invitation. The room was not very large but the bookshelves were full of books on all subjects, these had been collected over the years. Alain wondered if anybody had read all of them. When you are 8 years old, there is a lot to learn, so you have to ask questions. Alain certainly was persistent. However, he knew that once his father had gone into his Study, he would not be able to follow him unless invited; otherwise he knew what the consequences would be. To Alain's surprise, his father came to the study door and said, "Alain come and join me in the study."

Meanwhile, Marie was in the kitchen clearing away and washing up. Marie was a very good cook, for she knew that if they eat well, they would stay well. Pierre had a good business, so they were able to buy good quality produce from the local market.

When he was on holiday Alain would go with his Mother to the Village Market. The Butcher always delivered; in fact, when the Clement farm had livestock they sold much of their meat to the Butcher who now supplied them. The two men were sitting in the Study talking when Marie came in. They had not noticed that it had got dark, so quickly had the time passed.

"Bedtime for you now please, Alain. More talking time tomorrow," she said.

Alain said goodnight to his father and went upstairs to get ready for bed.

"I'll be up shortly to tuck you in," said Marie.

Marie went back out to the Lounge and collapsed into an armchair. One day she thought, I would have a maid to do all this Housework and the cooking. She looked up at the time on the Grandfather clock that stood against the wall by the Lounge door. By golly, she said to herself, I must get up to Alain. By the time she got to his bedroom, Alain was fast asleep.

Soon Pierre joined Marie in the Lounge. Marie had had a long, hard day, she had started to read and relax. Pierre too, felt tired and sank into his favourite armchair to the left of the fireplace.

"Pierre, you certainly spent a long time with Alain tonight, he must have asked a lot of questions."

"Marie, my love, that boy asks questions from morning until night. Now with this Horseless Carriage business on his mind, you can be certain he will have a lot more questions to ask. Unfortunately, I do not have the answers. I do like him asking questions, otherwise he will not learn. I would like him to try and find some answers himself."

"I guess so," sighed Marie.

Pierre looked at the Grandfather clock.

"Time for bed, my love, I have to deliver the Count's coach in the morning and Alain is joining me. Therefore, I will have to be up at the usual time to make last minute checks. See you upstairs soon."

On his way to bed, Pierre knew that his son was fascinated by the possibility of something that could go faster than a Pony and Trap, which on the local roads was the fastest thing around at the time.

The following morning, after a night of dreams of fantastic machines running through his brain, Alain could not wait to go with his father to deliver the Count's carriage. He was down early for breakfast and raring to go. He drank his milk and ate the freshly baked croissants without a word, lest his Father changed his mind.

"You alright son," said Pierre looking across the table, "you seem very quiet this morning."

"I'm fine father, just looking forward to this morning's special trip in that lovely coach."

Marie turned to the two men at the table and smiled. When they had finished their breakfast they made their way over to the workshop where the Carriage stood ready to receive its motive power, namely the Horses. Albert, Pierre's right hand man had been there for almost 30minutes and had selected two of their finest black horses to draw the carriage. Alain assisted the two men to harness up the splendid steeds.

Then when all harnessing was complete Pierre climbed on to the top of the coach and took the reins.

"Climb aboard Alain," yelled Pierre, "we are off now."

"Can I travel inside, please father?" asked Alain.

"OK just this once," responded Pierre.

Soon they were off to the Chateau. Alain felt like the Count, the ride was ultra smooth; the Carriage seemed to just glide along. Pierre was delighted with the new suspension he had designed. All too soon they arrived at the gates of the Chateau, and Alain's little daydream had ended. Pierre stopped the carriage; he beckoned Alain to join him on the driver's seat, for Pierre thought that the Count would not be pleased if he found Alain sitting on his plush new leather seats. The Gatekeeper opened the Chateau gates. The carriage then continued up the long gravel drive to the main house, where the Count was waiting at the foot of the stairs that lead to the main doors.

Count Guy de Longchamps was tall and of athletic build, with well-trimmed blonde hair, his wife the Countess Claudine had long dark brown hair, and a very trim figure. She was the daughter of the Count and Countess du Velay. Guy had met Claudine at a Grand Ball in Paris; they had fallen in love at first sight and were married within a year. Unfortunately, Claudine was unable to have children, but they were deliriously happy, and had a good relationship with the local villagers, especially the Clement family. They lived in a beautiful Chateau that had been built in the 17th Century by the Second Count de Longchamps and was situated on the top of a hill. Part of the hill been removed, this had produced a large enough area so that the Chateau, could have a flat area on which it could be built. It enjoyed a commanding view of the surrounding countryside. With its grand entrance gates, towers and turrets, Alain always thought it looked like a Fairytale Castle. Drawing closer to the imposing building, Pierre could see the excited expression on the Count's face; the Count had tried not to show it, but had failed miserably. As the coach drew to a stop, Alain climbed down and the Count greeted them.

"Good morning, Monsieur Clement," said the Count shaking Pierre's hand, "how does she run?"

"Good morning Sir," Pierre replied, "she runs like a dream. The best yet."

"Excellent, Pierre, excellent," replied the Count excitedly.

"May I introduce you to my son Alain, Sir? He is very interested in the Horseless Carriage. Asks lots of questions which sadly I cannot answer."

The Count turned to Alain, who by this time had climbed down from the driving seat.

"It is a pleasure to meet you Alain," said the Count shaking Alain's hand, "so young man you are interested in the Horseless Carriage are you?"

Alain looked up at the Count.

"Yes sir, I certainly am," replied Alain in a definite tone.

The Count looked down at Alain.

"So am I young man, so am I."

The Count returned his attention to the Coach, and after admiring it for several moments he walked around it and gazed at it from several angles, whilst Pierre and Alain watched him. Finally the Count broke the silence.

"Pierre, this carriage is absolutely splendid. This time you have really excelled yourself. I shall give you an extra bonus and I shall make sure that this lad of yours had a special treat too."

He then turned to Alain.

"Alain, your father and I have known each other for many years. He has made me such a magnificent carriage that I am inviting your parents and you to witness the very first competition for these Horseless Carriages, which takes place next Sunday 22nd July. The Race as they are calling it runs from Paris to Rouen a distance of some 126 kilometres. This is in addition to the bonus I am paying for your father's beautiful creation, and I will expect you all here at the Chateau at 7 a.m. sharp. The Countess

Claudine will join us then we shall go to a suitable place to see this historic event in my new carriage. It should be very exciting day, especially for you Alain. Especially, as you have a great deal of interest in this Horseless Carriage."

The week could not go quickly enough for Alain. Each day he would help with the household chores, which included tidying up his room. This in itself is a rare event. He spent time with his father in the workshop, chatting to the workmen also helping to repaint several wagons and a coach that had been in for repair. Alain was interested to see how various tools were used. His questions were endless, or so it seemed, Pierre thought he would never stop, but then Alain did have an inquisitive mind.

At last Sunday dawned, bright and clear, another glorious summer's morning, with just the faintest wisp of high cloud.

Alain had hardly slept at all during Saturday night, he was thinking about those fantastic machines that he had read about and would see on the morrow. He pretended to be asleep when his mother opened the door to his bedroom.

"Come on Alain, it is time to get up," said Marie, "I thought you would have been awake long before this. It is a lovely morning, breakfast is ready and I have prepared a picnic for us all."

Alain stirred and opened his eyes.

"Good morning Mother, thank you. I will be down for breakfast as soon as I can."

Alain dressed quickly, he was not going to waste one more moment. He was down to breakfast in record time and he ate with gusto. Soon, the Clement family was into their Horse and Trap and setting off along the gently winding road to the Chateau. Passing through the gates of the Chateau, Marie could not wait to see her husband's latest masterpiece. In a few minutes, the House came into view.

Then as they got closer, Marie now could see the carriage, it truly was magnificent, no wonder the Count was so pleased, and she smiled to herself. Pierre brought the Trap to a standstill. The Count had harnessed four of his finest black stallions to the Carriage; their coats were gleaming in the morning sun.

"Good morning, Mr. & Mrs. Clement, and to you too young Alain. Glad you could all come today. It will be an experience for us all."

The voice came from inside the carriage. The door opened and the Count emerged he looked very handsome in his tweed jacket, plus fours and laced up boots.

"Good morning Sir," the Clement family replied in unison.

"The Countess will not be long," replied the Count, "she is putting the finishing touches to the food we are taking with us."

Pierre knew this was not true as the Countess had servants to prepare her food. The Countess Claudine finally appeared a few minutes later in one of her many 'outdoor' costumes. Her long hair was swept up under a broad brimmed hat that was tied under her chin with a lacy scarf. She was dressed in a brown velvet coat, matching dress, and brown leather laced up boots. Marie thought she looked very regal, whilst she, Marie, felt rather dowdy by comparison. Then again, the Count was a rich man so he could afford to indulge his wife in her passion for gorgeous clothes. Alain too thought that she looked like a Queen.

On the other hand Pierre, who knew all about carpentry and mechanics, but very little about fashion. Ladies fashion in particular. He knew when something looked right; the Countess certainly looked right and very stylish to say the least. The Count broke the silence by saying,

"Ah! There you are my Love. Are you ready to go?"

He turned to the Clements and continued speaking:

"Pierre here has done such a magnificent work making this carriage, I thought we would all go to the Race in it. We shall be able to see how she runs. Have not given it a good run yet."

Pierre was speechless, in all the years he had known the Count the only time he had been inside one of the carriages was when he was making, testing or delivering it to the Chateau. He noticed that standing next to the Countess was one of her maids carrying an enormous picnic basket.

"Sir" began Pierre, "it will an honour for us to travel with you."

They all climbed aboard and settled in their seats. Claude, the Count's coachman, took the picnic basket and tucked it away in the back of the carriage. He then climbed on to the driver's seat cracked his whip across the backs of the two rear horses and they braced themselves, took the strain and they were off. The passengers sat back in absolute luxury as the carriage sped along as if it were on air.

Alain smiled to himself in quiet satisfaction that at last he was on his way to see his very first race for Horseless Carriages. The Count bent forward to speak to Pierre.

"Monsieur you have excelled yourself with this marvellous creation on wheels. This is by far the finest carriage I have ever travelled in."

Pierre felt both proud and embarrassed at the same time. He really did not know how to reply. In the end he just said,

"Thank you very much Sir."

Marie was looking out of the window watching the scenery flash by, she felt wonderful. Her husband, at last, had been recognised for all the hard work he had put in over the past few weeks. The Countess then broke the silence again:

"You must be very proud of your husband Mrs. Clement he and his team are very fine craftsmen."

Marie looked straight at the Countess and replied, "Thank you for your compliments, your Ladyship. My husband has always tried to keep up the standard set by his father and grandfather."

She turned and smiled at Pierre.

They were heading towards the small town of VERNON, which stands on the banks of the River Seine. From the windows of the carriage, they saw road signs pointing the way to where spectators could view the race.

They had been travelling for about two hours, when the Count said,

"I think that this spot will be ideal."

He knocked his stick on the roof lining of the carriage. The Driver Claude opened a flap.

"Yes Sir?" he asked.

"Please pull off the road somewhere convenient, Claude." Within a few minutes, the carriage turned off the road into a large field.

"This will do nicely I think," said the Count.

He looked at his pocket watch and thought for a moment.

"The Horseless Carriage should be along in about an hour, by my reckoning. I have seen a plan of their route, now there is time for us to partake of some refreshment."

They all alighted from the coach and Claude prepared drinks for them all. The next 60 minutes were the longest of Alain's life, he could wait to hear and see these machines, those magical Horseless Carriages. He did not hear the adult conversation all he could think of was the Motor Cars. The Count and Pierre spoke to him but he was in a world of his own. He sipped at his drink as if in a daze. His thoughts were suddenly shattered by a noise - a strange noise one he had not heard before. It seemed to come from over a nearby rise in the ground, some distance away, although nobody could see a thing. The sound gathered in volume, the horses in a field close by seemed to become restless, and then began to gallop around as if crazy. It must be a Horseless Carriage thought Alain; it could not be anything else surely?

The whole group then moved to the fence, which lined a very dusty road. In the distance they saw a plume of dust rising up, and then around the corner a small cart came into view. Alain thought it resembled something his Father would make. It was moving fast but without Horse, or shafts. Therefore, Alain thought, this is the famous Horseless Carriage that everyone has been talking about. The machine got closer; they now could clearly see the Driver and his Mechanic (which in those days they had to carry as part of the rules of the competitions). They wore their caps on back to front, goggles over their eyes and scarves across their mouths. They were clothed from head to toe in black leather with heavy boots.

The Driver held what looked like a walking stick (apparently this was called a tiller and this steered the vehicle), tightly gripped in his leather-gloved hands. The Mechanic fiddled with some levers. At the rear of the machine was a pipe billowing smoke; noise seemed to come from everywhere.

That must be the engine making all that noise thought Alain. The other members of the party looked in wonder, as this little machine spluttered by at 35 kph. Just it passed them the engine coughed, a cloud of black smoke appeared from the exhaust pipe, and the little car came to a halt. The Driver juggled with a few of the controls and the Mechanic got down from his seat. Walking round to the rear of the car, he lifted a panel up, fiddled with something, muttered something obviously not complimentary and for public ears. Alain wondered what would happen next. The Driver looked distinctly unamused, after all, they were losing time, and it was a race after all. The Mechanic scratched his head, and then raised his finger in the air as if he had received inspiration from above. He went around to the back of the car once more lifted the panel again, fiddled with something else, wound a handle around and the machine burst into life again with a great plume of black smoke. The Mechanic jumped back into his seat; there was a jerk, the car shot forward then slowly disappeared into the distance. Alain was transfixed; he knew that his love affair with the Motor Car had begun. He would love to drive and race one of these funny little things. It was some time before another Car hove into view, this time it passed without incident, but had only one person on board. Ten more then went by some struggling, others going really quickly. All the Drivers and Mechanics were leaning forward to reduce wind resistance. It certainly had been an exciting morning. They had all worked up such an appetite and at last, silence reigned. The Horses in the field had settled and started grazing again. Then, when they thought it was all over, a car travelling very slowly and noisily came into view and ground to a halt close by. The Driver and Mechanic spent some time trying to bring the machine back to life, but to no avail. So they sat by the side of the road to await assistance.

The Longchamps and the Clements were all tucking into the feast prepared by the Count's staff. It was absolutely sumptuous; there was fresh Lobster, Salmon, Beer, Wine and Cheeses of all kinds, freshly baked bread, salad, truly an outdoor feast. The wine flowed it was all most tempting, and not for those on a diet thought Marie. Having finished their grand picnic, Alain wondered how the competitors, whose car had broken down, were getting on.

"Why don't we offer them some food, we have plenty left," said the Count. Alain volunteered to go to ask the two men sitting by the car. It was a hot day, and they had taken off their outer garments, and were trying to repair the car. Alain walked towards them, one of the men stood up.

"Excuse me Gentlemen," began Alain, "the Count de Longchamps, he that owns that coach over there. Would like to know if you would join him for some food and drink whilst you await rescuing."

"That would be marvellous young sir," said the driver breathing a sigh of relief, "thank the Count very much."

Alain began asking questions as they walked along. The Driver and Mechanic were only too pleased to answer him, for many people thought that the Horseless Carriage was just a nuisance and those that drove them were crazy. The two young men that drove the little car were sweating profusely, and were extremely grateful to the Count and his Party for their kind invitation. They did not know how long it would be before help arrived. The afternoon wore on, two more cars chuffed by, but nobody seemed to take much notice now, for even the horses had got used to the noise. A Policeman on a bicycle came along to tell everyone that all the competitors had passed, and that the road was safe to use. He stopped and spoke to the Count and the Party.

He said that help was on the way for the stranded car. Therefore, the day was over now. It was time to pack up and head back to the Chateau. All agreed that it was a great occasion, a wonderful day. By the time the Clements arrived back at the Chateau, they were very tired. The Count congratulated Pierre on his wonderful carriage, whilst Alain knew that his love affair with the Motor Car had begun on that fateful day in July 1894.

Soon, Alain was getting ready for bed, he knew that what he wanted to do when he was old enough, he wanted to become a Racing Driver. As he fell asleep he began to dream about being World Champion and had won over 10 Races. Alain had only seen the cars pass; he was interested to find out more. The next day he had a good look through the Newspaper, his father always had one delivered, to find the report of this earth-shattering event. He read the account of the day's happenings. It seems that the event, which incidentally, was the first City-to-City race, was controversial. The winner was a Count de Dion in a car of his own manufacture.

He had covered the 126-kilometre course in a time of 6 hours and 48 minutes at an average speed of 18.53 kph. He was 3 minutes and 30 seconds ahead of his nearest rival a Monsieur Lemaitre in a Peugeot. The next three past the finishing post were also due to make their name as time went along, namely an H.Panard another in a car of his own name and an Emile Levassor also in a Panard. However, the winner was then disqualified. The Rules stating that cars must carry a mechanic. The Count de Dion, had it seems driven the race alone.

The next few months passed by very quickly; Alain was still studying hard at school. However, Marie had always wanted another child, hopefully a girl. Now that business was picking up for Pierre, they could now afford to raise another child. Marie hoped it would be a girl. Alain's life had changed on that fateful day, 22nd July 1894, now it was Marie, Alain's Mother turn to have her life transformed on the 24th March 1895, when she gave birth to a daughter. She blamed it on the Motor Race. There was too much wine, good food and over-enthusiasm by Pierre. Alain suggested that they called the new baby Emily, as it was a girl's name closest to one of the drivers in race. However, Marie had other ideas and they finally settled on Helene-Marie, named after Marie's late Mother.

As the years passed, Alain was still fascinated by the Motor Car; he faced his schoolwork with the zeal of a boy who had set his heart on becoming a Racing Driver. He always had his head in a book, and read any articles in the newspapers about Horseless Carriage races that took place. He read about the 1895 Paris to Bordeaux race, which involved a return run to Paris. It was a gruelling event over atrocious roads. The winner, Emile Levassor was disqualified as he had driven a 2-seater and the race was for 4-seater cars. The race over a distance of 1171 kilometres took Emile 48hrs and 48 minutes.

In 1896, on September 24th the race went from Paris to Marseilles and back this time the distance was some 1700 kilometres, the winner took 67 hours and 43 minutes. Certainly, an epic drive by any standard. Despite this, Alain had his mind set. This was something he had to get out of his system.

His school reports on some subjects would say - could do better or must concentrate. His best subjects were Mathematics and Science. He knew that to build his own Horseless Carriage - now known as Motor Cars - he would need these subjects and a lot more besides especially money. The Motoring World was still in its infancy. Pierre's business was doing well; the Count had ordered yet another new carriage. One day Pierre took Alain aside.

"Alain I know that you are doing very well in some subjects, but overall you need to improve. I know that after seeing that Motor Race some 5 years ago, your mind is set on becoming a Racing Driver. I want you ought to know that there is more to life than that. You need a real career."

Alain smiled for he knew what his father meant. He was now 13 years old, growing fast and soon to leave school. His father realised this and so continued giving advice to his son.

"It is all very well dreaming of success in long distance races, that is if you are blessed with a good deal of money. For all those who succeed in these races are wealthy men. You know that young Helene is growing up fast too, that is another mouth to feed. We must all try to learn as much as we can, in order to get a good job. Those Motor Cars are very expensive to buy and upkeep. There are several made in France but by specialist engineers, not by a simple coachbuilder like me."

Alain knew that his father was right; he had been daydreaming in class and knew that he could do better. Alain thought for a moment.

"Father, you are not just a simple coachbuilder, you build the best carriages in the whole of France."

"That may be true son," replied Pierre, "but one day in the not too distant future there will be thousands of cars on the roads in France and my trade will be out of date."

Alain stared at his Father in disbelief; he thought that the Coachbuilding business would last forever. Then, it dawned on Alain that he had better get down to some serious studying at Home and at School. Technology was moving fast, there were articles about flying machines and airships. The world of science was developing at a rapid pace. Pierre hoped that his son would pass the necessary examinations to qualify for entry to the Sorbonne in Paris, to become an Engineer with top qualifications.

The next few months showed a complete change in Alain's attitude toward his work; he hardly mentioned cars at all.

He spent long hours at home studying really hard, subsequently his school reports improved dramatically. His sister, Helene was now a real handful, she took up most of Marie's time, especially when she tried 'helping' her Mother. Before they knew it Christmas, the last one of the old Century was almost upon them, there had been a light fall of snow making the whole place look like fairyland. Pierre had been into Rouen buying special presents for all the family. There was also a big Party at the Chateau planned for New Year's Eve and Pierre and all his family were invited. The Clements were really looking forward to that grand event. Christmas was always a family affair. The Christmas tree was adorned with tinsel, fairy lights, and other baubles. The rooms were decorated with Holly and Mistletoe. Marie, although she liked Christmas, it seemed to get harder each year; she usually breathed a sigh of relief when it was over. The consolations were the smiles on the faces of her children, which always made up for all the hard work she had to put in. For 1899 was no exception, this would be the last Christmas of the Century, she had to make it special, and she did. That year the Clement family had their best ever Christmas, because there was money to spend. It was really enjoyable for all the family. Soon the festivities were over, now the talk of the village was the Grand Party at the Chateau. This would be Helen-Marie's first big occasion. Alain too was celebrating with an astonishing report, which assured him of a very good chance to go to the Sorbonne; all he had to do was to keep it up for another term.

Then came the day 31st December 1899, it was all excitement, no doubt one topic of conversation would be who wearing the latest fashions, and what the new century would bring. All those clothes, not worn very often, came out of the wardrobes. It had been very cold, so thick coats were going to be the order of the day. Pierre had bought Marie a new Winter Coat for Christmas. It was made of Black Wool with white fur trimming and a thick wool lining. She tried it on, felt so warm, it was the best present she had received in a long time, and she looked lovely in it. Her old winter coats had definitely seen better days. Pierre always liked his wife to look good, even though from time to time they had struggled financially. The Count's Party would be the ideal occasion to show off her new winter coat. Underneath, this she would wear her very best dress.

Pierre found a Dinner Suit he had not worn for some time, and the children had new clothes too. Together, they all looked very smart indeed. It was then time to set off to the Chateau in the family coach, in fact it was one of the Count's old coaches that he had given to Pierre as a present a couple of years before. So at least, the family could travel to the Chateau out of the cold. The night was clear and starry, but there was a real chill in the air. Marie and the children huddled together inside the coach, whilst Pierre who was also wrapped up well, drove them off to the big event.

On arriving at the Main Doors, they were greeted by the Count's Butler Charles, who took them into the Entrance Hall where their names were announced. Alain felt very important, it was the first time that he had attended this event. Helene-Marie felt all grown up in her new party dress. Marie felt a little embarrassed; the Count shook the Men firmly by the hand, kissed Marie on the cheek and bent down to kiss Helene-Marie who held her hand out for him to do so. The guest list read like a who's who of the local gentry. Pierre did not feel out of place, neither did Marie or the children, everyone mixed in perfectly. Everyone spoke to Pierre and Marie for they knew that his family had some standing in the Community. The food prepared by the Count's servants lay on three large tables in the Banqueting Hall, which was oak-panelled. On the walls were an array of pictures some of the Count's ancestors and French and German landscapes by famous artists. The ceiling was also painted with biblical scenes. The Ballroom was vast; Alain had never been into this part of the Chateau, he thought that this must be the biggest room in the world. The 350 guests had plenty of room to converse and dance.

At the end of the room was a raised stage on which was a small group of musicians, Alain counted six, that played music for dancing. The Clement family made their way into the Ballroom, a Viennese waltz - The Blue Danube greeted their ears. The dancers were swirling around so gracefully. Others were talking and moving around in little groups. The Count mounted the stage and called for silence.

"My Lords, Ladies and Gentlemen," he began, "the time has come for the Musicians to have a break, and time for us to move into the Banqueting Hall where you will be served with the finest food and wine."

The crowd moved slowly at first, but before long, the Count's servants were serving them all. When they had all eaten their fill, the guests returned to the Ballroom for more music and dancing. The bewitching hour approached and the Count mounted the stage again.

"My Lords, Ladies and Gentlemen," announced the Count, "it is almost time to say goodbye to the 19th Century. The 1900's are but a minute or two away. So let us charge our glasses and drink a toast." Those with empty glasses called over the servants to fill them again. "Everyone ready," the Count began again. "Right now, let us raise our glasses and drink to times past and times to come."

The throng then as in one voice they shouted out - "to times past and times to come". Everyone was wishing everybody a Happy New Year. Little Helene-Marie was fast asleep on a couch; Alain was dancing with one of their neighbour's daughters Adrienne. Pierre and Marie were having a wonderful time; they had never seen such gaiety. The decorations in the Chateau were the most beautiful and intricate they had ever seen. It would be a shame to take them down. All too soon, it was time to leave. Marie had to wake Helene and Alain was called over and told it was time to go home.

Pierre thanked the Count and Countess for their wonderful party. They then made their way home.

Winter gave way to spring; Alain was still studying hard at school, where his efforts were now really bearing fruit. The spring term was ending. The next event in the calendar was Helene-Marie's 5th Birthday; she was becoming a young woman, she had started school at the beginning of the spring term. She showed promise and could read well. The family had seen to that, encouraging her to start reading early and to take an interest in learning from books. For the Party, she had a new Pink Party dress and on the day, she had a pink bow in her long blonde hair. All the local people had been invited; about 50 guests amongst whom were the Count Guy and Countess Claudine de Longchamps. Alain was now almost 14 years old, he had matured a great deal in the last year, and he wanted to go to the Sorbonne as a junior student. He would be accepted in the summer, subject to an entrance examination. The Sorbonne had changed their rules on new students and he would not be eligible until they were 18.

The Count had written to the Director of the Sorbonne, saying that he would help pay the money required for Alain's accommodation, tuition and books that he would need.

Alain had been the most talented student of the year, had won several academic prizes in the past few months. His father was absolutely delighted; his son had done so brilliantly. However, he was sad to know that his son would have to wait another four years until he could be accepted, at the Sorbonne. The day belonged to Helene-Marie; she was the Belle of the Ball, the perfect party girl. The Party was held in the large garden of the Clement home. The Rose beds were still a bit bare, but tidy, the grass mown and all the edges straight. The trees that fringed the garden were breaking into leaf. The weather was perfect, a really gorgeous spring day with hardly a cloud in the sky. As Pierre wandered around seeing to his guests, he thought pity every day is not like this.

At precisely 3 p.m. the Count and Countess arrived in their new coach, built by Pierre of course. The paintwork was gleaming in the spring sunshine, the four white Horses that pulled the coach, were in peak condition. The Count always made certain that his grooms did their work thoroughly, for his stables were a real credit to his love of animals. Marie, Pierre and the Birthday girl greeted the Count and Countess. Helene-Marie was presenting a bouquet to the Countess with a curtsy. The Countess thanked the Clements for their gracious invitation, kissed Helene-Marie on both cheeks, and wished her a Happy Birthday. The Count stood behind his wife, and in his arms, he held a large parcel wrapped in pink paper with a big pink bow on it. He moved forward to be beside the Countess and said,

"Happy Birthday Helene - Marie, this is a present for you".

Marie was at a loss for words for a moment, then she gasped "thank you Sir for a wonderful present."

Now giving present to children was no problem for the Count. They loved children although he and the Countess had no children of their own. It seems that some years before the Countess had a miscarriage, her physician had told her that trying for more children could be a danger to her, even life threatening. The Count was sad, as he wanted to pass his title on to his children. He looked down at Helene.

"Why don't you open it," said the Count, "we would all like to know what it is?"

Pierre helped Helene take the bow off carefully, then as they began to remove the wrapping; everyone wondered what the present might be. The suspense was electric. Then as more wrapping came off, the present was revealed. It was a saddle for her new pony. It was dark brown leather, with the brass buckles that shone in the bright sunlight. The Count knew of Helen's interest in horse riding, he had heard that she recently had been given a Pony called Azure. On the side of the saddle, Helen's name was emblazoned in gold lettering. She looked at it in amazement. It was something she had really wanted, ever since she knew that she was getting a pony. It was the loveliest saddle she had ever seen. Her face lit up; she rushed over to the Count and gave him a big kiss. The Count now felt slightly self-conscious.

"Young lady," he said, "it is my pleasure to give you this saddle, for I hope one day you will represent France at Equestrian events."

The Party continued and all the other children gave presents to the Birthday girl. She was on Cloud Nine. Alain wanted to talk to the Count about Motor Cars. For he knew that the Count moved in social circles where, there was plenty of money to spend buying of motor cars. Alain managed to spend about 15 minutes talking to the Count; he was very interested to know that Alain had done so brilliantly at school. He was delighted, to hear that Alain would be going to the Sorbonne to continue his studies in Engineering, Science, and Mathematics, but sad, that he would not be able to go until he was 18 years of age. The Count said that these subjects were essential, should he desire to work in the new technological age.

The Count was surprised to learn that junior student's courses had been suspended at the Sorbonne. Alain said that he had read about Motor Car Shows, they were being held in Paris at the end of each year. The Count said would Alain like to go to see one of these Shows. The Count said that he too, would like to go as well, may be they could make arrangements to meet and go together when Alain went to the Sorbonne. This might be some time in the future. Alain thought that would be really terrific, but the Count said,

"Alain you must qualify really well in your examinations this term, and if you do, that trip to the Paris show will be my treat, as your reward. I will take you to a Restaurant I know where they serve the most gorgeous food. I sure that even you will not turn down an offer like that."

Alain knew that it would be a few years hence, but he had his eye on success. Alain was over the moon, being taken to a Paris Show and a great meal.

"Sir that is something worth working for," replied Alain enthusiastically, "I will succeed in my examinations and we shall go to Paris together. That is a promise."

"That is what I like about you Alain," responded the Count, "you have a very positive attitude. With that kind of determination, you will be famous one day. It has been very interesting talking to you; we must do this again soon. Come to the Chateau when you have time and we will discuss many other things. I see that the Countess is ready to go now. I must thank your parents for a wonderful party."

The Party had started to break up, but the children were having a great time playing in the sunshine. The Count and Countess walked over to where Pierre and Marie were talking to their neighbours and friends. The Count and Countess said to the Clements how much they had enjoyed the Party and that Helene was so delighted with her saddle. As the Count's coach moved away, it was the signal for everyone to help clear away the food, not that there was much left. The families began to leave; the sun began its journey towards the western horizon. Everyone agreed that it had been a terrific party. The Count and Countess attending had made it a simply superb. Helene-Marie could not believe that the Count had given her such a marvellous present. When her bedtime came around, she wanted to sleep with it on her bed. Marie had to say no. She did, however compromise and let her sleep with it beside her bed. Helene fell asleep dreaming of success, one day she would be the top Horsewoman in France winning International acclaim.

The future was still unknown for all the family, but the dreams of the children were the strongest. By the time Marie and Pierre were ready for bed, the Farmhouse was back to virtual normality. There were times during the day; Marie wondered how she would ever get as she always said - tidied up. Marie was one who liked everything in its place; she had a perfect melancholy temperament. Pierre on the other hand, being a professional artisan, always thought that as long as he put something down and could find it afterward, that was all that mattered. He did keep a tidy workshop, always hanging up the tools he used when finished. The Clements agreed that it had been a hard day, but both agreed that Helene-Marie should be spoilt for one day. It was her Birthday after all. The icing on the cake was the visit of the Count and Countess; their present to Helene was both thoughtful and useful. Now, she could ride her pony safely. It was late when Marie and Pierre finally got to bed. They were both exhausted and soon fell asleep.

Chapter 2

On that same day some 130 miles away, in the rolling countryside of England, another party was well under way; another child was opening a present given to him for his 6th birthday. The Event, was being held at Ashdown Hall, the family home of Lord John and Lady Victoria Ashdown. Ashdown Hall had been the ancestral home of the Ashdown family since the late 15th Century. The House had been styled on Knole house in the county of Kent. Knole, was one of the largest private houses in England, when Thomas Bourchier who was then Archbishop of Canterbury, built it in 1454. The 1st Lord Ashdown had been with King Henry V at the Battle of Agincourt in 1405, the King for his courage and valour in Battle had given him large tracks of land in Sussex near the hamlet of Horsham. It included several small settlements. On returning to England when the War with the French was over, he decided to build a large house on the land near the village of Horsham. He had grand plans for his 'palace' in Sussex, and to get ideas he went to look at several houses in the neighbouring counties. He heard about Knole and decided to have a look at it being built. He was now in the autumn of his life; his house was large but not palatial enough. In 1456, he began to design his dream palace; he died in 1457 with just the plans in his head. It was not until, some 120 years later that the 8th Lord Ashdown decided that the old house needed a good deal of work in the way of repairs.

He had acquired funds through various means; not always honest it can be said. Therefore, he decided to spend most of it before someone found out where the money had come from. He called up a prominent Architect of the day found the plans the 1st Lord had made, and asked if this large house could be built. The Architect said it could be done, but it would cost a good deal of money. The grand plan was started but after 5 years work, the House was still not completed. The money had dried up, and the project abandoned. Since that time, just a few outbuildings and stables had been added but the main building had never been completed. Above the entrance gates were the Coat of Arms of the family with the motto: HONOUR ABOVE ALL.

This motto considering their early family history, was a bit of a contradiction. However, since the days of the 11th Lord Ashdown the family had buried its murky past. Lord Henry had fought beside King Charles I at several battles in the English Civil War, including the Battle of Naseby, in 1645 there had many close shaves with the Roundheads. When the War ended he managed to keep his estates and began to brew local ale, which he distributed around the local hostelries. Over a period of time, this became very profitable. Every day you could see his horse and wagon with a driver plodding around the country lanes near Horsham.

The heirs and successors developed the Brewery until the 16th Lord Roger Ashdown began the modernisation of the Horsham Brewery, improve the quality product, and service to local hostelries. Lord Rupert the 19th Lord Ashdown had taken over several locally run Public Houses and tied them to the Brewery. The family were now wealthy and lived in style. They could afford the best. Lord Rupert was a shrewd businessman he had developed links with Vineyards in France, Germany and Italy to supply fine wines to be served in his tied Public Houses and distributed to local Hotels. The business flourished. In 1893, Lord Rupert was tragically killed in a riding accident, when John was only 23 years old. John who was a tall upright young man, slender in build with blonde hair, was a member of the Diplomatic Service in central London. He asked his Head of Department for compassionate leave to sort out his Father's affairs. The business suffered as a result, for neither John nor his Mother had the skills to run a large brewing and distribution business. It had to be left to the Brewery Manager and Lady Elizabeth to restore confidence and acquire the experience needed to return the family business to profit again.

During his father's funeral, he had met his future wife Victoria. She was tall, with a good figure and long black hair. She was the daughter and only child of the London businessman Sir Nigel & Victoria Hawkesley. Sir Nigel was an old family friend for many years and had invested money in the Brewery, when there was a need to rebuild and modernise. Although a solemn event, Lord Rupert's funeral brought Victoria and John together, previously they had hardly known each other.

At the funeral they consoled each other and love seem to blossom and the couple became inseparable. It was no surprise to either Sir Nigel or Lady Elizabeth - Rupert's widow that John and Victoria became engaged. The wedding some 6 months later, was a grand affair, with all the landed gentry present. John had been a rising star in the Diplomatic Service, just six months before his posting to India; their son Nigel John Ashdown was born on March 23rd 1895, a bonny baby with blonde hair. Their family life on the India sub-continent was a far cry from their life in England, where John had spent his childhood. Victoria too found life different, a life she could get used to, with servants at her disposal. Nigel was cosseted and protected, he was very lucky not to fall foul of the various diseases in this region that were prevalent at the time. Medicine in India was basic to say the least. John's duties included many social events and Victoria always looked as pretty as a picture in her gowns. Although she found it hard to come to terms with the insects, heat, humidity and the poverty in the region just outside their official residence. After three years service, the posting was over, the traumatic goodbyes had to be said, and one grand farewell party. On the journey home, by boat, the Ashdown's wondered what life would be like back in Sussex, how different would it be. In any case, they would have to adjust.

Whilst they were overseas, John's Mother, Elizabeth with the help of the Brewery Manager, James Colgate, had run the Brewery. It was a difficult time; Rupert had a great presence. Now that a Lady was now running the business, at meetings with Clients she was not always taken seriously. On arrival back at Ashdown Hall there was a grand family reunion; Elizabeth remarked how much Nigel had grown. She asked all about India and had Nigel been keeping up his studies. Nigel told his Grandmother, that he had private tuition and was looking forward to going to school in England for the first time. Elizabeth suggested that now they had returned, the Brewery had to be their first priority. They had a management meeting. James and Elizabeth apprised John of the present situation. It seemed a good deal of fence mending was needed. It would be hard work. John told James that he would be confirmed as Brewery General Manager and he;

John Ashdown would visit all their contacts both in England and in Europe. To build up the business once more and firm up all existing contracts.

Meanwhile, Nigel had settled down at the local school and family life had got back to normal. With the Brewery being so busy, John resigned from the Diplomatic Service to concentrate on the family business. His mother was relieved, as she was not as she put it getting any younger. In any case, she wanted to help Victoria in the House organising the servants, and any social events that might be required. Nigel had always been inquisitive, for he was interested in anything mechanical. John encouraged him, as he wanted Nigel to take over the running of the Brewery at some time in the future. By the spring of 1901, Nigel had started to mix with the children of local landowners; he enjoyed horse riding and had made lots of friends at school. So, it was that on Nigel's next birthday there should be a proper birthday party outside in the garden area, where any food dropped could be picked up by the local wildlife.

Nigel was now 6 years of age, and it was decided to hold the party on his actual birthday March 23rd. There had been little joy in the land for the old Queen Victoria had not long passed away. Lady Ashdown felt a little sad, after all was she not named after the Queen? They had attended the Funeral of Queen Victoria that was a glittering affair. It was not only an historic, but also a unique occasion being attended by the new King Edward VII, the Kaiser Willheim II, and the Czar Nicholas II with his lovely Czarina Alexandra, together with other members of Royal Families related to the late Queen. It would be the only time in history that all these relatives of the old Queen would be together. The International Press had a field day with all these crowned heads of Europe. However, it was the new medium of the moving pictures captured the unique images of the funeral procession.

As for Nigel's 6th Birthday Party true to the organising ability of the Ashdown family, all the local children were invited. It was stated on the invitations that no presents would be opened until 3 p.m. precisely, but the Party would begin at 12.30 p.m. With a sit down meal for all the children. The Parents were invited, of course, but for them there would be a buffet laid out in the very large conservatory. The time approached, for the merriment to begin, the local people who had invitations started to arrive. There must have been about 50 children and around 75 adults.

The children's laughter was certainly a tonic to the Ashdowns, and most of all Nigel who was having a wonderful time. He had lain awake for hours the night before, with eager anticipation of what presents might be forthcoming. The tables were spread with fine foods of all kinds for both the children and parents. The servants had been up half of the night making Cakes, Trifles, and bowls of Salad. There were cold Chickens, Turkeys, and Salmon, sliced Beef and Lamb. Dishes of cold Ham and Eggs, all of which were decorated with parsley, and other Herbs. Truly, a fine display of the culinary art, it looked too good to eat. Victoria toured around the tables before the feast began. John looked at the groaning tables and thought that they had prepared far too much food. However, he need not have worried, for by the time the meal was over, it was if a plague of locusts had descended. With some 125 people to feed there was precious little left. Nigel was reminded of the feast of the 5000 from the Bible. Here there were no loaves or fishes left over, just a few crumbs.

The minute hand on the clock tower nearby edged towards 3 o'clock, a crowd now gathered around the podium where the birthday gifts would be presented to Nigel. There were small packages, and large packages all wrapped in various coloured papers, which shone in the glorious spring sunshine. Then, the chimes rang out and they all waited with baited breath. Lord Ashdown took his son by the hand and led him up on to the podium. Nigel felt rather embarrassed; he was now the centre of attention. He had never before stood in front of a crowd of this size, although most of them were his friends. His big moment had finally arrived. What beautiful gifts lay underneath all those coloured wrappings? He would soon find out.

The ceremonial unwrapping began. The first present to see the light of day was a Bow and Arrow set and then models of all shapes and sizes. There were Coaches and Horses, Carts with Horses and finally the biggest present of all. Nigel could hardly wait to see what this present might be. It was certainly large. As Nigel began to remove the wrapping, the gift was revealed. It was a model Car big enough for young Nigel to pedal around. It was beautifully made, finished in Green and Silver, it had a leather-padded seat and a steering wheel edged in leather.

The wheels were spoked but with solid rubber tyres, of course. Nigel's eyes lit up as he removed the last piece of wrapping paper from this magnificent model. Nigel was speechless for a moment, but recovered his composure and walked over and kissed his father on the cheek

"Its really wonderful present father," said Nigel, "thank you very much indeed."

The crowd then sang "Happy Birthday" to Nigel.

That spring and summer of 1901, seemed to drag by, for young Nigel could think of nothing but Motor Cars. He was still doing well at School and was a very popular pupil. At weekends, he could be seen peddling around the grounds in his little green and silver car. The servants would sometimes have to chase down as far as the Gatekeeper's Lodge to find him. The Lodge was situated at the end of a long gravel drive. The only timekeeping device Nigel had was his stomach, this always told him when it was mealtimes. He always seemed to be in such a state when he returned to be fed, with dirty face, hands, and knees. His mother wondered what he got up to on his jaunts around the family estate. Along the edge of the wood, that fringed the southern boundary ran a wide stream with rushes on either side; during winter it sometimes flooded the nearby fields. It was the home of a wide variety of local wildlife including Frogs, Newts, and Fish. In the wood lived Badgers, Foxes, and Rabbits. Nigel often went there and there is no doubt, where the mud on his clothes came from. He was a typical lively boy of 6 years of age with a bottomless thirst for knowledge of all things.

Time passed and the summer wore on, Victoria and John decided that it was time to think about further education for Nigel. The local school was all very well, but he needed to be stretched. His reading standard was very good indeed; in the evenings he always had his head in a book. Cars, Toys, and playing around in the House were all very well during holidays, but one day John hoped that Nigel would take over the running of the Brewery. So, one evening, John, Victoria, and Nigel sat down to discuss the matter. They agreed that nothing should be done in a hurry, but that any further education must be carefully planned.

The Nanny that had looked after Nigel, since he was born. She had some teaching skills she had taught Nigel to read and write, but now, she could not equip him with all that he needed to know to survive in a commercial world.

John and Victoria had taken on Lily Green when Victoria had become pregnant, and had travelled with them to India. She was very intelligent, and could have been a college graduate but her family was poor, even after passing some examinations, she was unable to go on to a professional career. In her spare time, she had read many of the books in the Ashdown collection, both at Ashdown Hall and in their home in the hills near Delhi. Whilst they were overseas, Victoria always encouraged her to read and improve her Mathematics and English. They knew that she was an intelligent girl, and as Nigel grew, they could employ her not only as a Nanny, but also as a Tutor and a Governess. Lily had always been treated like a member of the family. She cooked and cared for Nigel as if he were her own son. She would read to him from time to time. Nigel always looked forward to a quiet time listening to stories read by this charming girl. John and Victoria thought that children who have stories read to them always benefited.

So, it was decided that after Christmas a Tutor would be engaged, one with University qualifications. This news had to be broken gently to Lily, as she might think that her position in the family was under threat. Victoria knew that there might be other children, who could benefit from Lily's knowledge. In fact, one of their neighbours had asked if she could hire Lily to do some tuition for her 5-yr.old. Victoria put the proposition to Lily, and she agreed. At the same time, they told her about the proposed Tutor. Lily was quite happy with that arrangement. Victoria told Lily that when the new Tutor arrived she could spend time with him in order to brush up her skills.

That Christmas of 1901, was a happy time for all the family. The House was full of colour with festive decorations in every room. Nigel's Grandmother, Lady Elizabeth, made one of her bi-annual visits to Ashdown Hall, for after the death of her husband, Lord Rupert Ashdown, she had moved to the London Flat in Kensington. She loved the social whirl of Victorian London. Now with King Edward VII on the throne the high life would no doubt continue and indeed, it did. She always said that Kensington was far more convenient, for the social whirl than that rambling house in Sussex. She usually brought her maid Dorothy with her. Nigel always thought that the pair of them looked 100 years old.

The big surprise was that Victoria's parents, Sir Nigel and Grace Hawkesley had cut short their holiday in the South of France to attend the festivities. In fact, they had a villa just 20 miles away from Lady Elizabeth on the Cote d'Azure.

The servants really had their work cut out now, with all these extra guests. They all expected to be pampered, no doubt. On Christmas Eve, there would be the traditional big party. Nigel was told that if he behaved himself, he could stay up late. The Party got into full swing around 7p.m. The first outside guests arrived, Lord John, and Lady Victoria welcomed them, and the Master of Ceremonies announced each guest by name. Soon, the place was buzzing with conversations and gossip. The band began to play in the Ballroom; soon the dancers took the floor. The food was laid out in the Banqueting

Hall ready for the guests to be served during the course of the evening. It was going to be a successful evening thought John and indeed, it was. The Party went on until the early hours of Christmas morning. Nigel was very good and so nobody told him to go to bed. Lady Elizabeth found Nigel asleep in the Library; she picked him up and carried him up to bed.

Overnight the temperature had fallen, the family awoke to find there had been a heavy blanket of snow, covering everything all fields, hedgerows and trees. When Nigel finally surfaced, he opened the curtains and looked across the countryside.

"It looks like Fairyland," he sighed.

He glanced across at the carriage clock on the mantelpiece. "Goodness me," he said to himself, "8.30 a.m. and a lovely Christmas morning."

He made his way downstairs, throwing on his dressing gown as he went.

"They all had a late night," he thought to himself, "so I doubt if anyone will have got up yet."

He slowly opened the big Oak doors and entered the Morning Room. However, he was wrong; there were his parents in front of a roaring fire. They turned toward the doors, and smiled as Nigel entered the room.

"Good morning son," they said in unison, "and a Very Merry Christmas to you."

"Merry Christmas father and to you too Mother," replied Nigel.

"We didn't wake you Nigel," said John, "for you were sleeping so soundly. Actually, we thought that you had forgotten it was Christmas. Your presents are over there under the Christmas tree. Why don't you go over and unwrap your presents?"

Nigel needed no other invitation as he made his way to the enormous Fir Tree that dominated the room. It was decorated with every device, tinsel, fairy lights and gaily-coloured baubles. He soon found his presents; the expression of delight on his face brought a smile of satisfaction to both John and Victoria, as he opened one after the other.

As the morning wore on the Christmas festivities continued with the family Service at their local church. Nigel never looked forward to the sermon given by the Reverend Ward, which in his opinion was always far too long. The family Christmas Dinner with all the trimmings was an event that Nigel loved, as he really enjoyed his food.

Sadly the Christmas holiday came to an end; the New Year of 1902 was now almost upon them. John had plans to extend the Brewery again during the spring. This would mean further prosperity for both the Ashdown Family and the Employees.

January began cold and grey. After dinner one evening John took, Nigel aside.

"Nigel," he began, "one day you will inherit the family business. I know your present school is adequate, and Lily has taught you so many things. However, over the past couple of months your Mother and I have been thinking seriously, about your future education. I have spoken to Nanny. She says that she cannot now cope; with all the extra information you need to know, and even that the school cannot teach you to the level that I know you can reach. To succeed in life you need a really good education. Mother and I do want the very best for you. A few days ago, I placed an advertisement in a London Newspaper for a Tutor. One with a University education, I have had several replies and hope to start interviews next week. I can see from your expression that you do not agree with this."

Nigel was frowning. John stopped for a moment to see if there was a response from his son.

"Father," replied Nigel, "will I meet the prospective Tutors?"

"Of course Nigel, we cannot have someone you do not like trying to teach you. After all if you do not like someone, how can you learn from them?"

Nigel seemed much happier now that his Father had reassured him. After such a wonderful Christmas and New Year, Nigel thought that his world would be turned upside down by this new Tutor. It now meant school all day, tutoring at night and weekends. When would he have time to play? There were other questions his young mind threw out. What sort of man would his Father employ? There were indeed many questions to be answered.

The days passed a succession of young men came to the Hall. Lord John and Nigel interviewed them in the Morning Room. Nigel did not like any of the applicants. Some were haughty and others just plain horrid. They were either too strict, too old and some did not even like children. Some gave Nigel some really funny looks. Obviously, thought Nigel they must have been thrown out of one University or another. Poor John Ashdown was at his wits end. Would he never find a going to find a tutor that both he and his son liked? Nigel did not mind too much, for him life went on as normal. Finding a Tutor was not as easy as John and Victoria thought. They had by this time almost given up on the idea.

Then, in the middle of February, John received a letter from a George Campbell, which said that he would like to be considered for the post as Tutor. The letter also stated that he had excellent credentials and would bring them with him. John passed the letter to Victoria, who having read it thought for a moment.

"Oh, well" said Victoria to John passing the letter back to him, "might as well see him, got nothing to lose have we?"

"I agree my love," said John putting the letter on a side table, "I will phone and make the necessary arrangements."

On the 27th February George Campbell came for his interview. John arranged for his chauffeur to meet Mr. Campbell at Horsham Station to bring him to Ashdown Hall. Charles the Coachman, who had never been asked to pick up an employee in his life, thought those that could not afford a carriage should walk or hire a Horse-drawn Trap. However, he could not disobey his employer so with good grace he set off to meet the London train. George's train had arrived a few minutes early. He was astounded, that a fine carriage with the Owner's Coat of Arms should be coming into the Station Forecourt. Charles stopped the coach, walked over to George, who was looking around to see who was meeting him.

"Excuse me young sir," replied George in a snooty tone, "are you Mr. Campbell?"

"Yes I am," replied George, "are you here to take me to Ashdown Hall?"

"I am Charles, Mr. Campbell, would you please follow me."

George followed in silence until they reached the coach.

"You may sit inside if you wish," said Charles haughtily.

George did not need a second invitation to this unique experience he opened the door and climbed in, and now he settled down for the journey to the Hall. The interior of the coach was the height of luxury as far as he was concerned. The coach pulled up outside the Hall and George alighted and rang the bell. Lily answered the door and asked George to wait in the entrance hall. After a few minutes, John appeared. He walked over and greeted George.

"Mr. Campbell," said Lord John shaking him warmly by the hand, "how good of you to come."

"Thank you sir," began George, "for sending your coachman to meet me at the Station. It is certainly a long walk, and I would have had some difficulty finding Ashdown Hall."

"Not at all," replied John, "I'll send for my son Nigel, as I have promised that he shall sit in on all interviews. You see Mr. Campbell, not only do I have to like you, but my son will have to like you as well. So please follow me into the Morning Room. By the way Mr. Campbell would you like a cup of tea?"

"Yes please sir," replied George.

The two men sat down in the armchairs and talked until Nigel arrived.

Nigel opened the door, and Lord John and George got to their feet as Nigel approached them.

"Nigel," said Lord John, "may I introduce you to Mr. George Campbell and as you may know, he has applied for the post of Tutor."

George shook hands with Nigel, "it is a pleasure to meet you Nigel."

Lord John suggested that they all sit down and informally discuss the question of Nigel's future education.

John and Nigel agreed that they both liked George, for he had a gentle but firm way and had excellent qualifications. At the end of an hour or so, John asked him what he expected from the position offered and told him the salary he was prepared to pay. John also told him that the post was residential, meals would be provided and he would have time off as well. John could not make out why such a clever and personable young man did not have a professional post in London. May be one day they would find out. Today was all about Nigel and his future. If this young man could bring out the flair that was hidden in Nigel, and then the money spent would be worthwhile. George sat for a moment in silence to consider the offer.

"Sir," he began, "I would be honoured to teach your Son. I can start if it agreeable to you, at the beginning of next week. In the meantime, I do have a few personal arrangements to make."

"Mr. Campbell that is perfect," replied Lord John, "I will arrange to meet you at Horsham Station off the 4 p.m. London train, on Monday of next week."

George was delighted and they all shook hands and George was hired and Nigel now had a full time tutor.

Lord John called Charles, and told him to drive George to the station. George sat in the London bound train as it chugged along pondering over his trip to Ashdown Hall. He felt that he had the right decision. He had no ties, and although living with the aristocracy might be a strain at first, he now thought of it as a challenge. George Campbell had been educated at Christ's Hospital in London, where his family was in the

Meat Trade at Smithfield Market. Their only son had been accepted at Christ's Hospital having passed the entrance examination. He had been top of his class, later had become a Grecian and finally Head Boy. He had then gone on to Cambridge University where he studied, English, History, Mathematics and Music. He could not wait to start his tutoring of Lord Ashdown's son.

The days passed quickly, George now was back at Ashdown Hall settling in to his new living quarters, which were more palatial than he expected. He even had his own bathroom, a luxury indeed. George and Nigel got down to working together. John thought that they made a good team. George had apparently learnt to drive at University, for one of his friends had a rich father who owned a Motor Car and George had spent some weekends with him.

John and George both hoped that Nigel would be able to go to Christ's Hospital that had just opened a brand new School, just a few miles away. It was fortuitous, that George had been a pupil there. However, they made enquiries, but they were told that Christ's Hospital only allowed children from less advantaged families were being admitted. There were other private schools including Eton, Harrow, and Marlborough. Seems as if they would have to examine all the options.

Time seemed to pass quickly; George and Nigel became firm friends. Nigel soaked up information like a sponge. George found it easy to get Nigel to solve the problems he set. They both shared a love of motoring and music. George was an excellent pianist; he could play all kinds whether classical, popular songs of the day or the new Ragtime music which had started to come over from the USA. He taught Nigel to play on the family's Grand Piano. Time spent with George did not seem like school to Nigel. The view from the Music Room out of the large Picture Windows gave a wonderful panorama of the rolling Sussex countryside, so when Nigel was playing, George could enjoy nature in all its glory.

In the spring of 1903, the Motor Car again, entered Nigel's life. His father came home one day in a large white Mercedes. He had managed to buy this beautiful machine through a business acquaintance, who travelled regularly through Europe. Nigel never did find out how much his father paid for the Car. He did know that it was called a Model "60" and that it was very fast and powerful. John Ashdown had asked his contact if two extra seats could be fitted, as the normal Model "60" was only a two seater. The extra seats were fitted at the factory and they were very comfortable. All Nigel and George knew was that it was the finest car they have ever seen.

There were one or two around the district, but this was the best of all. At first, John would not let even his chauffeur drive this new machine, until he had practised with George.

John was like a boy with a new toy. One afternoon, the Ashdowns all climbed aboard this magnificent vehicle. Nigel was really excited. The family seemed to spend ages getting really dressed up in thick Coats, Boots, Gloves, Goggles, Hats, and Scarves. Nigel was getting impatient, all this dressing up go just a few miles. When they went out in the coach the dressed in just ordinary clothes, so why all this? Nigel did not realise that the roads were so bad, for the car would kick up clouds of dust that would get everywhere. At last, they were ready to go. John reached under the seat and got out a piece of metal rod, called a starting handle. Fitting it into the front of the car, under the radiator. He then fiddled with a couple of levers, pumped another control, and gave a twist to the starting handle and the beast coughed into life. A cloud of blue smoke came from the rear of the car. John climbed on board again, pushed down a pedal, called the Clutch; there was a jerk and the Car shot forward. Soon they were doing 20 mph as the reached the Gatehouse. They then stopped at the main road, turned left and accelerated away heading for the open countryside. Nigel looked back to see a large cloud of dust, now he knew the reason for dressing up to go motoring. John accelerated, as he did so the size of the cloud increased. Looking to the side, Nigel noticed the fields whizzing by and the wind whistling past his ears. Victoria sat beside her husband as if she had travelled in cars all her life. She was enjoying every minute of it. By the time that they had reached the village of Five Oaks, they were doing over 40 mph. John slowed the Mercedes down, when they were clear of all habitation the speed increased once more. They turned right and accelerated, a Horse pulling a Cart approached, the Driver looked surprised to say the least.

The Horse reared up in its shafts; the driver shook his fist at John and shouted something. John could not hear him so carried on. Nigel looked back to see the driver still trying to calm down his Horse. Before them, lay a very long straight road, no other traffic, and no habitation. John accelerated again to see what this Car could do.

Soon they were doing almost 60 mph, John understood that this Model "60" could do over 80 mph, he knew he was well within the machine's capabilities. Nigel thought that they were travelling at the speed of light. He had never been so fast in all his life. All too soon the ride was over; they were all back home safe and sound. George asked Nigel what he thought of his trip. Nigel thought that it was absolutely magic. That hour on the open road changed Nigel's life, but for now, it was back to the studies. He vowed one day to have a car of his own. He would work hard to earn one of these fabulous machines. The wind on his face, the excitement of speeding along and complete freedom to go where he wanted excited him. It was a dream to be realised. It was there for the taking, but he had to be focussed.

Chapter 3

It was 1903 and a glorious Mediterranean Spring, 'would a young man's fancy turn toward her' thought 20 year old Carla Navarrio, as she strolled along to an Interview at the Bank of Italy in her hometown of Florence. The large Renaissance building stood some 200 metres from the Railway Station in the centre of the City. She was dressed in a dark Grey skirt, White blouse and her dark brown hair was tied back with a ribbon and on her head was a straw hat.

It was her first job interview, so she wanted to make a good impression on her new prospective employer. She needed this job, and wanted to prove to her family that the money, which they had spent on her education, was not wasted on a mere girl. She had talent and wanted to show it. Her father Guilliermo was a successful Engineer and still owned a large factory in Milan, where he also had a town house. However, being a Florentine himself, when he had the opportunity to expand his Research and Development Department he chose Florence. He had lavished both affection and money on his only child. Carla had not disappointed him. She was beautiful, intelligent, strong willed but also sweet natured. Her father always said that she could charm anybody, unlike many of her friends who possessed that fiery Italian temperament.

She climbed the steps leading to the large double Oak doors, which stood wide open leading to the lofty entrance hall. She walked, confidently up to the Reception desk. The Reception Clerk looked up.

"Excuse me," she said, "can I help you, Signorina?"

Carla explained that she had an interview and showed her the letter. The Clerk directed her to the first floor, where the Manager's Office was situated. She climbed the long marble staircase and found her way to a door marked Manager's Secretary. She knocked on the door and waited for a response.

"Come in please," said a woman's voice from within.

She entered a small Office with a desk, typewriter, and a filing cabinet. The woman at the desk looked up and smiled.

"You must be Signorina Navarrio," she said, "you must be here for your interview with our Manager Signor Borghese. Please wait a moment and I will tell him you are here."

"Thank you," replied Carla.

Carla looked for a mirror to see if her make-up and hair were all OK. She did not have any time to do anything, for the Secretary reappeared and indicated that Carla should go into the Manager's Office.

"Please come in," she heard a male voice answer.

Carla pushed the door open wider went in and sat down. Behind the large walnut desk sat a young man perhaps 21 years of age, looking as if he was the Bank Manager. He was slim with long dark hair slicked back with hair oil and he wore a dark blue pin stripe suit. He seemed too young to hold a position like that. "Please sit down Signorina," said the young man, "would you care for a coffee Signorina, whilst we wait for my Father? He is the Manager and will be joining us shortly."

As Carla sat down their eyes met, Carla tried to say something, but the words seem to stick in her throat.

"Sorry," began the young man again, "I should really have introduced myself. I am Dino Borghese, my father has the same name, but prefers to be called by his second name, which is Enzo, and I hope that is not confusing. My father calls himself Manager; really he is Vice-President of the Bank."

He rose from the high leather backed chair, came around the desk, and kissed Carla's hand. Carla blushed a little.

"Welcome to the Bank of Italy."

He remained standing, for at that moment, the door opened again into the Office appeared a tall man, greying at the temples, but very distinguished. He came straight over to Carla and kissed Carla's hand.

"Good morning, Signorina Navarrio," began Enzo, "I am Dino Enzo Borghese. I see that you have met my son, Dino. I am sorry to be a little late for our meeting."

Dino Borghese Snr. turned to his son.

"Would you please leave us please Dino, whilst I interview this charming young lady?"

"Of course, Father," said Dino Jnr.

Dino turning to Carla he said,

"I do hope that we shall meet again soon."

Dino Jnr. smiled and left his father's office. The door closed Carla felt a little self-conscious; she sat there wondering what would happen next. Dino Snr. soon put her at her ease.

"Just relax, Signorina Navarrio. I will just phone my Secretary and tell her that we are not to be disturbed."

He picked up the telephone.

"Maria, no more calls please."

Dino Snr. sat back in his chair, picked up a yellow file, and opened it. He gazed at it then his eyes went back to Carla.

"I have your letter," he began, "and application for employment with our Bank. Let me just refresh my memory."

He glanced back at the file again, looked at the papers and then paused for a moment. Carla wondered how the interview would go as she had said so little.

"I see Signorina, that you are well qualified with top marks from Pisa University. Excellent references too. What have you to say for yourself, Signorina Navarrio?"

By now, Carla had collected her thoughts together she knew that it was time to speak for herself. Her confidence was growing; after all, she wanted this job more than anything.

"Sir," she began, "first of all can I thank you for seeing me. I am a bit nervous and I can speak for myself. I do hope that you can offer me the position I applied for?"

"Let me assure you Signorina Navarrio that there is nothing to be nervous about. With your qualifications the job advertised was somewhat junior and it has been filled. It was really not suited to your talents. You could say that this is your lucky day."

Carla's feelings changed, what was on offer for her now? Was there a job or not? Was she being patronised because she was a young lady?

"If that is the case sir," replied Carla, "what position are you able to offer me today?"

Carla's mind seemed full of questions. Dino Snr. sat back in his chair thought for a moment and then leaned forward.

"Well let me explain, Signorina. My Son Dino is badly in need of a Personal Assistant, with your qualifications, you would be perfect for the job. It is yours, should you want it, plus it pays twice the salary of the position for which you applied. Dino Jnr. has to travel to all the other branches of the Bank. These are located in all the large cities from Naples in the South, to Turin and Venice in the North. When travelling with him, you would stay in first class hotels and all expenses would be met. The Bank has many Clients, some small others very big, it is Dino's job to visit them on a regular basis. Sometimes you will join him, other times you will look after Clients here in Florence." Carla felt that she had just won the State Lottery.

"In essence," said Enzo, "that is roughly what your job will entail. Will you accept this post?"

Carla could not contain herself any longer.

"I should simply love to do that job," she blurted out, "when can I start?"

Dino Snr. smiled and walked around to the front of his desk. "We would be delighted if you could start today Signorina Navarrio," answered Enzo, "if you are happy with that. My Son will now show you to your Office, where you will find all that you need, including a Secretary. I will arrange to draw up your contract."

Carla kissed Dino Snr.

"Thank you Sir," said Carla ecstatically, "thank you very much indeed."

Dino Snr walked to the office door with her. He shook Carla's hand once more.

"Welcome to the Bank of Italy Signorina Navarrio. I hope that you will be happy working here."

Dino Snr. was still standing in the doorway as Carla got to Maria's desk.

"Maria, would you take Signorina Navarrio along to my son's office. Then come back to me for I have some letters to dictate."

Maria Cassetti was a Florentine; she was tall, slim, blonde-haired woman and about 30 years of age. She had worked at the Bank of Italy for about 8 years, like Carla she had graduated from the University of Pisa. She had worked hard at the Bank; her promotion had been very swift at times, now she was the Personal Assistant to the Vice-President. She always accompanied Dino Snr. on his business trips, when they were out of town.

There was gossip that they had been lovers one summer, which was why her promotion had been so swift, however nothing had ever been proved. Sufficient to say that her wardrobe was far in excess of her salary. She had many designer outfits that were the talk of the Office. Her Gowns, summer clothes, winter coats, and furs would not have been out of place in the President's wife's boudoir, let alone that of a mere Personal Assistant. Maria gave herself airs, and graces feeling that she was superior to her colleagues. It was therefore, no surprise to anyone that she had a few friends at the Bank, all her cronies and associates outside the financial world were of a similar style to her, social climbers. They all liked to be seen in all the best places, you could say they were posers. Nobody ever saw her in male company, only female, there was stories put about of her sexual deviations, but most people guessed she swung both ways. In spite of all this, she was very good at her job. She chatted to Carla, looking her up and down, as they walked through what seemed endless corridors lined with paintings of famous people and landscapes.

Finally, they arrived at the main marble staircase. Waiting at the top was Dino Jnr., who was smiling.

"Good morning again, Signorina Navarrio and good morning Maria."

He turned to Carla.

"Follow me please to my office Signorina Navarrio. It is just around the next corner."

Carla followed Dino Jnr. to a large carved oak door, which Dino opened.

"This is my Department," said Dino Jnr. with a hand gesture.

Carla looked around the large room with its stucco ceiling and intricate freeze patterns, along one wall large picture windows ran the length of the room and looked out over the busy street below. Over at the far end of the room was another door. Carla wondered where that led to; she was soon to find out.

"Behind that door over there," said Dino Jnr. "that is where we keep our secretaries. My desk is here; your desk is over there."

There were two large walnut desks by the windows.

"Having our desks close the windows," Dino continued, "we always get the best light to work by. Don't you agree? We must always remember that the real world is out there. That is where the business is, that is where our Client's are. Always remember to keep the Client happy. Remember that the Client pays our salaries without them there would be no business. Always treat a Client with respect, even if you think that they are wrong."

Carla nodded her understanding. She had a lot to learn about the business side of things and doubtless, a good deal more to know about Dino. Little did she know how her future would turn out, but today, she felt simply full of the joy of spring, a new job, and money in her pocket.

Dino beckoned her to sit beside him on long leather Chesterfield, which was situated in the middle of the room.

"We have not spoken very much," said Dino, "but I am delighted that you have accepted the position. I need someone I can trust and work with. I have had both Male and Female Personal Assistants in the past, which have disappointed me. I know you can do this job, otherwise we would not have chosen you. I have seen your file and I think my Father explained your role here."

They continued talking, when suddenly Dino looked up.

"By the way can I call you Carla? Signorina Navarrio seems so formal as we shall be working together? Please call me Dino."

"Of course you may," replied Carla who seemed to have said little to this point.

"Then Carla, it is time I took my new Personal Assistant to lunch. I know a great Restaurant down by the Arno. We can talk there and be at our ease."

The two young people got up left the building and went off to lunch. The Restaurant was just a short walk away from the Bank. Carla was over the moon, but realised that this might be the only free lunch. Now, she had a position at the Bank with all the trimmings, plus lunch with a handsome Boss. She certainly had fallen on her feet. The Lunch was a leisurely one in a Restaurant close to the Ponte Vecchio; it was crowded with executives and their associates. Dino always got a table, as he was a regular

Diner. The Restaurant Manager, Roberto, came over and showed them to a table that was overlooking the river. Lunch progressed and as the wine flowed. Carla began to open up, responding to Dino's questions, in turn asking quite a few of her own. Dino knew he had chosen the right person. Here was a young lady with brains and intellect. He admitted there had been many applicants for this position. He reiterated, he wanted her to join him on his visits to other branches of the Bank. By the time they had returned to the Office, Carla's desk had been equipped with a telephone, pens, pencils, calendar, blotting pad, and ink. There was also a very comfortable chair for her to sit in. Carla began to settle in.

The door at the far end of the room opened, a young lady appeared she walked towards Carla.

"Good afternoon, Signorina Navarrio," said the young lady, "my name is Franchesca, I am your Personal Secretary."

Carla looked surprised, my first job and already I have a Secretary.

"Good afternoon Franchesca," replied Carla, "I am delighted to meet you, I am sure we can work well together."

Franchesca smiled and Carla asked her to sit down.

"Thank you Signorina, I will type all your letters, answer the telephone and take messages when you are out of the office. In fact, if you need anything call me. I am No.2 on your dial."

The two young ladies talked for several minutes and all too soon the day was over. At 5 p.m., Carla left the Office; she thought that really was some day. The rest of the week seemed to fly past, at the weekend Carla went off to see her family who lived in Fiesole, where her parents had a small weekend villa.

Carla's father was delighted that his daughter had found a really good job, her mother Florina, was also pleased that Carla was staying in Florence and would be living at home for a while. Jobs for women graduates were very hard to come by, especially those that paid a reasonable salary and offered prospects for promotion. Promotion usually meant that you had to give sexual favours to your boss. At least that is what the Media were saying at the time. Men always got the best jobs, women were supposed to stay home and have children; they were not suited for commerce.

Suddenly, the weekend was over and Carla was back at her desk, coping well with the new job. Dino announced that he was off to Milan on Tuesday morning to see a very important new Client. He told Carla that she would be joining him. This would be an excellent opportunity for her to meet Sandro Minardi.

The Bank's other Vice-President, not only would they meet their new Client but several other important existing Clients in the City. They would be staying at the home of Signor Minardi for a couple of nights. They would meet at Florence Station at 8 am, in the Booking Hall in time to catch the 8.30am train direct to Milan.

The next morning Carla awoke early, her mother having packed her suitcase the night before, much to Carla's annoyance, she liked to pack her own case. Carla hailed a taxi and was soon at the Station in good time. She wandered through the early morning throng. Everyone seemed in a hurry. She found her way to the Booking Hall and there was Dino. He looked very handsome in his dark blue suit, white shirt, and blue tie. Carla had on the dress she wore for her interview; she did have not the money to buy a new wardrobe.

"Good morning Carla," said Dino cheerfully, "you look very glamorous. We have about 25 minutes before the train leaves. Just time for a quick coffee."

He picked her suitcase and they headed to a nearby stall for a cappuccino. They settled into their reserved window seats as the train steamed out of Florence Station. It had been several years since Carla had been on a train; the last time was when she went with her parents to visit an uncle who lived in Padova. Carla looked out of the windows and watched Florence slip into the distance; she was on her first trip for the Bank. She said to herself, that she would maintain self-discipline, because she wanted to create a good impression on all the Bank's contacts. The train built up speed; Dino then fully explained the reason for the hurried arrangements. Carla was fascinated that she should be included. It seems one of his previous assistants had departed quickly, leaving a very important business operation in mid-stream. They had to close the business tomorrow or the deadline would pass. Dino got out his notes on the discussion that had taken place, whilst Carla watched the scenery rush by.

The first stop the train made was a Bologna. Carla had never visited this city, for only thing she knew was a Sauce that went over Spaghetti called Bolognaise. Dino finished reading his notes suggesting that Carla skim through them, so that if she were asked questions, she would have some background information on this case. The train steamed on through Modena, Palma and finally it pulled into Milan right on time. The new era for Carla had begun.

Outside Milan Station, Dino hailed a taxi and soon they arrived at the Bank. It was an imposing building in the Commercial quarter of the bustling City. They quickly went up to Signor Minardi's Office on the first floor. Sandro Minardi was a short, stout gentleman in his mid 40's. He greeted Carla and Dino with a kiss on both cheeks then led the couple in to his palatial office. It was late afternoon, even so, Sandro wanted to know all the news from Dino, and who was this new attractive Personal Assistant. Time seemed to just fly past. Their discussion was suspended, when Sandro's Secretary came in to the office to tell Signor Minardi that his car was ready to take him and his guests' home. The party made their way down to the front entrance, where the chauffeur was standing by a large black Fiat saloon. They sat back in comfort whilst they were whisked off to the Minardi home.

The Minardi's lived in a large villa in landscaped grounds surrounded by a stone wall. Carla thought that it looked magnificent, although she had seen pictures of Villas like this in magazines. They drove through the wrought iron gates and up the gravel drive to the main entrance. The car came to a halt, in the doorway, they could see the silhouette of a woman, and the light was behind her. Carla could not see her face, she wondered if it was Signora Minardi. The chauffeur opened the car door; the party alighted and made their way to the open door.

"Good evening, sir," said a woman dressed in a maid's uniform who curtsied.

"Good evening Maria," replied Signor Minardi, "these are my associates Carla and Dino who will be staying for two nights. Will you please arrange for their luggage to be taken up to the Guest Bedrooms?"

Maria curtsied again.

"Yes, sir," she replied, "Signora Minardi is in the Drawing Room."

On hearing voices, Signora Minardi came out into the Hall, where she kissed her husband and her guests on both cheeks. She hoped that their stay would be a pleasant one and that their business negotiations would be successful.

It seems that Dino came to stay once a month. Maria always treated him coldly but with respect; on the other hand, Dino looked upon Signora Minardi as Aunt Sophia. Dinner was served and afterward Sophia and Carla got deep into conversation. Sandro seldom brought guests home, especially female guests. If he did, usually they were Clients with their wives.

Sophia Minardi took an instant liking to Carla, something she rarely did with other guests. She said that if Carla came to Milan again, she must come to stay at the Minardi home. Talk went on into the early hours of the morning; the two men were totally engrossed in talking business. By the time they had decided to go to bed, Carla could hardly keep her eyes open, when her head hit the pillow; she fell asleep at once and slept like a log.

She awoke the next morning to the smell of fresh coffee, before her stood a young woman in a Maid's uniform.

"Good morning, Signorina, I am Catherina your Maid. Breakfast will be served in 30 minutes in the Breakfast Room. I have taken the liberty of laying out your clothes for the day."

Carla was astounded; life was getting better by the minute. Breakfast was not a leisurely affair, as Dinner had been. They had a very busy schedule, no time to waste. The big FIAT with the chauffeur was by the Main Entrance of the Villa waiting to whisk them back into the City for another hectic day.

Several large deals were concluded over lunch in a very swish Restaurant. This was the new Client, he was very impressed with the presentation, and said that it would lead to more business in other cities. This was indeed a very successful day. Carla really liked her job; she seemed to have got into the swing of things. Dino made sure that she was involved in all aspects of the business. After all, as his Personal Assistant, Carla would have to deputise for him when he was elsewhere. He felt confident that she could handle Bank business with authority, and would not make rash promises or indeed form agreements that would jeopardise Client relationships. The day just flew by; soon they were back at the Minardi home. Sandro asked how the day went. Dino said it could not have gone better. Carla has charmed one of the Clients, saying the right thing at the right time. It had been Carla that had closed the biggest deal of the day. All too soon, the trip was over and they were back at their desks in Florence with all the paperwork to complete, and reports to write. Carla could not wait for the next trip. Life had certainly changed for her since she crossed the threshold of that Bank.

In the weeks that followed, the young couple were starting to be the talk of the Bank. They went away together, to visit other branches of the Bank about twice per month. Then on Dino's 21st Birthday, his father bought him a Motor Car; it was a 1902 Mors. In this car, Dino spent many happy hours with local Ladies of his choice, doing what virile Italian young men do in the hills around Florence. With all the sexual activity that went on in that car, it was a good thing that cars cannot talk; otherwise that Mors would have a tale or two to tell. In fact, he made passionate love to a certain Isabella Ferrarino; she was the love of his life, well, for about a month or so. Isabella was very beautiful, with a well-developed figure, and she knew it. She always dressed in tight clothing, and low cut dresses especially in summer, that left very little to the imagination, but unfortunately for Dino, she had an extremely jealous nature. Her father Marco owned a famous jewellery shop close to the Bank. He was quite wealthy, and Isabella being his only child he indulged her passion for fine clothes. Isabella was walking towards her father's shop one day, when she happened to spy Dino walking along with Carla. She got extremely angry, raced crossed the street, and then started a blazing row with Dino in front of Carla. Carla tried to walk away, she had only walked a couple of paces when Isabella ran after her and stopped her. Then another argument began. Carla, being diplomatic said nothing. The way Isabella was behaving in public, nobody in their right mind would want her as a partner. Isabella stormed off, and that was the last Dino ever saw of her.

Dino caught up to Carla and apologised for Isabella's behaviour. Carla nearly asked the fatal question - was that your lady friend Dino. She felt that silence was best. Dino sat at his desk deep in thought. After her latest outburst Isabella was now history, he decided that he should cool things with the ladies and assess his situation. However, due to his Latin temperament any periods of celibacy last precisely a week. He had fallen head over heels in love with Carla. He always made it a rule never, to go out with young ladies with whom he worked.

After all, he had his own position to consider. He recalled the affair between Maria and his father; that was kept very quiet; he certainly did not want a repeat of this.

Gossip in the Bank was always rife, certain people were matched up, whether they were or not. Dino wondered exactly what these mischief-makers gained out of it. Several of the staff had been forced to leave because of viscous gossip. How much was true he did not know. Dino was frightened to tell Carla of his love for her, lest he lose a valuable Personal Assistant. Therefore, he felt that he had to suppress his feelings for her.

In the early summer of 1904, he plucked up courage to ask Carla if she would like to come with him for a drive on the following Sunday. They would take a picnic, enjoy some peace and quiet, and not talk business. Carla agreed, and Dino was delighted; he could not wait for the weekend. It was a beautiful Sunday morning; the young couple set out on a drive to Dino's favourite spot by the River Sieve. The picnic was spread out at a spot where they could see right across the valley. The swallows darted about catching insects that flew in the gentle breeze. Dino wanted to be careful, not to express his love for Carla too demonstratively, for fear of rejection.

By this time, unknown to Dino, Carla had become infatuated with him too, but feared that if she revealed this at work, it would expose her to scandal at the Bank. She was frightened any gossip, would no doubt soon circulate. Gossip was forever circulating at the Bank; the female staff seemed to love spreading it. They laid there in the sunshine, just enjoying life. Dino stretched out and touched Carla's hand, then raised himself on one elbow.

"I realise Carla," he began, "that we have only been working together for only a short time, but I feel I have known you all my life. I guess it was the time we did those deals in Milan, that I became aware of the fact that we were a team. Not only in business, but also in life. Please do not be offended, but I have fallen in love with you Carla."

Carla blushed, and had an idea of what was coming next.

"Oh Dino!" exclaimed Carla, "I have fallen in love with you too, I was afraid, in case you did not feel the same. I was also worried about my job at the Bank. I just love working with you."

They kissed passionately.

"Will you marry me?" said Dino when their lips finally parted, "we would be a terrific team together you and I."

Carla laughed aloud.

"Dino my love, I would be proud to be your wife."

They laid there their bodies entwined to celebrate their engagement. Dino thought that there would be one place he would not buy the ring, and that was from Marco's Store. They could now enjoy the picnic that much more; getting engaged certainly made them hungry. The day was now complete; all they had to do was tell the parents.

When Dino told his father that Carla and he were engaged, Dino Snr. and Sofia were absolutely delighted. Over the years, Dino had been out with lots of women some very jealous, others just as demanding. One they thought was a nymphomaniac, poor Dino used to come home worn out. Now, they were delighted that Dino had found a young lady, in the true sense of the word. She was beautiful and intelligent. Dino Snr. could see her dressed in the finest clothes plus being a real asset to his son and indeed the Bank.

Carla's parents were also very happy, that their only child had found happiness. They were looking forward to meeting Dino's parents. Dino had not even met Carla's parents. Therefore, it was decided that the very next weekend they should go to the Villa at Fiesole. The week seemed to fly by; with the weekend fast approaching he wondered how he would be received. Dino and his prospective father-in-law were professional men; maybe they would have something in common. Soon the day dawned, Dino called for Carla early on the Sunday morning, and they headed off in the Mors to Fiesole. The Villa was situated just outside the village, with glorious views across the Arno valley. On summer weekends, the heat, and humidity in Florence was unbearable. Guillermo and Florina were only too pleased to escape to the hills, to drink the local wine and enjoy the simple foods. Being away from the commercial whirl enabled both of them to relax and be themselves. Carla always did the cooking; to give her Mother a rest from 'toiling over the hot stove' as Florina called it. It was a bolthole with no telephone to disturb the peace.

As Carla and Dino approached the Villa, you could not help but hear the raucous exhaust note of the big Mors engine bouncing off the stone walls. Florina and Guillermo were waiting in the Garden as the car drew up. They greeted the couple with kisses on both cheeks, and invited them into their home.

Carla had brought very few of her young men home to meet her parents. In fact, Guillermo wondered if Carla could have a serious relationship, he thought that she was a career woman first and foremost, rather than let her affections loose. They had heard of previous boyfriends, most of them had been students at one University or another. However, Dino was the first young man with whom she had had a serious relationship. Both couples were soon in deep conversation, they were delighted that Carla was enjoying her position at the Bank and had concluded some very good business in partnership with Dino. He seemed to be an honest and sincere young man, with a secure position at the Bank, they hoped he would love and cherish their daughter. They then sat down to a feast of food and wine prepared by Florina and Guillermo, who was not a bad cook either. It had been a great day; Dino got on really well with Carla's parents.

They decided that to have a big Engagement Party later in the summer. It was their intention to get married on New Year's Day 1905. The Engagement Party that was held in a beautiful Restaurant on the banks of the River Arno, it was a very sophisticated affair. Carla showed off her Diamond and Emerald ring that Dino had bought. The presents were displayed beside a small stage, where a quartet played during the meal and for dancing later in the evening.

Now that she was earning a good salary Carla had moved into her own apartment, Dino had spent several evenings with her Carla even cooking for him. She had learned her culinary expertise from her Mother. Back at the office on the Monday morning, it was business as usual; however, they kept their engagement a secret. It was during the weeks that followed their love blossomed even more. The whole bank knew unofficially, that they were a couple. There were the Bank trips to Rome, Venice and Verona, where the Bank had just opened a new branch. The Bank was now getting very busy; there was much to do both commercially and personally. There seemed little time to spare as the summer disappeared and autumn came. Carla began to look through her wardrobe; some of her clothes were suffering the ravages of time. Her winter dresses, and coats had not been replaced for some time. Now, she had her own apartment there were bills to be paid.

She could not buy on impulse; as she had in the past, now she would have to calculate her expenditure very carefully.

The new winter fashions were in the stores; she had been window-shopping, 'Oh!' She thought how she would love some new clothes. She realised now that she had to look her best, especially if Clients invited them out. Dino said that now, as she was almost part of the family, and that now they should go shopping together. Being her fiancée, he would pay for all her new outfits, no expense spared. The day they went out into the fashion centre of Florence, Carla felt like a Princess. Dino decided that he would provide her with a complete winter wardrobe, starting with lingerie, daywear and eveningwear. She should have at least one fur coat and a suitably matched fur hat for those special occasions, and other Fur-trimmed coats to wear to the Office. All of her new clothes were to be designed by the top names of the day. When they got to the store, Carla could not wait to try on lots of different coats and dresses, each time she looked at herself in the mirror. She could not believe the transition; the new clothes certainly made a difference. It was not until she was wearing the one of her new evening dresses, together with a full length Silver fox coat, did Dino realise that Carla was such a beautiful young woman.

In view of the fact that Dino had spent so much money in the store, they gave Carla a Mink stole as an extra gift. Carla admired herself for several minutes, the softness of the fur against her skin gave her a sensuous feeling inside, and with the matching hat she felt like a princess. This was one outfit that she had to have, but Carla loved them all. Dino smiled and said that whatever the new clothes cost, she was worth it. Carla was to be his future bride and nothing would be too good for her. Next, there were bracelets, earrings, necklaces and watches by the dozen from which to select. Carla was dazzled by it all. It was like a dream. This day would be one that Carla would not forget. The day they were delivered by the Stores, Carla could not wait to try them on in the privacy of her Apartment; she could admire herself without feeling self-conscious. She spent all one evening trying on her new clothes, and she felt like a new woman, just like a beautiful butterfly that had emerged from a chrysalis.

She never did see the bills, she knew all these clothes, and the jewellery must have cost a fortune. In her new fashionable clothes, she realised how dowdy her old clothes were. It was time to throw them out. The new look starts here and now. Carla started to wear her new clothes to the office; she knew that Maria, Enzo's Senior's Secretary, would soon notice her change in appearance. The last thing Carla needed was sarcasm; Maria was very good at that. She had a habit, of staring at female members of the Bank staff, when they wore new clothes to work. It made her feel decidedly dowdy. Maria was the senior Personal Assistant, and felt that she alone should dictate the latest fashion to the rest of the women. Maria became very off hand and decidedly cold towards Carla. When Carla started to wear her new clothes to the Office, Maria gave her some very odd looks. Carla did not care; she now had new clothes, her man, whilst Maria was fast becoming a bitter old spinster.

Autumn gave way to winter; business volume at the bank increased, more new accounts came on line. Carla and Dino seemed to have little time to socialise together except at business meetings. Time passed so quickly, before they knew it Christmas was almost here. There was a big party at the Borghese villa with about 100 guests. There was food a plenty, music, dancing and of course merriment. The families of the happy couple were really getting on well. The whole evening seemed to pass in a kind of blurred mist. Dino and Carla realised that in a week or so they would be getting married. The arrangements for the big event were all finalised. Getting married on a Sunday was difficult; they had to get special dispensation from Cardinal Biaggi.

It was New Year's Day 1905 at last; Carla had been awake for hours, wondering if all would go well, what would the weather be like. Her Mother and Father had stayed overnight at Carla's apartment. The living room was full of flowers. Outside, the weather was very cold, a weak wintry sun shone down from a pale blue sky. Carla washed, and then got into her Wedding Dress, which was pure white with lace trimming and a very long train. She and her Mother looked in the Mirror. Florina could not believe how beautiful her daughter had become. She looked absolutely fabulous in her wedding dress.

Her father, Guillermo, resplendent in his Morning Suit, fortified himself with a small amount of alcoholic refreshment. Both Carla's parents were more than a little bit apprehensive on this big occasion, which was just an hour, or two away. In fact, they were more nervous than the Bride. Carla was their only child and they wanted everything to be perfect. Florina on the other hand, fussed around like the proverbial mother hen, trying to hide her nerves by being busy. The time came for them to depart for the Cathedral. In the street below, the closed Horse-drawn carriage awaited the Bridal Party. Carla threw her Mink stole around her shoulders as they got into the Carriage.

Florina put on her fur-trimmed coat over her blue full-length gown, whilst Guillermo helped her adjust her large fur trimmed hat. The carriage arrived at the steps to the Cathedral, Guillermo alighted, opened the door for Carla, who took his arm. There, waiting on the steps for the Bride was Dino Snr.

He took Florina's arm and smiled at her.

"You look lovely Florina," said Enzo, "I can certainly see where your daughter gets her looks from."

Florina blushed, and then thanked Dino Snr. for his compliment. Carla was waiting in the entrance; she could see ahead the congregation all of whom were friends and relations. She could hear the sounds of the organ, floating through the large half-opened doorway.

Earlier, not far away Dino was getting ready for the big day. Unlike, Carla the only person with him was his best man Mario. The last thing Dino wanted was his parents flapping around him on his wedding day. Mario had been his best friend for many years; they had met at University. Mario had been married for three years had a son two years old, and had moved to Rome where he was the Manager of the Bank. Dino and Mario set out early for the Cathedral arriving in good time and were settled in front row of pews. The ceremony was due to start at midday, which would be well after the morning service had ended. Dino looked at the High Altar, closing his eyes in prayer for a moment. Cardinal Biaggi, conducting the service mounted the steps leading to the High Altar. The organ sounded the first notes of "The Wedding March" by Mendelssohn. The congregation came to its feet, whilst Dino resisted the temptation to turn around to see his lovely bride walking down the aisle. Carla passed her Mink stole to her father. Carla with Guillermo on her arm walked slowly down the aisle. As they passed each row of pews, the guests looked with amazement at Carla's stunning Wedding dress Venetian lace veil and long train, held up by two pageboys. The weeks of worry as to the style, material and the making of the dress had culminated into a creation beyond the dreams of the bride and certainly her parents.

Dino and Mario looked round to see a vision of loveliness coming toward them. Dino thought, could this be the young woman that only a year or so ago he had employed as his Personal Assistant? She was indeed now something special to him. In a few moments, they would be joined together in Holy Matrimony. Carla, was simply floating on air, this was her day. She had been in Florence Cathedral many times, but this was special. It was like a dream come true. The Priest called the Party forward and the Ceremony began. When the service came to that point where there was the exchange of rings. Dino started to get very apprehensive and whispered to Mario.

"Have you got the ring?"

Mario searched through his pockets, then nodded that he had. Dino was certainly relieved. Neither Carla nor Dino heard half of the words uttered by the Priest. They both exchanged rings in a kind of trace. With the Venetian lace veil had covering her head; Dino could not see his bride's beautiful face.

Now that they were pronounced Man and Wife, Carla threw back the veil. Dino finally heard hear the words - you may kiss the Bride, so he did. Carla looked down at the third finger of her left hand, there was the band of gold, would it keep them together forever and ever? She hoped so; she had fallen hopelessly in love with Dino. They were a team; they had pledged themselves to each other on this day. Today would be the first day of the rest of their lives; they were the happiest couple in the world. They smiled at the assembled congregation, as walked up the aisle together, and then went into the side chapel to sign the Marriage Register. It was the first time she had written her new name Signora Carla Borghese. It seemed strange; she would no doubt soon get used to it. There was delight everywhere. It was not only a deliriously blissful moment for Carla and Dino, but also a very satisfying moment for both sets of parents. Finally, their children had settled down and hopefully they had found happiness together.

How long would it last nobody knew; only time would tell. Now that the formalities were over, the couple left the Cathedral. Carla had retrieved her Mink stole and Dino put it around her shoulders to keep her warm. The Carriage that had brought them to the Cathedral was waiting outside to take the happy couple off to the reception.

The Wedding Breakfast was being held in a Hotel not far from the Ponte Vecchio, there must have been about 300 guests. The Caterers put on a really magnificent Cordon Bleu feast. There were speeches from Guillermo extolling the virtues of his new Son-in-law and equally matching praise his for his daughter. Whilst Dino Snr. replied with an equally brilliant array of compliments for his new Daughter-in-law and said that his son could not have chosen a better lifetime partner. The Best Man gave a witty speech and read out the messages of congratulation sent in to the happy couple. The presents were displayed on a small stage for all to see, and what an array of glittering presents there was to be seen. Dino and Carla cleared the tables so that the dancing could begin lead. The musical quartet played tunes popular at the time.

There was a break when Carla and Dino opened the presents given by their many friends. It seems that Carla and Dino would want nothing for their new home that would be on the outskirts of the City. A three Bedroom Villa surrounded by a small garden was given to the young newlyweds by Dino's parents. The time came for them to depart for their honeymoon in Egypt; they would be gone for 4 weeks. They changed quickly into their travelling clothes. There was a tear in the eyes of Florina, tears of joy. The Wedding Party finally broke up and the guests started to leave, it would be remembered as the Wedding of the Year. There would be one more present on their return from honeymoon, the Bank President had given them a brand new bright Red FIAT, and so they could sell the MORS. In the closed carriage, Carla and Dino were at last alone snuggling in each other's arms. Neither Carla nor Dino had ever been to Egypt, so not only was it a honeymoon, but an adventure into the unknown. It was a chance for them to get to know each other. In Egypt, they made love under the stars, as well as enjoying the new sights, sounds, and smells of a new Continent.

They were so happy together that words could not express their feelings for each other. They felt that their marriage was made in heaven, they were both so in love.

The honeymoon over, the happy couple returned to Florence, where they carried on as they had left off. Maria, Enzo's Secretary, was now even more put out, for Carla was now a happy young bride, being sexually satisfied by her husband. Whilst Maria was lucky if she even got a kiss or a cuddle from her man friends, who saw her as a bit of a cold fish.

Carla often wondered if Maria preferred women to men. She always dressed in a provocative manner, to attract attention. She had even made advances to Dino and Enzo at one time. Carla wondered at times if Dino had married to right woman. Only time would tell.

Chapter 4

In the small market town of Weisloch, not far from the University Town of Heidelberg, was the ancestral home of the Von Lundenbergs. The family had moved to the Schloss Lundenberg in the late 17th Century. The magnificent Castle, had been a gift from a grateful Emperor for victories in battles against impossible odds in the 30 years War (1618 - 1648). The War had left some honourable scars on the high white stone battlements. There had been a siege, but despite heavy bombardment, the occupants had held out for several weeks. Food stocks had got dangerously low, but luckily, peace had come just in time.

In the spring of 1880, a son was born to the 11th Count Josef and his beautiful wife Margarita. The boy was named Rudolph Michael; he seemed to grow up so fast also he was very quick to learn. His tutor was hard put to keep pace with his thirst for knowledge. The Count knew that one day his son would go to University at Heidelberg. When the time came, Josef hoped that Rudolph would take over the reins of the family business of Iron and Steel making. Business was good, during school holidays and when not having private tuition, young Rudolph could be seen down at his father's office. He would go around the Departments talking to everyone from Shop floor workers to Directors. By the time he was 18 years old, he had grown into a tall, dark haired young man, and he had a long list of academic achievements. These had been obtained by sheer hard work at School. He was accepted as an Engineering Student at Heidelberg University in the autumn of 1898. He soon made many friends; he was a very sociable character. After classes, he could nearly always be found with his best friend of all, Hermann Ritter. They were about the same age, but from very different backgrounds. Hermann was thicker set with light blonde hair and his father was an entrepreneur. He had been an agent for Krups, the famous steel and armament manufacturer. He had done some arms trading, and so was a very rich man. The family lived in a large house on the outskirts of the city of Ulm.

Rudolph and Hermann were always burning the midnight oil, whether it was studying or, perhaps chatting to the local ladies in the Beerkeller. As you may know, Heidelberg is renowned for its drinking and singing. Rudolph and Hermann were good at the former, but had little expertise in the latter. After all, they were training to be Engineers not Singers. After a few steins of Lager, they reckoned they could sing anything. They had developed a reputation with the women of the town, which sometimes, got them into scraps with jealous boyfriends. On many an occasion, there was the odd black eye or bruise. The two young men often gave a good as they received. This did not deter them at all. The only thing they did take seriously was their studies; after all, their future depended on their final results. Their student days at Heidelberg were drawing to an end; it was time for both Rudolph and Hermann to consider their future. This could be bright, providing their examination results were good. Hermann had a deep interest in all things mechanical, including the Motor Car; after all, he was a trained Engineering Student. However, they were still a bit of a rarity on the roads of

Germany. In any case, only the rich could afford them. Rudolph knew that should his results not be as expected he could always work with his father, he too was interested in Motor Cars.

He had ridden in his Father's 1901 Mercedes and that was always a joy to him. He always wanted a Car of his own, but knew he would have to earn the right to buy one. They were very expensive indeed. He had learned to drive, although his father was reluctant to begin with. Rudolph soon became a very competent driver, his parents feeling very safe when he was driving and they were passengers. It had been seven years since the first City-to-City race from Paris to Rouen; every year there had been a City-to-City race, even a tour of France a distance of 2160 kilometres. All the races had been in France, and not one had started in Germany. The race in June 1901 from Paris to Berlin had even started in France. Although Mercedes had been manufacturing motor cars since 1899 and Benz since 1886, neither Company's cars had featured in the results of any important races. All the races, all the Cars, and Drivers were all French. Rudolph and Hermann thought that the French should not be having it all their own way. They were proud of their Fatherland; it was time that they made their mark in Motor Sport, to show the French that they could not have it all their own way. So, they sat down together and decided to write to the MERCEDES Company asking if there were vacancies as Engineers or Test Drivers. They posted the letters, not knowing if they would get an answer. They wrote with such enthusiasm, that in their hearts, they knew that they would not be denied. After all, they could charm the birds off the trees, couldn't they? Several days passed, then a week. Their hopes for employment with MERCEDES were diminishing by the day.

Both Rudolph and Hermann were home for the summer, now that they had completed their University Degrees. All they were waiting for were their results, and that letter. Then on a Tuesday morning of their third week home, a letter arrived at the Ritter household, in the top left-hand corner was the word MERCEDES. Hermann's Mother, Marlene, picked it up, and carried it to her son; he was reading in the Library. When he saw the envelope his face lit up, could this be his future or not? He opened the envelope with care and pulled out the letter. His eyes scanned it quickly and he gave out a wild yell.

"Mother, I have got it!" he exclaimed.

He punched the air with joy.

"That is wonderful, my son," replied Marlene, "why don't you telephone Rudolph. I am certain he would like to know."

Hermann re-read the letter, where it mentioned Rudolph, who would be joining him.

Rudolph too, was in the Library reading, but his mind was still on two things, a letter from MERCEDES, and those results from University. The telephone rang in the Hall. The Maid answered and then came into where Rudolph was sitting by the open window.

"Excuse me sir," said the Maid, "there is a telephone call for you. It is a Herr Ritter."

Rudolph picked up the telephone.

"Hello, Rudolph it is me your friend Hermann."

"Good to hear from you, Hermann. Had any news?"

"Rudolph, what news is that?"

Hermann got very excited.

"Rudolph, it is wonderful news have you heard?"

"Heard what exactly, Hermann?"

"I have had a letter from MERCEDES Rudolph. They want both of us."

"I have not seen the letter yet Herman. Maybe my letter is in today's post. I'll call you back later."

Rudolph put the telephone down and went to find the post that had arrived earlier. There on his father's desk in his study was the day's post.

Rudolph quickly went through it, until he came to a light grey envelope with the single word MERCEDES in the top left-hand corner. He opened the envelope very carefully indeed, as if it were covered in gold leaf. He removed the letter and read it slowly. It dawned on him now why Hermann was so excited. The letter contained quite a lot of detail, and he re-reads it to make sure he was not dreaming. There it was plain enough; MERCEDES were offering the post of Test Driver and Engineer. It was a new Department to be opened later in the year. The position would be subject to his Final Examination results being up to the standard required. It was all set out in the letter from the Managing Director. Rudolph punched the air in delight.

"Yes, I've done it" he shouted.

The letter said that he should reply within two weeks and advise them of his Exam results.

Both Hermann and Rudolph waited with baited breath for their results to arrive. They had already sent off their replies to MERCEDES. The week or so later, another envelope arrived for each of our two hopefuls to say that they had qualified with honours. They could not believe that at last their dreams were coming into view. They both sent their results off straight away, and said that they looking forward to meeting the Chief Engineer in Stuttgart. In their letters of confirmation, they were told to be at the factory on Tuesday 1st October at midday. This would give them time to travel from their respective homes. Josef von Lundenberg was delighted that his son had the job of his dreams, but sad that he would not assume his role in the Iron and Steel business. The thought passed through Josef's mind to get Rudolph to ask the Chief Engineer if his Company would buy some high quality steel from his factory.

Early on that fateful Tuesday morning, Rudolph got ready and took the taxi to Weisloch Station. It was a cold; grey October morning, as Rudolph stood waiting on the Station platform for the train to take him to Karlsruhe. Here he would change to catch that train which would take him to his future in Stuttgart. Some 80 kilometres to the east of Stuttgart at Ulm Station, Hermann was waiting for the express to take him to the MERCEDES factory. The wind blew cold from the east; Hermann pulled his collar up and he watched the clock above his head tick away.

Then, a train whistle could be heard and into view came a large black Locomotive hauling the Stuttgart train. Rudolph was well on his way now; he had made his connection at Karlsruhe in good time. Both trains arrived in Stuttgart within a few minutes of each other. It was 11.30 am, as promised by the ticket barrier was a chauffeur from the MERCEDES factory with their names on a large white card.

"Good morning, gentlemen. Please follow me," said the young man in the Company uniform.

They all walked out of the Station where they saw a large Black sedanca de ville (A car where the chauffeur sat in the open and the passengers were enclosed). The chauffeur strolled beside Hermann and Rudolph he continued by saying,

"You are very lucky today gentlemen; we are in the Managing Director's Car. I have just dropped a Client off. So whilst I was here at the Station, they asked if I would collect you."

They were then whisked off to the factory that was a few kilometres away. They settled into the leather seats in the back of the car, and chatted away about what they had been doing since they last met. Also how they should conduct themselves at this most important interview. The big Limousine passed through the factory gates, and then slowed, pulling up outside a large office building. The chauffeur alighted, then opening the door for Rudolph and Hermann.

"Gentlemen," said the chauffeur, "will please go to the Reception desk, where the Receptionist will contact Herr Schumann. Looking forward to seeing both of you."

He smiled, clicked his heels together, turned, and was gone. Rudolph and Hermann walked over to the lady on the Reception Desk where they introduced themselves. The Receptionist picked the telephone, rang a number, then indicated that they should sit over by the window and wait. A few minutes passed, these seemed like hours to our two young men.

The telephone rang again, the Receptionist picked up put it to his ear mumbled something and replaced the receiver.

"Herr Von Lundenberg and Herr Ritter," she said, "please go to the first floor, you will find Herr Schuman's office directly opposite the stairs."

They mounted the stairs and knocked on the door. "Please enter," a man's voice called out from the other side of the door.

Rudolph opened the door, inside was a very large office, on the walls were several large oil paintings, some were of MERCEDES cars in action, others landscapes and portraits by various famous German artists. Behind a very large leather topped desk, sat Gustav Schumann. He was in his mid 40's, heavy set, and going bald.

He looked at the two young men over the top of his half-glasses, stood up and walked around his desk then, shook them both warmly but firmly by the hand.

"Good morning gentlemen," said Gustav Schumann, "that's what I like punctuality. Look at the time, your interview was at midday it is now exactly 1159a.m."

The moment he had finished speaking, the clock on the wall close by chimed the hour.

"Have a good journey gentlemen?" began Gustav, "I understand that you Herr von Lundenberg have come all the way from Weisloch and you Herr Ritter from Ulm. Excellent. What do think about working for MERCEDES?"

There was a moment of silence before Hermann was the first to speak.

"Sir, I enjoyed the journey very much. It would be an honour for me to work for this Company."

Rudolph thought for a moment or two.

"Sir," said Rudolph, "my Father owns one of your cars. I learnt to drive it some years ago. I know that you produce very good cars indeed. I love the Fatherland and want to see our cars beat those French ones that seem to be winning all of the Races. I would love to work for a Company that build the best cars in Europe."

Rudolph thought that may be he had said too much already. Herr Schumann looked at him and smiled.

"That is the finest response I have ever heard from a prospective employee," replied Gustav. "No speeches of welcome Gentlemen, you are hired. However, you must prove yourselves. There is a lot of hard work to be done before we become the best.

A Company cannot run on its reputation. I feel hungry let's go to lunch. This I would add will be your only free lunch."

They all laughed at this joke. The young men were over the moon; they had started their dream jobs. Now they had to prove themselves. They all adjourned to Gustav's favourite restaurant, which was only walking distance from the factory. Over lunch, Herr Schumann told them exactly what was expected, they should return on the following Monday to start the real work. He told them that the lunch they were eating would be their only "free" lunch, so to speak. Meals were free to employees who worked for it. After lunch, they were shown around the factory, and were introduced to the Chief Engineer – Wolfgang Kessler. Wolfgang was a stocky man in his late 40's with fair close-cropped hair and a handlebar moustache. Hermann and Rudolph had lots of questions to ask him. Wolfgang answered all their questions, and gave them an overview of what was expected of them. The day was soon over; as they left the Wolfgang Kessler gave to them a small model of their latest machine. He looked forward to seeing them at midday on Monday. He would arrange accommodation for them in a local boarding house close to the factory. He told them once you are settled in, and then come to my Office. On their way back to the Station again, in a chauffeur driven car, they decided to spend a couple of days together. From the Station, Rudolph rang his father to ask if Hermann could come to stay for a few days.

Hermann then rang his father, to ask if he could go to the Schloss Lundenberg until Saturday. He would come home get ready, and then leave for Stuttgart to start his new job. All was agreed. Hermann changed his ticket at Stuttgart Station. Rudolph and Hermann were about the same build; Rudolph had an extensive array of clothes for all occasions. Therefore, Hermann was able to borrow some of Rudolph's wardrobe. They spent a night in Heidelberg to reliving old times, bedded a couple of local beauties, got drunk and really enjoyed their last few days of freedom. Then it was Saturday, Rudolph drove Hermann to the Station, and they parted. Soon they would be together again, working as a team for money. They wondered what the nightlife of Stuttgart might be like.

Monday morning dawned, Rudolph was up early to catch that 7 a.m. train, and it was raining and cold. Still, there was no more University, he was now an employee of MERCEDES, and the sky was the limit. The train arrived on time; luckily the whole journey had been uneventful. Rudolph arrived first and waited to be met, as Herr Schumann had promised. Hermann arrived some 30 minutes later, his train having been delayed.

The chauffeur took them to the Boarding House, where they were greeted, if that is the word, by the Landlady Eva Sulzbach. She was not a jovial lady. She read out to Hermann and Rudolph a list of do's and don'ts. Rudolph wondered when she had finished the list, if they needed permission to breathe. Hermann scratched his head and thought. I will never remember all that. They decided to try and stick it out for a little while, later they would then get some money together and rent a small apartment. This way they could have some space to relax and socialise. Having unpacked their bags, hung up their clothes, they headed for the MERCEDES factory. At midday, they were in the Wolfgang Kessler's Office.

"Well done boys," he quipped, "all settled in with the fair Eva? She's a lovely lady isn't she?"

The boys smiled and said nothing. For all they knew she could be a relative of Herr Schumann. Still nobody could be that unlucky could they?

The first few weeks at the factory were less than glamorous, as they familiarised themselves with the internal combustion engine. Hermann called it the infernal combustion engine, when things did not go right. There were mechanical problem solving exercises, oil changing, replacing drive belts, tyres and wheels, to stripping down gearboxes. The tasks seemed endless. The glamour of Motor Racing seemed a world away to them. One afternoon after a hard day's work in the factory the Chief Engineer Wolfgang Kessler, took Hermann and Rudolph aside.

"Now Gentlemen," he began, "might I give you some sound advice?"

"Yes of course," replied Rudolph.

"This might all seem a pain to you now," continued Wolfgang, "do remember this, when you are racing there will not be a team of mechanics following your every move. You may be miles from anywhere. Take the City-to-City Races for instance. The 1900 race from Paris to Toulouse and back to Paris. That race was over a distance of 1340 kilometres, where would the cars break down along this route? We don't know do we? We cannot have repair stations along the route every few kilometres. That is why the cars carry a mechanic and tools, to fix the car if they can. You cannot ring up the factory and say. Oh dear! My engine has stopped or I have a puncture, can you send someone to fix it. We breed racing drivers, not Gentlemen who want servants to repair their cars." Suddenly it came home to Hermann and Rudolph. This factory employed professionals of the highest order. They expected their Test Drivers and Racing Teams to solve their own problems on the road, and in the races, they took part in. So they stopped whinging, and got on with the training.

The words of the Chief Engineer were engraved in their memory for all time, and would stand them in good stead for the years ahead. Although, both Hermann and Rudolph had driven cars around their own hometowns, the Cars were low powered, so when the time came to drive the latest models from the Stuttgart factory, they had a shock coming. The Cars produced by MERCEDES were very basic by today's standards, but in 1902, they were simply just a big engine and very little else. Certainly, nothing in the way of comfort or weather protection for the driver and his Mechanic. Suspension was by cart springs, braking on rear wheels only, with narrow tyres it made car control very interesting indeed. In fact, a real struggle. Gustav Schumann had let them drive the lower powered cars to get used to the roads around Stuttgart, the traffic mostly being horse-drawn wagons. There were a few cars, but he did warn them that the pedestrians were not used to high-speed vehicles in the City Centre. It would be prudent for them to keep to the country roads.

Neither Rudolph nor Hermann had any incidents or accidents in the months that followed, since they had joined the Company. It had been a cold winter with a good deal of snow. Driving was not permitted on the days when it snowed or was foggy. Gustav Schumann knew he had a good team that would be ruined by foolishly going out in inclement weather.

Spring 1902 arrived; Gustav decided that it was time that his young protégés got to grips with some real driving in their faster cars. They would learn the tricks of the trade, sliding around corners and other racing tips. He appointed his Chief Test Driver, Helmut Braun to get the young men up to speed, so to speak. They had some new improvements to test for the Company's entry in the Paris-Vienna race was scheduled for 26th to 29th June of 1902. The course would be 985 kilometres. The Driver, Count Zborowsi had been to the factory several times watching his car being built. It was certainly a magnificent machine and should do really well; great care had been taken in the manufacture of every part. Nothing had been left to chance. Rudolph and Hermann wished that they could take part. Gustav organised two cars; these would test new ideas. Hermann and Rudolph were excited as they dressed in their leathers, goggles, gloves and boots. Gustav had introduced something new to his team, Crash Helmets. These would protect the driver's head in case of an accident. He had seen too many accidents in his time, where the driver's life would have been saved had he worn a protective helmet. Gustav had designed them and had them specially made by the company. Hermann and Rudolph, now resplendent in their 'racing kit', strolled through the large workshop, they saw the two cars that they were about to drive gleaming in the morning sunshine.

Helmut introduced them to the Company's official Racing Driver Ernst Stuck. He had competed in the 1901 Paris-Berlin race over 1100 kilometres that was run over two days. It was a gruelling event he was lucky to finish 7th, it took him and his mechanic over 19 hours to cover the distance. Rudolph would be with Ernst and Hermann with Helmut. They would change places later. The idea being that the young men would drive once they had left the City suburbs of Stuttgart and got out into open country. Rudolph and Hermann were asked to swing the starting handles and get the monsters into life. Immediately the big 4 cylinder engines fired and the sound was deafening. The Cars throbbed with power. Rudolph and Hermann climbed into their seats; they felt in another world.

"Goggles down, Gentlemen" shouted Helmut above the din.

He put the car into gear, released the handbrake and the machine shot forward like a bullet, whilst Ernst and Rudolph followed closely behind. They passed through the factory gates and turned left on the road to Esslingen. After about 15 minutes or so at speeds up to 100 kilometres an hour. Helmut, who was leading the way, signalled that he was going to pull in and stop. Ernst did the same.

"Now you can be the chauffeur," he shouted at Rudolph.

The drivers and passengers changed places. Now it was up to Rudolph and Hermann to start learning to drive in real earnest. Rudolph got behind the wheel and Ernst explained again the procedure for starting from standstill, reminding him to be gentle on the controls. He was in charge of a powerful machine and should respect it. Helmut was giving Hermann the same advice. Both cars pulled away gently, after having stalled, just the once. The speed soon built up to 50 kph both Rudolph and Hermann were asked to brake, as in emergency but without skidding and under control. This they both did successfully. This was a surprise to the professional drivers, so they congratulated both Rudolph and Hermann on a successful exercise. Next, they asked them to go as quickly as they could, bearing in mind the road conditions and the fact that the top speed of the car was 160 kph. The young men managed to get to 145 kph on a straight stretch of road that was clear of traffic. They drove all the way back to the factory. Rudolph was amazed how easy the car was to drive, once you got the hang of it. Ernst and Helmut reported to Gustav that he had a couple of great drivers in the making, possible 'naturals'. Practice would make them really great.

The time passed by quickly; Hermann and Rudolph were praised for their mechanical prowess, and indeed the progress they had made in such a short period of time. They learned that the car they had admired, raced by Count Zborowski had finished 4th in the Paris-Vienna race and only 27 minutes behind the winner. Yes, the Winner was another Frenchman a Marcel Renault in a car of his own manufacture, his brother Louis had taken part but had not featured in the top six finishers.

The factory was pleased with Count Zborowski's efforts and he was Guest of Honour at a dinner, it was a chance for all the team including Hermann and Rudolph to meet yet another famous Racing Driver. In all the past few months had been a learning curve for the young men. There was still much to learn, for they were welding together a team, which would go far and be needed in the days and years to come.

One day in late summer, Gustav called Hermann and Rudolph into his office.

"Good morning Gentlemen, please sit down," said Gustav.

Rudolph and Hermann were hoping that this was their chance to become part of the new Racing Team, could this be too much to expect? Gustav explained that the Company was entering a team of three cars for the 1903 Paris - Madrid race to take place on May 1st. Also later in the year on the 2nd July there would be the Gordon Bennett Trophy Race to be held at Athy in Ireland. A Frenchman in a French car had up to now, had always won this race that had taken place since 1900, and it had always started in Paris. James Gordon Bennett of the New York Herald Tribune Newspaper - European edition, had donated the Prize in 1899. Now with our superior cars, we intend to take the prize in 1903. Our top driver Camille Janatzy will be driving our No.1 machine. Gustav stopped for a moment or two. The young men were fascinated, but what about their involvement? There was a knock at the door, and Gustav's Secretary brought in coffee for them all. Sipping their coffees, Gustav said,

"I suppose you would like to know my plans for you two?"

The two young men sat up. Gustav continued, he informed them that they would act as Mechanics for Herr Helmut and Herr Ernst. He asked how they were getting on with his two top drivers. Rudolph replied, "I know I speak for Hermann as well as myself, when I say it has been a great honour to spend time and learn from those great men. We shall be delighted to act as their Mechanics. We will not let you down Sir." Gustav then said, "Remember this fact, if you succeed or if you fail, your names will be in the press. It all depends on you two, and of course, Helmut and Ernst as to the kind of publicity we will get."

The days passed quickly, and then Rudolph and Hermann were allotted a RaceCar. They had to know it inside an out. It was the latest MERCEDES 90 h.p. A beast of a machine.

With the help of the Racing and Development Department team, they stripped the car and the engine down to its hundreds of components then rebuilt it time and time again, until they could do it blindfolded. In fact, that had dreams about it. The team was developing a spirit of unity. Gustav could see this moulding into shape. Everyone had a job to do, they knew success or failure of the Company's entries depended upon all of them not just one individual, it had to be teamwork. The Cars were treated like works of Art; every part was polished and gleaming. Not a speck of dirt or drops of oil anywhere. They tested the Cars every day to try to find a weak part, then they stripped them down to see what wear had taken place. The whole operation was absolute meticulously monitored.

Several weeks before the race, Ernst, Helmut, Hermann, and Rudolph were invited to Gustav's office where they gave him a progress report on the whole operation. Gustav was delighted that all was going well. He had some special news for them. He had a plan to get one over on his rivals from France. He was going to send his drivers on a survey of the route. Paris to Madrid was a long way, the roads were bad, and as Chief Engineer, he had many decisions to make. The route had to be written down, so that his drivers would not lose their way. They would make notes as to where to put refuelling stations, for men and machines. They would do what he called 'pace notes'. This would tell his drivers where the fast and slow sections were. This would be a professional operation, no time for amateur tactics. He would run two cars, these would be the 60 hp. Models, speed was not the essence here, it was information he wanted. Ernst thought that this was a great idea. He said that he had lost a lot of very valuable time in the 1902 Paris to Vienna Race, when he was misrouted by a Policeman, took a wrong turning, reaching one of the check points very late. He also had to slow down on another section in order to save fuel. The refuelling point had to be moved some 10 kilometres further on, this being due to opposition from the local inhabitants. This year they had to win. They all agreed that perfect planning and preparation was the key to success.

One week later they set off for Paris, knowing that if, they struck problems, and then they would have a month to cure them.

The whole train had been chartered by MERCEDES. There was a great deal of activity at Stuttgart Station as the Cars, and the service vehicles were loaded on to covered wagons. The Drivers and their Mechanics settled down in their Compartments, the train got up steam and set off on its journey. The Four men were looking forward to

April in Paris. However, they would not have much time for sightseeing, for they had been booked in to their Hotel for one night only on a Dinner, Bed and Breakfast basis. It was a long train journey; some of their time was spent looking at the maps the Company had provided showing the route to be followed. Soon they were at the French border; the train slowed down and stopped. The Border Police came through checking their papers for the Cars and their crews. Soon they were on their way, passing through Reims on the way to Paris and the Gare du Nord. The train stopped in the Goodsyard where the vehicles were unloaded and parked in a large Warehouse. This building was locked to keep the machines away from prying eyes and even possible sabotage.

Meanwhile, the crews headed for their Hotel that was nearby. It had been a long day, but Hermann and Rudolph had other things to do after Dinner. They sat in their room and had to make out a sheet on which to calculate the car's fuel consumption and tyre wear. They looked upon this as a mock examination. Flunk this, then they could kiss goodbye to a career as a Racing Driver. They had slept a little on the journey, but now in a really comfortable bed they slept like babies. They were woken by Helmut at 6 am the next morning, and made their way down for breakfast. They stocked up with a supply of everything on offer including several cups of coffee and fresh croissants. A car was waiting for them for their short trip to be reunited with their cars.

A quick check was made of every part, and then it was time to make their way to the Eiffel Tower. Approaching the massive structure, they could not believe that mere men made this wrought iron lattice structure back in 1889. The Tower, which was disliked when it was first built, stretched some 300 metres up into the sky. Ernst reminded them that they were in Paris for serious Company business, not to see the sights.

It was now 8 am and the traffic was building up, there seemed to be people everywhere.

The cars were brought to a halt in the shadow of the Eiffel Tower, whilst the back up vehicles pulled in behind them.

"Right, Gentlemen let's go!" yelled Ernst.

He put the car into gear and off they went in a cloud of smoke. Hermann and Rudolph had the maps ready in order to shout instructions to their respective Drivers. Keeping within the legal limits, they headed for the outskirts of the City. So far so good, thought Rudolph, looking back at Helmut and Hermann. They were all dressed, as they had been for the practise, complete with Gustav's Crash Helmets. As they raced along Rudolph shouted out instructions, they turned left and finally got on to the main road that led to Orleans some 116 kilometres away. Here they would stop to review their progress and check timing etc. They pulled into the Town Square and waited for the back up vehicles to catch up. All had gone like clockwork; it had taken them about an hour and a half.

So far they had averaged about 78 kph, which in a car less powerful than their Race Car was very good. It was a warm day, so whilst they were waiting for the team trucks to arrive they decided to visit a local café to get a cold drink. Soon, the trucks arrived, the fuel tanks were topped up and they were on their way once more. The next City would be Tours with its grand spires. To Rudolph and Hermann this was like a high-speed holiday. The cars were running like clockwork, but they still had a long way to go. The remainder of the trip to Bordeaux was uneventful; they only hoped that that on Race

Day, all would go as smoothly. At last they had reached Bordeaux, time for lunch for after all; this was reconnaissance not a race. Along the way Rudolph and Hermann were making notes at every stop, these notes would be crucial on the day of the race. After lunch, they reviewed the route so far adding additional information to those precious notes. Then they pressed on; deciding to spend the night in Biarritz, by end of the following day should be in the Spanish Capital. After a relaxing night, the next day saw the scenery change dramatically. The road from San Sebastian to Vitoria-Gasteiz was tortuous and the average speed dropped to 60 kph. Finally, they made Burgos with a deep sigh of relief. The trucks had difficulty keeping up, so the cars had to stop from time to time.

This at least gave the drivers and their mechanics time to rest, although it did mean that the survey took that much longer. They eventually arrived on the outskirts of Madrid on the evening of their second day. They had covered almost 1300 kilometres, an epic journey for the time. True they had a few punctures, but considering the state of the roads, they had done well. They had averaged some 45 kph overall including stops for maintenance and waiting for those trucks. At times they had exceeded 120 kph in their Model 60's. It had been a great test for their cars. The factory had arranged for their return trip by train. They teams were delighted. The thought of driving all the way back to Stuttgart did not bear thinking about. The teams slept for hours on the train, the car journey had been a great strain. On Race Day, they knew that their nerves would be at breaking point. Would they succeed, only time would tell? By the time they got back to the factory, Gustav had laid on a meeting with all the Directors and Development Engineers, so that they might hear exactly how the survey went. Everything was discussed in detail, and plans made to try to cover all possible eventualities. Then a letter arrived from Camille Jenatzy to say that he would not drive in the Paris - Madrid race. He wanted to drive in the Gordon Bennett Race, as he felt that he would have a better chance of winning on a circuit race rather than the City-to-City event. In the Gordon Bennett Race, the event allowed for three entries from National Teams, the winning country would then organise the event the following year. (Fact: Camille Jenatzy was born in Belgium on 4th November 1868 and died 7th October 1913 - he was accidentally shot during a boar hunt.)

Therefore, our two teams who had been so diligent in their survey would now hold the key to success in the Paris - Madrid Race, just a week or two away. There was a lot of work to do. The RaceCars were prepared and were ready to be shipped together with the back up vehicles on Monday 27th April to ensure that everything would be in Paris for the early start on the 1st May. It was deja vu and again, Ernst, Rudolph, Helmut and Hermann were back in Paris. The mighty Model 90 was entirely different from the Model 60. This was one big, tough RaceCar, not for the faint-hearted. It needed firm handling, with only rear wheel brakes and thin tyres it was a real beast at high speed, as Rudolph and Hermann had found out when they were testing.

However, this was the real thing. Race day arrived and they joined the crowds down at the start under the Eiffel Tower. All the factory teams were there, De Dietrich, Mors, Panhard, and Renault. The list of the drivers read like a who's who of the Motoring World. Would Mercedes win the day? All they could do was try their hardest. At least

Ernst and his fellows had been over the course, admittedly not racing speeds. The flags of competing Nations were arranged on poles in the start area. The crowds were kept back by fence and the local gendarmes. Everyone wanted to catch a glimpse of these wonderful machines. The Press from several countries were there taking photographs and reporters talking to the famous Drivers, which included Ernst and Helmut. They were asked a battery of questions about their past, their tactics for the race and so on.

The time was fast approaching for the start. The Cars were to be set off in number order at intervals except it seems for Marcel Renault. He was allowed to start first. The event would be against the clock. At one minute to go, the starter mounted his rostrum, holding the French tricolour, as the large clock nearby struck the hour of 7 am; he raised the flag and with a flourish sent the first car on its way. The Mercedes were numbers 27 and 28, so they about 25 more minutes to wait. In the distance ahead of them, they could see Marcel Renault in a car of his own manufacture. He was one of the favourites to win this event.

One by one, the cars set off, every French car that went by there was a big cheer. Then it was the turn Ernst and Rudolph, together with Helmut and Hermann to start their engines. They swung their starting handles almost together and the beasts burst into life. Ernst and Rudolph moved up to the starting line, closely followed by their team-mates. The starter raised his flag, brought it down, and away went Ernst and Rudolph with a mighty roar. Rudolph called out the directions to Ernst; they veered left and right following the route by the River Seine until they were on the outskirts of Paris. The open road gave them an opportunity to give the car the freedom it needed Rudolph began to feel the wind in his face. Soon they were doing over 130 kph and heading for Chartres, where the cheering crowds waved encouragement to these daredevils.

The Mercedes boys were jolly glad that they had their crash helmets on, because when the crowd realised they were from Germany, several people threw missiles.

Soon Chartres was a dot on the far horizon. Rudolph looked around to see a cloud of dust that seemed to be catching them up. On the next hill, they passed a Panhard that come to a standstill. The radiator had boiled, and the crew were looking around for water, whilst they waited for the engine to cool down. Onward then to Orleans, they had passed several more cars. One had crashed into somebody's garden, and the crew was trying to get the Mors back on the road. Between Orleans and Tours, they came to a wooded area where the road was particularly bad, with several sharp bends. A car had gone off the road into the woods and had struck a tree. Ernst asked Rudolph the car number. "No.63" he shouted as they roared by. "That was Marcel Renault," shouted Ernst, "one of our main rivals." Hermann and Helmut were doing well, no problems so far. They kept well back from Ernst and Rudolph; otherwise, it would be like driving in fog.

Their first stop came at Orleans where the team had organised a pit stop. New wheels and tyres were fitted, the fuel and water tanks were topped up, and off they went again. On the way to the next town Blois, which was half way between Orleans and Tours, there was a big accident a Mors had not negotiated a corner. The crowd here had been over enthusiastic had moved forward to get a better view. The car had hit a building nearby, bounced into an area of the crowd and three spectators had been killed including a child. Seeing the mob ahead, Ernst and Helmut slowed right down to make sure that their way was clear. Once out of the town, it was full steam ahead once more.

Before they had reached Poitiers, their next pit stop, they had passed several more wrecked cars, and others that had wheels missing, some were in hedgerows. It was a sad sight. The two Model 90's were going like clockwork. Rudolph could not believe their luck. At Poitiers, again a quick check over and away they went. They still had some way to go. The day was heating up and the blinding dust seemed to get into everything. Each town they passed through the crowd seemed to be all over the road.

It made driving very dangerous; it was bad enough for Ernst and Helmut without the crowd getting in the way. At their pit stop in Poitiers, they were told that there had been other very bad accidents. It seems two soldiers; two drivers and a child had been killed. It was likely that they race may be stopped if any more accidents occurred. The two Mercedes teams had averaged over 110 kph. They were about 40 minutes behind the leader, who was Fernand Gabriel in a Mors. All the team could do was to press on and hope that the opposition broke down. They started off again, the engines sounded as good as ever. The must have been travelling at about 120 kph when the car started to swerve from side to side. Rudolph looked down it was a front wheel puncture. Ernst, being a professional brought the big old car to a stop. Rudolph leapt out of his seat and got out the spare wheel and within about 5 minutes had the new wheel in place. Helmut had passed them, giving them a wave. Rudolph indicated that he was solving the problem. Ernst then got the car underway and thundered after Helmut. By the time they had got to Saintes, there were more cars lying by the roadside. It had been just too much for some of the cars and their crews. Our heroes had driven hard and fast and finally made it into Bordeaux, where there was supposed to be a break of an hour. This would give them time for refreshment and for the service crews to attend to the Cars.

They pulled into the Parking area where an official raced up to them. He told them that the race had been stopped. The Organisers of the event gave the reasons as too many accidents, several of which were fatal, several drivers, mechanics, spectators, plus a child had been killed, crowd control was totally inadequate hence the fatalities. Ernst, Rudolph, Helmut, and Hermann climbed down from their cars. All the drivers were covered in dust from head to foot. They were stiff from sitting in one position; their seats were not all that comfortable. Rudolph and Hermann said that this was an area of improvement to be addressed and that the seats should be shaped for back support. They made their way over to the Chief Race Official. To ask was it true that the race had been stopped. The four men knew how bad the roads were in Spain. They agreed with the official, the race had been badly organised. They were extremely disappointed for they knew that they had a good chance of winning.

The next day the results were announced. The winner was Fernand Gabriel in a Mors his time 5hrs 14 mins 31.2 secs. For the 547 kilometres his average speed 104.2 kph. The Mercedes teams were the only 2-car team to finish and were placed 7th and 8th. It was a great result for the team. So, they went out into Bordeaux and partied on the local wine and the local ladies. In the morning it was headaches all round. Ernst got on the telephone to Gustav to tell him the news. He was delighted with the result, pity they had not won, or gone the full race distance, although they had won the official team prize. Arrangements were made for all the vehicles to come back by train. On the return trip they all agreed that the survey of the route had been a great success, without that they both could have both been casualties, like so many other competitors. Two days later they arrived back at Stuttgart and another conference with Gustav. He praised them for their attention to detail, also for the professional way in which they had gone about their reconnaissance of the route. To begin with, he had second thoughts about making notes on route. However, the drivers knew best and so it had all worked out well. He analysed everything; Gustav was a very methodical man. The cars were stripped down to every last nut and bolt to check for wear, and ways to improve the machine. The Drivers said they needed wider tyres, better suspension, and four-wheel brakes. Gustav promised all these things would be considered. In all it was a terrific team effort. They knew that they had a great car in the Model 90.

The next race for the team was to be the GORDON BENNETT TROPHY to be held in Ireland at Athy. Nobody in the factory had even heard of the place. It was decided not to send a team to take part in this event. However, the factory would support one car driven by Camille Jenatzy. Rudolph and Hermann were disappointed, but they had their moment of fame in Bordeaux. The race at Athy would be 3 laps of a 40-mile (Circuit A) followed by 4 laps of a 51.88-mile (Circuit B). The team thought only a foreign organisation could run a race like this. The race was run on Thursday 2nd July 1903.

The Mercedes factory teams were eager to find out the result. In the newspaper was a photograph of the winner, there was smiling Camille with the trophy, the Model 90 had done it again.

As the days passed, Rudolph and Hermann, did more and more testing, with new ideas dreamt up by the Development Department. They got their wider tyres, better suspension, as yet no four-wheel brakes. Ernst and Helmut drove them even harder. "Last race we had, you boys had the easy bit." said Ernest, "you just sat there and we did all the work. OK you did a good job. Now it is our turn to sit and you drive. Drive as fast as you can without danger to life or limb." That summer passed away with the team now having four really good drivers. They had exceeded their expectations. Summer gave way to autumn; they were still spending time around their new cars for the coming season.

The days were getting shorter and soon, the hours for testing were few. Rudolph said that he would like to take some time off to visit his parents. He had the odd weekend at his ancestral home. The team had been successful in the races, in which they had taken part. So it was decided by Gustav to close the Racing Department for a month until the weather improved. The 1904 season would mean even greater effort as the Gordon Bennett Race would be held in Homburg and they would be entering at least four cars. Hermann and Rudolph would be drivers this time. Therefore, we have new mechanics to train. Homburg was only a few hundred kilometres away, not in another country. The cars to be used for the event would be heavily modified Model 60's. They knew the Model 60, for they had used this model to survey the route from Paris to Madrid. It had been very reliable, but a bit underpowered. For the Homberg race, new engines had been developed to produce nearly as much power as the engine in the Model 90.

So, on Friday 11th December, Rudolph and Hermann packed their bags and headed home for a 4-week holiday. It would be great to be home for Christmas and New Year, with the prospect of actually driving for the famous MERCEDES TEAM in the New Year. It would also mean a huge rise in salary, plus a share in any prize money. On the train ride home both young men, could not wait to tell their parents the good news. On arrival home Rudolph's and Herman's parents were delighted to see them. Having read about the horrific events of the Paris to Madrid race, they were thankful that their sons had come through without a scratch.

Christmas and New Year were well celebrated by both families. The Ritter family went to the Midnight Service in the great Cathedral at Ulm, whilst the Von Lundenbergs celebrate with mass at their local church. Soon, the holiday was over and it was back to the grindstone. As winter turned into spring, Gustav started interviewing prospective mechanics. These were young men already employed elsewhere in the factory. In order to test their skills they were paired up with Rudolph and Hermann, who drove them very hard in every way. They instilled into each prospective candidate, that their lives depended on their skills with the very expensive machinery - namely the racing cars. Of the 20 interviewed, they whittled down the numbers to six. By having two spare mechanics they would have a full compliment should any of them fall ill. Each day they would be working on the cars, getting to know every nut and bolt. Ernst and Helmut would double-check all their work. They had to be professional and above all else reliable.

Rudolph and Hermann were now team leaders in their own right, they now had to compete against the best drivers around. Gustav allocated Christian Deutz to Rudolph, as they seemed to get on so well together, and Joachim Wagner was paired with Hermann. Gustav told them: "You have until June 14th to become organised. That is race day; it will be 4 laps around a course of 127 kilometres, a distance of almost 509 kilometres. This time there will be no survey of the circuit, but I have arranged for a service pit at the start and finish. So lads, it up to you to do the job." There was a great deal of competition between the four teams of drivers, each of whom wanted to be the best. Each day they were perfecting their wheel changing techniques, checking their cars engine, tyre wear etc. They would time each other around known roads in the countryside around Stuttgart. By the end of May, they had honed themselves into a real force to be reckoned with. Defeat was not an option. A race strategy was worked out. They would change tyres and refuel every two laps. Special extra large fuel tanks were fitted to enable the cars to cover over 300 kilometres without running low on fuel. Tests had shown this was possible even travelling at speeds more than 140 kph. It was possible to average around 100 kph over local roads. They were all looking forward to the race, and of course winning.

Gustav told them not to take chances and definitely do not to race each other. Team orders were to finish, the order was not important, but he did not want them breaking the cars, or cutting up other team members.

The last few days leading up to their departure for Homberg were hectic. It was all double-checking everything. Then, the day prior to race day dawned; they set off to Homberg and to the Hotel where they were to spend the night. That evening after dinner the teams sat down and worked out their final race plans. Early the next morning, the teams were at the Garage supervising the mechanics, checking that the fuel tanks were full, the tyres were inflated to the right pressures and that the cars were ready to race. The engines were started and there was a check for oil leaks etc.

Then cars made their way from the Garage to the Parc Ferme, (the area where the Race officials would inspect the cars participating in the event to ensure that they complied with the Regulations), around this area the crowds waved and cheered. This time the German entries would be the heroes. Gustav had told the Stuttgart boys that there were other Mercedes entries. The Rules of the competition were that National teams of up to three competitors could enter each with a Driver and Mechanic. Therefore, the additional three teams from Mercedes were from their Austrian factory. It was agreed that Ernst, who in fact was Austrian, would be driving for the Austrian factory team. There had been 29 entries, as host nation Germany had been allowed three entries; these had not been required to take part in the elimination race, which had taken place the previous weekend. The Austrian team had competed, and had qualified in the top six places all using the new modified Model 60's. So the race would not only be of national pride, it would also be a competition with the Austrian factory.

Tension grew as race time approached. The officials of the meeting had painstakingly inspected the Cars and now those that had qualified went down to form up on the starting grid. The competitors were told to start their engines; there was an enormous roar as the giant machines burst into life. There were a few minutes before the Starter mounted his rostrum. He raised his flag and brought in down and the race was on.

All the cars got away, some a little slowly, in a cloud of dust and fumes, the roar of their engines sounded like the end of the world. As the dust settled, the sound disappeared. Rudolph and his mechanic were doing well they were in fourth place, ahead of them was Ernst Stuck in third place, whilst behind was Hermann Ritter in sixth place. The wild card had been Camille Jenatzy, who had seconded by the Austrian factory; he was second at this stage of the race. Rudolph was going about as fast as he dared; the clouds of dust made visibility poor and trying to keep up speeds of 100 kph plus, were very hard work. The car was on song and was going like the wind. It was a gruelling course with hairpin bends, steep hills, and sections where the road twisted through wooded areas. Rudolph knew from bitter experience that several competitors in their haste would end up among the trees. There were some straight stretches too, here the cars could be given almost full throttle, and speeds of up to 150 kph could be achieved by the most powerful cars.

The first lap ended without incident, Rudolph waved as he passed the pits at high speed. The Model 60's were all going very well and had held station. Gustav watched them thunder by, their engines sounding music to his ears. He crossed his fingers and said quietly to himself, only three more laps to go. He went over to the pit crew to warn them to be ready when the cars came in. There was about a 6 minutes gap between each of his entries at this stage, so there was plenty of time to service the cars and send them on their way with new wheels and a full tank of fuel. The leader Leon Thery in his Richard-Brasier had gone through ahead of Camille Jenatzy in the Mercedes but he was some 15 minutes behind the leader.

As they started their second lap, Rudolph noticed several cars that had crashed, fortunately nobody had been hurt. The wooded section too had seen a couple of drivers trying to drive their cars back on to the circuit. The lap ended without incident as Rudolph car swooped into his pit for a quick service. Rudolph's team had the car topped up with fuel and the wheels changed. He engaged first gear and sped away. Then, the next Model 60, driven by Helmut, screeched into the pit for attention.

Hermann had made up some time, which he subsequently lost, as he had to wait for Helmut who needed some adjustments to his car. The radiator had sprung a leak, when a stone flipped up by the car in front had hit it. Hermann was annoyed, but could only sit there and wait. He lost seven vital minutes. As the race progressed, so Rudolph made up several places. He was only 3 minutes behind Camille Jenatzy, and Rudolph was trying his hardest, but he knew that if he got too close the dust would slow him up. He would not be able to see the hazards ahead. He carried on driving to his own limit. The third lap again was uneventful; those that had been trying too hard fell by the wayside. Rudolph passed several Panhards and Renaults that had cried enough. Others had punctures, and were struggling to change the tyres. In these early races wheel and tyre changing was a slow process.

Now it was the last lap, Rudolph and Hermann could not wait to see the chequered flag, this signified the end of the race. Rudolph roared around the last corner, and he knew he could finish. The Car had been excellent; it had not missed a beat. He knew he had not won, but he had tried his hardest and would finish with his Mechanic, Car, and himself in one piece. As he crossed the finish line, a loud cheer went up from the crowd in the Grandstand. The Pit crew and Gustav were cheering too. It was a great day for the team all of whom had finished. Rudolph had finished 3rd, a very creditable performance. The winner was Leon Thery in just over 5 hrs 50 mins an average speed of 87 kph. Camille was second some 11 minutes behind the winner, whilst Rudolph was just 2 minutes back from Camille. Hermann too had done well finishing 4th a further 3 minutes behind. The only non-finisher was Helmut; his car had broken down, when the engine overheated due to an empty radiator. In all, a good day for the teams. It was a matter of packing up and returning to Stuttgart.

The Managing Director called a meeting, which involved everyone in Management, Research, and Development. It was decided that the Model 60 had reached its limit as a Racing Car, now it would be sold to the public, in a detuned form as a road vehicle. The top speed would be 144 kph and would have four very comfortable leather seats, a windscreen some weather protection including mudguards and an optional fabric roof.

They had read the account of the Gordon Bennett Race at Homburg, and knew that they would have to find more power, speed, and above all reliability. The Austrian press had praised their drivers, but less enthusiastic about the German teams. The reverse could be said for the opinions of the German press, who said that the Mercedes Drivers were heroes of the Fatherland. The Managing Director Herr Vicktor Mansfeldt announced that they would develop a new machine for the 1905 Gordon Bennett Race, which would be held on Wednesday 5th July 1905 in Auvergne region of France near the town of Clermont-Ferrand. It would be a tough race as the area was very mountainous being in the Central Massif.

The Management's decision was to run three cars; the selected drivers would be Christian Werner, with Ernst Stuck and Helmut Braun. He felt that both Rudolph and Hermann had earned their laurels, of that there was no doubt. The drivers that Herr Vicktor had chosen had the most experience in mountain events. He had other plans for Rudolph and Hermann; they would build, develop, and test, in the New Year. In order to maintain their expertise they would be entered some National competitions that would hone up their skills for the future.

However, events had a habit of getting in the way of the best-laid plans, as most of us know. It was to change their lives during the months that were to come, not just Rudolph and Hermann, but the whole factory. Late one Sunday evening, Hermann, and Rudolph were strolling home from a local Beerkeller where they had been with some lady friends. They noticed smoke billowing above the rooftops. It seemed to be coming from the direction of the Mercedes factory. A Fire Engine rattled by; the machine was going full tilt the Firemen clinging on for dear life. Rudolph hailed a taxi, he asked the Driver to take them to their factory. As they got closer Rudolph's greatest fear was realised. Smoke and flames were lighting up the night sky. He and Hermann stood at the factory gates feeling absolutely helpless. The Firemen were fighting the massive blaze. The situation was desperate, but they were losing the battle. The fire had a stranglehold, as they watched the main factory roof caved in. Rudolph and Hermann both felt sick, but could do nothing but watch their whole world go up in flames.

One of the Firemen walking off the site; asked Rudolph if he worked at the factory. They spoke for a few minutes, and then the Firemen just stood and looked. The local fire brigades were helpless; they just did not have the equipment to control the blaze that by now was out of control.

By now, a small crowd of onlookers had arrived and they normally do, and in the midst of all this confusion a car screeched to a standstill beside them. It was Gustav; the local Police, who had a large presence there now to keep crowd back from the ever-enveloping smoke and flames, had contacted him. Gustav could not believe what was happening to his beloved factory he just stood there in complete shock, he shook his head and started to cry. He was not an emotional man, but this was tragic. Rudolph tried to comfort him and Hermann consoled his colleagues. After an hour or so, the fire seemed to die down. Gustav took the two young men home, and asked them to stay with him and his wife. They sat up half the night trying wondering exactly what they could salvage from this disaster. On other parts of the site, the fire fighters were still trying to put out the flames. Gustav's wife Elizabeth kept them all supplied with coffee; finally, they just fell asleep in their chairs absolutely exhausted.

Early the next morning, after breakfast, they made their way back to the factory. It was just a charred heap of twisted metal and burnt bricks. The workers had turned up, not knowing of the events of the previous night. Herr Mansfeldt had arrived early and stared at the ruins of his factory in disbelief. He got up on a low wall and addressed the assembled staff. He promised that they would be paid, their jobs would be safe and that like the Phoenix a brand new factory would rise from these ashes. The Firemen were there again damping down the smouldering mounds of material. He said the only consolation was that the fire happened on a Sunday night when there was nobody in the factory. No lives had been lost.

They searched the site, just one small garage remained untouched, and it was where the new car that was being developed, was stored. As luck would have it, Gustav had taken some of the technical drawings home on the Friday night to study.

They would have to get in touch with the Austrian factory to get other drawings in order to start production, once the factory was rebuilt. An Insurance claim had now been submitted, but this would take time. There had been little cash on the premises; luckily the workers had been paid. The rest of the money had been banked, except for about 120,000 marks that had been put in a fireproof safe in the small garage that had been spared.

There would be a full investigation, of course and the probability of arson could not be ruled out.

During the weeks that followed, thoughts of racing were far from everyone's minds. Everyone toiled endlessly. Ernst and Helmut did take part in a couple of local races, but they had to borrow cars from Private Owners. They were dark days; the factory managed to fulfil a couple of orders via the Austria factory. It was not a satisfactory arrangement, for the Austrian factory was competing with its German neighbour for sales. That Christmas at home for Rudolph and Hermann was not the joyous occasion that past years had been. Rudolph related the highs and lows of the year. Margarita and Josef were very pleased to know that their son had not been injured in any way by all that had happened. Hermann too was welcomed home at Ulm, his parents told him to put the events of 1904 behind him and look forward to the New Year and new beginnings. They asked did he have a special young lady, but Hermann would only say that he was playing the field. In any case, with all the problems they had in Stuttgart a permanent lady friend would not help matters.

The holiday ended and Rudolph and Hermann were back in Research and Development Department trying to get back to normality. It would be a hard year for everyone. They would succeed; it was in their minds to be the best. The New Year started and building began, the steel structures of the new factory were erected, and things looked like getting back to normal. The cause of the disastrous fire was at last found. Herr Mansfeldt had inaugurated an extensive investigation as to the cause. It turned out to be poor insulation on the lighting wiring that ran the length of the main factory roof. Sparks had fallen on some inflammable material, probably the Horsehair stuffing used for the seats.

Herr Mansfeldt said that an alternative material must be found to fill the seats. They needed to store any inflammable materials well away from wiring in order to eliminate this kind of disastrous fire occurring in the future. Luckily, their Insurance Company had paid up in full, plus a substantial compensation payment for loss of business.

The year of 1905 wore on, the new factory took shape, new facilities were added, the Research, and Development Department was extended with far better building and facilities. The factory was fully working by June; it had been a tremendous effort by all concerned. The Construction Company, had completed the work two months ahead of schedule, this was beyond Gustav's wildest dreams. Due to the fire, development work had been virtually suspended, except on the one car, which had survived.

This car was the only one salvaged from the fire and had been modified to be able to take part in the Gordon Bennett Race in Auvergne; Christian Werner would drive this. The team took little interest in the races that year for, as they could not compete, they were only interested in any technical advances that their competitors had made. It was no surprise that they read in the Newspaper that last year's winner had done it again. Christian Werner finishing 5th. He was over an hour behind the winner. The race was again one of attrition, and less than half of the entry completed the 500-kilometre race. This race brought to an end an era for Mercedes. For 1906, there would be a 1000 kilograms maximum limit. Cars would have to be lighter. So it would be back to the drawing board.

The factory heard about a race at Le Mans due to be held over 2 days on the 26th & 27th June. The race would be for the new formula. The race would consist of 12 laps of a course of 103 kilometres a colossal distance of 1236 km. There were tales of monster cars being produced especially for the event. Fiat had entered a 130-hp car, like a rocket-propelled wagon. Panhard and Renault too were developing machines for this momentous race. Mercedes decided that it was not possible to get a car built under the new regulations, in such a short time. Failure was not an option; their existing car did not conform anyway.

During one of their regular meetings, Gustav told his team: "Of course, the French would have cars ready. Think about it boys" he said to the disappointed drivers, "the French have not only written the regulations they are organising the event, and running it in their own country." The day after the race, Gustav could not wait to see the result. It was given little coverage in the German press. However, he managed to get a French newspaper the following day; it gave a full report together with a list of all the finishers. Again, there were few.

The Winner was Hungarian and born in a village that few could pronounce, let alone know where it was. Ferenc Szisz was 33 years of age and they predicted a very bright future for this man. He brought his Renault AK across the finish line in 12 hrs. 14 mins and 7 secs. He was over 32 minutes ahead of another, yet to be famous Italian driver Felice Nazzaro in a monster sized 130 hp FIAT. The winner had averaged over 100 kph, and magnificent feat of courage and endurance. (Incidentally - fact Ferenc Szisz lived to the ripe old age of 97. He was born in 1870 - that 1906 French GP was his only win. Felice Nazzaro died aged 60 in his home city of Turin in 1940).

Would the regulations change for 1907? Gustav would just have to wait and see. In the autumn came the news that for 1907, cars would have to have a fuel consumption of at least 9.4-mpg. So the factory decided to give the 1907 French GP a miss. It seemed that the French only wanted their own cars to win.

"Let us wait Gentlemen," said Gustav, "for the 1908 Regulations to appear we might even get a level playing field. In the meantime, let us produce good cars that the public will buy."

Therefore, for 1906 and 1907 the factory turned out a variety of models, which sold very well to the rich people of Europe, and even Royalty. Rudolph and Hermann got on with testing and development of both road cars and engine development for future racing machines.

Chapter 5

The new school buildings for Christ's Hospital were situated only a few miles from Ashdown Hall. Nigel had been granted special dispensation to go to the school. The Brewery had sponsored several scholarships at the school, since it moved from London in 1902, as recompense for their generosity, the school had allowed John Ashdown's son Nigel to become a pupil. He looked fine in his traditional uniform, with the long blue coat with shiny buttons and those bright yellow stockings. The school always had a reputation for excellence. It had been founded by King Edward VI in 1552, for the education of children of the poor people of London. (Fact: The original buildings were in the Grey Friars Monastery in Newgate Street, London. The King had founded several schools of this kind, but today Christ's Hospital is the only one left. The following year 1553, the King died aged 16 of tuberculosis.)

Among its former pupils were Poets, Mathematicians, Engineers, and many other famous men of learning. There had always been a great tradition here and although the buildings were new, you could tell that within these walls was talent waiting to be released. Around the buildings were 1000 acres of playing fields and woodland. There was a farm that would produce diary products for the school kitchens. The Staff lived in Houses within the grounds. (Fact: The school dining hall has a high wooden supported ceiling and high on the wall facing the entrance is the famous painting by Antonio Verrio (1639-1707) measuring 85ft by 14ft and commemorating the foundation of the Royal Mathematical School at Christ's Hospital by King Charles II in 1672. Every boy is told the story of the painting that is unique. There are special Verrio guides appointed who show both visitors and parents around the School and relate the history of the Verrio painting. To top it all the School has its own station, with the Railway line running through the school grounds.

Lord and Lady Ashdown knew the school well; they had watched it being built. They hoped that their son Nigel would pass the examination to qualify for entry to such a prestigious school. They had been to the "Open Day" and had met Mr.Swan who would be Nigel's Housemaster in Lamb House. Every house had different names of famous pupils of the past. Mr.Swan received Lord and Lady Ashdown in his study. He told them that their son would be treated just like all the other boys. He would make no special case for Nigel. He would expect him to obey by the Rules and conform to School Discipline. They had a Matron to look after them and do their washing. There was an Infirmary for the times when boys were sick. The Housemaster would always inform the parents if boys were ill. If at any time they were worried about their son's health or educational progress, all they need do was simply to telephone. Junior and Senior boys remained in the same "House", until they left Christ's Hospital to go on to University. After the interviews were over the parents were invited to attend a special meeting in the Assembly Hall. The Headmaster Mr. Augustus Coatbridge gave a welcoming speech and hoped that they had all enjoyed their day so far. Later they escorted around the school by a "Grecian." He was a boy in his last year at School. John and Victoria Ashdown were very impressed, and said so in their brief meeting with the Headmaster. They then went back to the Dining Hall for high tea.

So it was that Nigel began his Education at a school with a long tradition. He felt a bit strange in School uniform, which was certainly different from any school uniform he had ever seen. He would be a boarder, even though he lived just a few miles away. During the first night, he had little sleep; he was kept awake by some of the new boys who were homesick already.

As the weeks went by he made good progress in his studies, and was always near the top of his class in every subject. Mr.Swan, his Housemaster was delighted that he had taken to life at C.H.; it wasn't to everyone's taste. Several of those who had been homesick had now settled down. Only one boy in Nigel's house had left, it seemed that there was a family crisis and were unable to allow him to continue at the School. Nigel enjoyed sport, whether Cricket, or Rugby. He was now opening Batsman for his house team, and later appointed captain. Soon the winter set in and Christmas holidays were here once more. It was a welcome break for Nigel who felt he was under pressure towards the end of term.

John went to the School and brought Nigel back to Ashdown Hall. Nigel was pleased to sleep in a comfortable bed. The school beds were very hard, iron frames with wooden boards topped with a horsehair mattress. Nigel said they had a menu for meals, but he thought it just gave their Chef, and he used the word loosely, something to aim at. He sometimes even got close to what it supposed to have been.

Christmas was a great time for celebration, for all the family was now together. Nigel's reports showed that he had great promise, both an academically and in the sporting field. John Ashdown said that if his work continued in the same vein, he had something special in mind for the coming summer. It seems that construction was taking place for a purpose built Racing Circuit called Brooklands, the architect of this unique circuit was a Mr.Locke-King. It would be situated near the village of Weybridge in the County of Surrey. Brooklands was planned to be the first circuit in England that would enable the public to view racing in comfort and safety. He told Nigel that he had purchased shares in the Construction Company who would be offering him number of tickets to go to as many meetings as he wished and take guests. Nigel was really excited at this; after all, he had keen interest in all kinds of sport. This would be something special indeed. It seems that the King and Queen would be there at the opening on July 17th 1907.

Nigel worked really hard in the months to come. He was always last to leave the Common Room, then he went to bed he slept like a log. He did everything with an enthusiasm that frightened some of his friends. Some of who were a bit phlegmatic to say the least. Whether it was an examination or just a game of cricket, he had to be the best. Second place, nobody remembered he said to himself. Mr.Swan wondered if he would burn himself out in the first year, but he did not. At the end of summer term, he had surpassed even his expectations; his results were better than everyone in his junior house. His report showed - English 1st, Geography 1st, History 1st, Mathematics 1st and the list went on.

Now it was the summer holidays, John took Nigel home once more, it was just 4 days to go to the opening of Brooklands, and Nigel was very impatient. John had bought him a bicycle, for his old pedal car was far too small for him now. He would cycle around the Estate as if in a race. He would read in the evenings about new ideas, new inventions, and the exploits of the new breed of daredevils in Racing Cars and Aircraft. These were exciting times. The Newspapers were full of stories about the new Racing Circuit at Brooklands; there were pictures of its construction and items about the daredevils who would be taking part on Opening Day. Early on the morning of the opening, the family Daimler Limousine was brought to the front of the Hall. The invitations to this Grand Event were strictly limited; after all, you cannot have just anybody coming to an event like this can you? Aside from the Royal Party, the Lords and their Ladies, the only members of the public that would be allowed in, were those that had worked on the project from Managers to the Labourers. There was the unusual sight of John Ashdown behind the steering wheel and Nigel sitting beside him. They were of course waiting for Victoria to grace them with her presence. Nigel had been ready for ages.

Then Victoria appeared in one of her gorgeous dresses complete with parasol. At last they could go. Victoria settled back in the rear leather seats, the Daimler then set off silently down the long drive and away to Weybridge and Brooklands. Approaching the circuit, they noticed vast crowds lining the road, hoping to catch a glimpse of King Edward VII and his lovely Queen Alexandra. A Policeman waived John through the gates, an Official dressed in a Morning Suit, and Top Hat came over to ask them for their Official invitations. John was told to go to the VIP parking enclosure. Nigel gazed around the vast concrete bowl; the number of people crowded around the circuit astonished him. He had never seen such a crowd in his life. Nothing like this had existed in England before.

John went off and came back with two Official Programmes for the day's events. The Forward was by King Edward VII, that gave a description of how the track was constructed and expectations for its future. There was a programme of the day's events and their timing, profiles of the famous sportsmen who would be participating in events during the day. Another article mentioned the machines that people would be seen performing, together with a few technical details. It was all very exciting.

It mentioned the steepness of the Byfleet Banking and how dangerous it could be and Drivers should take extra care on this section of track. (Fact: Part of this circuit – the Byfleet banking can still be seen today).

Along the top of the banking were thick lines of trees and behind the trees a very steep slope, below that ran the main Railway line. It was not a section of track for the faint-hearted. It was a case of approach the banking at high speed, keep you foot hard on the accelerator and steer straight ahead.

Anyone who went over the top caught the next train to London; at least so it was said. It was very daunting part of the circuit, because of the angle at which the cars passed across this section of the circuit. If a car was going too slowly it could literally roll down the embankment, and possibly turn over. It seems that there was a technique to conquering this particular hazard. Competitors had to go very quickly, and drive high up on the Banking; otherwise you were left at the bottom and would be passed by faster cars. Then swoop down using the gradient as a down hill section to gain extra speed. The experienced drivers had this method to a fine art.

The programme would start at 10.30 am, with a flight around the new circuit by a well-known Aeronautical Pilot. Next a Balloon Race, following this a Demonstration by the Racing Team from Mercedes. The Napier team would be there to show the British flag. The Official Track Opening would be at 12 noon by the King himself. Once the opening ceremony had been completed, the Mercedes and Napier teams would be presented to the King. There would a break for luncheon, for certain invited guests. During this period, the pits would be open for a closer inspection of all the machinery present. Drivers would be available for conversation. The afternoon was set aside for racing. This was the kind of event that Nigel had only dreamed about. He was in his element.

Just before 10.30 a.m., a big cheer went up and along the track came a very large open Rolls Royce. It was none other than King Edward VII and Queen Alexandra, the chauffeur sitting bolt upright behind the windscreen. The car pulled up to where the Red Carpet had been laid out, which lead to the raised Platform set-aside for special guests. Nigel's perfect day was about to begin; there, only 50 yards away was the King and Queen of England. Nigel had seen photographs of the "Royal Couple" in Newspapers, but seeing them in the flesh and so close as this was indeed something special.

The King and Queen got to the top step on the Platform, where they turned to face the cheering throng.

The Band of the Coldstream Guards, struck up the National Anthem and everyone stood silently to attention until the last note sounded. Then another cheer went up, the King and Queen waved again to the crowd. Nigel focussed his gaze on the Royal Couple. Queen Alexandra looked stunningly beautiful in a pure white dress that reached almost to the ground. She wore a broad brimmed hat in pure white adorned with a purple band. The King was dressed in a Morning Suit with a Black Top Hat. The National Anthem ended, the crowd settled down and the programme of events began. In the distance, a sound could be heard. It seemed to come from a spot in the sky. At first, it was invisible to the naked eye. The sound increased in volume as the tiny dot became larger; its shape became recognisable as a small aeroplane. The crowd gasped as the fragile machine zoomed low over the enclosures. Nigel could see clearly the pilot struggling with the controls. Would he survive this daredevil act? The man flying this aeroplane was none other than Alberto Santos-Dumont; he was a wealthy Coffee Grower, who was just crazy about flying. The Programme mentioned that he had, the previous year, made several flights in Europe with this tail first 14 - bis biplane. All too soon, he had disappeared, the sound of his engine faded away. Then he reappeared passing over the crowd once more, waved and then landed his little plane on the grass in the centre of the circuit.

The next part of the programme would be a demonstration of high speed racing, by the Mercedes Team. Nigel could see the three Silver Cars over in the Paddock area. Rudolph von Lundenberg and Hermann Ritter had already been practising around the circuit on the previous day. The third car would be driven by Camille Jenatzy, the winner of the 1903 Gordon Bennett Trophy, and had finished in 2nd place in the same event in 1904. Camille was now an adviser to the team and at this time was not involved in competitions. The demonstration was to be flagged away by Mr. Locke-King. Brooklands had been his brainchild; today was the culmination of all his dreams and aspirations. The weather was perfect, the Royal Guests had arrived and so had all his star attractions. It would be a day that history would remember.

Mr.Locke-King mounted the rostrum; the Mercedes team came out on to the circuit, and made their way to the start line. He was a very proud man as stood there for a moment, wondering what deeds of heroism would be performed on this 2.8 mile circle of concrete. The cars were now below him, there engines bellowing out their exhaust notes, shuddering, waiting like Greyhounds in the slips, ready to show their pace along this wonderful track. This Model 90, had shown a clear pair of heels to many of the best cars that France could throw against them. The Union Jack fell and away they roared in line abreast away from the start line. At over 100 mph they hit the Byfleet Banking still three abreast, then one of them swooped down from the top passing the other two. This was Camille showing his experience to the other two newcomers. Then they took it in turns to lead, and after four laps, they were given the chequered flag to signify the end of their demonstration. The three cars crossed the start and finish in line abreast. This certainly impressed Nigel, who now vowed that one day in the not too distant future he would drive one of these monsters. The team did a lap of honour and a cheer went up from the crowd and the Royal Party, who had never before witnessed such a thrilling event.

The timekeepers had clocked the fastest lap at almost 90-mph., which was amazing. The event that followed was by any standards an anti-climax. It was a Hot Air Balloon Race. There was no noise and very little in the way of excitement. The colourful Balloons just wafted along in the gentle breeze. Then, they slowly disappeared from view. Nigel's thoughts immediately focussed on the Lunch interval, when there would be an opportunity to meet 'The Titans of the Track'. The King and Queen rose to their feet, as noon approached. He gave a short speech. He thanked all those that had worked so hard and long hours building such a magnificent racing circuit, which would be a great proving ground for the new British Car Industry. He thanked Mr.Locke-King for having the dream that had now become a reality. Then, he praised the Stars of the Track, who had come to England to show their prowess.

It was a day they would all remember for all time. He called up Mr.Locke-King and made a special presentation to him and then declared Brooklands open.

The King and Queen then made their way to a large marquee, which had been erected on the inside of the circuit close to the Paddock.

Dozens of gleaming machines were parked in the warm sunshine. Inside the marquee, the VIP's and all the drivers were being presented to the King and Queen and to Mr.Locke-King. The queue to greet the Royal guests was moving slowly along, and then John and Victoria Ashdown were introduced, John said to the King:

"Your Majesty, may I introduce to you my son, Nigel."

The King bent forward and said, "Do you want to be a Racing Driver when you are old enough?"

Nigel thought for a moment then, replied in a positive tone. "Yes, your Majesty, I do."

The King smiled and said, "Then young man I wish you good fortune and to win for King and Country."

The King gripped Nigel's hand and shook it firmly. The Queen smiled and Nigel bowed and kissed the back of her gloved hand. For Nigel this was the proudest moment in his life. He had met the King and Queen of England and spoken to them. What could be more exciting than this? As time passed other moments would no doubt follow. A cold buffet was now spread out before them; it was on a long table that ran the length of the marquee. The introductions over, the Royal Couple made their way to a special table prepared for them. The uniformed waitresses had been told that until the King and Queen began to eat, nobody would be served.

The Ashdown family were finally seated and served. The food was absolutely delicious and the variety of dishes was truly astonishing. The range of wines available was mind-boggling. From where they were seated, Nigel could see those fascinating machines. As soon as he had finished his lunch, John could see he was impatient. John said he would take him to the Paddock. Here they could view these machines at close quarters; they may even be able to speak to some of the drivers, who had thrilled them during the morning session. John asked Victoria if he could leave her with her friend from The Ladies Circle, Margaret Ludlow. Her husband Jack had a small Engineering Company in Horsham, and had supplied goods to the Brooklands Company.

They made their way towards the Paddock and the three enormous Mercedes cars. Nigel was looking closely inside the open bonnet at the mass of metal and pipes that made up the power plant of this giant of a car.

"Why don't you get behind the steering wheel, young man?"

The voice came from behind Nigel who felt both startled and embarrassed, he turned around and there stood the tall figure of Rudolph Von Lundenberg. Rudolph turned to John and smiled.

"I am sorry Sir," said Rudolph, "if I frightened your Son, may I introduce myself to you? My name is Rudolph Von Lundenberg. Please call me 'Rudy', my name, is how do you British say. Ah yes! A mouthful that's it."

John shook Rudy's outstretched hand, and Rudy clicked his heels in typical German fashion.

"I am delighted to make your acquaintance Sir," replied John, "this young man is my son Nigel."

Rudolph shook Nigel's hand.

"Hello Nigel, it is a pleasure to meet a young man who is interested in racing cars. Are you enjoying your day at this wonderful and unique racing circuit?"

"Yes sir," replied Nigel now full of confidence, "I am having a really terrific day here. I thought that your team's demonstration was excellent. One day I hope to be a racing driver just like you."

Rudolph smiled and helped Nigel climb up behind the wheel of the giant Mercedes racing car.

Nigel felt on top of the world. The seating on this car was very high up and his feet could not reach the controls. He sat there enthralled and daydreamed for a moment that he was winning races.

"Nigel," asked Rudolph, "did you enjoy sitting behind the wheel of my car?"

"Sir," replied Nigel, "it is a moment I will always remember."

Lord thanked Rudolph for letting him sit on this valuable machine, as Rudolph helped Nigel down from the driver's seat. Rudy then introduced Nigel and John to his colleagues. The five men were so engrossed in conversation that the Lunch interval just seemed to disappear.

A loud klaxon sounded to herald the start of the afternoon's programme of events. Rudolph was sorry that they could not continue with their interesting conversation. The German drivers seldom had the opportunity to talk to people who were outside Motor Racing, yet so enthusiastic. Rudolph's last words were:

"Please bring your family to Stuttgart some day soon, and then we can really try these cars out with you."

They made a promise to meet again soon, perhaps later in summer when Nigel was home from School. The afternoon session was devoted to a series of races for local rich Amateur Drivers, who hurtled their cars around the Concrete Saucer with all their might. Some got very overexcited and there were a few accidents, luckily none too serious.

"Father," said Nigel as they were driving home, "this is the most exciting day I have ever had,"

"Well, son," replied John, "I told you that if you worked hard at School you would get a super reward."

That night Nigel dreamt of being a World Champion. The noise, fumes, smoke and cheers of the crowd as he passed the chequered flag for yet another victory. He dreamt of thundering around Brooklands to see that chequered flag as the Number One.

Meanwhile, Rudy and the rest of the team were on their way back to the factory. There was a good deal of work to be done, if they were to compete in the 1908 series of races. Gustav, back in Stuttgart, had received the Regulations for the 1908 season. They had changed completely, and now it would mean yet another lot of modifications not only to the bodywork, but a completely new type of engine. The new rules were quite complex, and were bound in a thick volume. The Regulations stated that all cars were to be built to a minimum weight of 1100 kgs. For engines the cylinder bore for 4 cylinder cars would be 155 mm, and 127 mm for 6 cylinder cars. Gustav decided that the factory would build just two cars for the 1908 race to be held in Dieppe. The Automobile Club of France seemed to have written the Rules again. They had one more event for 1907, and that was the Kaiserpreis.

This event would be held on open roads in the Homburg to Weilburg area of the Taunus Mountains over a 120-kilometre circuit. If, there were a large number of entries, then there would be a qualifying event, to weed out the slow runners. This event would rival the French Grand Prix and would be run in August. It would be open to modified 8-litre touring cars. It was a challenge that Gustav wanted to meet. It would show these French and Italian drivers that the Fatherland could win another event in their own country. They would enter four modified Model 90's and he would give the good news to all his drivers when they returned from their trip to Brooklands. This would be their final event of the year, and indeed the swansong for the Model 90. The race would be over 8 laps a total distance of 960 kilometres. The strategies for this event would certain need careful planning. Gustav knew that teams from their main rivals Fiat, Mors and Renault would be participating. Together, they would be formidable opposition for there were some very professional drivers and mechanics.

The one thing that Gustav Schumann had learnt the hard way was simply never underestimate your rivals. This meant that the team had to pull together as never before. He had put a framed inscription on the wall above his desk. It read in large red capital letters the following phrase: -

FAILURE IS NOT AN OPTION

Gustav always pointed to this inscription in his Office, whenever someone came in whinging.

All too soon, the summer holidays were over for Nigel; it had been a marvellous holiday; the highlight had been that trip to Brooklands. He told all his friends back at School all about it. They were fascinated, they knew it was true, for they had read all about it in the TIMES newspaper and that, only printed facts. A local newspaper reporter had come to Ashdown Hall and wanted to know all about the Ashdown's day at Brooklands. Now it was back to the grindstone, so to speak. He was no longer a new boy; Nigel was now in his second year and had a new boy under his wing. It was nice being a kind of elder brother, for Nigel was an only child. Life got back to normal. Well as normal as it could be at Christ's Hospital. Nigel's charge was a bright boy from a poor family in Kent. His name was Charles Graham; his Father was a Farm Worker from a village near Canterbury. He was a bright lad and always cheerful. He had a good attitude, so despite coming from different backgrounds, Nigel and he became good friends. They would study together; this indeed helped young Charles really progress well. It also stopped him feeling homesick and being bullied by the older boys.

Chapter 6

It was the late summer of 1904 and it was Alain Clement's last few days at home, before going off to the Sorbonne in Paris, were very hectic. There seemed so much to do, and he knew that his life would change dramatically. His Father let him off the many chores that he had been "saddled" with over the years. Helene-Marie realised at last that her brother was leaving home, it was quite sad. They had become quite close these last few weeks. Paris, he told her was not that far away. She had seen photographs in Magazines of Monsieur Eiffel's Tower, which was built for the Great Paris Exhibition of 1889. The Steel structure towered over everything, and was the tallest building in the world at the time. She read articles about people committing suicide by jumping from its platforms. Intrepid Birdmen had tried to fly with improvised wings, and had fallen to their death.

Finally, the day dawned when Alain was due to leave for Paris. The Count called in to see him off, telling him they would meet up in Paris for the Motor Show in the autumn as promised. The Family said their fond goodbyes, but Pierre and Marie knew that it was the only way that their son could realise his dreams, of becoming a Qualified Engineer. The Sorbonne had an international reputation for producing students with extremely high qualifications. Alain was determined to be amongst the best. The Students were given a short settling in period, before the Tutors really started pressing them for results. Alain found student life rather different to back home. He had his own little small room in the Halls of Residence. Here he could study in peace, no interruptions, terrific! At first, it took him a little while to come to terms with his new way of life. There was much midnight oil to be burnt it seemed. Luckily, Count de Longchamps had provided more than enough funds for his needs. Alain was able to buy all the books he required. Some he managed to obtain second hand or Students that had completed their courses. Others he needed had to be obtained from Bookshops in the City. He spent some of his evenings in local street cafes, where he watched the world go by.

Other times he spent with fellow students, for he was a staunch member of the debating society. They were often putting the world to rights. The one thing Alain did now, he had to be focussed, and he must not fail any exam, however difficult it may be.

One evening there was a telephone call for him; it was the Count de Longchamps. He asked how Alain was enjoying the Student life, and what progress had he been making. Alain told him he was really happy at the Sorbonne. He was missing his family, but realised that his future lay in studying hard, it was the only way to achieve his ultimate goal. The Count reminded him about their date to see the Paris Motor Show; he said that it might help with his Engineering Studies. Alain said he was looking forward to the Show and seeing the Count once more. Alain thanked the Count profusely, for all his financial assistance. For without the Count's help, he would never have been able to afford to go the Sorbonne. The cost of books and living expenses in Paris was astronomical.

"Alain, just do your best," said the Count, "that is all I ask as a reward. I will meet you on the steps of the Exhibition Hall on Opening Day. I have VIP tickets for us. Take care, be focussed."

The Count rang off. Alain was thrilled, for he knew that the Count was backing him all the way. Little did Alain know what surprises lay ahead of him?

Alain walked up the steps leading into the Exhibition Hall, he noticed three other people standing by the Count. It was a very cold day and the figures were well wrapped up against the bitter wind. Their outlines seemed familiar. He got closer, he now realised they were his parents and the Countess, who happened to be staying at her Paris flat with friends whilst they attended the Paris Fashion Shows. Pierre and Marie were overjoyed at seeing their son; they threw their arms around each other and kissed. Alain's Mother was still wearing that black wool coat with white fur trimming that Pierre had bought for her some Christmases ago. The Countess allowed Alain to kiss her on the cheek too. The Countess Claudine was wrapped in a long silver fox coat, with a large collar that she pulled up around her head to shield her from the keen East wind. She wore a matching bonnet that made her look like the Czarina herself. The quintet made their way into the warmth of the Exhibition Hall.

Ahead of him, Alain, could see the mass of exhibits, he wanted to glean as much information as he could from the Representatives on the various manufacturers stands. He collected piles of brochures, each giving specifications and prices of vehicles he could not afford. The Count and Countess smiled, as did Alain's parents.

The Count whispered to Pierre that he son was certainly keen on getting all the information he could. Soon it was time for lunch, and they made their way to the Restaurant where they all sat down to a sumptuous meal. After they had eaten their fill, the Countess suggested to Marie that they go shopping, leaving the men to drool over the machinery. They would meet them back in the reception area in about 3 hours. The two ladies set off window-shopping, which in Paris is an art in itself. They were soon wandering around the shops especially those devoted to designers of the day. To Marie, this was another world entirely. She had always bought her clothes in Rouen, it had a wide variety of shops and prices were reasonable. Pierre had never restricted her on her clothing budget, but Marie was a level-headed woman, she always bought clothes that were both practical and sensibly priced.

She was not an extravagant type. Marie could not get used to the idea that in these expensive shops, the clothes did not have price tags. The Countess Claudine suggested that Marie try on a few dresses, gowns and winter coats in a particularly fashionable store. In several of the dresses, Marie felt like royalty, one in light blue velvet she wanted dearly. She admired herself in the long mirrors that were scattered around the store. Then, the Countess suggested that she try a particularly gorgeous coat, over the top of the new light blue velvet dress she had tried on. It was made of dark blue wool and reached almost to the floor. The coat had a deep hood that was richly trimmed all round with thick blue fox fur, and lined with pure padded silk. Marie, felt wonderful in it she admired herself again and again in the mirror, she felt like a Queen. In her mind she thought, I must have this coat and dress, but they must cost an absolute fortune, far beyond her means.

Countess Claudine looked at Marie, who she could see was drooling over this wonderful coat. After a few minutes silence, Claudine thought she should say something to Marie.

"Marie," she said, "that coat and dress look really lovely together on you? If you would like to have them both, it will be my pleasure to buy them for you as a present."

Marie was speechless and blushed bright red, as she was so embarrassed, she knew she could never afford a winter coat and dress like these.

"I would absolutely love them, Madam," she said quietly to Claudine, "but surely they must be very expensive."

"You deserve them my dear," replied Claudine, "I shall enjoy seeing you dressed in them. Do not put them away in a wardrobe."

Marie smiled, and Claudine knew that Marie was absolutely thrilled as she pulled the fur-trimmed hood over her head and gazed in the mirror once more.

The Shop assistant was standing close by, thinking the two ladies had made a decision at last, and she came over to them.

"Please be kind enough to put that coat and that dress on my account," said Claudine to the assistant.

"Yes Madam," replied the assistant,

"Now young lady," replied Claudine," I have not finished shopping yet as I shall now be making further selections from your wonderful selection of beautiful furs."

The assistant disappeared and returned in a few minutes with Marie's coat and dress packed in two colourful boxes tied with a ribbon.

The two ladies stayed in that store for another hour, whilst Claudine tried on several more dresses and coats. Claudine was well into clothes shopping, she was a professional. Whilst there she bought three more dresses, two full-length fur coats, a red fox and a blue fox; in addition, a mink stole.

The Countess turned to the Shop assistant.

"Young lady," she said, "we will take the blue coat and that blue dress, also would you please arrange for all our other purchases to be delivered to my Paris apartment?"

"Certainly, Madam," said the Shop Assistant, who then went away to wrap the garments that were being taken away.

The Shop Assistant must have thought that she had won the state lottery, for the commission on her sales would have more than increased her wages by some six times. Claudine looked at the clock, they had been just 3 hours, and both Ladies were delighted with their purchases. Marie was still embarrassed, but accepted the Countess's gifts gracefully. She had never before had such expensive clothes particularly as presents; she would show Pierre her purchases when they arrived home.

Meanwhile, the men were seeking out every corner of the Show, asking questions about the new models on display, making sure they missed absolutely nothing. The time flew by. Alain had been soaking up all the information he could get on this new technology. Soon 3 p.m. had arrived and they made their way back to the Reception area to meet the ladies. When the Ladies arrived, the Count was not surprised to see Marie carrying two very large bags. Pierre looked in amazement; he had not planned on spending money on clothes shopping. Still, he did not begrudge his wife having new clothes. The Count and Countess said their goodbyes to Pierre, Marie and Alain, for they were spending the night at their Paris flat. Claudine wanted to try on her new clothes as soon as they arrived.

Pierre and Marie spent the rest of the afternoon with their son following a meal in a local Restaurant they caught a late train back to Rouen, whilst Alain made his way back to his lodgings.

On arriving home Pierre was intrigued to see Marie's purchases, especially as they were wrapped and packed in rather expensive bags. He wondered how much of the family budget had been spent. Marie gave him a private showing; he thought she looked absolutely fabulous, in her new wardrobe. Her new Coat was fashionable and practical; it was agreed only to be worn on special occasions. Pierre agreed it was extremely generous of the Countess to pay for these new clothes. He had worked hard for the Count, so it was a kind of extra bonus. The next time he saw the Count and Countess, he thanked them profusely for the day and the gifts, especially Marie's new additions to her wardrobe. The Count said that it was his pleasure to give.

The time seemed to fly by at the Sorbonne. Alain studied hard for his forthcoming examinations, and was confident that he would get good grades. Many of his friends thought he was a bit of a kill -joy for he wasn't keen on going to a lot of late night parties, when he knew that he had to study. He had one or two lady friends, but they were not serious romances. His sights were set very high; he had goals to achieve. His focus was on personal development and improving the golden opportunity, he had to become the best he could be. He knew that next term would be even harder than the last; however, he was prepared to work as hard as he could to achieve his goals.

Christmas was fast approaching; he had noticed the festive decorations in the shops. Father Christmas seemed to have appeared in nearly every shop window. Alain's main concern now, was the examination results that would be published before the start of his Christmas holiday. When the list went up, he noticed that those that had partied hard were well down the list with poor marks. Alain on the other hand had passed with flying colours.

"Yes. I've done it," he cried out loud as he punched the air.

He arrived home with his news to the delight of his parents, who were pleased that the faith that they and the Count had in him was truly justified.

Away from the bustle capital, village life seemed a bit mundane. In fact, after the pressure of his exams, Alain was very pleased to get some rest and simply enjoy a true family Christmas. He knew that next term; the work would be even more demanding than the last. He would be ready for it. He had made a commitment to both his parents and the Count; he would not let them down at any cost. On Christmas Eve, the family attended the local Midnight Mass. It was the first time that Marie had, to show off her new dress and her lovely new winter coat that the Countess had purchased for her on their Paris trip. She looked fabulous as they set off for the Church. It was bitterly cold; it had snowed earlier in the day, now it was a clear night and the stars shone clearly from the heavens. Marie pulled the hood around her head to keep herself warm and cosy. The

Count and Countess always attended the Midnight Mass and the Count read the lesson. It was a perfect Christmas for them all, with a fantastic meal on Christmas Day.

Pierre and Alain agreed that Marie and Helene-Marie, who had helped her Mother prepared the festive feast, had done a magnificent job. Everyone had eaten their fill. The Fir Tree in the corner had been decorated in traditional fashion with lights and baubles. The presents had been given out earlier in the day. The Clement family felt on top of the world.

The New Year began, Alain was right; the work was getting harder at the Sorbonne, now it was a question of concentration, determination and persistence. He had grown into a very handsome young man; all the girls seemed to chase after him. He would socialise a little, and many of the ladies wanted to settle down with him. He was not exactly aloof, but his eyes were on the main prize, which was still a way off yet.

He did return some affection; after all, he could not appear to be anything other than a Red Blooded Frenchman. He sailed through his Finals with ease, confident of a First Class Honours Degree in his chosen subjects. He was top of his group in every subject and was awarded an assisted Apprenticeship with the Darracq Car Company. He would work with Senior Engineers, who would assess his work and prepare a series of exams for him every three months.

Should he get good marks, and then promotion and salary increases would follow. The course would last six months; he would then be offered a position in the Research and Development Department that had recently been expanded. Naturally, Alain took this opportunity with both hands.

He was at last getting the right kind of experience, which would lead him to a career in the French, motor industry. Hopefully, leading to fame and fortune. He was taught to drive by one of Darracq's racing drivers, who told him that he was a 'natural' and should consider joining 'The Glory Boys', as the racing team were known. First, however, he must get through the next six months of his apprenticeship to qualify for a high position. He had to know the Cars inside out. Should a car break down at any time, he must know the cause of the problem and be able to repair the part or replace it. Alain found a new enthusiasm, after all his studies at the Sorbonne; here he was getting real hands on experience. He was on the ladder to his dream, on the first rungs, it was true, but he knew he was going in the right direction. The plan had begun; the final destination was still a long way off. How the journey would progress was still a mystery. He knew that Darracq, were not the fastest car by any means, they were a keen company and had plenty of competition in the marketplace. The leading Manufacturer was Renault. They produced racing machines that had won many races. Darracq on the other hand produced mainly what Alain called 'cooking motor cars'. He knew that if he managed to get through his exams, then the position in the Development Department would be his. They could then produce vehicles that could compete with the best in France and Germany on level terms.

By 1907, Alain was 21; he had passed all of the examinations and tests that the Engineers had set him. He was now one of the most respected members of the Darracq

Development Division, as it was now called. His driving had improved beyond all recognition. He had competed successfully in several Rallies and Minor Races all over France. Despite being against very stiff opposition, he had performed brilliantly.

He had won several large trophies; these were on display in the Company Reception area in a large glass cabinet.

There were certainly room there for a lot more, Alain thought as he passed them each day.

Now that he had accredited himself really well in competition, the Chief Development Engineer, Marcel Rickard decided that Alain, should drive their Number 2 car in the forthcoming Kaiserpreis Race to be run in the Taunus Mountains. It would give him a chance to mix it with the best around. It would also be good publicity for the Company. Alain was thrilled to be chosen. He knew that the mighty Mercedes team would be there, along with Itala (from Italy), FIAT, Mors and Renault. The number 1 car from Mercedes would be driven by Rudolph Von Lundenberg, whilst number two would be in the hands of Hermann Ritter, both very experienced campaigners on the racing scene. He knew these drivers gave no quarter to their rivals. Pierre Louis Arnoux, who had been winning races for the last two seasons, would drive Darracq's number 1 car. The stage was set for a grand confrontation. The French Motoring Press had been singing the praises of the Renault team; they had a new car for the race. Louis Pechard had been promoted to Number 1, as Georges Merchant their top driver had broken an arm, when testing the new car. Otherwise, their team was the one that took part in the French GP a month or so ago. Alain knew that even with the best will in the world, his chances of finishing in the top three positions were a little remote.

He would drive as fast and as safely as he could, but unless the opposition had problems, he could not see himself taking home the silverware. However, he had overcome all previous hurdles, this was just one more. A little bit higher that is all.

Alain and his team of mechanics worked really hard, to prepare a car that would be competitive. Louis Pechard too, had his team burning the midnight oil. Neither driver wanted to let the Company down. They had chosen the best mechanics to ride with them too. The Regulations stated that the event would be for touring cars with engines up to 8-litres in capacity. The Darracq Company had produced a massive engine of over 7.5 litres with all the latest innovations.

They even tested a model with four-wheel brakes; this was unheard of in those days. The tyres were wider than on the normal car, these would give better grip. They had contacted the Hutchinson Rubber Coy. Asking for special high quality rubber and fabric combination to give the best performance. The Tyre Company had come up trumps, producing special tyres for the event. After all they needed the publicity too, why should Michelin, the biggest Tyre Company in France, grab all the headlines? Alain and his Mechanic Jean Pierre Gaston, spent days out testing the new car, the four-wheel brakes and the new lubrication and cooling systems, all worked like a dream. The engine gave fantastic performance all along its power band, and the four-wheel brakes meant that braking distances were so much less. Alain was very happy with the machine. Then about three weeks before the race, they started to get braking problems. They were pushing the car close to its limits, when the engine, brakes started to badly overheat, and they were getting brake fade. Alain and Jean Pierre just managed to pull up in time to stop the engine ceasing up. The brake drums were red hot and the linings were smouldering. They drove the car slowly back to the factory, which fortunately, was close by. Alain scratched his head all night, thinking how could they solve these two problems. Then it came to him. It was simply a matter of cooling down the brake drums somehow; also, they needed to do something about engine cooling.

He read an article in a technical magazine that had mentioned these very things. At the foot of the article, it gave the solution. Simple, thought Alain, we will increase the size of the radiator cooling area, and add another cooling fan. As for the brakes, let me see, we can increase the width of the drums by 30 per cent, put ribbing around the outside and ventilate them. These modifications were made and extensive testing carried out. It did the trick, problems solved with simple technology. The number one driver was not convinced, but the tests proved him wrong. He congratulated Alain on a brilliant solution. Louis Pechard said that now the modifications had given the car a much better performance, then he too would now drive the modified car.

All over, Europe manufacturers were producing cars for this prestigious event. In fact, 37 makes of car from seven nations had been entered.

There was a huge entry of 92 cars; this necessitated qualifying heats, the fastest 30 cars being allowed to start. The qualifying was over two laps of the 120-kilometre circuit that was on open roads. They would not be closed for qualifying, so there was a need to look out for a variety of hazards, for example: - local Horse-drawn and Motorised vehicles, loose Animals and of course local people. It would be a very dangerous race in many respects. Some of the entrants were, just drivers who had bought a fairly powerful car and hoped for glory. On the other hand were the Works Drivers, a group of hardy professionals. The strongest of all, at least on paper, seemed to be the Mercedes team. They had a wealth of experience and a strong back up crew. However, in Motor Racing nothing is certain until the chequered flag falls as the winner crosses the finish line.

In the year previous 1906, the young ITALA team was making news, by winning a unique new race over the Sicilian Mountains. The race was called the "TARGA FLORIO." Cars had to be production based, with a least 10 of the models built. Mercedes felt that they could not support this race, as it was a long way from their factory. In any case, they were still recovering from their disastrous fire a year or two before. The successful ITALA was a sturdy, shaft driven; 7.4-litre four-cylinder engine that was rated at 40 hp. It had been described in the Italian press as prettily "retouched," with a well-tuned engine and bodywork "relieved" of all fittings. In fact, it hardly had any bodywork at all. ITALA again had their name into the International Press, when one of the vehicles took part in the 1907 Paris to Peking race. This event was mind boggling. It was a veritable endurance affair demanding the stamina of a lorry. There were pictures and reports at the time, that astounded the reader with adventures and hardships endured by all that took part.

For the Kaiserpreis, ITALA had stretched their engine to 8-litres and with new overhead valves; it was rated at 72 hp, the massive engine generating its maximum power at 1200 revolutions per minute. The man driving it had started to become a legend, a Felice Nazzaro. There were already reports in the Newspapers about the dangers facing the competitors, even before the qualifying heats had begun.

They thought that it would encourage a bigger crowd, as most people always like to see others taking part in dangerous sports. Rudolph and Hermann felt confident that they would qualify well within the time allowed for each lap. Alain had the opportunity to go around the course several times, on order to get the lie of the land. Some surveying of the course had been permitted; after all, it was 120 kilometres of dusty, twisting roads, through very mountainous terrain. The Race would be over 8-laps a distance of 960 kilometres.

Practice began early one morning, with the top teams going off first. Rudolph set off toward the start line with his Mechanic Fritz Lang. He was new to the team and showed great promise as a possible Driver in years to come. The big 8-litre engine thundering out its challenge to the other competitors. Rudolph knew how to handle the beast. He had a plan to drive just fast enough to qualify; he did not want to go flat out, if he did then, there might be a chance of a crucial part breaking. Worst of all a tyre coming off at speed, or getting involved in an accident.

With all these thoughts in his mind, he eased the car up to where an official was sending off the early starters. The flag dropped, the big Mercedes sprang into life and they were soon up to 100 kph, heading for the first town on the route - HOMBURG, they had already passed three cars. Rudolph thought, well, there are three of the opposition gone. Hermann was right behind Rudolph and was keeping pace with him, but due to the state of the roads, huge clouds of dust were being thrown up. Soon, it was Alain's turn in the big Darracq. He was feeling a little apprehensive; this was about the biggest event he had ever entered. He was carrying the hopes of the factory on his shoulders. He was under starter orders, pushing down the clutch; he engaged first gear and the machine shot off in hot pursuit of the De Dietrich that had left 2 minutes earlier. He felt great with the wind in his hair; his goggles down, he gripped the steering wheel in a way that would not give him muscle problems in his arms or cramp in his hands and fingers. This he had learned while testing the beast.

He was now heading for Homburg, having already passed the car ahead.

The driver gave him a cheerful wave, as Alain went by him on a straight piece of road. Rudolph was doing very well; he had started in 8th place so, by the time he got to the hairpin bend at the village of Esch, he knew that he was now third. Still ahead was Nazzaro in that ITALA, and they way he was driving, nobody looked like catching him. The road to the next crucial spot at Emmerhausen was extremely difficult, with a series of tight bends through forested areas. A slip here could be fatal. Rudolph was making mental notes as he sped along, reminding himself that he had to do it all once more on the next lap. Now they had reached Eiserhausen, where the road took an extremely tight right hand turn. This section had to be approached with extreme care. Breaking for the corner, Rudolph noticed a car in amongst the trees; it was a Mors that had started ahead of them.

He had obviously misjudged his braking point and had ploughed down the embankment. The Driver and Mechanic signalled to Rudolph that they were OK; Rudolph acknowledged them and then pressed on to complete the lap. They were relieved that they had survived one lap; they just had to do it again. Meanwhile, Alain was now making excellent progress thanks in part to the modifications to the brakes, engine and tyres that had made all the difference. The Darracq was going like a train; he had passed several more competitors who were having either mechanical problems or slight accidents. The section through Weilburg back to the start and finish was quite a fast with a series of bends to test out the unwary. Rudolph swooped through these corners, the big Mercedes sliding nicely on the loose surface but well under control. Hermann could see his team mate ahead, so was able to copy his line through the corners. The crowd watching the practice could hear a thundering exhaust note of the first car away, and bursting into view came Felice Nazzaro in the big ITALA with his mechanic hanging on for dear life. He crossed the finish line just ahead of Vincenzo Lancia in the big FIAT, hard on Nazzaro's heels.

Then came the two Mercedes, followed a few minutes later by Alain in the Darracq. All the front runners were going well. Of the 92 that had started the race, only 54 had completed the first lap.

There were a variety of failures, mostly crashes, several had engine problems, and others had chain-drive failure. The also-rans were having a bad day. The second lap for the leading vehicles was just a repeat of the first. When Rudolph and Hermann returned to their garage, Gustav was quite excited. He had timed them on their second lap; they had averaged over 80 kph. Both drivers reported that the cars had gone well without any problems; they also said that they had driven well within their capabilities. Both cars were stripped down and found to be in almost perfect condition mechanically. The tyres it seems were just about worn out; this meant that they could only go two laps before a pit stop. Alain drove into the Darracq garage and was met by the familiar face of the Chief development Engineer.

Marcel Rickard, Darracq's Chief Development Engineer decided that as it was the Company's first event outside France, he would oversee the Kaiserpreis operation. The Company's cars had done very well in the French GP at Dieppe achieving 5th and 6th places. They were some 25 minutes behind the winner, but at least they had finished. Here his cars were up against some stiff opposition. Having heavily modified their cars, that had done so well in the French GP, Marcel Rickard was hoping for better results, but could they stand up to 8 laps of this punishing course. Alain felt that the car had performed well, the new tyres, braking system and other changes had made the car more agile. Therefore, providing the engine was not overstressed in the early stages, and then they had a good chance of finishing in the top six. Alain had qualified in 5th place. Marcel was very pleased with Alain, but they should not be complacent. He told Alain: "Every one of the drivers that have qualified want to win this race. You have the ability to win, you can do it." The race was to be run a few days later. Those that had fallen by the way side were licking their wounds. Several drivers and mechanics were patients at the nearby Hospital. Mostly minor injuries and a couple of broken arms. The teams that had failed were packing up to leave. Alain sat outside a local café, drinking coffee and brandy. He was relaxing for once, and watching the world go by.

It was a beautiful evening and the sun was setting, he had just finished a most enjoyable meal. He felt at peace with the world.

The next day, he knew that he would be back at the garage fine-tuning his machine ready for the race.

Early next morning, Alain reported to the Darracq garage to look over the car. Jean Pierre, Alain's mechanic had already started polishing the car, this way they could see if any parts had become loose, and whether there were any oil leaks. They checked the tyres, wheels, and then made a list of the spares they had to hand. They had come well prepared. Whilst they were working away, Alain noticed a shadow on the wall nearby. He turned around to see a rather tall young man with dark hair.

"Bon Jour Monsieur, can I help you?" said Alain.

"Guten tag. I have come to wish you good luck in the race tomorrow. My name is Rudolph Von Lundenberg. I am with the Mercedes team."

Alain stood up and shook Rudolph's hand.

"I am Alain Clement and this young man is my mechanic Jean-Pierre."

Rudolph went over to Jean-Pierre and greeting him warmly.

"I am pleased to meet you Jean-Pierre. Look after your driver he is very good."

Rudolph looked intently at the car and scratched his head.

"Ah!" he exclaimed, "so you are the man with the four-wheel brakes. Very good. We shall see how you shall perform in the race, it will be very interesting. Au revoir."

Alain waved to him as Rudolph walked away back to his garage. When Rudolph entered his garage, all the mechanics were hard at work. Hermann asked Rudolph, where he had been. Rudolph said he had been to see Alain Clement, who was driving the Darracq with the four-wheel brakes. Rudolph then told Hermann that if the Darracq were successful in the Kaiserpreis, then he would suggest that the Development Department try this system on next years Mercedes racing cars. The rest of the day went quickly, as all the teams burnt the midnight oil, once more in order to get their cars to the starting line for the actual race in perfect mechanical condition.

All of the drivers that had qualified had a fitful night of sleep; they knew what was expected of them. Those competitors that had been around these 120 kilometres of twisting roads knew the score. Some of the surfaces had been tarred, where it went through villages and small towns. Most of course was dusty, rutted tracks. It was more like a rally, than a road race. It had been a hot summer; there had been little rain to lay the dust. Most of the experienced campaigners knew the problems that dust clouds caused. Dangers were not seen until it was too late to take avoiding action.

The morning of the race dawned, and all the crews were ready to go. The 30 fastest cars from qualifying made their way from their garages to the starting area. They were lined up in pairs, with the fastest cars in the front. In the first row was Felice Nazzaro in the big FIAT; next to him was Vincenzo Lancia in another FIAT. Then came the two Mercedes of Rudolph and Hermann, behind him was Alain Clement in the Darracq. Beside Alain was Fernando Gabriel in the Lorraine-Dietrich; a surprise entrant and he had qualified well. Next in line was Ferenc Szisz, in the Renault AK, his qualifying time was disappointing, and Renault had high hopes of being the best in qualifying. The rest of the field was made up with a variety of makes.

The big clock on the Grandstand showed that there was 15 minutes to go. The cars would go off en masse. Time ticked by, the mechanics made last minute adjustments, and made sure that everything was just right. From the pits opposite the grandstand, everything was being readied for the first pit stop that would take place at the end of lap two. Then it was two minutes to go, and the car engines were started. The starting area cleared of everyone except Drivers and Mechanics. There was a deafening roar as 30 engines burst into life. The large crowd in the grandstand waited with baited breath, they were all anxious to see the start of the race. The Starter walked up the stairs to the starting platform, and the roar of the engines reached a crescendo. The noise was deafening as it bounced off the grandstand. All the crews were eager to go. The Starter raised the National Flag and with a sweeping action, he brought it down. The noise was now unbearable; all the drivers fought to get their cars into gear, to be first in front of the dust cloud which no doubt would follow them all of the way around the circuit. The front runners streaked away and were gone before the crowd realised it. Several competitors stalled their engines and took time to re-start; three could not even get off the start line. Their pit crews came out to try to get them going, but it was no good. The engines had died, and they were pushed off the circuit. Meanwhile, those that were still in competition were going great guns.

Felice Nazzaro was setting a hot pace and close on his heels was Vincenzo Lancia in the second FIAT.

Rudolph and Hermann were holding station behind the flying Fiat's, whilst Alain was well in touch, the Darracq handling and braking well due to its wider tyres and four-wheel brakes. He could see the dust clouds ahead of him and was keeping pace. By the time they had reached the town of Esch, Alain reckoned he had made up about 500 metres on the front runners, any closer and he would be driving in a thick dust cloud, with visibility but a few yards. Jean-Pierre looked back to see the Lorraine-Dietrich not that far back. Then came the treacherous section that all the drivers remembered from the qualifying session. It was from Esch to Eisenhausen. Alain, Hermann and Rudolph recalled seeing several cars off the road into the trees. From Eisenhausen back to the start was a faster section where they could show the car's speed potential, and gain some time, especially through the series of fast bends from Weilburg back to the start and finish line. The front runners steamed on, taking care through the dangerous sections.

By the end of lap one, the Fiat's, Mercedes and the Darracq, had opened up a gap. Szisz and Gabriel were having a job to keep up. Rudolph, Hermann and Alain gave thumbs up as they went by the pits. On their second lap through the wooded section, Rudolph noticed that two cars had rammed into each other trying to pass on the way into a corner. They had gone off the road into the trees. The drivers had been injured, and the cars written off. At the end of Lap 2, the front runners came in for fuel, new wheels and were away in a matter of 7 minutes. Alain was held up as they had a problem with one of the wheel nuts; he knew he could make up time, for even though he was in the pits for almost 9 minutes not one other car came by. He then started to go even quicker, but still driving within the capabilities of his car and himself. He soon caught up Hermann who was struggling with the Mercedes, and on a straight section, passed him, then set about catching Rudolph. He saw his dust cloud in the distance and now knew he was in fourth place. Unless the cars in front struck trouble this was probably the best, he could hope for.

The race wore on and more cars fell by the wayside, with punctures, overheating or over-enthusiasm by the drivers. At the end of lap 4, Szisz's Fiat would not restart following his pit stop.

The Mechanics checked underneath the car and discovered a massive oil leak. Therefore, his race had ended. This gave Alain third place, but he had half the race left to do. By the time, they entered the last lap there were only six cars left. Felice was well ahead now by some 14minutes. Rudolph was still in hot pursuit, hoping that the Fiat would break down. Alain's Darracq was still on song and only one minute behind Rudolph, whilst Hermann had dropped back a further 5 minutes but still held 4th place. The Mercedes was loosing power and their brakes were overheating badly.

In the grandstand by the finish line, the excited crowd were looking to see who would take home 1st Prize. In the distance could be heard the distinctive note of the Fiat of Felice Nazzaro who, crossed the finish line as the starter brought down the chequered flag. It was over, now who would be second. Rudolph had made every effort to impress on the final section of the course. He knew Alain was breathing down his neck, he whizzed across the line to beat Alain by a mere 20 secs. He was only one minute behind the winner. Felice had averaged 84 kph, and had taken almost 11 hours and 30 minutes.

The fastest lap was put in by another FIAT this one driven by Vincenzo Lancia who had rocketed around the course in just under 1 hour and 22 minutes averaging almost 88 kph. This was amazing feat by any means. The organisers gave a massive trophy to the winner; the Kaiser presented the award personally. He was not amused that an Italian had won it, but he congratulated Felice on a magnificent performance. Rudolph and Alain too received their prizes from Kaiser Willheim. They turned, stepped down to face the crowd, brandishing their trophies for all to see.

Walking back toward their pits, Rudolph and Alain were talking to each other.

"Alain," said Rudolph, "that was some close race. Frankly, I thought it would never be over. Congratulations it was a great contest."

Alain thanked him for his praise and said that he was sure that they would meet again in competition soon. They shook hands and parted. However, it was decided that the race would not be run again. Many of the drivers were relieved to hear that. After the presentations were over, the crowd began to leave.

The Kaiser and his entourage had long gone and Alain was resting in his garage. He lay there daydreaming, he thought back to that day not so long ago, when as a small boy he watched a car chug by on its way to Rouen. Little did he know then, how fate would change his life, for today he had met the Kaiser, the Crown Prince of Germany. He and the Darracq had not won the event, but they were up there with the best. The modifications were successful and had been race proved.

Meanwhile, back at the Mercedes garage Rudy and Hermann were analysing what went wrong. It was obvious to Gustav that they too needed to modify their cars if they were to win more races. "Gentlemen," said Gustav as he addressed his drivers and mechanics, "we have tried our best, nobody can say otherwise. Well done! However, the Darracq team seems to have pulled out several technical advances, in areas we should have obvious to us. Next time we will not be caught napping."

Rudolph and Hermann told Gustav about their car's lack of power. They said that Nazzaro just drove away from them in the FIAT. For try as they might they were unable to not catch him. Gustav agreed with his drivers about the lack of power and speed. However, until the cars were stripped down at the factory, he would not know how much harder that they might have been driven. One thing he did agree on was the search for more power.

Alain on the other hand was the hero of the Darracq team; they had not expected to finish, let alone in the top 3 places. They thought that they would have very little chance against teams like FIAT, ITALA, MERCEDES and RENAULT. Alain had driven an intelligent race, if he wanted the contract, he could be their permanent No.2 driver. He agreed readily. His suggested innovations regarding the 4-wheel brakes and wider tyres had given Darracq an edge over their competitors. It was an edge, which would not last unless they came up with performance modifications for the following season. Lessons had been learned by everyone that took part in the race; it would mean better cars for following season.   The teams would find out soon, exactly what competitions there would be for 1908. There would be the Prince Henry Trials, which inherited the long-distance rally role from the Herkomer Trophy.

The rules were curious and it seems that the winner would get some hideous trophy and there would be few money prizes. Therefore, the Darracq and Mercedes teams decided not to enter. Instead, they wanted to enter a more prestigious International event to be held on July 7th 1908 at Dieppe. It would be the 3rd French GP run over the same circuit as the 1907 event.

The rules were as follows: -

Cars to be 1100 kg minimum weight. Cylinder bore limited to 155mm for 4 cylinder engines for Cars with 6 cylinder engines the Cylinder bore was restricted to 127mm.

So for many factories it was back to the drawing board. Still they had the winter months and spring too to develop a racing-winning machine.

At Christmas, the Darracq factory closed for just over a week. Alain, at last, after an extremely busy season went home to see his family. Pierre met him at the local Station. It was a joyous meeting as Alain had not been home for some months. It was very cold; Alain's journey had been a long one, for the train had been delayed by a derailment. There had been a light fall of snow, and from the appearance of the clouds above, there would a lot more to come. The Count had sent his Car and Chauffeur, so that Pierre could have a warm and comfortable ride to meet the hero of the village. Alain's exploits in the Kaiserpreis were the talk of the village and celebrations were planned.

Pierre was grateful for the Count's generosity, as it had been a very cold day. Pierre was not relishing the thought of standing on a cold station, should the train be badly delayed. Wrapped in warm blankets the two men sat inside the big Renault as it made its majestic way back to Alain's home. Pierre thanked the chauffeur for the ride and not to forget to thank the Count for his generosity. Immediately they got inside the house, all the family started to fire questions at him. They wanted to know everything about everything. Alain felt tired and all he wanted to do was relax.

"Ask me as many questions as you like later," he began, "I have had a long, tiring journey. I am sorry all I want to do at present is eat, drink and rest by this lovely roaring fire."

He sat down in an armchair in front of the roaring fire started to fall asleep. He seemed to be dozing for a few minutes when Helene shook his shoulder to wake him up so that he could eat. It was the next day before he had sufficiently recovered, then he gave all the family an account of his exploits. They listened with interest, and then it was time for Pierre and Marie to give Alain all their news. Alain had noticed how much Helene-Marie had grown, since he was last home. She told Alain how much she enjoyed Horse-Riding, that she had won several Rosettes and other prizes at local Gymkhanas during the past summer and autumn.

Marie was very concerned for her Son's safety, especially as the Newspapers had reported all the gory details of the Racing Car accidents, together with photographs, including those that occurred in the Kaiserpreis. They wanted to know all about his meeting with the Crown Prince Willheim, and what their son thought of him. Alain could not say much, after all, he only presented him with an award; it was not as if he had had a conversation with him. What Alain did say, was that there was a comradeship amongst the drivers that was very strong. If there is a problem, or an accident, the passing driver will always try to get help, or even stop.

Pierre told Alain:

"Your Mother wants more children, but the Family Doctor has warned against it. After Helene was born, she had many medical problems; it is most likely that a further conception would endanger her life. It is because you are our only Son, Alain, that she worries so much about you. You will be careful won't you?"

Alain told him about the new safety measures being brought in by the Company. He mentioned to his Father that the Mercedes team had worn a form of Crash Helmet; it was to protect the head in case of an accident. He would be asking his team Manager if all their drivers could have such a piece of equipment. Pierre thought this very sensible. After all, a soft hat would be little protection in case of a crash. These racing cars were capable of speeds more than 140kph.

They could now look forward to a really great Christmas; all the families were together again. Alain was bringing in good money and had a healthy bank balance. The House had been decorated with a myriad of paper chains; tinsel and baubles hung from a large Christmas tree. The Turkey had been plucked and the merriment would begin.

There was great joy in the Clement household. They would of course attend the Midnight Mass, and Marie could again bring out her new Fur-trimmed Winter Coat. Alain too, had added to his wardrobe with a new suit, and a large fur-collared woollen overcoat. This he had bought in Germany on their trip to the Kaiserpries.

Times had changed for the Clement family; this was after all the festive season. They were going to enjoy their time together as never before. Alain was looking forward to the next season and the new cars being prepared. They would enter the French GP of course, to uphold the honour of the Tricolour. The event would be held over the same course and distance the 1907 event, he knew that to average at least 120 kph or more over 770 kilometres would be no mean feat. Alain discussed this with Pierre, who assured his son that with his engineering skills, plus the innovations he had brought to Darracq, it was not impossible. Alain had been doing well financially, especially with the prize money he had received. For the first year, he had bought 'special' presents for all the family. They were hidden away from prying eyes. The family would he thought be surprised, at their gifts all purchased in Paris.

Chapter 7

Across the English Channel, at the home of Lord and Lady Ashdown, the preparations for the Yuletide celebrations had long been underway. The Brewery had enjoyed a fantastic year; the crop of hops and Barley had been especially good quality and plentiful. The long, hot summer of 1907 had dried the throats of the good folk of Sussex. Beer Sales had increased by almost 20 per cent. John Ashdown had sent a personal letter to all his workers, congratulating them on their splendid efforts. The quality of the beer had been first class, the best year ever. Then this was topped off with a magnificent Christmas Party at the factory canteen.

Whenever he was on holiday and his studies were over, Nigel was allowed to go with his Father to the Brewery. Therefore, it was natural that he went together with his parents to the Staff Christmas Party. He sat on the top table, next to his Mother; on the other side of him was The Managing Director James Colgate. As he sat there he felt sure that his Mother would be keeping an eye on his liquid refreshment intake. He was very proud, when his Father got to his feet to give a short speech. Lord John announced that the Management was giving all the Staff a Christmas Bonus, plus an extra week's pay, in view of their good work during the year. At the end of John's speech, one of the shop supervisors stood up. He proposed a toast to the Chairman and Managing Director. The workers all stood up and sang, "for he's a jolly good fellow." John felt slightly embarrassed when the singing ended; he got to his feet and said a simple thank you. One of the young women who worked in the Accounts office presented Victoria with a large bouquet of silk flowers.

When the meal was over, the Hall was then cleared, a small band came on and everyone danced the night away. The family then had a day or so to recover from this event, before any partying began at Ashdown Hall.

The Christmas Parties at Ashdown were legendary. It was the Winter Social Event for most of the landed gentry.

Definitely, the place to be seen. Nigel wondered what present he would get this year. His school report had been excellent; again, he had far exceeded even his own expectations. His room was already crammed with Toy Soldiers, Castles and Model Cars. He was now 12 years old and had grown quite a bit in the last year. Life at Christ's Hospital obviously suited him. He had selected and played for both the House Cricket and Rugby teams. He had all the Sports Kit that he needed, including an Autographed Cricket Bat signed by the Sussex County Cricket Team.

It was traditional, at the Ashdown Parties that family gifts were given out at the Christmas Eve Party, rather than on Christmas Day around the Christmas Tree. The idea being, those partygoers could give gifts to the family directly. The Party would not break up until the early hours. Although, everyone would be expected to attend the Christmas morning service at the local church, again this too was traditional. Before the guests started to arrive, Nigel was admiring the Christmas decorations. This year, they seemed to have excelled themselves. The whole house was ablaze with colour. The Banqueting Hall, where the Party was to be held had been decorated with the skill of an artist. It was truly magnificent.

Soon, it was time to get ready, around 7.30pm. The guests began to arrive; John and Victoria welcomed them, after Charles, who was acting Butler for the evening, announced them. Everyone was chatting, and a small group of musicians assembled on the raised stage and played background music. At 8 pm., precisely, Charles announced that Dinner would be served in the Dining Room. The guests made their way to where a sumptuous feast was laid out ready for them to be served by John and Victoria's staff. After the meal was over, the guests reassembled in the Banqueting Hall for the presentation of gifts. Victoria and John began to distribute the presents. One by one, the young children came forward to receive their gifts. It was traditional for all children who attended the Ashdown Parties, to receive a gift. Nigel noticed the number of gifts remaining was reducing by the minute. He had a horrible thought, could his parents have forgotten him? As John picked up the last present, he motioned Nigel to come and stand by his side. He called for silence and as the hubbub of conversation died down, John began his speech.

"My Lords, Ladies, Gentlemen first of all let me thank you all for coming to the Party on this festive occasion. It may have come to your notice, I know it has to my Son, that Christmas is just a day away, and a time for remembering good deeds and of course the giving of presents."

John looked down at Nigel who had a puzzled look on his face. Various thoughts went through his young mind, what could his present be this year? John continued, "my son Nigel has done extremely well at Christ's Hospital. He has had top marks in nearly all his examinations. So far he hasn't had a present from Victoria and I."

Nigel felt somewhat embarrassed and was wondering what his Father would say next. He did not know whether to be excited or disappointed. There was silence in the Hall, so much so, that you could hear a pin drop. John carried on letting Nigel stay on tenterhooks. John looked at Nigel again and winked.

"Now my friends, do you all think that my son deserves a really good present?"

John raised his hands to get a response.

"Of course he does," the assembled guests responded in one voice.

There was deafening applause. Then John held his hand aloft, Silence reigned once more.

"You are right, my friends," continued John, "he does really deserve a special present this year."

He turned to Nigel, who was still waiting to find out what his present actually would be this year.

"Well, my Son they are correct," said John smiling at Nigel, "we have not forgotten you. However, there is one small problem, and that is the present I am giving to you this Christmas. It is rather large and we cannot get it into the Banqueting Hall. So, Nigel and assembled friends, shall we venture outside to view Nigel's present?"

The guests made their way out into the Courtyard. Whilst they filed out into the cold night air, they too were wondering what this large present might be. John had certainly raised their curiosity levels. There at the foot of the steps stood John's 1904 MERCEDES Model 60.

"Well father where is my present?" said Nigel, looking around. John pointed to the car.

"There is your present my son. I am giving my MERCEDES. It has been overhauled by the factory and I will teach you to drive it safely."

Nigel was simply amazed; he really did not know what to say. He had been crazy about cars since that day at Brooklands, which had been the highlight of his life so far.

After a few moments, he realised that the car was his. He embraced his Father and said a hearty thank you. John was absolutely thrilled to see the expression of surprise and joy on his son's face. He knew he could not have given a better present to Nigel if he had tried.

Nigel climbed up behind the wheel of the pure white machine. He felt the luxury of the 4 leather seats. The factory had upgraded the two large acetylene headlamps, which now shone bright in the darkness lighting up the nearby buildings.

By adding two other smaller lamps and wider mudguards, which would protect the driver from mud and water. John had also a windscreen fitted to stop being windswept, as the car was capable of over 70mph. As he gripped the steering wheel, he pretended he was racing for the Championship, for this car was the greatest present of all.

"Its terrific Father!" exclaimed Nigel who was almost speechless with excitement, "how can I ever thank you for such a wonderful present?"

John paused for a moment and gave his son a big hug.

"Nigel, just be your best at everything do. There is no substitute for a good Education. You have shown the potential to do great things at School. As the years pass, those things that you have learned will show great benefit for I am sure you will become a great driver, but also a great teacher to others in later life. Be positive, be focussed."

John felt like he was giving his son a sermon rather than an answer.

The last four words were emblazoned on Nigel's brain: -
BE POSITIVE. BE FOCUSSED.

After the initial shock of the present had subsided, Nigel climbed down from the car and asked that question that all sons ask at a time like this.

"Father, when can I start to learn to drive?"

John looked at his son and realised that this question was going to be asked.

"As soon as the weather improves Nigel. Now I think we should go inside now as my guests are freezing."

The chauffeur came across, and drove the car back to the garage. As the guests made their way back to the warmth of the Banqueting Hall, John put his arm around his son's shoulder and asked him to be patient. The merriment continued and everyone was dancing.

The midnight chimes began to ring out, and then everyone went around wishing each other the compliments of the season. Then it was back to the dancing for another hour or so. John and Victoria were waltzing around when Victoria whispered in John's ear.

"Darling, what did you buy me for Christmas? Now that Nigel has his wonderful present."

John blushed slightly, for many years past John, had given his wife her present, along with all the other family gifts.

"Later, Darling, later," he whispered in her ear, "you will not be disappointed."

Victoria was intrigued. Was he doing 'a Nigel' on her as well, surely not? What could it be? This present John had for her, maybe it was something very personal. Her feminine curiosity was starting to get the better of her. John was usually open about most things. He was now being secretive; this was not in his nature. Still, it must be a present well worth the waiting. Perhaps it was something both special and personal. The hour grew late; Nigel was nodding off in a quiet corner, but still aware of what was going on. He did not want to miss a thing. After all, he did not have to get up that early on Christmas morning, but no sleeping until lunchtime, for he would be expected to go to the Christmas morning service along with the rest of the family.

It was a yearly tradition. The guests began to leave. Nigel decided it was time to go to bed, it had been a great party, soon, and he was fast asleep. He kept dreaming of racing his car around many circuits, collecting prizes and being adored by the crowd. Finally, the last guests departed, thanking their hosts for a superb evening. At last, John and Victoria were alone. The servants had cleared away everything, but they would be up early next day preparing Christmas Dinner for the family.

Victoria was still wondering what her present could be; she was bursting to know. How much longer could John keep her waiting? John led his beautiful wife upstairs to their Bedroom; she now had little time to wait. She could not even guess what it might be. There on the four-poster bed lay three boxes; one very large and two smaller ones wrapped in gold paper each with a big red bow on them. On each of them was a label; each of them had the message - To a really wonderful, beautiful wife and mother.

Victoria was impatient to find out what articles were contained in each of these mysterious boxes. She pondered for a while, wondering which one to open first. John stood back and smiled. Victoria decided to go for the biggest one first. She carefully removed the wrapping, bow and then slowly opened the box. She squealed with delight, for inside the box was the most beautiful, full-length silver fox coat she had ever seen. She quickly tried it on admiring herself in the mirror.

Then she opened the second box; inside was a pair of dark grey leather boots fur-lined and topped with silver fox. The third box contained a bonnet and gloves that matched her coat exactly. She tried on all her presents, looked again in the mirror, then went over to John and embraced him passionately.

"My Darling Husband," she gasped, "these gifts are really wonderful. How did you know that this is what I really wanted?"

My darling," replied John, "a little bird told me."

John had heard from one of Victoria's friends that she always wanted a silver fox coat and matching accessories. Victoria was not a lady who demanded a great deal in the way of personal possessions from her husband. She knew that sometimes business profits could rise and fall. John always liked to give Victoria the best life he could; she had a good wardrobe of fashionable clothes. They were expected to be the leaders of fashion around Horsham. Victoria loved hats, and they were the talk of the town. These new presents would certainly make heads turn. John had managed to get the coat, boots and bonnet through his business contact in Germany. John had been expanding his Wine Import business and, on a visit to Stuttgart when was negotiating for his new Mercedes, he met Count Gerhard Richter a prominent winegrower in the Rhine Valley. The two men got talking, and John struck up a friendship with him. They had started doing business; wine sales had gone really well. Gerhard said that he had a friend in the fur trade. He said on many occasions that should John want, a Fur coat for Victoria, of excellent quality then he could arrange it, just give him a call. With Christmas approaching, John wanted an extra special present for Victoria. So asked if Gerhard could get him a full-length silver fox fur coat with matching bonnet, gloves and boots to be made in time for Christmas as the special present. Everything was agreed, John was particularly excited and could not wait to see the expression on his wife's face when she opened her special presents early on Christmas morning. The three boxes had arrived by courier a few days before Christmas and John had problems trying to hide them from his wife. Otherwise, it would be no surprise.

Victoria still could not believe that she had the coat that she had always dreamed about, it felt so soft against her skin. She had a special feeling she had never felt before and could not explain it at all. She wrapped herself around John once more.

"My dearest husband, I'll do something special to you to thank you for these wonderful presents. Of course, I shall wear it to Church tomorrow. Incidentally, where did you buy this beautiful coat, my love?"

John explained that he had overheard her talking to her friends, that it was about time to buy a new winter coat and matching accessories. So John made an arrangement with his business associate Count Richter. He was able to have the presents delivered by courier in time for Christmas. Victoria was overwhelmed by it all; she did not want to take off her new presents. However, they had both had a tiring day and were soon in bed and fell asleep at once.

Victoria, soon started to dream she was a Queen, dressed in all her furs with her loyal subjects all around her.

The next morning servants woke them with their usual tray of tea. Victoria and John dressed, and then made their way down to the Breakfast Room. The servants had been up for hours, no rest for them. It had been a late night, now an early morning preparing Christmas Dinner, in the large Kitchen that faced out on the Kitchen Garden. John Ashdown's Father had started the garden when local produce had been in short supply. John had developed, enabling the Hall grow most of the vegetables needed for the household. The Head Gardener, Henry Brown took great care of his pride and joy, for any weeds were soon dispatched to the incinerator.

John and Victoria entered the room; they noticed Nigel was already tucking into a steaming bowl of porridge. He looked up and saw that his Mother was smiling.

"Good Morning Mother, Good Morning Father" he said.

"Good Morning Nigel," replied John, "I trust you slept well?"

Nigel said that he had and noticed his Mother was still smiling. He thought, that it must have been an extra special present, that his Mother had received from his father. They talked for a while, and then it was time to get ready for Church. Victoria was so excited, that soon she would be wearing that lovely silver fox coat, bonnet and boots.

Victoria pulled on her new boots; she told John that they were the most comfortable boots she had ever worn. After all, they were made to measure. Then carefully applying her make-up, she was looking forward to putting on her new silver fox coat and bonnet. At last she was now, wearing all her furs she felt wonderful, sensual and looking as pretty as a picture. While she was gazing into the mirror that strange feeling, she had felt the night before returned. It was a feeling that she could not explain.

John, who had been in his dressing room, came in to see her posing in the full-length mirror; she was dressed in her new furs.

"My darling! John exclaimed, "in your new furs you look without doubt the most beautiful woman I have ever seen."

Victoria turned towards him and blushed.

"You just wait until later, my darling, I am going to give you a present," she whispered.

John wondered what he would get later. Victoria certainly had a surprise in store for John, but he would have to wait. After all, she had to wait for her present, now he had to be patient. She composed herself and after one longer look in the mirror she turned to John.

"I guess I am ready now to go downstairs, otherwise we shall be late for Church."

The Couple descended the staircase.

Nigel was waiting; he looked at his Mother as she descended the staircase.

"You look absolutely beautiful Mother in your new furs."

"Thank you Nigel," she responded.

Victoria blushed again; it was something she could not stop. Nigel thought his mother looked stunning, but like most young lads, he was not given to extravagant compliments. Nigel too had a new overcoat; he had outgrown the one he had two years ago. The new coat was similar in design to the one that his father wore; it was dark grey wool with an astrakhan collar. They descended the outside stairs where Charles the Chauffeur opened the door of the family Limousine and the trio climbed inside.

The overnight snowfall had left a layer of white across the countryside. It was a very cold morning; a wintry sun hung there is a pale blue sky, with just a wisp of cloud. Victoria peered out of the windows at the scene that looked like fairyland. She was cocooned in furs and in the warmth of the Limousine. She was feeling wonderful as warm as she had ever been in her life.

The Daimler came to a halt outside the little village church, where Rev. Hubert Ward greeted them. He had been Vicar of the local Village Church for some 15 years and had in fact christened Nigel. He was delighted to see him again, and asked how he was getting on at Christ's Hospital. Nigel spoke to him for a moment or two, and congratulated him on his success at School. Rev. Ward then shook hands with Victoria.

"May I," said the Rev. Ward, "wish you and the family a very Merry Christmas and a Happy New Year Lady Ashdown? Can I also say you look absolutely stunning?"

"Thank you Reverend," replied Victoria, feeling more than a little self-conscious. John shook hands with Rev. Ward as the family passed through the Church Porch, and then took their places in the family pews, main body of the little Norman Church, which was now full to capacity.

The Rev. Ward was usually a man of few words and rarely passed compliments on his parishioners. Victoria knew she felt special, but that was being vain and that she was not. The Rev. Ward climbed the steps to the pulpit and then launched into one of his long sermons, Nigel thought he never knew when to finish. John took a sly sideways look at his wife; she had that far away look in her eye. John was wondering what she was thinking, for this was always tricky. She was certainly paying no attention to the Rev.Ward. His sermon eventually ended; there were two more hymns before the service finished. In true tradition, Victoria, John and now Nigel joined the Reverend outside the Church porch to say Merry Christmas and a Happy New Year to all their friends and neighbours. With the entire congregation now departed, the Rev. Ward wished the compliments of the season to Victoria, John and Nigel. He trusted that his compliments on Victoria's attire had not caused her any embarrassment. She assured him that it had not. On the way home John turned to Victoria as he could see she was still daydreaming.

"Anything wrong, darling," he asked, "you were miles away when the Vicar was giving his sermon?"

Victoria still wrapped up in her gorgeous furs and felt absolutely wonderful.

"No, darling," she replied, "just thinking how lucky I am that's all."

John knew there was something he did not know about, perhaps it was what he called, woman's thoughts. Nigel too was miles away, staring out of the window. Not another word was said until they pulled up outside Ashdown Hall.

John reminded both Victoria and Nigel that Christmas Dinner would be served at 3pm precisely. He would be reading in his study until then.

Victoria went up to her boudoir, closed the door and locking it behind her, for she wanted to be alone with her private thoughts for a while without disruption. She knew that there would be about an hour or so before Christmas Dinner would be served now there was time to daydream. Standing in front of the mirror, gazing longingly at her reflection quite unable to believe how good and different she felt. She did not want to take off the coat, gloves, bonnet or boots. Admiring herself is something she very rarely did, although she took a pride in her appearance, but vanity was not in her nature. Her new winter furs were transforming her thinking completely.

Now she felt like a young girl again, with desires that had lain dormant for so long. She just stood there looking. She had noticed how the Bonnet and Coat complimented her dark hair, also how the boots matched her coat. No wonder the Vicar had praised her appearance.

There was a knock on the door. Victoria looked at the clock on the nearby mantelpiece; gosh it was almost 2.30pm, she could not imagine where had the time gone. A Man's voice was heard outside her bedroom door.

"My love it is me," called John, "are you alright?"

There was no answer from Victoria for a moment or two.

"Sorry darling," replied Victoria, "I will be with you in a few minutes. Just tidying my hair."

"See you downstairs then," said John, who then walked down to the Dining Room.

Victoria was still wrapped in her furs. She said to herself: 'This is silly, I can wear all these lovely furs whenever I like'.

She quickly removed them, joining the rest of the family who were gathered in the Morning Room. John was seated by a roaring fire, chatting to Victoria's parents who had just arrived from London. Victoria's father, Sir Nigel Hawkesley had been on a business trip to Edinburgh; he had only just arrived back in London on Christmas Eve. Lady Alexandra Hawkesley, had spent time with friends in London whilst her husband was away, and had been on one of her famous shopping excursions in Mayfair. There was a good deal of gossip and news to catch up with, for they had not met for several months. Victoria and her Mother - Alexandra Hawkesley were very close, sharing many secrets. Victoria now had a new secret; she was keeping this one strictly between herself and her husband. Victoria was Nigel and Alexandra's only child so they tended to be very protective.

The Grandfather clock in the corner chimed the hour, and as the sound died away, Yeats, the Butler announced that dinner was served. Nigel took one look at the groaning table full of festive fare, and thought, this amount of food would feed the Biblical five thousand with a good deal over. There was a hubbub of conversation as the staff served wine to the family and honoured guests. Then John Ashdown got to his feet and said grace; the servants came in to serve the various courses as the meal progressed. By the end of it, Nigel felt fit to bust; he had eaten so much.

The Port was then served; the Ladies then withdrew to the Drawing Room. Nigel's best friend Andrew Crowley and his parents had been invited over for Christmas Day, it was nice that the boys could get together. Andrew, was the son of Sir Peter Crowley the Managing Director of a local Glass Manufacturer, his Company supplied all the beer bottles for John's Brewery. He and his wife Elizabeth had been lifelong friends of the Ashdowns. Although Andrew was a year younger than Nigel, they shared many common interests. Andrew heard that Nigel had a car, may be one day he would have one too. When time allowed, Andrew and Nigel were inseparable they had decided that whatever happened in the future; they would be bosom friends. Now that Nigel was at boarding school, time together was strictly limited to holidays and the odd weekend.

Time quickly passed as they played together; all too soon Victoria came to her son's playroom and announced that Andrew's parents were leaving. The two boys decided that providing their parents would allow that they would meet at Andrew's house the very next day. Victoria said that would be OK, and that she would arrange for Charles to take him over in the car. The boys then went downstairs to join their parents. The Crowley's having gone home, the Christmas Day entertainment was rounded off, in traditional style, with a musical evening. Victoria showed off her talents by singing, whilst being accompanied on the Piano by George Campbell. Victoria and John always tried to encourage all their staff to take part in the musical soirees. Several of the maids had good voices and sang in a local choir. George apart from his talents at the piano keyboard had a good baritone voice.

The evening was ending, everyone had enjoyed the day, none more than Victoria, she had all her family and friends around her. It was her favourite time of winter, for she had a very loving and faithful husband, who had this year, excelled himself, with a marvellous gift that she would constantly enjoy. Now it was time for bed. Victoria had her plans for John's present clearly defined; she knew that John would be completely surprised, just as she had been with her new furs.

It had been a long day, Victoria was feeling tired, and made her way up to her boudoir, opening the door, and locking it behind her. Then she saw her new silver fox coat, and bonnet hanging on the wardrobe, the boots below them. When she had worn her furs earlier in the day, she had a feeling within her body that she had not experienced for some years. She simply could not describe it.

She thought, 'I must try that fur coat on again, before I go to bed.' She undressed, removing the corset she wore. This garment was more of a nod to fashion rather than a necessity, for Victoria had a very shapely figure. Many of her friends had a need for this item of lingerie, due no doubt to their way of life. Soon, she was naked. First of all, she put on her new boots, then stood gazing at her figure in the full-length mirror. Then, walking a few steps, she slowly removed the silver fox coat from its hanger, and slipped it on. Immediately, that sensual feeling returned to her body in a trice. She stood there looking in the mirror once more, turning this way and that. Then putting the silver fox bonnet on her head, tying the leather straps with the furry balls at each end tight, then tucking them under her chin.

Now she feasted her eyes on her reflection, and let out a hum of satisfaction. There was a knock at the door; this brought her back to reality. What should she do? She was supposed to be getting ready for bed, and here she was in her beautiful Silver fox Coat, Bonnet and Boots and naked underneath.

"Who is it?" she called out in a sexy voice:

"It is me darling, John".

"Just a moment, darling" she replied.

Then she thought, I will let him come in after all he is my husband. I may be able to create the feeling that I have within me to him. She unlocked the door.

"Come in darling" she cooed.

John opened the door and entered the room. He had got ready for bed, and was wearing his Dressing Gown over his pyjamas. He looked at Victoria somewhat surprised.

"My love," he said, "your silver fox coat looks absolutely fantastic on you, darling. I must admit I did not get a really good look at you earlier. With that Bonnet and Boots it is a wonderfully sensual combination. By the way, I thought we were going to bed my love?"

Victoria just looked at him through with those flashing eyes of hers. Then from under her fur bonnet she smiled and whispered, "we certainly are going to bed, my dearest."

John was taken aback for a moment.

"In your lovely furs?" asked John.

Victoria gave him that look again and murmured, "you just wait and see. I am preparing your present."

She pouted her lips. John was astounded; he hasn't seen his wife like this since their honeymoon some 14 years earlier. This was certainly something unexpected.

Over the past few years their sex life had been on the back burner, so lovemaking sessions were few and far between. They were deeply in love, but the physical expression of their love for each other, had taken second place. Victoria had now found the catalyst, to rekindle those sexual feelings within her. Now she hoped that it would also light the fire of passion within her husband. Now she had her golden opportunity and she would grasp it with all her might. John realised at that moment, what could happen next, now he was really longing for out and out expression of love, physical love.

He came closer to her.

"Kiss me darling," she cooed, "just feel the softness of this beautiful fur against your skin. Mmm, doesn't it feel sensuous?"

"Yes my dearest," sighed John, and moved closer to her side.

They kissed passionately and sensually. Victoria's tongue searching inside John's mouth. She was now giving him a strong message, that she wanted him totally. It was time to relax and enjoy each other's bodies. They were locked in a firm embrace, the prelude to their sexual union.

Their bedroom lit only by a fire flickering in the Adam fireplace, which created a romantic atmosphere, sending shadows on to the closed heavily embroidered curtains.

Outside, a full moon shone down from a midnight blue sky. They were alone together at last. John was feeling the softness of the fur against his skin. Victoria was right; it was sensual in the extreme. Their lips parted and John broke the silence.

"What are you wearing under that coat, my love?"

Victoria answered his question by parting her furs. John looked a little surprised; for now he knew now what his wife had planned for his Christmas present, it was something no one else could share. Tonight, would be pure unbridled passion. Their lips met once more and as they kissed, Victoria started by feeling around inside John pyjamas. He was certainly getting aroused, for his sexual cravings had not been satisfied for some time. It was so simple for Victoria to seek out and caress him into what she had in mind. John felt a tingling in his loins; his passion had begun to stir.

In the mirror, she could see her husband's expression change, from one of surprise to one of pleasure. This had been a facial expression, which had been in short supply of late. John stood in front of her; she gently caressed his manhood with her fingers and furs. His male member rose to her touch, she held it and led him on the four-poster bed. Then lying beside him, she lowered his pyjama trousers to expose his muscle that was ready to give her pleasure. She knew that her body was ready for him. Then, moving her fur clad body on top of his, she gently guiding him into her. She felt wonderful, sighing with pleasure, as the large stiff muscle entered her; they both felt that special tingle.

Their union continued with vigour, she knew nobody would disturb their night of passion, for they were Man and Wife again. Victoria came to orgasm several times, John too was ecstatic, and kept having climaxes. He felt marvellous; the furs he had bought his wife were more than just presents, for they had unlocked a passion that had lain dormant for too long. They were both insatiable in their appetite for sexual satisfaction that night. They made love for what seemed like hours, their sighing and moans of pleasure filled the room. Outside this room of passion, not a sound could be heard. They finally fell asleep, exhausted by their sexual romp. The next morning, Victoria was woken up by a knock on the door. It was one of the servants bringing the tray of tea.

Victoria sat up, and could now see herself in the mirror. She had fallen asleep wearing her furs. Beside her was John, still fast asleep. Victoria quickly took off her boots and hung up her coat and bonnet. As she did so, she recalled their night of ecstasy most vividly. She never knew that John could make love that way. At last, she had found his fetish and his sexual Achilles heel. Their sex life had never been as good as this since their honeymoon.

Victoria knew that this was a new beginning, for their desire to strengthen their marriage. Perhaps, these silver fox furs would be the golden key to many more nights like this. It was new and exciting. Victoria had heard stories from some of her lady friends who made passionate love on a regular basis. The bawdy tales they told amongst the gathering of her lady friends usually involved a lover, not their spouse. Some of her friends, when they got together would soon spread gossip, just to see what the results would be.

Most of it was harmless fun, but occasionally, the gossip backfired on them. These sexual cravings that Victoria had for her husband and his new fetish would be their secret alone. After all, they had a very profitable business, so the last thing they needed was rumours flying around that she and her husband were sex mad.

Victoria now knew that she had a way of keeping her man happy. John had never strayed; goodness knows he had plenty of opportunities. He was tall, handsome and his long blonde hair made him attractive to women. During his many business trips throughout England and Europe, John had been introduced to many beautiful ladies, who would be been delighted to have bedded him. He knew that this would be dangerous to both his marriage and business. Rivals could easily spread gossip, if he had affairs he was certain that his world would come crashing down on him.

One of his business rivals in Germany Count Peter Von Gutenberg had an affair with the beautiful Maxine Klein. She had an insatiable sexual appetite; she had reputation as a man-eater and had an extremely jealous nature. Count Peter set her up in an Apartment in Linz, a City in Northern Austria, where they had a torrid affair for some months. Then a rival, for her affections, came on the scene and began to spread gossip about Maxine's affair with the Count amongst a few of her friends. In a few short weeks, the rumours got to the ears of Briggita, Peter's wife. Then followed a fearful argument, and Brigitta screamed a torrent of abuse at Peter, for she was an extremely jealous woman, who kept Peter on a very tight leash. Being very financially astute, she made certain that their business empire fell into her hands. The divorce that followed was very acrimonious. Briggita took all her husband's money with her and made him sell their home as well. She told her version of the story, of course, with lots of elaborations concerning of his infidelity, to all his business contacts and his friends. In a few short weeks everyone had shunned him. He was a broken man. However, he was not a defeatist; he had a strong will to survive.

He was left trying to get his life and his business back together. Victoria knew Peter's wife Briggita quite well, she was a lovely lady but sexually frigid, she was also a very vicious woman when and if she was roused. She had controlled her husband for years, wanting to know his every move. They had no children; sex was something she avoided like the plague.

The poor Count had been so frustrated that to relieve his sexual cravings, he had started the affair with Maxine. She was gentle, loving was sexually very active, adored the high life, and receiving expensive gifts. The Count did his best to keep the arrangement a secret, but someone saw them in a Restaurant in Linz and told his wife. When Briggita found out, she went absolutely crazy. Then she hired a hotshot Lawyer, and before Peter knew where he was, he was out on his ear. When Maxine, found out that her rich lover was going to lose everything she dropped him, like a hot coal. Victoria knew that to keep her husband satisfied, she had to be herself, and not restrict John's access to her body.

John awoke with a start; he could not believe what had happened last night. However, seeing the silver fox coat hanging on the wardrobe brought back the thoughts of their night of passion. He sighed with satisfaction and gave a smile. It was certainly not a dream, it was true, and he felt great. If this was the present that Victoria had for him, then he was certainly looking forward to playing more such sensual games with her. Victoria was now dressed, they made their way down to the Breakfast Room. Nigel was already there tucking into his bowl porridge to be followed by Bacon and Eggs. Nigel certainly enjoyed his food. Sir Nigel and Lady Hawkesley then came into the room, they saw Victoria sitting there holding her coffee cup, with a smile on her face. With last night's events behind her, she wished that she could have had a silver fox coat long before now; it had brought to the surface John's hidden sexual fantasies.

Lady Hawkesley looked at Victoria who was still thinking about her lovemaking with John the previous evening.

"Good morning Victoria," said Lady Hawkesley, "you look radiant this morning?"

"Good morning mother," replied Victoria, Alexandra's words bringing her back to earth, "did you sleep well?"

"I slept like a log," answered Alexandra.

Victoria smiled, then walked over and kissed her Mother good morning. Having finished breakfast, Victoria sat at the table reflecting again on her night of sexual pleasure.

Life could get no better now, she thought, they could enjoy each other's bodies with a renewed vigour. Nigel looked up from his empty plate, having now finished his Bacon and Egg.

"Good morning mother," said Nigel, "you look happy this morning?"

Victoria returned the greeting and smiled. She started eating, and was really enjoying her breakfast, but in her mind, she knew that it would now have to wait until tonight, when again her sexual needs would be gratified. When she had finished breakfast, Victoria made her way back to her boudoir, when she stroked her silver fox coat and smiled.

"Thank you," she sighed, "thank you so very much indeed."

She gazed towards the bed and knew that it was their bed of love. The day seemed to go slowly to her, whilst Sir Nigel, John and Nigel were spending some time together discussing various topics in the Study. Victoria was tempted to dress up again, but resisted it; instead she put on her day clothes and went down to see her Mother, who was still finishing her cup of coffee.

"Victoria," asked Alexandra, "you went off to bed quickly last night? You must have been really tired?"

Victoria blushed, she had to think carefully before replying, and after all, she could hardly tell her Mother the truth.

"Yes I was tired Mother," replied Victoria, " The party was tiring, Christmas Day had been a long day too."

(It had been a long night of love, but that was something Victoria would never tell her mother). The Ladies then sat down together in the Breakfast Room talking about things that interested them.

As the day wore on; Victoria could not get her thoughts away from her night of passion with John. Lady Alexandra could sense that she did not have all her attention. However, she was her daughter, so she forgave her. It was Boxing Day thought Lady Alexandra; no doubt, my daughter has a lot on her mind. Victoria had something on her mind but there was no way she could tell her Mother. Victoria now knew John's secret desires; together they had the furry secret that would be theirs alone. Her silver fox coat and bonnet had intensified their sexual desires and love. Lately, Victoria had wanted to make almost violent love to John; especially when she was going through a period of frustration. Every time they wanted to be alone, there was always something or someone to alter their moods. It was either friends or events. Even during the holidays, there were guests staying, sometimes John's business acquaintances would stay over. There were times Victoria did not have John's full attention; business had taken up so much of his energy he just wanted to relax in the evenings.

Now at this Christmas time, she had his full attention, with her new Furs and John's awakened sexual desires, she would ride this situation for as long as she could. She had the key now; that would open the door leading to sexual delights and the relief of frustration and stress for them both. The day passed and soon it was bedtime. For Victoria this could not come soon enough, she had planned a return visit to that silver fox coat and to give John another night of pleasure. When John entered the Bedroom, he knew exactly what to expect. Victoria stood there waiting for him dressed for pleasure. He too was now aware of the fixation of inhibitions that had been previous been hidden. Her body was now ready another night of passion. Just as last night, Victoria gently massaged him to try to enlarge and encourage her now favourite muscle. They lay back together, with the lovely Victoria on top riding him for all she was worth. Neither of them counted how many times they climaxed. They both knew that this had cemented their love for each other. Every night could be like this. This was Christmas night all over again. Victoria fell asleep for a while, John's organ that had given his wife so much pleasure had got smaller, so she aroused it again with her furs, and enjoyed entering her once more, it was an indescribable pleasure.

The next morning Victoria there was the knock on the door. Victoria sat up, she still had that coat on and there was John half awake with a smile on his face.

"Good morning, my Darling Victoria. You certainly know how to satisfy me. That silver fox was cheap at the price."

John smiled and Victoria then kissed him passionately.

"I now know your secret now my darling John. How did you know that a beautiful silver fox coat, bonnet and boots are something I have always wanted? You are very naughty. Apart from sexually arousing me, they will keep me warm during the day, and you heated up at night."

They both laughed aloud. Victoria still in her Fur coat put her hand between John legs and caressed him.

"That" she said, "that is a little bonus, and I shall want more of the same tonight, please."

"I promise," replied John, "that we will make love every night over the holiday."

"I will keep you to that promise my love," cooed Victoria.

Victoria then told John that her New Year Resolution would be that they should make love at least four times per week. John willingly agreed. Victoria knew that she had a willing partner who loved her very much. To both John and Victoria the family was paramount. Victoria wanted another child; she would keep making love until she was sure that she was pregnant. She hoped for a little girl, but as long as the baby would be healthy, that would be absolutely wonderful.

The holiday seemed to go by in a flash, whilst every night Victoria would weave her magical furry spell on her willing spouse John. Victoria felt with her new 'weapons' she had rekindled their love, which had been burning on a low flame for some time. She now realised they had not known such physical attraction for years.

They would wake up every morning feeling terrific, ready for whatever the day might bring, for at the end of it would be another night of passion and tenderness.

The old year 1907 ended; the final Party was a dazzling affair. The decorations that had gone up at the beginning of the Christmas holidays had stood the test of time. The tall Fir Trees with their myriad array of coloured lights, baubles, tinsel and crowned with angels stood in the corners of the Great Hall. In the Minstrel's Gallery above, a Quintet played a Strauss Waltz. John had his love in his arms as they whirled around the floor amongst the other couples.

"Victoria my lover," he whispered to her, "have you made any more New Year Resolutions that you intend to keep?"

Victoria thought for a moment or two before replying:

"Well, my lover, I have made only one that I did mention to you. Don't tell me that you have forgotten already?"

She blushed a little.

"No my love, but just remind me." replied John

Victoria whispered in his ear. John smiled; he knew exactly what she meant.

"Victoria Ashdown," answered John sensually, "this is my answer to you."

He kissed her rosebud lips. She had her answer. John knew that she was the only woman he had ever really loved. Their lovemaking boundaries had been widened, now that she knew that they both had a fur fetish. This had brought them closer together. Their love could now stand the test of time.

Victoria had been the perfect wife through good times and bad. There were some occasions in India, when local tribesmen had threatened their lives. There had been years, just after they had returned from India, when John had spent weeks away getting the brewery business back on track, that she had felt abandoned. There were times when the business had been in danger. They may have lived in a grand mansion, but money was very tight. She had despaired; her wardrobe was definitely second hand. Now with all the hard work they had a very successful business. This was due to teamwork by

Management and Workers. The help given by Victoria's Father, now a shareholder in the business had meant security at last.

Her wardrobe had been completely replaced with new gowns now; as for the Silver fox furs these were the icing on the cake.

She felt that they had arrived socially, rather than feeling like second-class gentry. They could hold their heads high in the community, for they had good reliable investors who were earning very good dividends. Everyone was happy, now Victoria was ecstatic; she had her love, her family and a future.

Nigel had been a credit to the family; he had taken to life at Christ's Hospital like a duck to water. He took his studies very seriously and had focussed himself for success. John on the other hand was proud that he had a very intelligent son, who would really carve out a future for himself and the family. He had not even thought about having more children, until now. Victoria had got broody, and John had his sexual desires brought to the surface and this excited him, and given a boost to his love for Victoria. The Party continued and the merriment unconfined. As John and Victoria danced the night away, their minds were full of beautiful thoughts; Victoria was looking forward to yet another night filled with passion. The New Year Resolution starts up there, she thought, thinking of the bedroom. The Quintet became silent; the dancers stopped as the Midnight Chimes rang out the old year. All the dancers joined hands to sing - Auld lang syne. Then a shout of "HAPPY NEW YEAR" went up.

Everyone embraced to wish each other Happy New Year. John took Victoria up on to a small stage, raised his hand and called for silence. He gave thanks to the musicians for the wonderful music, all the guests for attending, and a special thank you to all the staff for their hard work through Christmas and the New Year. He turned to Victoria whose was standing by his side.

"Without this lovely Lady by my side in my life," began Lord John, "I do not think I could have got through the last 12 months. She has been a tower of strength. I have my wife who is also my lover by my side, a successful son and great friends. What more can a Man ask for?"

Then through the throng came Sir Peter Crowley and he mounted the stage.

My Lords, Ladies and Gentlemen" he began, "I cannot let this moment pass without an enormous vote of thanks to the greatest couple we know. This has been a tremendous Party, for those that were at the Christmas Party they will know of all the work that has gone into our enjoyment, not only from our hosts, but from their staff as well. I will ask for three very hearty cheers for our wonderful hosts. I give you John and Victoria Ashdown." Three cheers rang out, followed by they are jolly good fellows, then a standing ovation. John and Victoria were astounded at level of praise that was heaped upon them. John came forward and said, "Friends, all I can say is thank you for all your support, through good times and bad from the bottom of our hearts."

The Party began to break up; Victoria hoped that her New Year Resolution would not go unfulfilled on the first night of the New Year. She was filled with anticipation that another night of sexual activity was just minutes away. Finally, the last guest had gone. Only Victoria's parents and John's Mother were staying and they were now locked up tight in their rooms, they were not likely to roam around the house. Nigel too was now fast asleep. John and Victoria had done their duty to all their friends. It was the final Party of the season. John and Victoria would go to their bedroom, now they would hold their own private party where pleasure and sexual desires were all that mattered.

The outside world would stay outside. They would be alone together at last. John knew that Victoria's New Year Resolution would be granted he would guarantee it. He would have the greatest pleasure in making her wishes come true.

Victoria made her way up to her Boudoir, with John following behind her. He always admired the way she managed to keep her figure, without resorting to excess foundation garments that seemed to take ages to remove. Victoria had a good appetite; she always ate sensible diet and managed to maintain good health. John entered the Bedroom; Victoria was ready and waiting for him. She knew she had the magic to weave her spell. Looking down at John's crotch, she noticed there was a swelling. He was getting excited at the prospect of what was to follow. She looked into his eyes; she could see that he was mentally undressing her. He was thinking, one day that coat will have something to answer for, and that would be the constant sexual gratification with my wife. He undressed quickly; Victoria caressed his crotch until he had finally removed all his lingerie. She then began to gently touch him and he responded to her touch. He got that tingle again; he knew that he was ready to satisfy Victoria's sexual appetite. This was ecstasy and even better than before. John now felt at last, that his sexual desires had been awakened.

She sighed with pleasure, this was the man she had married, and the man she would always want to please her in bed. Victoria was full of anticipation of the delight that was to come. Victoria gripped John's hand and led him to their bed. They lay there with Victoria on top of John. He had started to reach new heights of excitement; he was waiting to do his duty as a loving husband. She thought back to their honeymoon all those years ago, recalling that they could not get enough of each other. Time and events had stemmed the flow of physical love. She now knew he was a true and faithful husband, she was about to submit her body to him once more, and would continue to express her love for him in the ultimate way. Likewise, she was his only love; this new joy of sex had shown him that Victoria was not only a good wife and mother, but an excellent lover too. Victoria felt a quiver it had given her a special feeling, she had noticed it from the time that she had put the coat on, when she had been nude. Now her whole body was ready for penetration. Her whole being yearned for her husband to satisfy her sexual craving, this was just moments away.

She must wait, or could she? Their bodies were now entwined; Victoria guided John's large erect phallus into her, she had to wait no longer. At last, my love, she thought, now we can make love to our heart's content.

She rode him with fervour in excess of anything they had done on previous nights. This was the zenith of sexual gratification, and they came to climax together, and then continued to until they were exhausted. This was unthinkable; for she was determined to enjoy every last drop of life giving fluid from John's body. So she prepared to excite him again and to her delight her touch was magic. She gently massaged John watching her favourite muscle grow and grow until it was ready to satisfy her once more. She felt insatiable. Victoria wanted another child; she was making sure that she would become pregnant. So she continued to ride on top of John, and kept erecting him until at last she could not raise him anymore. She tried one last time, but the supply of semen for that night had been exhausted. John had not been sexually aroused like this before, this was something really special and sexually exciting. They had sex on honeymoon several times a day but not to this. Their new-found ways to the art of lovemaking were about to wake up their marriage and instil a greater love for each other.

Before they fell asleep, John turned to Victoria whose expression was one of absolute bliss.

"My darling," said John, "what a perfect New Year Resolution we have kept it for one night, now there is only 365 to go."

"Well I hope you can keep it up?" Victoria replied, "I'll certainly do my part, as I love you so much."

They then fell asleep, Victoria still in her furs. She closed her eyes wondering if there would be a chance to do it all again in the morning. She felt simply marvellous.

In the morning, the winter sun peeped through the drapes; it was going to be another cold winter's day. John woke up first and threw his dressing gown around his shoulders, he saw Victoria lying on top of the eiderdown still in her furs. He smiled with pleasure, kissed her and she woke up. She reached down to stroke his crotch.

"Darling," he said his male member stirring at her touch, "that feels wonderful. Please do it again, please."

Victoria did not need to be asked twice she began her caressing with her fingers and fur until John's erection was complete.

Victoria felt that her luck had changed for the better over the Christmas and New Year, for her new presents from her husband, had such an effect on him that it surprised them both. She knew that John would never refuse her with a New Year Resolution. Particularly the one she had agreed with him. This one they had made together would be one that they would enjoy, unlike most people who make resolutions only break them after a day or two.

Each night she continued to weave her sexual spell, with John as the very willing subject, caressing him gently as the muscle flexed itself ready to perform, for she realised that another supply of semen had arrived and she wanted it delivered now. She was feeling excited and ready to receive him, as he entered her, she groaned with pleasure, satisfaction, and came to orgasm. Victoria desire for lovemaking increased, she realised that there were other places to make love apart from their bed. So she undressed and went into the Bathroom to soak and reflect on a night and morning of unbridled passion. John opened the door and climbed into the bath with her. The Bathroom was large, the tub easily big enough for two people.

"Our New Year Resolution is surely the best New Year Resolution we have ever made together."

Victoria smiled and kissed John passionately.

"I knew that we could enjoy this resolution," she said as their lips parted, "for when I opened those boxes and saw all those lovely furs, I knew that you had a fur fetish that I have had for years. We can share and enjoy this together. It will be our secret."

John nodded in agreement.

She bent forward and kissed him passionately. In her heart, she knew that she would become pregnant now. They must have been the happiest couple in England, they had a shared sexual secret, and they were to keep their resolution every night. They were more in love than ever, both mentally and physically. The family bond between them showed to everyone. Nigel was delighted that he had devoted parents. Some of his school chums, came from broken families, others had parents that argued and beat each other. Some were on the breadline almost, and their appearance told its own story. John of course knew that his wife wanted another child, although he had taken pleasure from her body, he longed for a companion for Nigel, whether boy or girl. John being an only child, he had been quite lonely at times. The reason being that his Mother had a difficult birth, the Doctor had told her that to have more children would be life threatening. When Nigel was born it was a very easy birth without need for forceps. He was a bonny baby and full of the joy of living. John had a son of whom he was really proud. The holiday had now ended; it was time for Nigel to go back to School. Life started getting back to normal. For Victoria and John they continued to keep up their New Year Resolution for as long as they could.

Nigel got down to some serious studying; he knew that he had a lot of hard work ahead of him. He was determined to achieve his goal of being accepted at either Oxford or Cambridge University. He hoped for an Engineering Degree, for this would help him in his future career, either in the Family Brewing business or as an Engineer in the world outside.

Victoria and John's lovemaking continued and as the days and weeks passed. Victoria started to miss her periods; finally Doctor Vernon the family physician was called. He diagnosed that she was indeed pregnant, and had been for about three months. She began to show and was proud of it. She was 33 years of age and very healthy. He predicted that there should be no problem with her carrying the baby, providing that she did not overdo things. She hoped that this did not mean giving up sexual intercourse, that she loved so much. He said that providing she was careful, there would be no problems, except for the last two months perhaps.

Chapter 8

Alain's driving prowess had made him a local hero, although Darracq were not the best or indeed the fastest racing car in Europe, at least they had given Alain a chance to show his worth. He had worked hard testing, racing and designing at the factory for many months without a break. The Research and Development department had backed him with his ideas and design changes. They had a car that could compete against the best, but still did not have the performance to win. The car was reliable, and Alain felt safe behind the wheel. He had been looking forward to the Christmas holidays and now would be able to spend more quality time with the family.

Normally, the factory only closed for a week over the Christmas holiday, but due to Alain's successes, they said that he need not return until after New Year. Alain was delighted for it gave him time for rest and relaxation, which he badly needed. There had been precious little of this in the past months, during the racing season the team always seemed to feel pressurised and there were targets to meet. Alain did not seem to have a moment to spare, for the problems that keep arising seemed to need instant solutions. The challenges seemed endless.

Alain's homecoming was always a joy to the family, especially to Pierre who wanted to hear all about his racing experiences. Marie, his Mother always asked whether he had any ladies in tow, Alain always said that of course he had lady friends, but nothing serious. He said that some had given him small presents, but his main passion was racing motor cars. There would be time for romance later, when he had established himself. Marie was content that once again her only son was home unharmed. Young Helene was growing up fast and was very proud that her big Brother was becoming famous, even had his name in the papers. She told him that she had been taking part in some trials for the National Young Rider Championships. They were to be held in Rouen in the autumn, she had been chosen to represent their district in one of the area heats in the spring. She showed him an article in a local newspaper. Alain was delighted that his sister was winning prizes. Helene was becoming a very accomplished young equestrian, and she was top of her class at school. She was determined to be the best. It was great to relax with the family.

Then just before the evening meal two days before Christmas Eve, Pierre announced that they had all been invited to the Chateau for the Count's Christmas Party. The Party would begin early, the invitations suggested that guests arrive by 5.00 p.m., the early start would mean that the children could have their fun and food before the adults began their festivities. The Clement family was very excited at the prospect of an invitation to one of the Count's Christmas Parties. They were the talk of the local gentry. Gossip was passed down as to who said what to whom; Lady so and so said this and that. There was talk of who was wearing last year's gowns, and who was there in the latest Paris fashions. It kept the local's going for weeks after Christmas had long been forgotten. Marie Clement had heard all this gossip in the Village, especially in the Village stores that were the focal point for the gossipmongers. She wondered how much of this chit-chat was fact and how much was fiction. Local villagers had a habit of adding on extra pieces to the gossip to spice it up. After all, who wants to hear dull gossip? Marie put very little store by anything she overheard in the village stores, or indeed anywhere in the village. Now by going to the Count's Christmas Party; she could now get the facts for herself. If the news were important enough, she would be told.

Marie was very excited and proud at the prospect of being invited to this prestigious event. It was an honour to receive an invitation. Now she would have a chance to show off her new evening gown and her winter coat, neither having had any outings since that day they were purchased in Paris, by none other than the Countess Claudine herself. Soon as lunch was over, the family started getting ready for the big event. Alain was wearing his first dress suit, and looked very handsome indeed. Pierre too had on a new dress suit; the two of them looked like twins. There was a lot of activity in the Clement household, but by 4.00pm, they were ready to go. Marie felt special in her new clothes; she pulled the hood up over her head to keep out the winter weather, as she climbed into the family coach. The day had been very cold, overcast and there was snow in the air.

They were all wrapped up ready to face the short coach journey to the Chateau. The horses were hitched up to the coach, Pierre climbed up into the driver's seat tapped the reins on the horse's backs and away they went. Approaching the Chateau, they noticed several other coaches in front of them. It took them some minutes before they were able to pull up outside the Chateau's grand entrance. Pierre climbed down and opened the coach to allow his family to alight.

Then the coach was driven away by one of the Count's grooms. They walked up the steps into the Entrance Hall where they approached one of the Count's flunkies, who took their coats. They then joined the queue of people waiting to be introduced to the Count. Finally, it was their turn. The Count smiled and shook Pierre by the hand.

"Pierre," said the Count, "it is a great pleasure for me to see you and the family here tonight. This invitation has been long overdue and I apologise for not inviting you and your family here in previous years. I do hope that you will have an enjoyable evening."

Pierre then went on to kiss the Countess's hand.

"Countess Claudine," said Pierre, "I really cannot thank you enough for your kindness toward my wife."

The Countess Claudine smiled and kissed Pierre on both cheeks.

"Pierre," she replied discreetly, "your wife looks lovely in that dress and giving her that coat too has been my pleasure."

Helene looked lovely in her long pink party dress; she curtsied in front of both the Count and Countess. Finally came Alain. The Count shook him firmly by the hand.

"Alain," said the Count, "I am really extremely proud of you, you are the son I did not have. You have exceeded all my expectations. I know that you have big dreams and you will be successful in all that you do. I am certain of that. Darracq is a good stepping-stone to get to the top. Have a great evening and enjoy yourself, you deserve it."

Alain did not know what to say.

He thought for a moment and then thought out his reply.

"Thank you Sir, for your invitation and all your support. I will live up to your future expectations and my dreams. A Very Happy Christmas to you and your Lady."

Alain then kissed the Countess's hand and moved into the Ballroom. The queue subsided and the Countess moved to her husband's side.

"Darling, what did you say to Alain Clement?"

The Count told her what he had said to Alain.

"Yes, I would have been proud of a son like Alain," she replied, "he has achieved a great deal and I hope that we can help him in the future too. I think my love we had better join our guests now, otherwise they will think we are neglecting them."

There must have been about 150 guests including all the children. The Count had about 12 cousins, all of whom seemed to have children. The Chateau's festive decorations were absolutely fantastic, with balloons, streamers and of course an enormous Christmas trees covered in tinsel, baubles, lights and on top of each one was a large star. The guests read like a list of a local who's who. The Children were doing their best to misbehave, whilst their parents were desperately trying to keep them in order. It is very difficult to suppress excitement in children especially at the event of the year. The children's party got underway with a sit down meal for all the children, with all the usual connected chaos. An Entertainer brought in to keep the children amused followed this. Alain was asked to help for a while, he was happy to do so. It gave him a special feeling being amongst so many smiling faces. Most games ended with a prize for the winner. Alain presented the prizes and then retired to the Library, where the Count wanted to know all about his racing experiences.

The other Male guests in the Library were intrigued, for Motor Racing was something new to them. The Ladies, meanwhile, had been in the Morning Room, admiring each other's fashions and talking about various events. Marie was new to all of this, so the Countess introduced her to several of her friends, who despite from being landowners were very nice people and did not patronise Marie in any way. In fact, they invited her along with Pierre and Alain to visit them after the Christmas holiday was over. Marie felt she was among friends.

At 7.00 pm. precisely, the Count's Butler sounded the gong in the entrance hall to denote the fact that the Children's Party was over. The havoc subsided; the children were then lead away to another part of the Chateau, or in some cases taken home.

Helene went over to her Mother who was really enjoying the party.

"Mother," said Helene who was really excited by all the glamour, "this is the best party I have ever been to."

Marie said she must now go with the other children whilst she and Pierre had their Party. The Adult's Party was about to commence in the Ballroom.

The musicians that the Count had engaged mounted the small stage, set up their music stands and began to play a lively tune, inviting all the guests to take their partners for a dance. The Hall was soon full of whirling couples, the ladies showing off their long dresses, which were a fantastic mass of ever changing patterns and colours.

The Count and Countess had deliberated long and hard over the seating plan for the meal, that would take place midway through the evening. They tried to separate the ladies and men so that they would mix rather than just be in small cliques. Most of the guests were couples, most of who knew each other. Alain as far as the Count knew had no lady friend, and certainly, he was at the Count's Party alone. Therefore, he hoped that his 'seating plan' as far as Alain was concerned would work out. Only time would tell. The Count saw him standing close to the Ballroom door looking a little 'lost', as he was gazing around at the swirling dancers. The Count walked over and spoke to him.

"Are you enjoying yourself Alain? I have noticed that you do not have a partner with you?"

"Yes, sir, I am enjoying the evening, it is wonderful to see so many people enjoying themselves. Sadly, I do not have a regular lady friend, although I have several whose company I enjoy when I am able to socialise in Paris. At the moment nothing serious."

They talked together for a few moments, and then the Countess came over to them. Alain asked the Count if he might dance with the Countess. He gave Alain permission and Claudine led Alain on to the dance floor, as the Quartet started to play a Viennese Waltz. Alain was a good dancer, he held his partner firmly around the waist as they mingled with the other dancers. Alain gave a strong lead and so she was able to follow so easily. They made a handsome couple; the Count smiled to himself as they passed. The Countess seemed to be enjoying herself as they continued the dance. The music came to an end and Alain escorted the hostess back to her husband.

"Alain," said the Claudine, "that was wonderful, you are an excellent dancer. Thank you very much. I will expect you to dance with me again before the evening ends."

Alain thanked her, for he said how much he had enjoyed dancing with the loveliest lady in the room.

Time passed quickly, the Master of Ceremonies mounted the stage, and requested that all the guests were now invited to go into the Banqueting Hall where, a feast was prepared for their delight. Alain followed his parents into the Hall where tables were laid ready for the servants to bring in the various dishes. Alain found himself on a table away from his parents, the chair next to Alain's was vacant.

Alain was about to sit down when the Count came over to him; beside the Count was a very attractive young lady.

"Alain," said the Count, "may I introduce you to Francoise de Villeneuve. She is a niece of a very good and dear friend Henri de Villeneuve. Francoise, this is my very good friend Alain Clement; he is a racing driver. I hope that you will both enjoy the rest of the evening."

That evening would change Alain's life forever, although he did not know it yet. Alain was always full of confidence, and felt that he could make a conversation with this lovely dinner partner and still feel at ease. Alain was first to speak:

"Good evening, mademoiselle, my name as the Count said is Alain Clement."

Francoise's gave Alain a wonderful smile.

"Monsieur Clement, I have read about your exploits in the newspapers. The picture I have seen of you. It does not do you justice."

Alain felt extremely embarrassed, but soon regained his composure.

"Please call Alain, Mademoiselle, and thank you for the compliment."

"Alain," replied Francoise, "I am forgetting my manners; my name is Francoise de Villeneuve. I live with my parents who own a Farmhouse with a vineyard near the village of Duclair some 15 kilometres from here. Would you please call me Francoise?"

Alain bowed, took hold of her hand, kissed it.

"Francoise, replied Alain, "if you do not have an escort for the rest of this evening, then it will be my pleasure to be your partner."

"I think," replied Francoise "that others have arranged that already."

As soon as Francoise had sat down next to Alain they began talking whilst they enjoyed a most sumptuous feast, hardly noticing the other guests at their table. There were a few glances from them, but they realised that the two young people were totally engrossed in each other. The meal ended and the dancing began again. Francoise thought it correct to introduce her new-found partner to her parents, Henri, and his wife Justine. Alain spoke positively to Henri, who thought that Alain had embarked on an unusual career, but one that had enormous potential. Alain then introduced Francoise to his parents. They were delighted that he had found such a lovely young lady, and they certainly did not know that the Count and Countess had done the matchmaking.

The young couple spoke intimately as they danced the night away as if in a dream, to the Count and Countess they certainly made a lovely couple. The evening drew to a close and the Count knew that his invitation for both Francoise and Alain to stay the night in the Chateau was the right one.

Sleeping arrangements and attire were found for them. Francoise and Alain could not wait for the next day, so they could meet again. Was it love at first sight? They both had a feeling that it could be. They made their way through the Chateau's corridors to their respective bedrooms. At Francoise door, Alain tried to give Francoise a quick kiss but they held each other close and the kiss lingered on their lips. Françoise's outer feelings were telling her to let Alain into her bedroom; she wanted to spend the night with him. Alain had the same feelings; he had fallen in love for the first time. Here was a woman who was charming, warm hearted and beautiful. Rushing things might well spoil his chances with her. This he did not want. Françoise's inner feelings gave her the same signals that Alain was receiving. Their first kiss was no doubt the start of many more no doubt.

"See you in the morning, sleep well," they whispered to each other after another goodnight kiss.

They parted and arranged to meet the next morning at breakfast. Both Francoise and Alain soon fell asleep, both had dreams of each other, it was very frustrating to know that they were just a few metres apart, but separated by a wall. The morning could not come soon enough for either of them. They had dreams that night only new lovers have.

Next morning, Alain was down early for breakfast. The Count had promised them, the night before that they could use his horses to go riding. When Francoise appeared a little later, Alain was still eating. He got up, held her close and kissed her.

"Bon jour, Mon ami," said Alain, "you slept well?"

Francoise seemed very happy and was smiling.

"Yes my Alain," she replied, "I slept well dreaming of you."

"Francoise," asked Alain, "perhaps after breakfast you would like to go riding with me?"

"I would love that Alain," answered Francoise, "the countryside around here is excellent for horse riding."

They finished breakfast together and went up to their rooms. The Count and Countess had informed the servants to lay out suitable riding clothes for his two special guests. They dressed and walked together down to the stables, where the grooms had two horses prepared for them. Their ride took them out of the grounds of the Chateau to the woods that ran along side the River Seine.

It was a lovely crisp morning; the sky was cloudless as the two young lovers galloped along beside the river. It was a perfect start to the Christmas morning. They could not be out too long, as they were expected, along with the Count and Countess and other villagers to attend Morning Service at the local church. This would start sharp at 11.00 am. Alain looked at his watch and signalled to Francoise that they should start back, so that they would not be late for church.

They arrived back in plenty of time, for Francoise had to freshen up, put on her make up, best dress and winter coat. When they met down in the Entrance Hall; Alain could not believe how beautiful she was. Her outfit was stunning, her coat was full-length of red fox with a large hood, and underneath she wore a burgundy velvet dress that made her look like a fashion model. Alain felt decidedly underdressed, but he took her arm and proudly walked out to where the coaches were waiting to take them to Church. The Father Canard welcomed them all into his congregation. On that Christmas morning, the tiny village church was absolutely full, with everyone in good voice and spirits. The Count and Countess took their usual places in the front row of pews. Alain's parents were delighted that their son and his lady had decided to go to Church rather than roam the countryside on horseback.

Alain and Francoise sat quietly in the knave of the church, holding hands. The Church Organ started up and the congregation began singing the first hymn. Then came the sermon. Alain used to hate long sermons, now he could hold hands with his new love, so Father Canard could talk all day, as far as he was concerned.

The thoughts of Francoise and Alain were far away from the words of Father Canard. Soon the service was over and the congregation left. Alain told his father that the Count had invited him to stay on for a day or so, and Francoise would be there too.

Pierre said that he and Marie had been invited to the Chateau for Christmas lunch, where they would be introduced to Françoise's parents. Alain knew that the Count had been matchmaking. The Count had tried it before with one of his other nieces, but it had not worked out.

This time he had judged the situation to a tee and he hoped that the two young people he loved the most would find happiness together. Back at the Chateau, the Count introduced Pierre and Marie to Henri and Justine. Purely by chance, they had a lot in common and got on really well. Neither parent wanted to rush their children into any matrimonial decision. After all, they had only just met. It was plain for all to see that a flame of love had been kindled, whether this would burn into a flame of passion and true love, only time would tell.

With lunch over, they all retired to the Morning Room; a roaring fire burned in the vast fireplace, while the late winter sun cast its shadows across the room. The meal and the wine that accompanied it mellowed the conversation. Henri and Justine were intrigued about Françoise's new beau. They had of course heard about Alain, they knew from their meetings with Count Guy, that here was a young man of integrity. He was certainly making his mark in this new dangerous sport of motor racing. They wanted to know all about his exploits and what his prospects would be with Darracq. Alain told them that he had a new contract for the coming season with more money as a basic salary and bonuses should he feature in the top four places in any event he entered. As their Number 1 driver, he expected to do very well and the future looked bright.

The sun had now dipped below the horizon and the Maid arrived to turn on the lights. Soon after Butler announced that Dinner would be served at 7 p.m. They had not realised how the time had slipped away. Alain had it seemed created a very good impression and now he knew a little about his lady's parents. The Count suggested that they all get ready for dinner, where the conversation could be continued. Alain escorted Francoise to her room and said he would meet her and take her down for Dinner. Francoise was very excited as she undressed and the maid ran her bath. She had had several boyfriends, but nothing serious. Her Father had introduced her to the some of one of his rich customers at a Bank function. His name was Jacques Chaumet, he was tall handsome young man, and he knew it. He had broken hearts all over Paris, and spent money like water. He always showered his lady friends with lavish gifts, Francoise was no exception.

He had given her a diamond bracelet that must have cost several thousand Francs. Their affair lasted about four months, for he treated her as if a piece of jewellery that could be worn, or indeed left at home, as the mood took him. He was effeminate; Francoise could tell that by his mannerisms. His Father Jules and his Mother Marie were owners of a famous perfumery - Chaumet. Jacques always used perfume, and it was alleged that he wore ladies undergarments, but it was never proved. Francoise stopped seeing him when she saw him kissing one of his male friends on the lips, in the street, in broad daylight. She said he never once made any sexual advances. She told her Father, who stopped the affair, right there. She was afraid of 'ditching' him, because the CHAUMERT account was very profitable to her father's bank.

Francoise mulled over the past five years since her 15th Birthday whilst she soaked in her hot bath. Trying to think of her past boyfriends, apart from Jacques. She saw Alain in a different light; here was a man with whom she could relate. She had never thought of falling in love at first sight, but this time she had a strange feeling that she had. Whilst she dressed the maid hung up her clothes and fussed around her. Francoise took a long look in the full-length mirror and asked the Maid how she looked. The young maid said she looked beautiful.

Francoise blushed a little, then as she opened the door. Alain was waiting for her, and the young couple made their way down to the Main Hall where Françoise's parents and the de Longchamps were waiting for them. The Butler appeared outside the Family Dining Room and announced that Dinner was served.

Alain held the chair for Francoise, as she sat opposite her Mother. This was something rare for Francoise as manners had not been the strong suit of some of her previous beaux.

The meal began, and Alain thought it would be good manners to ask Henri about his business interests. Henri then gave him a complete autobiography, stopping just short of a full family history. Justine glared at him a couple off times, but glared back and continued his tale. He was a very popular sanguine. He told Alain that he had started at the Bank of France as a boy and worked his way up to Vice-President and next year he would become President when old Charles Duval retired. He went on to tell Alain how he and Justine had met and that he had known Guy since their days at the Sorbonne. He was interested to know that Alain had been to that French Institution too. They had enjoyed many riotous evenings together and suggested that at a more private time that Guy relates a few of their adventures. Guy suddenly went bright red in the face; this was something he had not expected. Obviously, Alain had asked the wrong question, which it seems was the key to a very long story. This time Justine glared even more at her husband and wondered in her mind what Henri would come out with next.

She raised her eyes to the ceiling, and Guy looked at her as she did so. She had that expression wives get when their husbands are on 'a roll' so to speak. Thinking no dirty linen in public please. Henri went on to say that he had met Justine at the Annual Bank Ball in Paris. She was the daughter of the Manager at their Paris Branch, whilst he was under-Manager at their Branch in Versailles. They had fallen in love and were married in Paris in the summer of 1886; Francoise had been born in the summer of 1888.

In 1890, he was promoted to Manager and moved to Rouen, and by 1900 he was promoted to Vice-President and moved back to Paris. As President he would stay in Paris, but would still maintain his country house at Rouen. He invited Alain to come to stay any weekend. Dinner was now over; the ladies withdrew whilst the gentlemen enjoyed their Port. Alain begged that he take their leave and went off to find Francoise. He found the ladies in the Morning Room and asked Justine, if he and Francoise might spend some time together.

Justine said that of course he could spend some time with Francoise, who smiled and together hand in hand they made their way to a quiet place in the Chateau.

She told Alain that once her father got going with his life history it was difficult to stop him. They kissed and held each other tightly. Francoise told Alain that she was falling in love with him. Alain told her that he felt the same. They talked of the past and how neither of them had ever given themselves fully to another human being. They kissed a long lingering kiss.

They were both tired and decided that bed was a good idea, they wanted to sleep next to each other, and this no doubt would be tricky if someone discovered them with very little decorum. They agreed to meet for Breakfast and go riding again. Alain said he would arrange this. So they kissed again and Alain took Francoise by the hand and went with her to the door of her room. Then more good night kisses. Alain made his way downstairs where the men were still chatting. Alain asked the Count if both he and Francoise could go riding the next day. The Count said he would arrange it for them.

The next morning Alain was up early, he had slept like a log; Francoise had sweet dreams of the new man in her life. Alain was already tucking into his breakfast when Francoise appeared; she still looked lovely, even first thing in the morning. Soon they were both finished eating and were dressed ready for riding. Alain led his lady on his arm to the stables where the horses were ready for them, and helped her mount her steed. The weather was sunny and cold so they were well wrapped up. They galloped off toward a Mill that Alain knew; there they would not be disturbed. They needed to talk. By the time they reached the Mill on the banks of the River Seine, the wind had brought colour to their cheeks. Alain dismounted and helped Francoise down from her mount. They tied their horses securely to a nearby post and walked towards the Mill that had been closed for the winter. Alain led Francoise by the hand until they were inside the building, for out of the cold wind, it was a good deal warmer in there. He told her he used to come here when he was a boy and watch the Miller grinding his corn. During the guided tour Francoise hung on every Alain's every word. When the tour was over, she pulled him towards her and kissed him passionately and held him in her embrace. They found an area used as a bedroom by the summer occupants. The beds were still there but the mattresses had been removed.

Francoise was at that moment the more adventurous of the two, and was starting to remove her clothing, when a strong gust of cold wind blew across the room, this stopped her. Alain now knew that this was the woman with whom he wanted to spend the rest of this life. His brain sent a clear message - DO NOT RUSH THINGS IT COULD RUIN EVERYTHING.

They lay there embracing each other, there was no doubt, they were lovers and their senses had them in a vice like grip. Each wanting the other, but in reality their common senses telling them that intercourse at this time would spoil their relationship. They lay together side by side for quite some time. However, when they heard the horses whinnying, this brought them back to reality.

"Alain," said Francoise getting up, "I fear that the time is getting on and I think we should make our way back to the Chateau."

They kissed again and walked back to where the horses were pawing the ground. Alain helped Francoise back on to her mount and soon they were back at the Chateau. The next two days went by in a blur and soon it was time for Alain and Francoise to part. They knew they would meet again soon. They would write to each other every day. It was a lover's parting. Count Guy knew he had made a love-match.

Henri and Justine before they left the Chateau had spoken to Count Guy about Alain. They knew that here was a sincere young man who would love their only child. Justine let slip that she was sorry that Alain did not come from an aristocratic family. Justine agreed that Guy's recommendation of Alain's character was good enough for her too. She tended to be a bit of a snob. She did admit that Alain was really genuine and a person she could get to know and love like the son they never had. They all hoped that the future would be bright for Francoise and Alain. Wedding bells soon perhaps?

When Alain arrived home, the family wanted to know all the things that had happened to him whilst he was at the Chateau. They could tell from his expressions that their Alain had fallen in love with Francoise. They all agreed that she was a lovely and sensible young lady with good manners and breeding. No doubt, she would make Alain a very good wife when the time came for them to wed. The next day Alain packed his suitcase and said his goodbyes to the family. Pierre drove him to the Station, for it was time to start work on the Cars for the new season's racing.

During the period running up to the Christmas break, Alain had attended many meetings with the Darracq Research and Development team as they struggled to improve their cars for the coming season. So how could they beat Mercedes?

They had put forward some very interesting ideas to be incorporated into the 1908 cars, for they had been the third most successful team, thanks to Alain who drove with intelligence and panache.

His technique was driving his car with skill, rather than trying to be a daredevil. He would try to win races by cunning, anyone could drive flat out, and he would drive quick enough to win. Most times the public came to watch the races to see exciting crashes rather than exciting competition between rival teams. Pierre and Marie still worried about him, but they knew that it was in his blood. He was a natural driver; he was fast but never took unnecessary risks. Pierre now had a car an old Renault and the two men chugged through the lanes and finally arrived at the station in good time. They sat and chatted about the wonderful party at the Chateau and family matters. All too soon a train whistle could be heard in the distance and the locomotive with its 6 carriages came into view.

"I'll telephone to let you know I have arrived safely," said Alain as embraced his father.

Pierre was standing on the platform as the train pulled out and was finally lost to his view. Alain sat back and thought about Francoise and how much he had enjoyed her company and how well he had mixed with her parents. This was an unknown quantity, and can be difficult in a new relationship. There were challenges ahead that he would have to meet head on. The season ahead would prove that he was capable of new heights in his career, providing the car was up to it, he would be on the rostrum as a winner. The journey soon passed and before he knew, he was back at his lodgings.

Chapter 9

The 1907 racing season had been a successful and busy one for the Mercedes team, so they had called their Drivers and the Development Engineers back to the Company Headquarters in Stuttgart. There had been endless meetings to discuss the plans and tactics for 1908. Their defeat in the Kaiserpreis had been a shock; after all, they were favourites to win. They certainly had the best car, something had gone radically wrong, Gustav was determined to trace the cause and rectify it. There was a kind of end of term party for all the staff that ended in the early hours of the morning. Those that had to travel some distance were accommodated in local Hotels; these included Rudolph and Hermann, who were heading home for the holiday. During the summer, Hermann's father had moved from Weisloch to Ludwigshavan to a larger house for his employers had opened new premises and Karl Ritter had been promoted to General Manager.

His wife, Hermann's mother Eva, had always been a snob and now with her husband's raised status, she would no doubt be in her element. With the move, she would now create a circle of friends suited to her husband new standing in the community. She always dressed to impress; at least that is what Hermann always told Rudolph. The Ritters had been invited to spend Christmas at their cousins' new house in Karlsruhe. So, as Hermann and Rudolph arrived by taxi at Stuttgart Station, they purchased their tickets at the Booking Office, as they parted, they were full of excitement about the Christmas holidays. Now they would be looking forward to the new season and success for their team. Hermann had to go to the far side of the Station to catch his train. They wished each other a very Merry Christmas and a Happy New Year.

Rudolph looked up at the arrival and departure boards nearby; he had some 20 minutes to wait for his train. He then made his way to the Station Bookstall and bought a newspaper. Then he made his way to the platform and sat down on a seat. He opened and starting reading his newspaper, then looked up as he heard Hermann's train arrive.

He glanced around looking at the passengers passing by, then just a few metres away he noticed a lady dressed from top to toe in a beautiful blue fox coat. She did not seem like the average train traveller. He looked at her more closely; she had a pair of very expensive fur topped blue leather boots, a leather bonnet trimmed with blue fox and matching gloves. He had not noticed her when he had first sat down; from her stance she seemed a bit anxious, as if something was troubling her. He could not see her face as this masked by the upturned collar of her fur coat. On the ground beside her was a large blue leather suitcase. Rudolph thought she had a bit of an air of mystery about her. He refolded his newspaper, and then slid it into the straps around his suitcase. His train steamed into the Station and shuddered to a stop. He opened the carriage door. The Fur coated Lady walked towards him, and began to climb the steps into the carriage; she seemed to be really struggling with her suitcase, which looked very heavy.

"Excuse me, Madam," said Rudolph assuming she was a married lady, "may I help you lift your suitcase on to the train?"

Thank you young man," replied the fur-coated lady, "that is very kind of you. I am sorry it is so heavy."

Rudolph picked up the suitcase, which was quite heavy, and put it on the floor of the carriage. The mystery Lady turned, smiled, and then disappeared along the train corridor. Rudolph walked along the corridor of the train, until he found an empty compartment, where settled down to read his newspaper. He had been sitting there for a few minutes, when the compartment door slid open.

"Excuse me," said a lady's voice, "do you mind if I share your compartment?"

Rudolph looked up. There in the doorway stood this lady cocooned in her furs with a suitcase in her hand. Rudolph stood up.

"Madam," replied Rudolph, "I would be very pleased to share this compartment with you. That suitcase is quite heavy; let me help you with it. Are you catching this train as far as Weisloch?"

Rudolph took the suitcase and placed it in the overhead locker, then slid the compartment door shut. The lady sat down next to Rudolph.

"Thank you Sir for helping me with my suitcase," said the lady. "I am travelling to Rohrbach about four Kilometres from Heidelberg where my Husband Michael has a business. At present he is away in England seeing various Clients he will not be returning until the beginning of February. I shall get off the train with you, for I have a car meeting me at Weisloch Station."

She put her hand to her mouth, realising she may have said too much already. Rudolph could see that she was still a bit concerned. So he tried to put her at her ease.

"Madam, may I introduce myself my name is Rudolph von Lundenberg. May I know your name? Of course, I do appreciate the problems ladies have travelling alone, and worried about being with strangers, and may be prefer to keep themselves to themselves."

The Fur coated lady thought for a moment then replied.

"My name is Catherina von Braun. I remember you Herr von Lundenberg from reports in the newspapers of your prowess in the Motor Races. You drive for the Mercedes team."

"That is correct," replied Rudolph. "I feel honoured that you have remembered my name. Please call me Rudolph?"

"Very well," replied Catherina, "and please call me Catherina."

Catherina removed her bonnet and her long blonde hair cascaded down over her fur coat, which she now unfastened and again sat beside Rudolph. He had guessed her age to be between 23 and 26; she had very green piercing eyes and turning her head towards him she gave a lovely smile.

"Rudolph," she said, "I would not consider sharing my journey with anyone else but you."

Rudolph felt a little embarrassed, but recovered his composure. The train began to move giving a jolt as the locomotive took up the slack, and so the journey began. Catherina asked if Rudolph would pull down the blinds on the windows that looked on the train corridor, so that they might have some privacy on their journey of some one and half-hours.

Rudolph lowered the blinds and returned to sit beside this lovely lady. She pulled him towards her and kissed him full on the lips. Rudolph was a little startled; this was something he had not expected. Her kiss was like something he had never felt before; he had kissed quite a few ladies in his time, but never was the first kiss one like this. It was like the first kiss that lovers have.

"That my love," whispered Catherina as their lips parted, "is the first part of a very big thank you from the Fatherland. I bet your team Manager didn't thank you like that."

Rudolph did not know what to say in reply, he was completely taken aback. He was speechless for once. "Don't look too surprised Rudolph," Catherina continued, "I am certain you have been kissed like that before. A handsome young man like you must have the girls flocking after him."

Rudolph thought carefully before replying, after all, here was a young lady who obviously wanted male company.

"Yes Catherina," replied Rudolph, "I have had a few affairs with ladies, but nothing serious nor is there anyone at present. Travelling around and living in lodgings, does not help, when you are dating someone. My landlady is very strict and does not allow her lodgers to bring any ladyfriends back. I am going home for Christmas to the Schloss just outside Weisloch to see the family."

Catherina pulled him towards her and kissed him again. Rudolph noticed that Catherina was enjoying this, and he was getting to like this too, but he still felt uncomfortable, for after all this beautiful lady was a married woman. He had always made it a rule never to get involved with married women; there was always trouble in the end. A love triangle was something he did not need at any time. Catherina decided to open up a little to her travelling companion.

"Rudolph, I live in Rohrbach, in a very large house. My husband Johann is a good deal older than I am, he is in his late 50's, all he thinks of is business, business, and more business. Well, you may know how that makes me feel. He does not consider me at all. He is hardly ever home. I think that he may have a mistress, I am not certain. We met and married just over a year ago, when his wife died of pneumonia. I am his partner's daughter. He buys me all these lovely clothes, furs and jewellery. We have a lovely home, but he has kept many his wife's things, as kind of mementos. I still feel like the daughter, rather than the wife. He has never made love to me. I get very frustrated. Most of the time I am alone, as I will be over Christmas and the New Year. Would you please come to stay with me for a few days?"

Rudolph was shocked for a moment, although he did not show it. Here was a lady of exceptional beauty asking him to go to her home, and who knows where that might lead, but he was already weakening. Normally, he would never have expected this kind of approach from a lovely lady such as Catherina, especially as she had given him an invitation to be with her. She was married and he was about to break his own rule. He quickly recovered his composure.

"Catherina I have to spend Christmas and Boxing Day with the family. I would love to come to stay with you on the 27th December until after the New Year. I have 2 weeks holiday from the factory."

"That will be wonderful, Rudolph. There are many things we can enjoy together during your stay with me."

Rudolph thought that you do not need to be a genius to know what that included.

The train rattled on and the two young people were oblivious to their surroundings. Catherina's frustrations were now coming to the surface very quickly. Their lips met and their hands started searching each other's body. Catherina had found the buttons to open Rudolph's trousers. Catherina had no idea why she had the impulse to do this; she had never in her life done something like this, with a man she had only just met. There seemed to be a signal from somewhere within her, that here was a man she had to please.

She eased out his male member, rubbing the end of it with her furs, again this was new to her, but seemed right somehow. Rudolph felt it stirring and it stiffened up quickly, then she kissed him lovingly and longingly.

"We shall save all that for later, my love," she cooed, "after Christmas you will get some special presents from me."

Rudolph kissed her once more. Then she tried to put back Rudolph male member into his trousers, which was proving difficult for her, but also exciting. Meanwhile, Rudolph was massaging her ample breasts, whilst his tongue now searched the inside her mouth. They were both completely oblivious to their surroundings and eager to make love. Their bodies entwined, time seemed to stand still. Rudolph's thoughts now, were that this would be the first Christmas that he had spent with the family, where he wanted the celebrations to be over quickly, so that he could be with this exciting woman. He did not care if she was married or not. He wanted her and she wanted him.

The train slowed on the outskirts of Weisloch this being its first stop. They stood up adjusted their clothing, Rudolph still had a bulge in his trousers and Catherine gave it a little rub.

That's some magic lamp you have there," she said with a little laugh, "I hope to see the genie soon."

Rudolph laughed too at her joke, for he could see she was very happy. Then she rubbed Rudolph's crotch and kissed him longingly once more. Rudolph helped her on with her coat as the train slowed right down. Rudolph removed Catherina's suitcase from the overhead rack, he now noticed that all her luggage was monogrammed in gold with the initials C von B. Rudolph then let up the blinds, as he could see that they were already getting close the Station. Soon, he would have to say a fond farewell to Catherina and he knew the days could not pass quickly enough. Catherina put on her fur lined and trimmed bonnet tying the straps under her chin, the big fur balls at the end of each strap covering the front of her neck. Rudolph put his coat on and got down his suitcase. The train was going very slowly before it finally shuddered to a stop. A Guard was calling out to advise all passengers alighting at Weisloch to leave the train as soon as possible. Rudolph held Catherina in his arms and they kissed passionately.

"We must say goodbye here rather than on the Platform," she said as their lips parted, "my husband knows a number of influencial people around here. At present the last thing I want is to be 'discovered' with another man. I want us to keep away from prying eyes. If we are seen together, you can imagine how the gossip will spread."

"I agree," answered Rudolph, "gossip about you and I could be disastrous."

They made their way out of the compartment on to the Station platform. Rudolph put down his suitcase as Catherina beckoned to a nearby Porter, who picked up her suitcase and together they walked toward the Barrier. Rudolph's eyes watched Catherina in her beautiful blue fox coat and bonnet as she strolled sensuously along the Platform and across the Station concourse until she was finally out of his vision.

Rudolph said to himself, "That is one very sexy lady."

Rudolph picked up his suitcase and walked towards the barrier he was still daydreaming about the gorgeous Catherina. At the barrier the Ticket Inspector asked for his ticket, and Rudolph handed it to him. He was now outside Weisloch station, Catherina was just getting into a closed car, and she turned her head to give Rudolph one last look. He was still thinking of her when his Father - Count Josef and the Chauffeur Karl came over to him. Count Josef gave him a big hug then the Chauffeur picked up Rudolph's suitcase and they set off for the drive to the Schloss. They wanted to hear all his news. Rudolph kept off the subject of Catherina. It did not know how his parents would react. In any case, when he did tell them he would not mention the fact that Catherina was married, this would definitely not go down very well.

His Father, the Count congratulated him on the successes that he had had with the Mercedes team through 1907, and said that 1908 would no doubt be even better. He told Rudolph that a truly wonderful Christmas had been planned, and relations, would be coming from far and wide and staying over the holiday. However, Josef told his son that on the 27th December he had to travel to Bavaria for a business meeting. He would be away for a few days and may not return until after New Year.

He hoped that Rudolph would look after his guests. At this stage, Rudolph thought it prudent; not to mention the fact that he had been invited to stay with Catherina at Rohrbach. He would have to play this carefully and choose his moment. The festivities were being prepared as the Car swung through the gates; it crunched to a standstill on the gravel in front of the stairway leading to the imposing main entrance of the historic building.

The chauffeur grabbed hold of Rudolph's suitcase and took it into the Entrance Hall where all the family were waiting to greet the conquering hero. They all wanted to ask questions. However, Rudolph just wanted to 'freshen up'. He had spent quite a while travelling, but now he wanted to relax in a nice hot bath.

That evening, there was the traditional family dinner and reunion. The relatives from far and wide had arrived; all of them seemed to be talking at once. Nobody seemed to be listening. Rudolph was being asked so many questions, most of them on two subjects, his Motor Racing experiences and his love life, that his head was in a spin. On the Racing he chatted freely, as to his love life, he said that he was still browsing. This caused a few laughs. They all asked about his meeting with the Kaiser, as this had reported in the papers and also about his exploits in England and how he had met King Edward VII and his beautiful Queen. After dinner, all the relations snared him, but still, Rudolph could not get Catherina out of his mind. Fortunately, he was able to give the answers expected of him and did not let the cat out of the bag.

The guests were too busy to notice that Rudolph was not 100% with it for most of the time. The rest of Christmas Day went by in a bit of a blur to Rudolph. Then on Boxing Day morning he went into his Father's study, he found his parents in there discussing a serious matter. Time was running out and he must tell them of his visit to

Catherina, but how could he break it to them? Rudolph entered the study; his parents turned their heads towards the door.

"Mother, Father I want to tell you something," said Rudolph, "is now a good time?"

"That," replied Josef, "that depends on what you have to tell us."

"Well," began Rudolph, "I have met a friend, who has invited me to stay for few days from tomorrow. I hope that you do not mind."

"That's good son," replied Margarita, "I am glad you have found a friend. We hope that you enjoy your stay with him."

He dare not tell them it was a lady and that she was married, on top of that he husband was in England and not due back for over a month. He must also keep his passion for her a secret too, for he did not know whether his parents or any of their guests would reveal his secret. Now he could not wait for Boxing Day to end and the next day to begin. He longed to see Catherina again.

Rudolph woke early on December 27th and looked out of the window. There had been a dusting of snow overnight, but he decided that rather than take the local train he would drive the 8 kilometres to Catherina's home. He got dressed and ate a hearty breakfast, packed a small suitcase, then got dressed in his fur lined leather coat, helmet and gloves. The drive was but a few kilometres, but he knew how cold it could be, after all, he was a professional driver.

He made his way down to the garage, where the chauffeur was polishing the family cars. Rudolph told Karl, that he would take the open top Mercedes. Karl told him it was ready to go and that the fuel tank was full. Rudolph climbed aboard the Model '60' put his suitcase on the back seat, whilst Karl was ready to turn the engine over with the starting handle. One turn and the engine burst into life. Karl was an excellent mechanic and a very good driver. He had been trained at the Mercedes factory some years before and could have been a racing driver, but for the fact that he did not get the opportunity. Rudolph swung the car out of the garage and made his way to the main road. This road would lead him to his new love's house, for she lived about 2 kilometres off the main road to Heidelberg. Rudolph went at a leisurely pace, for he was certain that Catherine was not a lady that rose too early.

Catherina, in contrast to Rudolph, had endured a very miserable Christmas. Her husband had left for his trip in the middle of December; he had not even left his beautiful Catherina a present. He felt that she had all she needed; she had a boudoir full of clothes and fur coats and jewels so why clutter the place up with more gifts. There was not even a Christmas tree or any festive decorations. Johann, Catherina's husband, had given all the staff, including the chauffeur, Otto, a holiday over Christmas and New Year. He thought well, he was not there so, Catherina could fend for herself. He had left her plenty of food in the large larder. If she needed anything, she could always send her Maid to the local village before she went away for the holiday. The only one thing that kept her spirits up, was the fact that she knew that a new man was going to come into her life. He was tall, dark, handsome and virile, exactly what she needed.

On the morning of the 27th Catherina was up early, she ran a bath, soaped and soaked herself. She lay amongst the suds just thinking about the way her life had gone over the last 12 months, hoping that the future was going to be a lot better. Fate would no doubt decide her future, at present moment she was in control. However, when her husband returned it would be a different matter. He dominated her life in all its aspects. These things ran through her mind as she lay soaking away, looking forward to the next few days. She was hoping that they would bring at least temporary happiness and relief from the frustration of a really awful Christmas. The house had been empty and not a sign of cheer anyway, and even the servants were smiling as they left for their holiday. For some, it was the first Christmas they had spent with their families for years. Michael was a hard taskmaster, devoid of passion and compassion; he was completely self-centred and devoid of humour. His was not one for small talk, you could say he was a man of few words, and most of them were not nice.

Catherina emerged from the bath; she caught her reflection herself in the full-length mirror that covered the wall opposite the enormous tub. She saw breasts were full and firm, her body trim, she knew she had the ability to please a man; after all, she had aroused Rudolph on the train, but what next? She would just follow her instincts. Up to now she was merely a decoration, carried around by a husband who did not appreciate her one bit. He was always comparing her to his late wife Eva, who was it seems nothing short of perfect in every way. They doted on each other, but Eva could not have children, and was unresponsive sexually. She and her husband were well matched in this area. When she had died of pneumonia, Johann was devastated. He had devoted his life to his wife and his business. He became a bit of a recluse, but after a few months of mourning and moping, his partner George had suggested that he marry again, so he introduced him to his only child Catherina, who was 30 years John's junior. They married within 6 months. Catherina reckoned he only wanted someone to take out to social events and not a wife; in any case he did not like children anyway.

Catherina looked at the time; it was already almost 9.00 am. Her Rudolph could be here at any time. Should she dress or surprise him. After all, she was sure they would make love almost as soon as he crossed the threshold, so why waste time dressing. Then, she thought it would be fun to meet him at the door dressed in her furs, as she had been when they first met. So she opened her boudoir doors and got out her blue fox coat, slipped on her boots and strolled down to look out of the breakfast room windows and await the arrival of her lover.

She did not have to wait long, coming up the drive was an open car with just one person in it, was it her Rudolph? She prayed it would be. As the car came closer her heart started racing, for now she was very excited. The depression of the last few days had gone; she was a different person, her whole body was now pulsing with excitement of what was to come. Rudolph alighted from the car and walked to the large oak doors, before he could knock Catherina had thrown wide the door. As Rudolph crossed the threshold, she wrapped her arms around his and kissed him, with her tongue searching inside his mouth.

Rudolph the door closed behind them, putting down his small suitcase he stood back.

"My darling Catherina," he said passionately, "you look wonderful. I have missed you so much."

Catherina moved back into his arms.

"Dearest Rudolph," she cooed, "these few days I have with you will make up for the dreadful Christmas I have had. Let us enjoy them as much as we can. There are no servants to tell tales and gossip, I have given them a holiday, for I want you to satisfy me in every way possible."

Rudolph could not believe that this was the mystery woman of a few days ago.

"My beloved Catherina," replied Rudolph emotionally, "I shall ensure your utmost pleasure. Anything you want to do, then I am willing to do that with you."

Catherina took him by the hand and led him to her bedroom, closing the heavy drapes. She wanted everything; she was so excited now that her lover was here with her.

She enthusiastically helped Rudolph remove his clothes; she could now enjoy his muscular body for her ultimate pleasure.

The bedroom was cold, for there had been no fires in the room since the servants had left. Rudolph now naked and began to shiver, and so Catherina suggested that he put on one of her fox jackets to keep him warm. The combination of the soft fur against his naked body and the thought of what may soon come aroused his sexual passions.

"My Love," said Rudolph, "you are still in your furs do you feel cold too?"

"Yes," answered Catherina, "wearing them makes me feel 'special', especially with what I have on underneath my furs. Now more talk it is time for love."

She opened her coat and she too was naked, taking Rudolph's manhood in her hand, Catherina played with it until it had become stiff and thick, caressing the end with her furs. Rudolph had never known a woman like this, for those ladies he had made love to wanted a very quick in and out, usually before anything 'messy', as they called it, occurred.

However, this beautiful lady wanted all he had to give her and more, she certainly knew how to please him, and for a lady who had little experience of sexual foreplay she had mastered a technique with amazing speed.   Rudolph found her soft spot, moving his fingers in and out, whilst Catherina sighed with pleasure. This was a new sensation to her and was enjoying every moment, now she felt the moment had arrived, they we both in the mood for making love. They eased gently towards the bed with Catherina on top of her lover; her body rubbing against his. As he entered her cavern of pleasure she squealed with delight, this felt absolutely wonderful. Whilst he moved in and out she felt something welling up inside, Rudolph was in seventh heaven, for he was in a grand house with a lovely lady, who had found his Achilles heel. He just loved her and dressed in those beautiful furs; it gave Rudolph that extra sensuous feeling for the woman he wanted above all else. He had never felt this way with a woman before, and he was certain that Catherina felt the same. Now they were together in sexual union, it was sheer bliss.

Catherina was now in absolute ecstasy, whilst she often had overheard some of her husband's friends talking about lovemaking, she had always felt a little embarrassed, particularly as her husband had never shown interest. Having only heard second hand, about 'the pleasures of the flesh', as most of the women in whose company she had been, had called it, she often wondered why women talked about it so much. To some of them, it was a 'naughty' thing, a sexual pleasure not always done with the husband. Now she was releasing all her pent up passions and frustrations that had dogged her marriage to Johann. This one 'affair' would not be broadcast or boasted about. Those women that talked about it most, were those who were rich and frustrated. They usually 'performed' with much younger men, boasting about the sexual abilities in the bedroom.

Catherina's father, George, had kept her on a tight leash, many suitors had come to woo his daughter, but her Father's overbearing and pompous attitude, had frightened them off. Now she was experiencing it all at first hand, every emotion and feeling that previously she had been denied. Her mind could not think of words to describe her new sensations, and indeed the happiness she felt at that moment. Now she was with a man, she wanted more than any other. Then from within, came what felt like an explosion, she had at last had her first orgasm, there was a little blood. The intense pleasure she felt totally outweighed the slight pain. She told herself that was probably because being a virgin, this her first time with a real man, she did not know really what to expect. It was certainly the most fantastic physical feeling she had ever experienced. Now she was with someone that she loved and respected, she could express her love to Rudolph with both her body and soul. The next time they made love, which she hoped would be very soon, she would enjoy it even more. They continue their love making until they were both exhausted. Catherina could not wait until the next time. Rudolph was the man she wanted in her life now. They got up and stood beside the bed, she rubbed his crotch, he sighed with pleasure and they kissed yet again. Catherina had discovered lovemaking, now could not get enough of this wonderful feeling, that set her emotions on fire. Catherina pulled out a full length Red fox coat from her wardrobe, saying that it would be warmer for Rudolph to wear around the house.

After all, what would be the point of dressing? They then ran a bath and soaked in it together. Feeling hungry after their sexual pleasures they made there way down to the kitchen, where together they prepared lunch. This was the first time that Catherina ever helped prepare a meal. They sat at the table together, as Catherina told Rudolph her life story, and she poured out both the joy and the sorrow.

Catherina admitted to Rudolph that her real name was Catherina von Bismarck; her husband is a distant relative of an important man in the German Government. Therefore, until the time is right they must keep our relationship very secret. Her husband was still politically active, should he find out about her love affair he could cause immense problems for them both, complications that did not even bear thinking about. Rudolph agreed that this was the best course to take. Her father, whilst a good friend and partner in Johann's business knew very little about his private life. Having visited the couple, he was disgusted to hear how his so-called son-in-law had treated his lovely daughter in such a degrading manner. Michael had told George that she lacked experience in all matters, and more or less to mind his own business in the matter of his marriage.

Whilst he had to work with Johann, her father never visited their home. She was very sad, as before her marriage she had been very close to her father. In retrospect, George felt really that she should have married a very much younger man with a future, rather than an older man with no interests in family life, only business. She hoped that Rudolph would not be angry after hearing her life story. After all, this was her first affair and did not know whether to tell Rudolph the truth, or keep something back. Even though she had known him for only a very short time, Catherina had the feeling that here was a man who she could trust with her secrets. Rudolph was surprised that she had been so open with him after just a few days.

" I am not angry my love," he said when she had finished, "I am overjoyed that you have so honest with me, after knowing me for such a short time. Our love must remain concealed. Should anyone find out, as you have said who knows what the consequences will be? I want you in my life and I will certainly not jeopardise anything that we have. I love you so much it hurts."

Catherina felt much easier now in her mind. She had not been certain how to handle this part of her new relationship, but it seemed to her that she had a loving, willing partner who was prepared to listen. She knew he loved her and understood the problems that might arise. She had idea that there would be challenges, together they would meet and overcome all of them. Secrecy was paramount. In her brief married life, she listened to many tales of sexual prowess from some of her husband's business acquaintances, until it became utterly boring. Most of them had many affairs, even boasting about them, particularly when their wives were not around. She felt that nearly all the men had exaggerated the numbers of women that had succumbed to their sexual charms. The wives too told similar tales, and no doubt embroidered on their sexual adventures. The one thing they obviously did not do with their wives was to share their experiences in strange bedrooms. It was without a shadow of a doubt that, some were the fabrication of a sexually fertile mind. For want of a better word, the 'less physically attractive' husbands did not want to feel, as if they were unattractive to the opposite sex. However, most of the attraction, according to Catherina, usually came from the thickness of their bankroll.

She knew some of the wives must have used their avaricious sexual appetite to overcome the shortcomings in their physical beauty, to put it mildly.

When lunch was over, the two lovers went back to the bedroom to enjoy each other in the many ways of sexual intercourse. This was true love, not lust. Catherina was now making up for all those years that she had been denied. As the day passed they just lost count of the number of times both of them had reached their climax. They wanted to express their intense love for each other, mentally and physically. They were now deeply in love, but how could they be together with Johann, Catherina's husband still on the scene. During the days, that followed Catherina and Rudolph played sexual games, satisfying each other in every way they knew. Catherina told Rudolph that being alone with him was the very best Christmas present she had ever had. Rudolph, following their first night together, lit fires in the Bedroom and Breakfast Room. They both wore furs the whole time, in case they got cold, at least that was Catherina's excuse. The days and nights they spent together were the expression of their burning passion for each other. Catherina then had the thought what happens when Rudolph leaves her, what would the future hold for her with this man she adored? They were both totally besotted with each other and could not get enough of the physical love they felt. Then came the day that Rudolph had to part from his beloved.

It was a tearful parting, but they knew that love would find a way. Rudolph knew the only way they could be together involved some very fancy footwork. As Rudolph's car went off down the driveway Catherine felt alone, this was her first experience of parting from a man she truly loved. Tears came to her eyes, she had enjoyed true unbridled physical love in all its forms, and finally she now felt a new woman. She was determined somehow to be with Rudolph for the rest of her life, but how? That was the question uppermost in her mind as the servants appeared after their so-called holiday. Catherina settled down to normal life at the von Bismarck residence, even though her husband was still supposedly in England on business. When the servants returned from their Holidays, the Maid asked if her mistress had enjoyed her Christmas.

"It was certainly different," replied Catherina.

When he arrived back at Schloss Lundenberg, his parents noted that he had an extra spring in his step, they were curious as to how he had enjoyed his few days with his new found friend. He seemed happier than he had ever been in the post Christmas period. They asked him questions on what he had been doing at his friend's house. Rudolph did not lie, that was not in his nature; he was just a little evasive. After a while the questions stopped. His parents knew that their son had a secret to keep, and would tell them about it when the time was right.

All too soon, it was time to return to Canstatt and his lodgings. Once unpacked his thoughts turned to the beautiful Catherina, he just could not get her out of his mind. One evening after a long day at the factory, he and Hermann went out to a Beerkeller for a drink or two. Rudolph was quiet and Hermann asked him what the problem was that he had on his mind. Hermann was sure it was a woman. The winter days seemed so short now, and the factory was busy developing the new cars for the season. He had not heard from Catherina for almost a month. She had sent a letter just after Rudolph had left her, saying that he should not write to her as he letters were sometimes opened by the servants. Her husband was an extremely jealous man and could at times get violent, particularly if he had the slightest suspicion that she was having an affair. She had posted the letter herself in the village, but even going down there was tricky. Rudolph had kept this letter close to his chest. He wondered when he would see his love or hear from her again.

One evening Hermann and Rudolph came back to their lodging after a particular difficult day at Mercedes, when the Landlady handed Rudolph an envelope. It bore the crest of the von Bismarck's. Now Catherina's only letter to him had no such crest. He went to his room and locked the door, then sat at the small table by the window. His thoughts raced, could this be a letter from Johann, who had found out about the days and nights he had spent with Catherina? That could be disastrous for their relationship, and would certainly put Catherina's life in danger. Perhaps she had forced to reveal their secret. The only way to find out would be to open the letter. He put the envelope down, and then paced the room. He was worried that the only woman in the world that he wanted would now not be his. He could wait no longer, picking up a paper knife he slit open the envelope slowly unfolding the paper, which bore the family crest. He eyes glanced quickly over the handwriting that he recognised as Catherina's. He read it very slowly absorbing every word, which was etched, into his brain. It was the letter he had hoped for and it would change his life forever.

The letter was dated 16th February 1908 and read as follows: -

My Dearest Darling Rudolph,

> *I am writing to tell you the very sad news that today I had a letter from the General Manager of the London and North-Western Railway in London. The letter concerns my husband Johann. It seems that he was passenger travelling on a train from Glasgow to London on the night of February 4th. At 2.30 a.m., the train left the track just outside Crewe Station. Seven coaches were derailed and rolled down an Embankment. My husband was among the 25 people killed. I have to go to London to identify the body and bring it back to Germany for burial.*

> *I cannot do this alone, my darling I do hope that you will be able to travel with me. Fate has intervened in our lives, now we can be together. My body yearns for your touch and I want you by my side always. Those intimate moments we shared will live forever in my memory. I cannot live without you my dearest. I treasure every moment spent with you. Making love with you was simply wonderful.*

> *Please telephone as soon you can, I long to hear your voice, and be close to you.*
> *Your ever loving,*
> *Catherina.*

Rudolph read the letter several times, and then ran downstairs to use the telephone to speak to his Catherina. He picked up the earpiece and the operator answered. He told her the number he wanted and the ringing tone began. After a moment or two, it seemed like ages to Rudolph, a familiar female voice answered.

"Hello, who is calling?"

Rudolph's heart missed a beat as he recognised Catherina's voice.

"Its Rudolph, my darling. How are you my beloved?"

"My darling Rudolph, your voice is like a breath of fresh air to me. I feel wonderful now that I have heard from you."

"Catherina, I have your letter. I can't wait to be with you every moment on that trip to England. I will speak to Gustav, my Team Manager tomorrow and will be at your home on Friday evening. Goodnight for now my love."

Catherine was now crying with emotions of both sorrow and joy. Now she could be with her love at last.

"Good night my Rudolph, until Friday when our bodies will meet in a night of passion."

That night Rudolph had the best night's sleep he had enjoyed since his time with Catherina. She was now very excited, at last she could be with the man she truly loved with all her heart, she could hardly wait until they were together once more.

The next day was Thursday, so when Rudolph arrived at the Factory, he decided to see Gustav before he got involved in the day's work. Rudolph knocked on Gustav's office door, and was invited to come in. He explained to Gustav the situation that he had met a lady friend, who had a Brother working in England.

There had been a train crash and the Brother had been killed. The lady had no other relatives and had asked him to go with her. She had to identify the body and accompany it back to German for burial. They would have to make last minute funeral arrangements

In order to catch the ferry to England; they would have to catch the train very early on Saturday morning. They had been informed that the mortuary could only hold the body until Monday at the latest, as they closed at midday on a Sunday.

"Being as this is an emergency situation," said Gustav, "and a sad one, you can take a week's compassionate leave, I know how long these things take to arrange."

"Thank you Gustav," replied Rudolph, "my lady friend needs support at this sad time."

Rudolph had been hard at work of trying and testing new parts for the new season's cars, since his return from the Christmas holiday. Hermann knew that a lady had come into his life. However, Rudolph was not about to let Gustav or Hermann into his secret concerning Catherina just yet.

It was Friday midday when Rudolph left the factory. He picked up a small suitcase from his lodgings, and then made his way to Stuttgart Station. He bought a newspaper and sat on the same seat on the same platform, that he been on when he had met his Catherina. He gave a quick look around. This time, no fur-clad lady to be seen, no chance of deja vu. The train steamed in, Rudolph climbed aboard and found an empty compartment; there seemed to be very few passengers on this train. He settled down and read his newspaper from cover to cover. Then train slowed as it came into Weisloch Station, he alighted, and walked out to the Taxi Rank, then climbing into cab the driver off they sped to the Schloss. Rudolph's parents were delighted to see him, and indeed very surprised, they wondered why he was home. He told them the same story he had told Gustav. They both thought that this was a very noble thing to do, for Rudolph was relieved that no one had asked many awkward questions. He asked his father if he might take one of the cars as the lady lived near Heidelberg. Rudolph apologised for the fleeting visit, but there were arrangements to make once he got to the lady's home.

He said his goodbyes to his parents, then, climbing aboard the Model '60', having donned his fur-lined leather coat, helmet and gloves, for it was a very cold day, he set off for Catherina's home. She heard his car coming up the drive and was ready in her furs waiting for him. Throwing the door open she leapt into his arms then door slammed behind them. She could now be with her darling Rudolph, as she knew she could find happiness at last.

The young couple went up to the Bedroom and enjoyed each other until they were exhausted. Catherina knew she wanted Rudolph from the first moment they had met on that train. It seemed ironic that a train had brought a new love into her life, and another train had taken away a husband that had never loved her. They could be together at last, now there were no obstacles to overcome.

They decided that after a month of mourning, they would announce their engagement.

Neither of them cared what others thought; their happiness was all that mattered. Their energetic lovemaking had made them hungry for food. The Cook, Marlene, had prepared a substantial meal for them; she did not seem to worry that a new man might come into her mistress's life. It seems she hated the Old Master, for he had treated her quite badly and over a long period too. He had not paid her properly for years, and expected her to work all hours. She showed no emotion when Catherina told her that the old Master had been killed. Catherina introduced her to Rudolph. Marlene hoped that at last she might be able to serve someone who would appreciate her and no doubt pay what she worth. During dinner, Catherina and Rudolph discussed the travel arrangements, for now she knew that Rudolph would be with her on this trip. She felt relieved; she could never have made it on her own. She hoped bookings now confirmed would all go smoothly.

They would catch the early train from Weisloch; change at Cologne, then the long haul to Ostend catch the ferry to Dover and finally London. They had Hotel Reservations at the Waldorf Hotel in London, a double room of course, for two nights. It would be a sort of pre-honeymoon. They were both excited at the prospect of a long journey together. They could relax and be themselves.

After dinner, Catherina introduced Rudolph to the remainder of the staff; they greeted him with a certain amount of scepticism. Here was the new man in their mistress's life, they did not know whether there was a future for them all at the von Bismarck household. Most of them had been with Johann for many years, he had been a hard and mostly unfair taskmaster. He was upper class; the servants were nothing more than peasants. Catherina had always treated the staff fairly. Michael had her castigated for it, sometimes in front of the servants.

This had undermined her authority. Now, the old Master had gone they hoped things would change. The staff was looking for better conditions, pay and a little bit of appreciation.

Catherina and Rudolph slept soundly; her Maid; Anna woke them very early. She told Catherina that she had packed a small suitcase, and reminded them that the train left Weisloch station at 6.30a.m. This was the only train that connected with the express at Cologne, to take them to the ferry at Ostend.

It would indeed be a long train journey. Catherina dressed herself in a full-length silver fox coat complete with bonnet and boots, whilst Rudolph wore his fur-lined leathers. They looked a handsome couple as the chauffeur; Otto whisked them off to catch their train. The journey went well; at least they could rest, relax and talk. On the express from Cologne to Ostend, they had a private compartment, so they could make love and indulge themselves. They caught their connections with time to spare and on the ferry to Dover; they watched the Belgian coast disappear. Soon they were aboard the train at Dover heading for London.

At Waterloo Station, a Porter wheeled their luggage to the taxi rank and finally they arrived at the Waldorf Hotel. They unpacked, and dressed for Dinner. It was a delicious meal that they both appreciated the food on route being far from exotic. Then it was bed at last, for it had been an exhausting day; they were even too tired to make love.

After a hot bath together and breakfast in their room, they got dressed and went to reception. Catherina tried to look as if she was a widow weeping for the loss of her husband, but she still looked absolutely stunning in her furs. The Doorman raised his top hat to her as he hailed a taxi, and they made the short journey to Euston Station. They were shown the way to the Station Master's Office; here they met Mr.Harold West, the Assistant Station Master. They explained the reason for their visit. He was sorry for her loss, that a lovely lady such as Frau von Bismarck, should have to come all the way from Germany to collect her husband's body. There had been a full investigation, and a report was being prepared as to the cause of the train crash. The insurance company was at present resolving the matter of compensation.

Mr. West told Catherina that she should have a letter from them soon that would explain matters together with a cheque to cover their liability.

In the meantime, the London & North-Western Railway would cover any costs involved in shipping the body back to Germany. He phoned the Mortuary and having spoken to Dr. Desmond Craft, the Chief Mortician, confirmed that arrangements would be made to send the body back. He asked Catherina if she would visit the Mortuary to identify her husband's body. Rudolph led her by the arm. Dr. Craft pulled back the sheet and there lay Johann, stone cold and grey. She had not even seen a dead body before this; she shuddered, covered her face and pulled away.

"Excuse me Madam," Dr.Craft asked Catherina, "is this the body of your husband?"

Catherina broke down sobbing, whilst Rudolph comforted her.

"Yes Doctor Craft," Catherina answered through her tears, "that still body lying there is my husband."

"Then Madam," replied Dr.Craft, "I will complete the necessary documentation including the death certificate and arrange to ship the body back to you in Heidelberg for burial. The cause of death is known, so there is no need for the formality of a post-mortem. There is no need for you to accompany the coffin unless want to, I can make alternative arrangements."

"Dr.Craft," answered Catherina, "I would rather not accompany the coffin, as this would be a reminder of the sadness I feel. Can I be notified when the coffin has arrived at Heidelberg, and in the meantime I will make the funeral arrangements."

"Very well Madam," replied Dr.Craft, "leave everything to me. May I say I am sorry for your loss?"

"Goodbye Dr.Craft," replied Catherina, "thank you for your kindness. I appreciate that."

The young couple left the Mortuary with Rudolph hugging Catherina who was still very upset at the death of her husband. Tears of joy and sorrow filled her eyes. Rudolph kissed her eyes and took the tears away.

Once outside in cold Euston Road, they would change from being mourners and become tourists. They had a chance to see the sights of London. They hailed a taxi and visited the Albert Memorial, Buckingham Palace and the Tower of London. They had lunch in a very good Restaurant. Catherina was relieved that at last she could relax, be herself at last. This was something she had not done for a long time, as her late husband Johann only took her to places to show her off as his lovely wife. They had never visited an interesting City unless it had been on a business trip and that was only in Germany. She had never left the Fatherland, and this trip to England had been a breathe of fresh air, with new sites and sounds. Here she was with the new man in her life acting like a tourist, taking an interest in her feelings and loving her for herself. They were in a foreign country and she felt marvellous, as if a great weight had been taken from her slender shoulders. Her face filled with colour and she was free at last to enjoy life to the full, for she was the Princess and Rudolph her Prince Charming.

The day seemed to end so quickly, they were enjoying themselves so much. The sun began to set as they made their way back to the Waldorf Hotel for Dinner. That night they made passionate love, with Catherina naked under her silver fox furs and she aroused her lover just as before. That night their lovemaking knew no bounds. She felt that she had laid the ghosts of the past and now could get on with her life at last; she could have a proper relationship with a man she loved above all others. The journey home to Germany was less traumatic; the lovers in sexual union for every moment that they could. The only thing left to do from her past life was to bury her husband.

On arriving home, a letter awaited them addressed to Catherina, it had a London postmark. What could this be she wondered opened it? She read it quickly, and then passed it to Rudolph. Rudolph could see that Catherina was upset, as he began to read the letter. It was from a Henrietta Bonallack, from Flat 2, Glenholm Mews, Kensington. Henrietta explained that she had been Johann's mistress for some years, she had heard of his death. She had read the report of the train crash and the names of the dead in the Newspapers. As her money supply had dried up she was asking for money to pay the rent on the London Flat. Rudolph shook his head in disbelief as he passed the letter back to Catherina, who started to cry. She put her head on Rudolph's shoulder.

"Darling how could Johann treat me so badly, and have the audacity to have a foreign mistress," she stuttered through her tears,

"I am both sad and very angry. How dare she expect me to pay her rent? How dare she, how dare she?"

Rudolph tried to console her.

"That my darling is the past, we have the future before us now."

"You are right my love," said Catherina as she tore the letter into little pieces and threw it into the fireplace.

She threw her arms around Rudolph and whispered in his ear.

"Damn this Henrietta Bonallack to hell, she will never get a pfennig from me. Let us forget her and go to bed and make love under my furs."

Rudolph smiled as she led him to her Bedroom for pure unadulterated love.

Two days later Catherina had a telephone call to tell her that the body of Johann arrived at Heidelberg. A funeral was quickly arranged, as Rudolph had to return to work. Catherina decided to invite her parents to the funeral. They replied that they were reluctant to come as they felt they could not pay their respects to a man who had treated their daughter with such disdain. However, at the last minute, they changed their minds. Rudolph wondered how George and Ingrid would receive him, for Catherina had spoken little about her Mother.

The Funeral was held a week later on a Saturday in Catherina's local church. Catherina's parents sat at the back of the church in the last row of pews, as if they wanted to distance themselves from the service-taking place. There were just a few mourners in the little church in Rohrbach, for Johann had only a few friends, and although Catherina had contacted them, not one of them came to the funeral. In the front row on one side sat the house servants, whilst in the pews on the other side sat Catherina in her silver fox furs holding hands with Rudolph. Father Hans Heinrich conducted the service, and whilst Catherina had spoken to him regarding saying a few words during the service, with recent events she felt she could not. The service was somewhat brief and having finished, Catherina introduced Rudolph to her parents. They were not at all, as he imagined them. They were very friendly and said that they were delighted that their daughter had found a young man who would love their Catherina as she deserved.

The coffin was taken outside carried by four of the servants, to the little graveyard that surrounded the Church. It was followed by Catherina and Rudolph, George and Ingrid. Catherina and Ingrid pulled their furs around them against the cold wind. Father Heinrich said a few words at the graveside as the coffin was lowered into the ground

The cars that had brought them from the house took Catherina and Rudolph and now with George and Ingrid back to the house.

Here two couples sat down and had long conversation. Catherina's late husband Johann was not capable of reasonable conversation. As the afternoon wore on Catherina's parents warmed to Rudolph, for here was a young man with personality, drive and a real love for their only child, his future with Mercedes was rosy. Ingrid said it was a shame she had not met Rudolph before she met and married that monster Johann. They invited him to spend time with them at their home in Heidelberg when time allowed. His parents asked many questions, but Rudolph was still evasive. He would only say that he did have some news for them soon. The day that Catherina was dreading had passed so quickly and the hour was drawing late, so Rudolph took his leave of Catherina parents and said he hoped to see them soon. He gave Catherina a long passionate kiss and then returned to the Schloss.

Then it was back to work and the difficult job of getting the cars in tiptop shape. Early morning testing and stripping of the cars to ensure, all the new parts were working perfectly began again. Then one morning, Rudolph and Hermann were called into Gustav's Office. With Gustav was one of the Company Directors Albert Himmler. Rudolph knew him only by sight, as he was involved a Sales Director in another part of the Company works. The both looked very serious. Rudolph hoped that he was not in some sort of trouble. Thoughts flashed through mind. He had been away for a week. What could have happened? Why wasn't Hermann there now? His questions were soon to be answered.

"Rudolph," said Gustav, "please come in and sit down, do not look so worried; you are not in any trouble. Let me explain."

He picked up the telephone and spoke to his Secretary.

"Please send in three cups of coffee, and no calls."

He put the telephone down and looked straight at Rudolph.

"As you may know my friend," continued Gustav, "we had hoped to supply our new engine to the Zeppelin Company for their new Airships. It seems that our rivals Maybach have won the tender. Your friend Hermann Ritter has decided, in his wisdom, to join that Company in their development section."

Rudolph wondered what other revelations there would be, and how the change would affect him. Rudolph thought he better say something.

"This is all news to me Mr.Schumann, for as you know I have been away to England to help a very good friend collect a dead body. Of course wish Hermann luck at Maybach."

Then all of a sudden he saw Gustav's face changed, Rudolph realised that he had said the wrong thing.

"Well Rudolph, I do not wish him any luck at all, I am angry, not at you Rudolph. You are a loyal employee and a credit to the Company. He was a good driver and we have lost him. We shall have to find a replacement and he has to be German. That is the present Company policy. What I would like you to do is this. Go to as many of the smaller races as you can. Try to spot a new driver that you consider worthy of joining us. Take as much time as you like at weekends and use a Company Car, and even go with a lady friend. Please feel free to see me at any time, should you see anyone with talent or who can be trained, if they are not German we shall have to assess their potential."

Rudolph had not told him about Catherina, he knew that soon he would have to.

On his next weekend visit to Catherina, he told her about Hermann's defection to Maybach and how Gustav had asked him to find a replacement. Would she come with him to a race? She said she would love too, providing Otto; the chauffeur did the driving, for they could snuggle up together in the back of the car. Rudolph agreed. There was a race the following day run over part of the old Kaiserpries circuit, with the start at Wehrheim. This Rudolph said would give him the chance to scan the entry for talented drivers. It was a race for amateur owners and drivers. Rudolph picked up the telephone and called the organisers. All was arranged for Catherine and Rudolph to be guests of honour at the event.

Early on the Sunday morning, they breakfasted and dressed in their warmest furs and were met outside by Otto. It was a lovely April morning, but there was still a chill in the air.

The big Mercedes roared into life as they set out on the 120 kilometres to the start of the event. The journey took them just under two hours; a dust cloud followed them most of the way. It had been a dry spring so far. On arrival at the start the President of the Organising Committee an Adolf von Stern met them. He was thrilled that the top driver from Mercedes and his lady would be gracing their amateur event. Rudolph told him that the winner of the event would be given a test drive with Mercedes. This would be in addition to the Trophy and cash of 150,000 marks. He would also like the names of the two runners up, as they might be worth considering as Test Drivers.

The race was over 4 laps of a course of some 40 kilometres. There were 24 entries a mixture of Adlers, Fiats, Mercedes and Opels. Some were spotless; others looked as if they had seen better days. Rudolph having seen some of the cars wondered if they would last one lap.

Adolf showed Catherina and Rudolph around the pit area; Rudolph thought what a vast difference to the professional race pits, for it looked so basic. These fellows were doing it for the love of the sport. Adolf handed Rudolph a race programme and he glanced down the list of entries. Only two were non-German drivers. The fastest in practice was Fritz Lang; he was young and very quick. He drove an immaculate 1906 Model '60' that sounded better than new. Rudolph thought that this was one driver to keep an eye open for in the race, that was due to start in about 15 minutes. There was a big roar from the large crowd of some 5,000 that lined either side of the dusty straight road, as the cars went down to the start line to await the fall of the starter's flag. Rudolph noticed that Catherina was getting quite excited.

"This is really quite thrilling my love," said Catherina, "I must come and watch you when you race."

Rudolph put his arms around her and kissed her full on the lips.

"My Darling Catherina, it would be wonderful if you will be at my side when I race."

The starter mounted a bank at the side of the road, raised the German flag and brought it down with a flourish. The noise from the cars was deafening as they engaged gear and sped into the distance. Then all was quiet for a while until the first car hove into view. It was Fritz Lang; he already had a good lead over Manfred Wurtz in an Opel, closely followed by Ralf Shultz in another Model '60'. The rest were miles behind. After 4 laps, the three of them were very close together Fritz winning by just 3 seconds. Catherina presented the trophies and even kissed the winner. Rudolph went over and spoke to all three, inviting them to the Mercedes factory for interviews.

They were absolutely thrilled, saying that they looked forward to meeting Rudolph at the factory. The day ended with Adolf inviting his guests of honour for tea at a local Hotel. Adolf was very interested in the way professional teams were run; he was delighted to meet the lovely Catherina and hoped they would meet again soon. Rudolph and Catherina took their leave of Adolf then made their way back to her home, which she would now share with the love of her life.

On Monday morning Rudolph went into Gustav's office and told him the story of his visit to the Motor Race on Sunday. He slipped out the fact that he had taken a very lovely lady with him.

"This lovely lady Rudolph," asked Gustav, "will she be a permanent item in your life?"

"Well, I do hope so. She is a lovely lady with a very gentle and loving nature."

"Excellent," replied Gustav, "now to the race you visited yesterday, this Fritz Lang and the other two young men you mentioned, do you think they will be able to meet our high standards?"

"Gustav, they looked to have great potential, especially Fritz. I have invited them for interview to ascertain their mechanic knowledge and a driving test tomorrow. They all live in the Rhine Valley, Fritz lives in Karlsruhe."

The following morning, bright and early Fritz Lang arrived for his interview. Gustav and Rudolph conducted it, they were happy with what he had to say for he was quite familiar with the mechanics of the motorcar. The interview over, it was time to find out his driving talents. Rudolph took him on the factory test route. This covered all types of terrain away from civilisation. It covered 50 kilometres and normally took Rudolph about 20 minutes. It took Fritz about 5 minutes to get used to the 'Model 90', which was quite a handful to say the least. They whizzed around the circuit and were back in 22 minutes. Rudolph was impressed, for Fritz was both quick and safe. They walked back to the Office where Rudolph gave Gustav a report on the trial run. Gustav suggested that Fritz went to his office and had a coffee. Later in the morning, the other two drivers that Rudolph thought may be suitable, Manfred and Ralf arrived together, and they had come by train. They both showed up well at interview and on the road circuit were within one minute of Fritz's time. Gustav was very impressed indeed. Finding three drivers was indeed a bonus so he decided employing all of them. They were all trained engineers, two were working the other Ralf had been recently made redundant. Soon the new boys were put to work. Gustav had a system and he stuck rigidly to it, for this was his secret of success.

At the end of that week, Rudolph and Catherina decided to announce their engagement.

Rudolph had casually mentioned to his parents that he had a lady friend, but did not tell them that it was a serious affair. It felt that was now time for them to meet Catherina. He did not know how this news would be received. When could he tell them the truth about Catherina? May be in a week or so, when his parents had got used to the idea that their son would soon be married. Rudolph arrived home on the Friday night for his weekend leave, he sat down with his parents after dinner and told them that he had met the most wonderful woman in the world and wanted to marry her. He would like to bring her home so they could meet her. At first, his Mother was a little shocked, as this seemed a sudden decision, because Margarita and Josef had been introduced 'properly' as she put it through friends. They had 'courted' for about two years before getting engaged.

"Well my son," said Josef, "if you adore this lady so much and you think that marriage to her will make you both happy. Then certainly you have my blessing. Do you agree Mother?"

"Yes my love," replied Margarita, "we would love to meet her. Why not bring her over tomorrow for lunch and we can meet her properly She can stay for the weekend, sleeping in the Guest Room."

"Thank you mother," replied Rudolph feeling relieved, "thank you both I am sure that you will adore her."

The next day Rudolph drove over to Catherina's house, she was thrilled that at last their love could be in the open. Now there were no more secrets. She was really excited at meeting Rudolph's parents at last. Rudolph had told her all about them, so she would feel she would be not meeting strangers. She donned her most attractive dress, not one that would make her look 'overdressed', put on one of her fur coats and then climbing aboard Rudolph's car they set off for Schloss Lundenberg. The Count and Countess who welcomed her to their home met them at the top of the steps. They all sat down in the Morning Room and coffee was served.

Rudolph's parents wanted to know all about Catherina. Rudolph had already discussed with her what she should say at this stage, leaving out their lovemaking escapades, plus the fact that, when they met she was still married. They would not lie; just withhold the truth until a more appropriate time. Catherina was very beautiful indeed; Josef and Margarita took to her immediately, something they rarely did. She told them that a close relative had recently passed away and had left her in his will, a very profitable shipping business in Northern Germany, together with several wineries in the Rhine Valley.

She owned her own house with servants and was very deeply in love with Rudolph. They had met on a train when she was travelling alone from a business meeting. She had asked Rudolph if she could share his compartment, he looked kind and thoughtful; she was concerned that travelling alone a male passenger might accost her. He was her 'White Knight'. Rudolph pulled a small leather box out of his pocket and gave it to Catherina. She opened it her and her eyes lit up, inside was the engagement ring, it was absolutely dazzling. In the centre was a large Emerald surrounded with an array of Diamonds. Catherina slid it on her finger and then kissed Rudolph. Count Josef and Margarita were very surprised at their son's sudden engagement. Josef having recovered his composure went over to Catherina and hugged and kissed her. Margarita could see that Catherina and their son were very happy.

"Catherina," said Josef, "welcome to our family. I can tell you love our son very much, I can see it in your eyes."

Then Margarita also hugged and kissed Catherina.

"Catherina," said Margarita with tears of joy in her eyes, "I know you will make my son happy. I have not lost a son, but gained a beautiful daughter-in-law. We will arrange a party soon. Can I ask when you plan to marry?"

Rudolph looked at Catherina who looked very surprised.

"Catherina and I did talk about this," said Rudolph, "when I asked her to marry me. As for the wedding, we shall have to fit it in between races. We thought perhaps the first Sunday in June if we can arrange the ceremony?"

"Excellent" said Josef, "then we can arrangements for the engagement party here at the Schloss and later the wedding. I do hope that you are getting married in our local Church?"

"Yes Father," replied Rudolph looking at Catherina who was radiant.

"I will speak to the local priest Father Reinhardt tomorrow," said Josef, "and arrange everything together with the wedding breakfast. This will be a wonderful occasion for us all."

The Butler came in to announce that lunch was served. In the back of his mind Josef hoped that Rudolph would find a young lady and settle down, may be they would have a son to carry on the dynasty of the von Lundenberg's. Catherina was thrilled that she had created a very good impression with Rudolph's parents. She had been worried about this for a while

The weekend seemed to fly by, although sleeping in separate beds was something new to both Rudolph and Catherina. The weeks flew by and before they knew it the day of the wedding dawned.

It was the 7th June 1908, and the little village church at Weisloch was filled to overflowing with guests and the whole place was filled with flowers. Catherina's parents, George and Ingrid looked delighted that finally their beautiful daughter and her beloved Rudolph were getting married. It was a glorious June morning, the sun shone down from a cloudless blue sky. The Bride and Groom had been up for hours getting ready for their big day. Catherina looked absolutely stunning in her pure white silk bridal gown trimmed with lace and its long train. A fine lace veil would cover her face.

She had spent her last night as a single lady in one of the Guest Bedrooms. From tomorrow, she thought I will sleep with the man I really love. Originally, Rudolph had hoped that Hermann would be his best man, now he had moved away, that was a problem.

When he told Gustav of his engagement, he was not so surprised, he knew that there was a lady in the background. Rudolph asked his Team Manager to be his best man and of course, his wife was invited too. Gustav said he would be delighted to act in that capacity and that his wife Elizabeth would be thrilled to be there.

Gustav lived in a modest house on the outskirts of Stuttgart; he had been married for about 18 years. They had not ever been to a wedding like this. Rudolph suggested that they arrived on Friday and stayed for the weekend. The Castle had plenty of bedrooms. Therefore, everything was in order, for the best man had the rings and the bride ready. Gustav and Rudolph walked down to the local church to join the congregation. They sat in the front row to await the arrival of the bride. Father Reinhardt Gessler had been the village priest for only two years. His predecessor Father Helmut Zuller had been holding services in the little church even before Rudolph was born. In fact, he had officiated at the wedding of Josef and Margarita and was a family friend. He had retired to Bavaria where he continued his hobby of landscape painting. Father Reinhardt had soon become a part of village life; he was short with fair hair and really cared for his parishioners. The organ played whilst the hubbub of conversation continued, then it struck up "The Wedding March" by Beethoven, as the bride escorted by Count Josef entered the Church. Everyone turned around to see her walk up the aisle. Catherina felt a glow inside, this was her day. At last she would be joined in holy matrimony and would become part of a real family at last. The service all went to plan. The happy couple was showered with rice as they passed under an arch of copper pipes that Gustav had brought along.

The Banqueting Hall rang to the sound of laughter whilst a band played on a small stage. Rudolph introduced Gustav to his parents and guests. All the team drivers had arrived for the Wedding Party. Catherina and Rudolph said it was the happiest day of their lives. Then it was time for the Bride and Groom to set off on their honeymoon.

The big white Mercedes was decked with streamers and a large banner that read: JUST MARRIED. As they waved goodbye to the assembled guests, Margarita started to shed a tear, a tear of happiness. The newlyweds were to spend their honeymoon on the shores of Lake Zurich in the tiny resort of Meilen. Here at the Grand Hotel they had a beautiful room en-suite with a balcony that gave a wonderful view of the Lake. They swam in the Hotel Pool, motored around the mountains and made passionate love to their hearts content. These were happy days, which they were to recall when darker days came into their lives.

The end of the honeymoon came all too soon and it was back to reality, for Rudolph work at Canstatt. There was a lot still to do for the next race was only week or so away. Catherina was now back home and deliriously happy with her new husband. The old servants were retained, and felt warmth towards Rudolph, and life settled down once more. Catherina now knew happiness that before was denied her, and Rudolph thrilled with his new wife who he loved and adored and she him. They decided, whilst on honeymoon that they should buy a small house near the factory, so they could be together everyday rather than just weekends.

Two weeks later Rudolph moved in to Catherina's home, now they were together at last. There were many aspects of Catherina's life that Rudolph did not yet know. She was now able to share with him the Business Empire left to her in her husband's will, and indulge in all the other pleasures previous denied her. This would be her future as well as Rudolph's, they were now a team that would surmount all obstacles and their love would stand the test of time.

Josef and Margarita were frequent visitors to Rudolph and Catherina's home, they could see how happy they were together and this gave them a warm feeling inside.

Chapter 10

Since their return from their Egyptian honeymoon, life had been idyllic for Dino and his lovely wife Carla. She had never known such happiness, her job at the Bank meant she could spend as much time with her new husband as she liked. Not long after they returned Carla became pregnant, she and gave birth to a son Dino Gulliermo on 10th October 1906. He was a happy child, the Bank was sympathetic and Dino only went on a few long trips during the early part of 1907. True he visited Venice, Milan and Turin and when possible he took Carla and baby Dino with him. They stayed in the best hotels, and Carla loved Venice particularly in the spring. They bought a house in the village of Fiesole early in the autumn of 1907 and celebrated little Dino's birthday there, with a party for the local children. Carla had enjoyed choosing the decor and the furnishings for their new home. There was a small garden to the rear of the house and Carla even redesigned that too. She liked everything to be just so, in this her first home with her new husband. They planned a small summerhouse at the end of the garden, for then it would enjoy sweeping panoramic views across the Arno Valley towards Florence. It was certainly a beautiful spot. For in summer, they could escape to their retreat from the heat and humidity of the City, and delight in the cooler breezes that would filter down from the Tuscany Apennines, whilst Florence sweltered in the heat of the day.

By late spring 1908, everything was complete, a rose garden had been planted, and by May, the builders and decorators had left. This was the Borghese's dream house, with room for guests and a playroom for young Dino, now growing up fast. In June, Carla thought that she and her husband would now have a summer they could share together. He had not been away on a long trip for weeks now.

One day Dino came home and told Carla that the Bank was sending him on a special course for 3 weeks. It would be held in Rome and would be residential, although he would be staying in a Hotel; Carla would not be able to join him.

She was sad, but accepted the inevitable. On June 30th he left for Rome from Florence Railway Station, Carla and Dino Jnr. were there to see him off on his journey. A few tears were shed, as the Rome Express steamed out of the station, and disappeared up the line. Dino settled down in his seat, opened his briefcase, and started to read the paperwork about the course that he had to take. The journey was uneventful, and he was staying at Grand Hotel in the centre of Rome. Dino checked in and the reception clerk gave him his key, and the bellboy led Dino to his room. He tipped the bellboy, unpacked, and headed for the shower, then down to the Restaurant for the evening meal.

The Restaurant was a large room with a high ceiling, over to one side was a small stage and to create an intimate atmosphere the management had placed potted palms and flowering plants to create colour. In the centre, was a large fish tank and the whole place had an air of opulence. The Restaurant was full, so Dino approached the maitre d'hôte to enquire about an available table. Close by there was a table for two, with a vacant chair. Seated opposite the empty chair was a very attractive lady, who appeared to be dining alone. The maitre d'hôte asked Dino to wait a moment, he would ask the lady if she was expecting a guest to fill the empty seat. The maitre d'hôte went over and spoke to the lady. Dino could not quite hear what was said, but he did hear the word Countess. The maitre d'hôte returned to where Dino was still waiting.

"The Countess," said the maitre d'hote "would be delighted if you would join her for dinner. I will return to the table to take your order when you are ready."

He turned and walked away. As he got closer to the table Dino had not taken a good look at his dining companion, but as he was about to sit down, he decided to greet her.

"Good evening Countess, I am sorry to intrude on your privacy. I hope that you do not mind that I share this table with you?"

He then took a good look at his dining companion. She was the loveliest woman that he had ever seen, her complexion was perfect. She had the most penetrating blue eyes; her long blonde hair was swept up was held by a diamond clasp. Around her neck hung a multi-strand row of real pearls; her dress was embroidered with precious stones that glinted in the glow of the lights of the Restaurant. Her breasts were perfectly shaped, and in her cleavage on a solid gold chain hung a large diamond and emerald brooch.

Her clothes thought Dino must have cost a small fortune. She looked at Dino and smiled sweetly as Dino sat down.

"Good evening Signor," she replied, "it will be a pleasure to have you as my table guest. I am in Rome for 3 weeks and I like to see the Opera and the Theatre. I live in Venice and if I may be so bold, to tell you that my name is Maria."

Dino introduced himself, and told her that he was in Rome on Banking Business. The conversation then began to flow freely and they enjoyed their sumptuous meal. When they had finished their after dinner drink, the Countess asked Dino to escort her to her room. She was fatigued, having travelled from Venice that day, she felt tired and wanted to sleep. They arrived at the door of her room and as they were about to part, she turned to Dino.

"Dino, why don't you come in for a night-cap?"

"I would love to Maria," he replied.

They entered Maria's room; it was not on the same floor as Dino's or in the same class. Maria had rented a suite of rooms that was the finest the Hotel could provide.

"Now Dino, I am just going to slide into something more comfortable. Please, make yourself at home and be a darling, pour me a drink. I would just love a Martini with ice and Lemon and whatever you would like."

Dino walked over to the massive drink cabinet and poured out Maria's Martini and one for himself.

Maria reappeared from the bedroom wearing a very revealing; almost see through nightdress and negligee, which left very little to the imagination. Dino could now see her breasts were full, and inviting with a deep cleavage. She went over to the sofa and patting the cushion beside her.

"Dino, come over sit by me and relax. It seems to me that you have a very demanding course ahead of you. So in the evenings, if you were not too busy, I would simply love you to accompany me. I am here in Rome all alone, it is my first visit and I need a man to protect me and show me the sights. I will cover all the expenses and be extremely grateful."

Dino said that he would enjoy showing her Rome, for he knew it quite well. They chatted for a while, then slowly but surely, Maria moved closer to Dino. Then Maria put her arm around Dino, and kissed him full on the lips with her tongue searching inside his mouth. Up to this point Dino had made no advances, but it seemed to him that Maria was about to open the floodgates of passion. Dino responded, then wondered if he had done the right thing.

He had a quick thought or two about his wife Carla, and his baby son back home in Fiesole. Then his Latin temperament took over, the odd kiss or two would be harmless enough. In any case, who would know apart from the lady herself, and she was not likely to meet Carla was she? Dino was surprised at Maria's direct approach; she was a world apart from some of the ladies of his acquaintance, prior to his marriage to Carla. Was he out of his depth with this mystery woman? He was soon about to find out. Little did he know then what the Countess Maria had in mind for him; she had barely scratched the surface, so to speak. She wanted to see what response she could get from this red-blooded Italian boy. It was almost exactly as if she had planned it, and written the script herself. She was very manipulative, as Dino would later find out to his cost.

However, for now, to Dino it was a bit of fun with a lovely lady, who after his trip to Rome could be forgotten. Maria on the other hand, was using a different set of rules. She began to caress Dino's thigh, then her hand slid higher to his crotch. Dino started to relax his guard, responding by rubbing his palm across her breasts. Maria sighed with contentment; she loved this, and her eyes closed. Suddenly she got up, and this startled Dino.

"I am sorry Maria, have I offended you in some way?"

Maria just smiled and wiggled her ample figure.

"My darling Dino, you are a naughty boy," she said sexily, "I think it is about time you slipped into something more comfortable. Why don't you freshen up our drinks?"

Dino freshen the drinks as she led him into the bedroom, where he put the drinks on a dressing table. Maria then helped him undress. Dino started to feel ill at ease, but tried not to show it. He kept telling himself that after 3 weeks this affair would end and that it would be history.

At that very moment, his conscience went out of the window, and he threw caution to the winds. Maria helped him throw it too. Maria had already unbuttoned his trousers that were soon around his ankles. Her eager fingers sought out the thing she really wanted inside her, and that was quickly revealed. She played with it, whilst Dino tried to remove his underpants.

This was the kind of foreplay that Dino loved; he started to forget Carla, as his passion plus his male muscle rose to the occasion. Maria was an expert at foreplay; she placed Dino's hand between her legs, whispering instructions in Dino's ear. Dino followed these instructions to the letter, while Maria sighed with pleasure.

Maria then lifted the hem of her night-gown and Dino could now see her soft spot. She told Dino that it was there for him to use, as he wanted. She had played him like a fish on a hook. He could not wait any longer; he had to satisfy her and himself. He entered her, wrapping her legs around him, while he carried her over to the bed. She rode him hard and long, she was determined that he would have the best sex of his life. That he would be back for more every night, not only for the 3 weeks, but long after they had left Rome. Dino had not enjoyed a woman like this for years. He had decided that she was better in the bedroom than Carla had ever been. He had come to this decision after the first night. Now he was reaching new heights of sexual fantasy, and this was real. He was certain that his affair could be kept secret. Little did he know that Maria had other plans for Dino? They both came to climax keeping going until they were completely exhausted. Maria had a sexual appetite that had to be satisfied and Dino might well be the man to do it.

Maria turned to Dino and kissed him passionately.

"Darling," she gasped, "that was the most wonderful sexual experience, I have ever had."

They fell asleep there and then. Dino had dreams that he was still making love to Maria until the morning sun started shining through the windows. Dino woke up with a start. He looked around and realised where he was. Maria was still fast asleep. Dino looked across at the clock on the mantelpiece, it was 7.30 am, he dressed quickly, and then made his way back to his room. Here he showered, then hurried down for breakfast. By the time he had finished, Maria was still nowhere to be seen. So, Dino made his way to the Reception, where asked the Doorway to call him a taxi. He arrived at the Bank of Italy building with plenty of time to spare, then made his way to the room where the course was being held. The day seemed to drag by, his mind was not completely on his work; it was in that room in the Hotel with Maria. When he arrived back at the Hotel, Maria was sitting in the Hotel Lounge. She wandered over to him, gave him a long lingering kiss.

"Hi there Cara Mia," she said, "had a good day? I think we should go to my suite and have a little rest and relax. It will do you the world of good."

Dino did not need a second invitation; he knew exactly what she meant. They spent time together making love; it certainly took away Dino's stress. Later down in the Restaurant, Maria insisted on paying for the meal.

"It is my pleasure," she cooed.

That night was exactly like their first one together. Dino was absolutely infatuated with Maria, who knew how to please him. She was a nymphomaniac; she could not get enough of Dino's body. Every night was the same, during the day at weekends they would go for a drive into the country, find a lonely spot, and then make love under the summer sun. It was idyllic. By now, Dino had almost forgotten Carla, although he did telephone her once every week. She said she missed him terribly and was longing so much for him to return home. Finally, the course ended and the lovers had to part. Maria had invited Dino into her web like a Spider attracts a fly. After dinner on his last night, they enjoyed one final night of sexual pleasure; this one topped all the others by far. Maria knew she had Dino hooked now; she would draw him into her life. She had yet to play her ace; she had time and could wait. Dino would be a willing student, and she would be the dominant teacher.

On the Saturday morning, they both checked out of the Hotel sharing a taxi to Rome Station. Maria had told Dino very little about her private life, perhaps one day she would. He guessed she had been married at some time, but she had never mentioned a husband at any time, even during their most sexual moments. They would be travelling on the same train to Florence, where Maria would stay on the train that went on to Venice Mestre. They wanted to make love on the train, but it was too crowded. During the journey, Maria told Dino, that she had been widowed some two years earlier when her husband, Marco had drowned in a boating accident. He was rich, and owned several wineries together with businesses in other countries. The train slowed as it approached Florence, Maria kissed Dino goodbye, and she intimated that she would see him again. Now Dino had to face Carla, he could see her waiting for him at the barrier. It was back to reality, but for how long? He strolled slowly along the platform, thinking about those nights of sexual pleasures with Maria. He now knew that she was rich, had a forceful personality and of course, heaven in bed. He could not tell Carla anything about his trip, for the consequences for his marriage would be dire. Maria was well ahead of him now; luckily Maria did not know what Carla looked like. Carla did give a glance, to a very attractive blonde woman in a rather expensive coat that passed her. She waved as Dino came closer; Carla opened her arms they held each other tightly and kissed passionately.

Carla was delighted to see her husband; this was the longest that they had ever been apart. Carla asked Dino about his course. Dino decided that least said soonest mended would be the best action to take, so he told Carla that it was very interesting and informative, and would no doubt help his promotional prospects at the Bank. He told her that he had burnt a good deal of midnight oil, but at the end of it all he had emerged with flying colours. In his heart, he yearned to see Maria again; she had created a big impression on him, doubtless that was due to the fact that she laid on top of him during lovemaking. Dino smiled as this thought passed him by.

Carla meanwhile, had not been sexual satisfied for over three weeks, so she and Dino had some very wild sexual capers. At one stage, Carla wondered where Dino had learned some new foreplay; after all, they had been married for some time, and she thought she knew all of Dino's techniques. Perhaps, she thought he is trying something different because he missed me. However, Dino could not get Maria out of his mind; she was rich, beautiful and paradise in bed.

Young Dino was growing up fast and was a real handful, demanding constant attention. Therefore, Carla decided to employ a nanny. She would be careful not to have one too attractive, as she might be competing for her husband's affections. If pretty she could attract young men to come calling. She hired Sofia, a plain but sensible young woman with good credentials. Young Dino took to her, and she played with him for hours. This certainly freed up time for Carla, who could now relax more knowing that her son was safe.

Several weeks passed, Dino was worried; he had heard nothing from Maria. He was certain that his fling with her for three weeks was just that. He had not forgotten her. Had she forgotten him?

He became despondent; even Carla noticed his change of mood. She asked what was wrong. He told her that nothing was wrong; it was just the strain and pressures of the job. Then one day a pile of mail arrived on his desk. He sorted through the envelopes; among them was one bearing a coat of arms. It was a crest that, he did not recognise, it had been sprayed with a perfume that he did not immediately recall. Who could have sent this letter?

He put the other correspondence aside. He carefully slit open the letter addressed to him as private and confidential. The letter was from Maria; she expressed her undying passion for him in the most explicit terms. She also invited him to spend a weekend with her in Venice; this would be the weekend after next. If he would not come to her, Maria would come to visit him. On top of that she would 'spill the beans' about their affair in Rome, to his wife. That would no doubt help end his marriage. This letter worried Dino. What could he do? He was caught in a difficult situation. What excuse could he give Carla? Would she believe him? He had no answer to these questions. If the affair continued, then he would have to lie to Carla. If he tried to end the affair, then he would be subject to sexual blackmail. As he was trying to compose himself, the telephone rang, it was the receptionist.

"Signor Borghese," she said, "you have a private call, it is a lady. She would not give her name, but she says she knows you."

"Hello, my beloved," said the lady on the line, "have you received my letter?"

Dino recognised the voice as Maria's.

"Yes Maria, I have your letter in front of me."

"Don't get upset, my sweetness," said Maria sexily, "I am saving my body just for you. See you in Venice on Friday week. I'll be waiting ready for your love and your body."

Dino really did not know how to answer, but then capitulated.

"Very well my love," he answered, "I will see you at the Villa on Friday."

Maria blew him a kiss over the telephone and hung up. Dino had committed himself now. What excuse could he give Carla for going to Venice?

The days passed, it seemed that Dino was no nearer to a solution to his problem. Then an idea came to him.

He would tell Carla that he had to visit his cousin Luigi. He told Carla that Luigi had been unwell and he wanted Dino to resolve some of his financial problems.

True, Luigi lived in Venice, but he was not ill, nor were his finances in a poor state, for he was an Accountant. Anyway, Carla always believed her husband. So far she had suspected nothing.

On that fateful Friday morning, Dino had packed his case and said goodbye to Carla. As he was leaving for the office, he told her that he would be catching a train at lunchtime so that he could be at Luigi's by nightfall.

Dino sat at his desk, the morning seemed to drag by, and he was excited at the prospect of seeing Maria again. At midday, he told his Secretary that he was going away for the weekend and he could not be contacted. He took a taxi to the Station, bought his ticket and boarded the Venice train. He settled back into his seat, he then daydreamed about the forthcoming sexual activities that he would perform with Maria. He felt quite excited, as the train sped on to its destination. Maria's villa was but a thirty-minute taxi ride from Venice Station. Now, as the taxi drove along, Dino wondered what entertainment Maria had prepared for him. The taxi pulled up outside Maria's villa. She was waiting for him, dressed in one of her very provocative fur trimmed outfits. The taxi driver smiled as he drove away. Maria threw her arms around him, kissing him as her tongue searched the inside of his mouth.

"I knew you would come," she whispered, "my body just yearns for you. I have been so lonely since we parted in Rome. I will show you to your room."

Maria grabbed Dino by the hand leading him to an upstairs bedroom. It had an enormous four poster bed and around the wall were large oil paintings by famous artists. The one on the ceiling Dino recognised was by Rubens. Dino was still looking around the room admiring the art and décor.

"I hope you like our room my Dino, I am sure we shall enjoy ourselves amongst the old masters."

Dino walked towards the large picture windows. The view was fantastic, for beyond the driveway was a small walled garden with a fountain playing. The ground sloped gently down to a small copse. Over to his left Dino could see a large landscaped garden.

Whoever had designed and built this beautiful Villa certainly had good taste and plenty of money.

Dino unpacked, and Maria's expression changed. Dino knew she was about to say something serious.

She had moved away from him and sat herself down on a chaise long that was over by the windows.

"Dino," she began, "I would like to tell you a little about my family background."

She told him that the Second Count had built the Villa, in the late 1600's. He was a nobleman who had been a soldier of fortune. He had made his money by hook and by crook, and had married into a rich family. He had inherited the title when his Father the First Count, had been killed in one of those European Wars. The Doges of Venice had awarded the title for services to the City.

Dino looked around the walls that were filled with paintings by Italian masters; they were originals not copies. There were 20 rooms and the décor was of the late 1600's. Maria took her leave and Dino ran a bath. Having soaked away the cares of the day, Dino made his way down to the Library where Maria was waiting for him. That room too was like an Art Gallery. They sat on a sofa and talked of many things. Dino thought it was about time that he confessed to Maria about being a married man. So he explained the situation, whilst Maria listened with interest. Maria seemed to take it all in her stride, after all she was the one who was looking forward to being sexual satisfied. However, in the back of her mind she knew that she wanted to control Dino. So she thought out her answer very carefully rather than cause an argument.

"I fully understand that Dino," she replied, "I do not have a problem with that."

Dino felt much better now. He had got over the marriage problems, so he had thought. However, he had not reckoned with Maria who was an intelligent and a very cunning woman. She would wait her opportunity to pounce like a Cat on a Mouse. Dino did not realise that he was the Mouse. After her husband Marco, had died, she consolidated the business expanding it, controlling her Clients with the skills she had learned from her husband. She told him that on the next day, they would be guests at a grand party in a Palace on Grand Canal. There would be some influential people there.

Dino discovered that here was a woman who was intelligent and beautiful, although Dino tried to resist her; he found he had fallen for her charms and was hopelessly in love with her.

That night Maria gave Dino the sort of sexual experiences he could expect if their arrangement became permanent. Dino gave it all he had, but Maria wanted more, that meant they got very little sleep, but plenty of sexual exercise.

They bathed together the next morning and by mid-morning they were ready to go to the Party. This was from Noon until late. A Carriage took them to the Lagoon, where a Gondola carried them to the steps that led into the Palace. The Party was one of the events of the Venetian social calendar. The guests were not so much quantity as quality. Maria introduced Dino to a Count Benito di Fontazo, who was besotted with the Motor Racing, and had recently become a Director of the FIAT Motor Company. He spoke at length to Dino, who had a FIAT, himself now.

The Count asked Dino if he followed Motor Sport. Would he be interested in driving for the factory on an amateur basis? Dino said he would love to. It looked so exciting, much better than working for a Bank. The Count said he would make enquiries and write to Dino at the Bank.

The guests were now invited into a Banqueting room where a feast was laid out before them. It was a triumph of gastronomic artistry. Dino eat and drank the finest fare he had every consumed. A quartet played in a corner to soothe the gastric juices. The Party went on late into the night. There were a number of beautiful women at this event, so Maria kept a tight reign on Dino to make sure he did not stray. Dino had no idea that Maria was a very jealous woman, for at the moment she was showing her good side, acting like the perfect lady. She knew exactly what she wanted and would make sure she got it. That night was one that Dino would remember for many years. As the guests took their leave, Maria joined Dino on the balcony above Grand Canal. Together, they watched the lights twinkling and a full moon shining on the water. It was all very romantic. They kissed passionately and Maria took Dino's hand as they made their way down to the steps and on to the gondola and back to the Villa. The next day, Dino had to return to Florence and Carla. Maria knew this and that night their love juices flowed as never before. There followed a night of pure lust, which Dino would long remember. Maria was certain that she had now 'captured' Dino. She would do all in her power to have him for her own. Dino was ecstatic, and reached so many climaxes, he surprised even himself. The next morning they parted, with Maria giving him a final thrust into her body. Dino was very tired and he looked it.

On the way to the Station, in the taxi he tried putting his thoughts together.

What excuse or explanation could he give his wife for his appearance? No doubt, he would think of something. The big problem would be if Carla actually contacted Luigi, for then there would be trouble indeed.

When arrived home Carla hugged and kissed him.

"You look tired very tired my darling," said Carla when their lips parted, "did you have a tough time with Luigi?"

Dino thought carefully before answering.

"Yes my dearest Carla. His accounts were worse state than I thought they would be. At least his health has now improved."

Dino hoped that Carla would not ask too many questions.

He wondered how long he could keep up the pretence. No more was said, and Dino breathed a sigh of relief. He had won round one.

A week or two passed, and then a letter arrived for Dino at the Bank from Benito. It invited Dino to the FIAT factory in Turin on the following Monday at noon. It was fortuitous that Dino had an appointment on that Monday at the Turin branch of the Bank. Now, he could kill two birds with one stone. He chose to travel on Sunday morning catching the direct train and stay overnight in the Michelangelo Hotel. He bade farewell to Carla, who knew he was on a genuine business trip. Dino arrived at the Hotel and checked into the Company suite No.126. He opened the door and went into the Bedroom. He was struck dumb; there in all her naked glory was Maria. She had just emerged from the bath.

"Welcome to Turin, my darling," said Maria.

She sighed. Dino did not know what to say. She approached him, with one arm around his neck and the other unbuttoning his fly and started to arouse him. Dino was dumbfounded. How did Maria know that he would be in Turin? The only answer he could come up with was that Count Benito must have told her. Soon they were both naked and on the bed together. Maria began showing him some new sexually exciting tricks that she had up her sleeve. Later they called room service, after all said Maria; even lovers have to eat.

The next morning after a long night of sexual activity, Dino made his way to the Bank and concluded his business. Maria then met him as they grabbed a taxi and went off to the FIAT factory to see the Count. Maria hoped that the meeting would seal a friendship between the Count and Dino.

The meeting at FIAT went well. Dino told Benito that he would only drive for the factory, as and when his commitments with the Bank would allow. Benito said he would keep in touch, prepare a contract and send it to him at the Bank. Maria was delighted that the two men had got on so well. Benito and his wife Lisa had stood by Maria when her husband had been so tragically killed. Dino had to travel back to Florence straight away, so there was a tearful parting with Maria at Turin Station.

As the days went by Dino wondered if he would ever get a drive with FIAT.

Then one Tuesday he received a letter from Count Benito with a contract to sign, he had been entered into an event organised by the newly formed Motor Club of Florence. The date would be mid-September, and although it was for amateurs it had attracted a first class entry. This would give Dino his first taste of competitive Motor Sport. He was really looking forward to it. Should he take Carla? Would Maria be there? Fortunately, Carla had other plans. She had decided to take young Dino and to visit some friends; she was not that keen on going to a Motor Race meeting. It would be noisy, and no doubt very dusty.

Dino was entered at the back of the field of 50 cars. The winner would receive a large silver trophy and a cash prize of several million lire. All those that finished would get a certificate from the Club. It would be on a time basis, and the winner would be the one that completed the course in the shortest time. The start was in the centre of Florence. The course then ran through the Arno valley to Arrezzo, turned north through Bibbiena and back to Florence via Pontassieve. It was a tough course and would stretch driving ability to the limit. Dino knew most of the roads being used and felt he had a slight advantage. Benito did not expect Dino to win, only put up a good performance. It was a warm September morning as Dino made his way to the starting area. There was Benito with Maria, dressed up in all her finery. Benito greeted Dino and took him over to the car, where the mechanic, was carrying out a few checks. The early starters were already at the start line. Dino had about 30 minutes to wait before he would be starting. The time flashed by, and then he had to he leave to take up his starting position on the line. Maria kissed him and gave him a token. It was a lace handkerchief, just like the knights of old carried into combat to defend their lady's honour. Benito wished him good luck as Dino made his way to the line. Now it was Dino's turn to show his driving skills. At first he took things fairly easy, he was getting used to a different car. Once out in the countryside, he opened the throttle and let the car show what it could do. They soon began passing the drivers who had started before them. Dino felt great, although on some of the corners, the mechanic Georgio was a bit apprehensive as to whether they would complete the course at all. Dino was in his element as he passed car after car. Some had gone off the road, others had broken down. Then he sped across the finish line to the cheers of the crowd.

After a while the results were announced. Dino had finished in third place. The Count and Maria were delighted, and headed off to a local Restaurant to celebrate. After a very sumptuous lunch, Dino before he bade farewell; Maria asked a very personal question as she leaned over to Dino.

"I would simply love to meet your wife and son," she said enthusiastically, "I could come to Florence and you can introduce me as one of your rich customers."

Dino was flabbergasted he was wondering how long it would be before things got out of hand. Dino was delighted with his silver trophy, for now he had proved to FIAT that he could at least race reasonably well. Now Maria had asked this question, whatever answer he gave would be the wrong one. He contained his guilt, but when he arrived home Carla could tell that there was something wrong. She was thrilled that he had won a prize for his efforts and that he would be driving for FIAT. That night over dinner, Dino was quiet, which was unusual for him, plus the fact that they had not made love properly since his trip to Rome. Carla thought that if she dressed up in the clothes that normally turned her husband on, then perhaps things would get back to normal. Carla got Dino got really aroused, and was ready for him to ravish her. They made passionate love, but at the moment of climax he made his first and biggest mistake.

"Darling Maria," Dino called out, "that was wonderful."

Dino realised what he had said, but it was too late. Carla was absolutely stunned. She had just given her body to her husband, and they had enjoyed the most intimate pleasure, and his sudden outburst at the moment of ecstasy, cut her to the quick.

She got very angry and her face and whole demeanour changed.

"Dino, I know you are having an affair, but to call out the name of some tart, when we are in a moment of extreme sexual pleasure is the death blow to our marriage. I am utterly speechless."

Dino knew that his affair was a secret no longer, for now had to pluck up courage to tell Carla that he had met another woman. Almost as soon as he realised that had said that very first word, it was too late to retract it. He knew that he would regret it for the rest of his life with Carla. At first, Carla could hardly believe what she was hearing. Then she put two and two together, and the sum total completely shattered her faith in Dino and their marriage.

First of all, there was Dino's trip to see Luigi and when he returned looking tired and exhausted.

Following that, the fact that he had not called her each evening on his trip to Rome, for this was not like Dino. She was sure that he was faithful and loved her and she in turn adored him. Now she was the mother of his child, this gave him a family responsibility. Why was it all going wrong? She would now confront him to try to find out the truth. Carla sat on the bed beside Dino.

"Dino, I want to know truth about your affair from start to finish, no lies?"

Dino began and told her the whole story, he was a very bad liar, and she could tell that he was bending the truth. By the time he had finished, Carla was extremely angry to say the least. She was dumbfounded that her husband could be so stupid. Dino left out most of the details of the sexual gratification, which he had been enjoying when he was performing with Maria. Normally, Carla was a calm woman, as nothing seemed to ruffle her feathers. Now she was shouting at the top of her voice, she used words that Dino had never heard her utter. She sounded like a street woman from the poorest parts of the City. With clenched fists she hit Dino on the body and around the head, and then threw saucepans and plates at him.

Finally she burst into tears, and sobbed.

"After all we have meant to each other Dino, how dare you enjoy another woman's body? I bet she is some tart you picked up in Rome. Well, I hope you get some nasty disease. You will never come near me again. I am leaving you, and I shall tell your father what you have done. I shall see that you are sacked from the Bank. Go, leave this house tonight, and I do not want to ever see you again. Get out of my house and out of my life forever. I shall never forgive you for this, for it has brought disgrace upon this family. You did not give one single thought to our son, who will never know his father; you are not worth anything. Go back to your tart if she will have you. You will hear from my solicitor in due course."

After she had finished her tirade of abuse, she collapsed on to the sofa, and burst into tears. Dino tried all her knew to comfort her and tried to apologise for being such a fool, but he could see it was pointless. Now he had burned his boats, for he realised that Maria had won. If Maria changed her mind, the rest of his life would be in ruins. That night Carla hardly slept at all, she cried most of the night. Dino now thrown out of the bedroom slumped on to the sofa, he had very little sleep and knew that he had been playing with fire, and got very badly burnt in the process.

He had ruined his family's life, for the sake of a taking a few nights of sexual pleasure with what he considered to be an exciting woman. He kept thinking back over the events of the past few months, when it all began. Dino did not think that what had started out as dinner with an attractive woman, could have turned into a sexual affair, which had now virtually ended his marriage. He had to face the fact that, there was no turning back, and he was certain that Carla would never forgive him. When his parents got to hear about his indiscretion, who knows what the consequences would be?

The next morning, Carla woke early, she was still extremely angry, and simply could not understand why her husband had behaved in such a way. She had the feeling, that this Maria that Dino had been with, had got some kind of hold over him, perhaps even blackmail? The simple fact was that her husband had cheated on her, and this she could not forgive. At their marriage ceremony they had pledged themselves to each other, until death parted them. Before the birth of their son they had only themselves to consider, now there was young Dino too.

Dino finally appeared, he looked and felt terrible. He knew he was guilty, as he came into the Kitchen where Carla was pouring herself a coffee; she just turned and just stared at him.

Carla suggested that they went into the Lounge. Carla was first to speak and was desperately trying to contain her anger in the tone of her voice.

"Dino, I can never ever forgive you for what you have done. You are either a complete idiot or just plain stupid. How could you do such a thing, is simply beyond my comprehension. Obviously, this Maria is much better in bed than I am. I suppose you thought you could get away with it? Well, I have news for you. From the first moment your affair began, you obviously did not give one single thought to your son and least of all me. All you were interested in was having sex, which presumably you did not pay for initially. Now by God you are going to pay, in a very big way indeed. When you were in Rome I expected you to call me at least every other night, not just once a week. You have not only ruined our life together, but also your son's and your own. I hope that you are completely satisfied with your irresponsible behaviour; you do not give two figs for either your young son or me. Perhaps that Maria will look after you? For after I have telephoned your father, you will be sacked from the Bank I can assure you."

Dino was surprised that Carla could actually discuss the matter of his infidelity so calmly, especially after her viscous attack on him the night before. Dino did his best and tried to explain the situation to his wife.

"My love, I never intended that it should go this far. It started out as empty place at a table in a crowded Restaurant. The waiter showed me a table where this Maria was sitting alone. He asked her if she minded a dinner guest. We got into conversation over dinner and I walked her back to her room, as a Gentleman would, to make certain that she got there safely. Then she invited me in for a drink, and before I knew it she was undressed and sexually arousing me. Like a fool I played along with her. I just thought it would be just a one-night stand and it would be all over. Then she pursued me every evening, and of course you know what happened. I fell for her charms. Now I want to end it, she is getting very heavy. I am in a situation; of my own doing it is true. The only thing I can ask is for your forgiveness."

Carla thought for a moment, trying desperately to recover her composure.

"Dino," she began, "I cannot ever forgive you for what you have done to young Dino and I. When we married we vowed to be faithful to each other until death do us part. You do remember that I presume? Now you have broken that vow. However, although I will never forgive you I will compromise, for the sake of young Dino. I suggest that we shall have a trial separation for a month. Then, you might come to your senses and forget this other woman.

If I hear anything about you with that Maria, then I shall immediately start divorce proceedings. In the meantime, young Dino and I will move out to stay with my parents in their Florence home. Is that clear to you?"

Dino listened carefully to Carla and agreed that this compromise seemed the best solution. Later that day, Carla moved out and Dino was left with his thoughts. Most of his thoughts were of Maria; he was thinking more of her than his family. His brain had moved to below his waist, he was thinking as a single Italian man rather than a family man. His responsibilities to his family had been forgotten; from the first moment that he had entered Maria's room on that fateful night in Rome.

The next morning, Dino got ready and went off to the Bank to start another day. He was not prepared for the reception he would he was about to receive.

He thought that now he had agreed a separation period with Carla that his problems were over, at least temporarily. He got a very cool good morning from his Secretary, who put the post in front of him. Then his telephone rang, it was Enzo, and he was sounding very angry indeed.

"Dino," said Enzo curtly, "come and see me at once."

Then, the receiver was slammed down. Dino walked along to his father's office, knocked on the door and went in. Enzo Borghese was sitting behind his large leather topped desk and he looked furious. He motioned Dino to sit down.

"Dino, I have just had my daughter-in-law on the telephone. Carla has told me all about your affair with this Maria person. She also told me that she has left home with young Dino. I am not interested in anything you have to tell me. This sexual behaviour of yours has brought disgrace on the family."

Dino tried to reply to try to give an excuse for his sexual straying.

Enzo took no notice and continued, "Dino you are a complete fool. I cannot have a son of mine involved in a scandal like this, that will no doubt spread very quickly, and it will bring the bank's reputation into question. What will our Clients think of us? This matter has got out of hand, and there is no way we can control it. You will leave the Bank immediately. Clear your desk. Get your Secretary to bring all your current files to me. Do not even think of another position in Banking anywhere in Italy, Furthermore, I forbid you to set foot in any branch of the Bank of Italy. Your assets in the Bank are frozen until you have settled matters with Carla. Is that clear."

Then standing up, he shouted at Dino,

"You idiot, you have ruined this family with your stupidity, thinking with your balls instead of your brains. Get out of this Bank. I do not ever want to see you again. Get out now!"

Dino had never seen his father so angry. He got up and left his father's office feeling really ashamed. All his years at the Bank, and the hard work building up business and Client relations were gone. The moment he had sex with Maria, he had kissed his family and his career goodbye. Dino returned in his Office, he just sat there and stared at the wall. His secretary came in; she did not say a word, just looked at Dino in disgust. Obviously, the word of his affair was already common knowledge throughout the Bank. With all the shouting that had gone on in Enzo's office, even the people in the street outside could probably have heard as well.

His Secretary began opening all the filing cabinets; she collected all of Dino's files and carried them into Enzo's office. Dino meanwhile sat at his desk feeling shell-shocked, when the door opened again; it was Gino, his father's assistant. He had been at the Bank for some 20 years, and had known Dino since he was a small boy, he recalled the very first day when Enzo had brought his baby son to the Bank. He sat in the easy leather chair beside Dino's desk. Although a loyal member of the Bank's staff and especially to Enzo, he felt like an uncle to Dino. He looked at Dino's dazed expression and said,

"Excuse me Dino; I have just had a meeting with your father. He has told me that you are having an affair with a lady who lives in Venice. He was discreet enough not to mention her name. I hope that you do not think that I am interfering, but if you need to talk to anyone, please contact me at home."

Dino swung around to face Gino.

"Gino my friend, I have always thought of you as an Uncle. I do not think that you are interfering at all. It is times like this when you need understanding. I know I have done wrong, but I do still love Carla and young Dino. This lady Maria has come into my life and I cannot say that I do not love her. She is a very beautiful lady and she pleases me, if you know what I mean. My father has told me he does not want to see me again. I will comply with his wishes. I have not told Mother, no doubt she will know by now."

"I suppose Dino; I told you so might be about right. I will still be there should you need me. After all some of us do stray at times, but it is the trick is not to get found out isn't it? However, your father has asked me to make sure your office is cleared. It should include all your personal effects. You are not to touch any correspondence, and your Secretary will place all non-current files in the safe in your father's office. Your keys are to be handed to me. It is sad that after all your work, a lady comes into your life and ruins your career. Now I must escort out of the building."

Walking down the stairs with Gino, he thought of the first day he had met Carla. He really loved her, but his sexual cravings on that trip to Rome had got the better of him, and now he was out of work, possibly without a future. He went to a local Restaurant and had lunch with several drinks. It was late afternoon by the time he got home. He felt he was now living in an empty shell, for his wife and son had gone. Would he see them again?

He hoped so, only time would tell. He sat there on the balcony watching the sun set. He drank a little then a little more, until he fell into a fitful sleep.

He awoke the next morning; feeling dreadful and the first cup of coffee started to perk him up. It now dawned on him that he had to do something with his life. Finding a job would not be easy, now that any job in banking had been denied him. He was on his second cup of coffee, when the doorbell rang. Dino could hear a car driving away; he hoped it might be Carla and his son having changed their mind? When he opened the door there stood Maria. He was dumbstruck, how did she know were he lived? He looked at her dressed in all her finery with a white fox fur stole around her shoulders.

"Well Dino," she said in a sexy voice, "aren't you going to invite me in? I thought you might need cheering up?"

Dino knew now that he had cooked his goose.

She stretched out her arms and hugged and kissed him.

"Well my love, I presume your wife and son are not here?"

Maria marched in, and then taking Dino's hand she led him into the Bedroom.

"Cat got your tongue?" she quipped.

Dino was still speechless.

She began to undress as Dino watched her fascinated.

Dino's willing hands soon had her naked, whilst she admired herself in the full-length mirror. Then she smiled and rubbed Dino's crotch.

"Time to wake it up," she sighed.

Dino could wait no longer. He thought he might as well be hung for a sheep as a lamb. They were soon making love with all their might. Moving slowly up and down on her new lover loving every movement.

"I have missed you so much my dearest darling," she gasped, "I have yearned for your most interesting muscle that makes me feel like a real woman."

Dino now knew he had sealed his fate; there would be no going back now. He was now enjoying sex so much with Maria; he did not care what would happen in the future. He was in seventh heaven once more with a lady who wanted his body, and he would give it all he had. Following a day of sexual gratification, they sat down to eat, and he discovered that Maria knew all about what had gone on with Dino and his father. It seems she had a good friend that worked at the Bank.

"Don't worry, darling Dino," she whispered, "I have a plan as to how we can be together. You can to live with me in my villa in Venice. There is plenty of room,"

To Dino this was the best news he could have had. After the meal, he rode Maria for all he was worth until they were both exhausted. They made a bargain; he would be her lover and a kept man. Dino thought this was a great bargain, and agreed to her suggestion, after all his life was now in tatters. What he did not know was exactly what Maria had in that inventive mind of hers. She was a very cunning woman, and very adept at pleasing her man. She knew exactly what she was after, and would use all her sexual abilities and guile to get it. Maria was sure that she had snared Dino, now he would be a very happy and willing victim. He had walked right into the sexual trap they she had carefully planned.

Carla had been at her parent's house for about a week. Sophia, her Nanny, was looking after young Dino, so Carla had some time to sit and try to sort out her future. Then one morning she had a telephone call from the Bank, it was Enzo Borghese. She was a little surprised to hear from him, for she had not heard from him since Dino had been sacked.

"Good morning, Carla," he said, "how are you? I am sorry that I have not contacted you, but since Dino has gone, life here is very hectic. By the way have you heard anything from Dino?"

"Good morning father. I am bearing up, and to tell the truth I do miss Dino, despite what he has done. I will not forgive him ever. I have told him if he does not come back to me within a month, then I will file for divorce."

There was silence for a moment. Carla wondered if Dino had contacted his Father, to prevent her working at the Bank as well.

"Carla, would you like to come back to the Bank as my Personal Assistant? You would not only work with me but also Gino."

Carla thought for a moment.

"Father, I would love to come back to the Bank and work with you. My nanny Sophia is excellent, and I can trust her to really look after young Dino. When can I start?"

Enzo suggested she came in the next day for a few hours to get acquainted with all the work involved with her new position at the Bank. When she put the telephone down, she was really excited. Her career, when she was with Dino was going nowhere, now there was a chance for her to get back into the workplace. The next day Carla was at the Bank as it opened and Enzo and Gino were delighted to see her. She soon got into a routine and as the days passed the pile of paperwork in the in trays diminished.

They agreed that without Carla they would be weeks behind with their paperwork. Carla had heard nothing from Dino. The month had passed and she went to see a Solicitor, a gentleman recommended by Enzo. His name Franco Bonatto, he was known as a very professional legal operative and had a reputation for squeezing the guilty party dry, financially speaking. At their first meeting, Carla ran her scenario by him. Franco said it seemed straightforward enough. He could get her good terms and that her husband would have to suffer the consequences of his actions.

The meeting was short and Carla felt that here was a man who she could trust to get the settlement she wanted. When she returned to the Bank, Enzo asked about her meeting with Franco. Carla said it had gone well, she felt happier now. She would be able to get on with her life. Sophia asked if she could spend Christmas with her family in Sienna. Carla agreed, for she now had her parents to help over the festive season. Working at the Bank had taken Carla's mind off the troubles that seem to surround her, for now she threw herself into the work and spared hardly a thought for Dino.

She was sure that sex was the only reason that she had left her, and she had felt that their relationship had changed since the birth of their son. Perhaps Dino could not handle the responsibility, although she knew that Dino loved the little boy? This was a question to which may never know the answer.

Christmas approached, the decorations went up in the Bank and the shops in the City put up their coloured lights and festive displays. Florence was a mass of colour, and of course innumerable Father Christmases. Carla did not feel the least bit festive at all, for this was her first Christmas without Dino.

Meanwhile, Dino had moved into the Villa in Venice with Maria. Maria kept him busy doing things around the home, for she definitely was not into housework. Now that she had Dino with her at the Villa, she no longer needed her personal maid, cleaner, cook and handyman. Why pay out good money to servants, when you can get your live in lover to do it for nothing except devotion, and sexual favours. Her late husband had not done any outstanding repairs to their home for some time. So Dino was put to work as a Househusband.

While he was working around the house, Dino noted that there were no photographs, paintings, or indeed any reminder of Maria's first husband. This seemed strange to him, after all she may have loved him and wanted some reminder that he had been part of her life. When he asked her about it, her reply was quite cutting.

"Dino, he was useless when he was here, so why I should remind myself of a man like him? I know he had a mistress; he must have got his sexual satisfaction from somebody. He got little from me. He has gone and I am delighted. The money he spent on me was the only consolation I had."

She was quite angry when she said it. Dino thought she must have hated him. Probably as a treat Maria would allow him to make love to her only when she felt he deserved it or when she was feeling the need. She knew that Dino had a good business brain and she would use it to her advantage.

One afternoon, whilst on her veranda when they sipping wine together, Maria decided that it was time to put her lover to work in the commercial world. He would be more than just her plaything. She told him that she had been thinking of how they could plan their future. She explained that, since her husband's death she had spent little time on the family business. He had an Office on the outskirts of Venice, with a Sales Assistant called Enrico Cigna, and two young ladies, Benedetta and Elsa, who one day he would meet. She had been a woman of pleasure, and it had been her husband who had built up a large wine business, with contacts in most European countries, including England. When she had met Dino in Rome she had been to see a few of her Clients, so that she could try to maintain the lifestyle to which she had become accustomed. Now she felt it was time to visit her contact in England, about the importation of wine into that country. She continued by telling Dino that apparently, Marco had been in negotiations with Lord Ashdown just prior to his death. She had written to Lord Ashdown and told him of her bereavement. She would contact him again, when her husband's affairs had been settled. She showed him a letter from Lord John Ashdown addressed to the Di Gigli Wine Company. It said that Lord Ashdown wanted to meet the Countess, to discuss terms for a contract and delivery. She had written back to Lord John telling him that she would make plans to have a meeting in Italy as soon as she could.

Lord John had replied that he was sorry for her loss and suggested a meeting in Milan on a date to be agreed. He said that wine was very popular with his clientele and would be expanding into the retail market. The meeting would be on Tuesday December 1st 1908, at the Grand Hotel in Milan at 11am, and Maria asked Dino to go with her. He readily agreed for it was his first business trip since the Bank had sacked him. Maybe now, life with Maria would change, and perhaps there could be much more to life with Maria than just sex and housework.

He knew he was sure to enjoy the journey even more now that he was with an extremely sexy woman.

Now as well as his body, she wanted his professional advice and support in her business dealings. Maria was of course, was indeed delighted that Dino was interested enough to join her on this trip, for she knew that she could rely on his financial advice. This area of business that was new to her. The accounts had been in a mess since her husband had passed away, for she had no head for figures, except her own and the one lying next to her. She felt that the company's accountants, were 'ripping her off', because she was a woman alone in business. Their charges seemed extremely high. Maria asked Dino to look the accounts over, and he agreed that the Accountants had made exorbitant charges for the work done. He checked things through and found a number of anomalies. He made the necessary corrections and got the accounts up to date. Dino told Maria that the Company was in a fairly healthy financial position, but needed to expand its operations.

Maria insisted that all this paperwork had to be done at home, for Maria was not ready to let Dino loose in her office, at this stage in their relationship. Dino did not know much about wine production and sales, but he did know how to consume it. He was a wonder with figures, and knew how to deal with people to get the best out of them. Maria suggested that when spring arrived that they visit the vineyards that supplied her Company, and then he could improve his knowledge of the products. Travelling with Maria would be a pleasure for them both. His thoughts were taken up with the exciting prospect of being both a marriage and business partner to this beautiful woman. In the short term, it would be business and pleasure only until Dino's divorce was made absolute.

Then he was sure that Maria would marry and he could be a true partner in all senses of the word, but in truth he had no idea what in Maria's mind.

The meeting with Lord Ashdown had come at a fortuitous time, for just prior to her husband's death they were talking about linking up with the British Brewery. Lord Ashdown was now quite happy to deal with Maria, who he had had met on several previous occasions. She had a good head on her shoulders, but she always felt that her husband was not the driving force behind the business, although he controlled the finances. Maria seemed always to be pushing him, sometimes not too gently.

Maria suggested to Dino that it might be better to stay overnight in Milan. Dino's eyes lit up.

"I thought you would enjoy that Dino. We can be lovers. So need I say more?"

Dino smiled and nodded in agreement, as he thought of the sexual pleasures to come.

The day before the meeting was cold and grey. They would have to wear their warmest clothes. Dino knew what that meant, for Maria had an immense collection of clothes, furs and jewellery, so she had plenty to choose from. Maria decided to wear her new sable coat, bonnet, and her best sable fur topped leather boots. Underneath a brown velvet dress, she wore some very revealing lingerie. She felt wonderfully warm and looked just like a queen. Dino wore a fur lined winter coat with a deep silver fox fur collar to keep out the chill winter weather and a beautiful fur hat to match. Maria had given this to him; it was one of her husband's coats, which had never been worn. Underneath he wore a pure wool blue suit. Together they looked a handsome couple as they got into the taxi to take them to Venice Railway Station. Maria had booked a private compartment, so they would not be disturbed on the 5-hour journey to Milan. Dino locked the compartment door and they settled down into their little private world. The train began to pull out of the station and they were on their way at last. So Dino started to loosen his clothing. Maria gave Dino one of her looks.

"Business before pleasure young man."

"Spoil sport" retorted Dino.

Maria just smiled and kissed him.

"Don't worry my lover," she replied, "there will be plenty of time for play. I can assure you."

Maria loosened her sable coat and removed her bonnet, then opened her briefcase. Together, they went through all the documents relating to their meeting with John Ashdown.

They had drawn up agreements in Italian and English, and had made notes on various points that they needed to discuss with Lord Ashdown. Their discussion was so intent that they failed to notice the glorious Italian countryside flashing by outside the window. The railway line passed along the southern end of Lake Garda, but they were too busy to notice the snow on the mountains that fringed the Lake. They felt the train slow down as it approached Brescia.

They had now finished their business meeting, was there time for pleasure? Dino asked the obvious question.

"Is there time for pleasure my love?"

"Of course, my love," whispered Maria, "it will not take me long to arouse you."

She smiled as only she could, and in a flash she had removed her leather gloves and unbuttoned his flies and began searching with her long nimble fingers. She stroked her chin and thought for a moment.

"Let me see," she said, "a good deal of foreplay I think before the final thrust of pleasure."

Dino could not wait; his trousers were around his ankles. He was aching for it, but Maria made him wait. She talked about all the things that always got him aroused. Then as he was about ready, she stopped. Dino was taken aback as he had expected Maria to continue.

"No, not now," she cooed, "I have changed my mind. I do not want it now thank you, Sir. Perhaps later."

Dino stood there, his trousers still around his ankles. Maria knew exactly how to please him; she lifted up the back of her dress and let her pantaloons drop, so he could see her flesh and roundness of her bottom. Then she pulled them back up and Dino was almost in pain trying to hold himself back. He could hardly stand this much longer. Something just had to give; for time was running short they would soon be slowing down and arriving in Milan. Just as he thought he could try again, Maria turned to face him bent down and kissed him. This was just the very start of the games would play with Dino over the next few years. Dino was almost ready to give forth as Maria stood up.

"There now Dino, I've kissed it better."

Dino realised that she had teased him for the first time. He had difficulty pulling up his pants and trousers. While he was doing so, Maria was smiling.

"Dino, that is a nasty swelling between your legs!" She exclaimed, "I will do something about that later."

"What about now?" asked Dino.

Maria laughed out loud.

"Little boys," she said waving her index finger, "must wait for their treats. You must control yourself, and then the pleasure will last that much longed. I want long periods of sexual satisfaction, not just quick in and out. Don't worry I will teach you all you need to know about being a great Latin lover."

Dino felt a bit silly. In the past he was always in a hurry, usually it was a quick grope here and there, and may be even the odd 'quickie', but as for a long drawn out session, he not even had that with Carla.

Now he had all the time in the world to learn the ways of pleasure, Maria would be a good teacher. She knew that later she would have her way with him. Now she knew that like her, he too had a fetish for the sensuous feeling of furs, and she would always exploit this to her advantage. She was certain that he had other sexual desires, which would no doubt surface with her instruction. He would not be disappointed; she would guarantee his complete satisfaction. She had a complete hold over him now, and that grip she would tighten as time went on. She would make him her financial adviser, her plaything and lover all in one. They got dressed, and after a little while the train slowed as in came into the outskirts of Milan. Maria looked in the mirror; she was once again looking as pretty as a picture, by now even Dino had tidied himself. They left the train and made their way to the Taxi rank for they had booked into the Grand Hotel some five minutes ride from the Station. It would be here that they would meet Lord Ashdown the next day.

Maria had booked a suite; she always liked plenty of space, and of course, room service. She undressed, then picked up the telephone and ordered a late lunch. Then she asked Dino to unpack both of their suitcases and put all her clothes away. She knew the thought of him seeing her sensual undergarments would turn him on. She was right; she could already see that swelling again, particularly as he hung up her sable coat. She now really had him 'hooked', and she was now in control. For not once, during the past month had he even mentioned Carla. Soon after lunch was over, Maria started to play out just one or two of her sexual fantasies with Dino, who was thoroughly enjoying these new sexual experiences. Maria noticed that very slowly but surely, that her lover was learning to control his sexual urges. Even so he had to go the bathroom a couple of times when things got too much for him. Maria had hardly started to tease him properly; she had barely one toe in the waters of her desires. With dinner finished, she gave in to his constant pleas.
She swanned around the suite in nothing other than her Sable coat for quite some time, before finally she let him have his way with her. She made sure that every drop of fluid in his body was released, and finally he lay back exhausted. Maria on the other hand wanted to find his sexual limits, and so she continued to excite him to new sexual heights and he loved it. That night that slept like two logs. Dino felt that he was on honeymoon again. This was indeed the honeymoon period; he had no idea what Maria had in mind and what was yet to come. That night he went to bed with a smile on his face, whilst Maria was still thinking of new fantasies.

The next morning, after breakfast they made their way down to meet Lord Ashdown. Maria greeted John with a kiss on both cheeks, then she introduced Dino as her new partner. John asked the Receptionist if there was a small business room, where they could have their meeting in private. The meeting went well and they agreed on all the points in the agreement. It was decided that the contract would be for 12 months renewable. The Brewery would take 15% of all the Di Gigli Company's wine output. It would be delivered in casks and bottled in England under licence and the label design would be that of the Di Gigli brand. So the deal was set, the contract signed and everyone was happy. It was lunchtime, so they all decided the next thing would be lunch. Over lunch, John explained that sometimes his wife Lady Victoria joined him on his business trips. However, he had just become a father of a lovely baby girl, and she was still getting over the birth and wanted to be with her daughter. John told them, that as he would not be leaving until the next morning, but he had managed to get tickets for the Opera that night. It would be a fitting conclusion to a great business deal. Maria and Dino said that they would be delighted to join him.

That evening, Maria donned her velvet dress and sable coat, then together with Dino they all went off to Milan Opera House and enjoyed Mozart's Magic Flute. John Ashdown particularly enjoyed the evening, for he admitted over drinks afterward, that due to the birth of his daughter, and the pressure of business, he had not had time for the Theatre or the Opera. As they parted, Maria and Dino said what a pleasure it was to do business with a true English gentleman. Contracts would be sent to England within a week, signed, sealed and certified by the Company Solicitors.

Later, Maria and Dino celebrated the deal with an extra special night of sexual delights. Maria was proud of Dino, for he had the business and negotiation talents that she lacked. This deal with Lord Ashdown was something she really wanted, and it would be her first business deal outside the mainland of Europe. She was thrilled, and showed it in her sexual appreciation with her willing student.

The following morning, John left for London, whilst Maria and Dino decided to see if they could have a meeting with Benito, her friend at FIAT. They telephoned, but he said that was too busy to see them, but he did have a few moments to speak to Dino. He told him, that there was no driver vacancy in their professional team, and that he would have to remain an amateur for at least 12 months to prove his worth. They would supply a car for him and give expenses, but no paid contract or retainer. Dino accepted this fact, for now he would help Maria expand her business. He talked it over with Maria on the journey home.

"I agree with Benito," replied Maria, "just take your time. It seems that you will have a divorce coming along next year, which alone may affect your driving skills. We do not want a lack of concentration at high speed, do we? I have found you and want to keep you my love."

Dino thought carefully, and in his heart he knew she was right. So Dino and Maria settled down wondering what Christmas and the New Year would bring, for the festive season was now almost upon them. Dino decorated the Villa with lots of coloured streamers. In the Lounge, there was a Fir tree with lights, tinsel, a fairy on the top of it, and small coloured packages hung from its branches. This was the first Christmas for years that Maria had been truly happy.

On Christmas Eve, Maria decided that she wanted Dino dress up in a Santa Claus outfit, which she had especially made for him. She loved charades, and this would be a real beauty. She told him, that she had never met Santa Claus, even as a little girl, and that her parents had told her that Santa did not exist. So she was determined that Dino would play Santa Claus for her, it would give her and him a great deal of pleasure. Dino was puzzled as to what she meant by that, but he was soon to find out. Once Maria had an idea in her mind she soon planned how to execute it.

On Christmas Eve afternoon, Maria brought down a very big box covered in golden wrapping paper; it was tied with a wide red ribbon and presented it to Dino.

"This is my special present to you," she said excitedly, "so please open it now as I want you to wear it especially for me."

Dino opened the box; and removed the contents slowly piece by piece, and finally he stood back looking at the Santa suit. Turning to Maria he hugged and kissed her.

"Thank you so much my darling Maria, this is a wonderful present. It is the most beautiful Santa Claus costume I have ever seen. I absolutely love it. What can I give you in return?"

Maria smiled sweetly, for she had already designs in her mind for Dino.

"Do not worry my love," she replied, "you do have something I really want. It will be a special present that we can both enjoy. I can assure you will absolutely delight at what I have in mind. Just wait and you will see."

The Santa Claus outfit she had bought for Dino was bright red, made from soft crushed velvet with real white fox fur lining throughout the jacket and trousers. They were also thickly trimmed with white fox around the hem and cuffs of the jacket, also along the bottom of the trousers. The pockets were fur lined too. Down the front were big white fur buttons. The ensemble was completed with fur boots, hat and gloves to match. The costume included a long white beard with side-whiskers. Maria told Dino, that he had to wear costume, without anything underneath and this was just one the conditions on which she had given him the present. She told him that he must dress up now, and not take it off until they had finished exchanging presents well after midnight. She would be wearing her "special" apparel at that moment, and then he had to give her the present that she most desired. Dino could not wait to see what that present might be. Maria insisted on watching Dino dressing up and made sure that he wore nothing underneath; when he had finished he put on the beard. He felt marvellous, absolute bliss; looking at himself in the mirror he started getting aroused. Maria came across the room, looked down at his trousers. Seeing the big mound there, she gave a wry smile.

"I see you like your present," she remarked, "or are you just pleased to see me? You look a really sexy Santa. Ooh! I really fancy you. However, I am going to have to make you wait until later, for my special present. I always fancied having my own Santa at anytime I liked and now I can."

Dino was delighted to play Santa and to be given a special present, as well as this lovely costume. He strutted around the Villa feeling wonderful, and he kept looking down to see the mound in his trousers. He felt really turned on by this present. He had only seen a Santa Claus in the Department Stores in Florence, but had never played the part himself.

He had sat on Santa's knees as a small child, but now he knew how it felt to be a real Santa. However, no Santa ever had a suit like this surely?

Over the past few weeks Carla never even crossed his mind. In this Villa, they could indulge in all kinds of sexual games and pleasures of the flesh, without giving a thought to the outside world. Dino had never played dressing up games like this. Maria's world was all new to him, and she still had a lot games yet to be played. She was certainly permanently obsessed, with all kinds of sexual deviations. She wanted to do everything, but only with men. She would take her sexual gratification, when she wanted it, and how she wanted it. After all, she was now in total control of her man, and he had do as she directed.

There were times, when Maria wondered, how and when these sexual urges had first begun, for now she was indulging herself in different kinds of sexual pleasures. In the past it had never even occurred to her to do all these things. Now she was finding that it was a delectation she could not do without. Her late husband Marco never turned her on sexually, nor was he particularly interested in having sex with her. She was simply an adornment. So, Maria started collecting books and magazines, those that related and showed in graphic detail, all the various different ways of pleasing yourself and men. Then as a substitute, for sexual fulfilment, she began to buy expensive designer clothes, in order to fill up her wardrobes. It must have cost her husband a large fortune, but he obviously did not care, for being very rich, money meant nothing to him. So, Maria did her best to help him spend it. Within her suite of rooms, there was a large boudoir that was full of furs, day and evening gowns, lingerie and jewellery, all of these things being especially designed for her.

She disliked most women, they were competition. One day, she knew she would meet a man who would satisfy her in every way. He would have to be a willing partner, to join her in all the sexual games she desired to play, in a costume of her choosing or out of it. She was not worried if he was rich, as long as he was not poor, but he had to be handsome and well endowed. For now she had Dino, who was an ideal student for her to teach and dominate. Maria had now realised, that she had started to release Dino's innermost sexual desires. He simply loved it all.

Dino had never encountered this kind of sexual behaviour in anybody he had ever known. He searched deep in his unconscious mind and he asked himself the question. Was this the kind of intimacy he really enjoyed? He decided that it was, he would still do anything for Maria. He posed in front the mirror once more, as these thoughts passed through his head. He looked down and the mound was still there.

Maria meanwhile, was in the bedroom preparing her present for Dino. She was having thoughts of the ecstasy to come. She was already naked and gazing longingly at her body, in the long mirrors. She had a matching Santa outfit that was a dusty pink, lined with the same soft white fur throughout, and trimmed with white fox. She was exciting herself once more by rubbing the soft fur against her breasts. Her gloves were lined with silk and the outside covered in white fox. She pulled the fur hood up and then down. Then pouting her lips, she admired herself in her mirror.

"Dino my love," she said quietly to herself, "your present is almost ready for you. You will be exhausted by the time you have finished playing with it."

She pulled up the deep fur hood up around her head so that he face was hidden and gave a twirl. She felt ready to give Dino her special present. He would now have Maria's permission, to enter her body for the sexual satisfaction of them both, she would tell him when to start and when to stop.

Outside, the sun had long disappeared below the western horizon. Dino wondered how much longer he would have to wait to give his present to Maria. He looked down; he could still see that mound that Maria had seen earlier, and he was simply aching to get into his lover. He had a feeling in his toes, which he had not felt for a long time, he hoped that Maria would be ready for him soon, for that certain part of his body was telling him that it could not wait much longer. Then, her moment came.

"I'm in the bedroom darling," she called out in a loud voice,

"I want give you my present now. It is ready, and I am waiting my love."

Dino did not need a second invitation; he could hardly control himself as entered Maria's boudoir. He burst into her boudoir and there was Maria, in front of the mirrors in her Santa suit. He stopped and stared at her. She stood a little way away him slowly and tantalisingly opening the front of costume to give him a glimpse of what he could expect. She was really aroused and hungry for Dino to satisfy her in every way. Now seeing her lover dressed as Santa Claus complete with a long beard, made her think she was giving her body to someone other than Dino. This excited her even more.

Maria was wide-eyed and pouting her lips.

"I am," she said, "your Mistress Christmas. Come here my Santa, I want to feel your lovely sack."

Dino stood in front of her. She ran her gloved hands down inside his trousers.

"Ah," she exclaimed with a squeal, "there it is!"

What happened next even Dino could not have even guessed. She pulled down his trousers, and led him around the room. Dino was ecstatic. Having played some more of Maria's other sexual games; they made love as never before. When they had finished, Dino was told to sit and listen to what she had to say.

"That," she said, "is the best Santa I have ever had. We will wear these costumes all the time over the next few days. You have a lot more to learn from me. These Santa suits certainly makes me feel - well I am sure you know by now very special. I have now come to a decision that you will really adore. Since that first moment we met, I knew exactly what would turn you on sexually. From now on I will instruct you when to change into and out of your Santa costume.

From now on I will want to dress up in my clothes and my furs, for I know you, are really longing to wear them, aren't you? You naughty little boy. I want you, to shed all of your inhibitions and thoroughly enjoy yourself all the time. I will make sure you relieve all your stress, amongst other things. In fact, you will not be permitted wear any male clothing at all for I strictly forbid it. I have thrown out all your male clothes. I am having a complete wardrobe full of 'new' ladies clothes, boots, shoes, slippers and lingerie plus some gorgeous furs especially made for you, and ready for you to wear. Your beautiful clothes will be here in a day or so. Then you will always be able to dress the way that I tell you. You must wear a maid's outfit when you are doing the cooking, housework and the gardening; every uniform comes with the most alluring underwear, and a suitable wig. You will really love it, my darling. When we have dinner, I always choose a suitable gown for you, and a sensuous nightdress with a negligee to sleep in. If I want you to change your clothes, then, I will choose what you will wear. I will instruct you how to walk like a lady especially in your high heels. You will make me extremely happy, and you will do these things for me, my darling. I am your teacher and you will be my very obedient pupil and servant. For the moment this will all be our little secret.

Is that perfectly clear to you? I certainly hope so. From now on I will call you Dina. That is your new name. I trust that what I have said is clear to you."

Dino just stood there and could not believe what he was hearing. Until that moment the thoughts of cross-dressing, had never crossed his mind. Now that Maria was telling him exactly how to dress, he was already getting aroused at the thought of becoming Dina.

He did not realise that these were the first steps in Maria's grand plan of complete humiliation. He was very animated, and very willing to perform all her instructions to the letter. In fact, he had promised her that it was his earnest desire to do anything to please. She certainly had some different ideas and it had opened up a New World to him, and it was one that he was willing to explore to its limits with Maria as his personal guide.

"My darling Maria," replied Dino who was now very excited, "I love the thought of becoming Dina, and I will do anything you ask of me, except murder of course. I must confess that the things you want me to do, and the way that you want me to dress will give me a great deal of pleasure. Can we start straight away?"

Maria smiled and waving her index finger.

"You" she answered, "must be a good boy and wait until I have finished with Santa, before you become my extra special Dina. After Christmas you will be my maid, and do as I tell you."

Dino agreed to all her instructions, for now he was very aroused by being her Santa. She gave him a kiss and her tongue did its searching, before leading him to her bed to perform for her ultimate pleasure.

Later Maria took Dino over to her wardrobe and dressed him in her sexiest lingerie, a frilly blouse, and skirt and her red fox furs. He then had to parade in front of her. He got very aroused indeed, and had to rush to the Bathroom. Maria knew that she had found his Achilles Heel, and it really excited her as he showed her Dina for the first time. Once she was satisfied, Dino was told to become her Santa once again. Maria of course, would constantly be suggesting new ways, to sexually arouse her man to keep him from straying from her.

She had now told and shown him how he would have to dress, and that he had to always perform for her pleasure on her slightest whim. She could now completely dominate him and knew that she had not even scratched the surface yet. After all, in her bureau she had reference books on the subject, and she had not passed page two yet. Dino had never known a woman like this. This entire scenario he found very sexually exciting indeed, this would be the best sex and Christmas he had ever had. For Maria was insatiable and she would ensure that Dino was going to adore every minute of it. He always dressed as she directed, and did her bidding whatever she wanted, and it was true it made both of them extremely happy. Maria informed Dino that she did not make New Year Resolutions, for these could be broken, and usually were. The fact was that now Maria had Dino exactly where she wanted him, and knew he would never return to his family. Carla was now a distant memory; he was not missing her or even thinking about his son. He had not even bothered to send any Christmas cards, presents or even get in touch with Carla or young Dino.

Maria would always make sure that she kept 'her student' under her spell, for as long as she wanted him to please her. Dino wore the Santa outfit for several days, and Maria obliged him with long sessions of foreplay, sexual games and always ended with intercourse.

With Christmas over, Dina's wardrobe arrived and having been allowed to open every package that arrived he could not wait to crossdress as Dina. Maria gave him full rein, and made comment on every outfit that Dina wore. Dina could not wait to try on his new furs, and there were lots to choose from, the red and silver fox furs coats and jackets were sumptuous, as Maria had excellent taste. These really aroused Dino, as he modelled and twirled in front of the mirrors. After the luxury of the furs came Dina's working clothes.

When he became Dina the housemaid, personal maid, cleaner, cook, and handyman, she him treated like a servant. He always had to wear the correct outfit. If the jobs were not done to her liking, Maria would physically abuse her Dina by taking down 'her' frilly bloomers and giving 'her' a good spanking, and task had to be done all over again. Maria kept her servant busy, but not so tired that she/male did not have the strength to satisfy her sexually, when she felt the need. On some days this was pretty often, and on other days not at all, when she would just tantalise her Dina. She was very demanding and Dina loved it all. For Dino thought this was part of a penance he had to pay for leaving Carla, but one of pleasure and not of pain.

Dino now realised that leaving Carla for Maria was not that painful. Maria always ended the day with a 'treat' for her lover, one that she had carefully thought out all day, this way she kept them both in an erotic state. Maria was seeking true happiness, for this had been the one thing missing from her life. Now she had found it with Dino, and by dominating him, she felt she could hold on to a love, that had previous been denied her. Maria was certain that now she had him totally under her control, which was precisely where she wanted him. While she was giving him plenty of sexual satisfaction, she was sure that their relationship would be permanent. She felt marvellous, and she knew that now as Dina he was thoroughly enjoying life under her rules.

He was always aroused each time that he had to dress in a new 'uniform'. Maria always made sure that he was suitably rewarded for being what she called 'a good little Dina'. They made love even as the old year 1908 passed into 1909. Dino had not given any thought to what might happen to Carla or young Dino. The last meeting that they had convinced Dino that there would be no compromising with his family. He had not been in contact with Carla within the timeframe, that she had lain down, so he now knew that divorce proceedings were underway.

The only time he had tried to contact Carla, just after he had left the family home she had shown real hatred towards him. May be one day, she would understand, but in his heart he doubted that he would ever be forgiven. He had made his bed, now he had to lay in it. It seemed that Dino's future lay with Maria. She satisfied his every desire mentally, physically and sexually.

Now that he was involved in her business operations, he knew that they would be a team with a future.

Chapter 11

The year 1908 had been a busy one for Rudolph. The early part of the year had been endless testing, then in June he had married his beautiful Catherina, and now the most important race of the calendar, was only a couple of weeks away. He was not amused to hear from Gustav that Christian Lautenschlager would be driving the number one car for Mercedes. Gustav did tell him that there would be no team orders. If he could beat Christian so well and good. He also suggested that Catherina might like to go with him to Dieppe to see the race. Rudolph accepted the inevitable the fact that he had to prove himself against his fellow countryman. Catherina was delighted that she would be able to accompany her husband. She joked that she might even see the beach and do some shopping. The travel arrangements were made and all was set for the journey, which was uneventful. The last thing the team needed was a drama on the way to Dieppe. There would be enough challenges in the race.

They settled in to the Hotel de Plage, their room had a balcony from where you could see the promenade and the beach. So, the young couple settled into their room and later made their way down to the Restaurant for dinner.

Alain Clement had enjoyed his year so far. He had met the woman of his dreams, but he had the headache of trying to develop the Darracq racing car to be really competitive. It had been a critical year for the Company. Alain had worked really hard on the innovations to make the car faster, also to improve the road holding and braking. There had been a great deal of midnight oil burnt in the development department prior to the French Grand Prix. Being French the company needed good results; it was a matter of national pride. They hoped that the publicity would help them sell more road cars. So, they gave Alain all the help they could. He spent many hours out on the roads around the factory, testing new ideas. Some of them worked and some did not. Alain had a kind of gut feeling that Darracq had gone as far as they could with development of their racing cars. Without a radical redesign of the whole car, they would always be chasing the top teams.

However, whilst he was still under contract. He would use all his endeavours to secure a win, or at least finish in the top three places in any event in which he competed. Alain was looking to the future, and thought he should apply for a position, with a company who wanted to develop a successful racing machine. Alain knew the chances of driving for a foreign team such as Mercedes, was out of the question they already had their top drivers. He had read in the Motoring press, that Peugeot intended to form a team to beat the other European Car manufacturers, in both Grand Prix and other motor sport events. One evening he sat down and wrote to the Managing Director, a Charles Orly. May be he would be chosen, from among the many applicants that they would no doubt receive. In the meantime, there was the French Grand Prix to think about. A good finish there would no doubt enhance his chances of driving for Peugeot if the contract with Darracq ended.

He was confident that he would receive a positive response. In the free time that he did have, Alain would see Francoise. The team was working flat out to prepare the cars for the Grand Prix at Dieppe. Francoise asked Alain; if she could come with him to the Race, after all the start was only some 50 kilometres from Rouen. Pierre, Alain's father said that he would like to take the whole family to the race. So, it all was arranged they would meet Alain the day before the race, at the Hotel de Plage in Dieppe. Here they would stay overnight, as the race started early the next morning. Alain had put the finishing touches to the car just a week before the race. He knew it would be a gruelling contest, after all he recalled the 1907 event. He hoped that he could finish, maybe even in 3rd place as he had done the year before. The distance would be the same 765 kilometres, and would be held on 7th July.

The evening before race day, the family met at the Hotel de Plage. The family had rarely been together since Christmas, and it was the first time that Pierre had the opportunity to see his son race. Francoise was proud that her fiancée was amongst the best drivers taking part in this prestigious event. The Hotel was full of drivers who were participating in the Grand Prix. Alain pointed out to Francoise the Mercedes No.1, driver Christian Lautenschlager, Rudolph von Lundenberg and the other team members.

They had an excellent evening meal and afterwards they enjoyed dancing to a small group.

They all slept well except for Alain. He was still apprehensive of what the morrow might bring. He and his team of mechanics had done all they could to the car. They had brakes on all wheels and wider tyres. The car looked and sounded right. Early next morning Alain was down in the Restaurant with the other drivers eating breakfast for he was keen to get down to the start. The rest of the family arrived just as he had finished. He told that they he would see them at the starting area. Alain found his way to where his team had their garage and almost next door to the Mercedes team garage.

As he passed Rudolph gave him a wave; Alain returned his greeting and then got down to last minute preparations before the race, which would start in about 30 minutes. Meanwhile, Pierre and the family had made their way to the Grandstand that ran along by the start and finish line. They found their seats and settled down to watch the excitement. They had a good view of the action; they had a programme and looked down the list of entries, which was very impressive.

It was time for Alain and his mechanic Gaston, to make their way down to the starting area. He was starting in 5th place and all the cars were now on the starting line. Rudolph and Christian Lautenschlager were in the first two places, followed by Otto Salzer in another Mercedes and Carl Jornes in an Opel. Pierre agreed it was an all star line up. He was surprised that Renault had not fared better in the start line up. The starter mounted his rostrum with the French flag, and with a flourish he brought the flag down and the race was on. There was a barrage of sound that defied description. Pierre could not believe the noise made by these cars. There was an enormous cloud of dust as the entire field sped off into the distance. Alain was doing well keeping in 5th place, travelling behind a large dust cloud. Rudolph meanwhile was close behind Christian who was going like the wind. Then as the race progressed, Otto Salzer, who seemed to have found some extra speed from somewhere, overtook Rudolph. However, after a couple of laps, his car gave up the ghost and it expired some way from the start and finish. Every time the cars sped by, Pierre looked out for his son Alain and the whole family cheered as he completed each lap.

On lap four Alain came in for fuel and new tyres. The old ones were getting threadbare. Rudolph too pulled in for fuel, as Christian left the pits to start lap 5. Pierre and the Family went off in search of refreshment behind the Grandstand. Alain managed to swallow some water and wipe his goggles as the team did their work. Rudolph was taking time to refresh himself before starting out on the next lap. It was a long hard race. Many had fallen by the wayside. The race wore on. Alain was trying everything to catch up with the leaders, after a very fast lap he had overtaken Carl Jornes and was now running in 3rd place. The race ended that way. It had taken the winner Christian Lautenschlager 6 hours 56 mins, with Rudolph some 9 mins behind him. Alain had again finished a very creditable third, some 2 minutes behind Rudolph. The Mayor of Dieppe presented the trophies in front of a large crowd. Pierre was proud of his son, and Francoise was thrilled, that Alain would have another piece of silverware to add to his collection. Christian held his trophy high up for all to see. Rudolph knew that if Christian had not been given the better car, he would be receiving the winner's trophy. He was not jealous after all; this was a race where anything could happen. He turned and shook hands with Alain. The Clement family celebrated the third place along with the other drivers at a big Party held at The Hotel de Plage.

Catherina was thrilled to see her husband finish the race even though it did take over 7 hours. He collected his large Silver Trophy and was given a big hug and lots of kisses from Catherina. All the team joined in the celebration party at the Hotel. After a good night's sleep they made their way back to Stuttgart. The season from then on was pretty barren of good quality racing. The team felt frustrated, but the testing went on. The season ended with a kind of 'end of term' party. This was being held at Mercedes Headquarters in Stuttgart. Catherina went shopping in Stuttgart for a suitable ball gown. Rudolph came with her and they decided to go to a designer store where Catherina was a regular customer. The Proprietor, a Karl Fischer welcomed them to his store and asked his assistant to make coffee. He personally showed Catherina many of his finest gowns.

"Countess," he said, "if you have time, I can design a gown especially for you."

Catherina said that the event was a month away.

"Countess," replied Karl, "if you would like to choose the materials and design and I will make sure it is ready in two weeks. However, you would need to come back in a week for the first fitting."

Catherina looked through his design book, and the sample of materials. After careful consideration, she made her selection. Catherina was happy with her choice and then looked around for a fur stole to go with her new gown. In the end she chose a short white fox jacket, it matched her choice of material. She was happy with her purchases and so they went home. It was the weekend, so they took off to see Rudolph's parents. Count Josef and Countess Margarita were delighted to see their son and daughter-in-law. It was the first time that Rudolph and Catherina had been to the Schloss since their wedding. It was a time for celebration.

Rudolph had enjoyed a successful season and his contract had been renewed for another four years, with an increase in salary and bonuses. Catherina's business was flourishing too and they were very happy. Life was being good to them. Rudolph promised that they would be home for Christmas and the New Year, so that they could both enjoy the famous "von Lundenberg" Party. Count Josef was delighted that the family could all be together again.

Alain meanwhile, had returned home to Rouen to spend the night with his fiancée, and his family. He was proud of the trophy he had won. He could not have asked for more. The car was just not quick enough, true it had innovations, but it lacked top speed, but at least it was reliable.

The next day Alain headed back to the factory. The Team Manager was delighted that they had managed third place. The Development Manager, Marcel Rickard who had taken over at the beginning of the year to act as Team Manager. He told Alain that there would be a meeting later in the morning to discuss future plans. Around 11am, the telephone rang in Marcel's office. It was the Managing Director, Bernard Jutant. He had been appointed by the board of Directors to turn the Company around, as sales were down and money was tight. Alain and Marcel went to his office and invited them to sit down. He ordered coffee for them and said that what he had to say was not pleasant, but it needed to be said.

"Alain," he began, "we are thrilled that you have once again brought home the silverware from the French Grand Prix. Your efforts to secure a good finish with a car, let us face it, which is not good enough to beat the Germans; we need a vast input of funds. The new ideas and the innovations you have made to this racing machine will one day be fitted to our road cars."

He picked up a letter from the organisers of the French Grand Prix and showed it to both Alain and Marcel.

"So, gentlemen", he continued, "you will see that there will be no prestigious events for us to enter either in next year or the two years that follow."

Alain and Marcel wondered what was coming next.

"It is therefore, with regret that I cannot renew your contract Monsieur Clement. Please feel free to offer your services to any other Company. In view of your success, and your ability to produce performances from a car that was not competitive is nothing short of a miracle. So, the Company will keep you on full pay, until you find alternative employment. As for you Marcel, I shall have to transfer you to the road vehicle department. You will assume control, as Charles Duprey is retiring."

The coffee arrived, and the two men did not know how to respond. Alain had not the heart to tell either Marcel or indeed anyone, that he had approached Peugeot, who were developing a Grand Prix team.

They drank their coffee in silence. It was a blow to Marcel, but Alain knew that he could not see his career at Darracq being a long one. The development department had spent quite large sums trying to beat the opposition. Each time they thought they had the answer, Mercedes would pull out a few stops, and more power would result. Alain wanted to marry Francoise, but now the future was not quite so clear. He now waited with baited breath, for the reply from Peugeot. He thought it fortunate, that had he not married Francoise before the position at Darracq had terminated. His financial status could have been very difficult. A few days later, Alain received a letter from Peugeot, inviting him to visit their Paris Offices, for interview. They knew of his prowess as a racing driver. At his meeting with the Managing Director Charles Orly he would be able to meet the Finance Director Henri Dinard and the new car's designer Nicholas Bocage.

Alain telephoned Monsieur Orly to confirm his visit. Alain felt better now that there was a chance to further his career in motor racing. In the last few days of September Alain spent three days at the Peugeot factory.

On arrival at the Peugeot's Paris prestigious offices, the receptionist directed him to take the lift to the 5th floor, Michelle, who was Monsieur Orly's secretary, would meet him.

Charles Orly was a tall, dark haired man in his late 40's he had been with Peugeot for about five years. He was a keen Motor Sport enthusiast. He was the driving force behind the Company's desire to make a name for themselves in a competitive sport. He greeted Alain warmly, and immediately ordered coffee and biscuits for them both.

"Monsieur Clement," Charles began, "or may I call you Alain. I have been following your career with a great deal of interest. You have a talent, which this Company badly needs. The word that springs to mind is - professionalism. You will no doubt realise that we have had a flood of applicants for our new grand prix team. Most of those who applied had never featured in the results of any major motor sport event. We cannot afford to take on drivers who do not have either the will or the skill to win. You are a class apart. You were able to give those Mercedes drivers a good race, in a car, which let us face it was less than competitive. You produced new ideas, which with the right combination of good engineering and a more powerful engine, would have resulted in more wins. Sorry, I am forgetting my manners. You are here to talk to me, not listen to one of my speeches."

"Thank you Sir," replied Alain, "for your compliments on my efforts to secure a win for Darracq. I have a feeling that, the Darracq car without serious redesigning cannot go any faster. It is reliable but not quick enough. May be I am a bit selfish, but I want to win. Nobody recalls who was second or third. I feel that Peugeot has the engineering talent to produce cars that will regain for France the supremacy we once had. I hope that we can come to an agreement. I would love the challenge of a new team with fresh ideas."

Alain could see that Charles Orly was very happy with his reply.

"Alain," replied Charles, "to be brief, we want you in our team, that is certain. I have taken the liberty of drawing up a draft contract for your consideration."

The coffee arrived. Charles passed the documents to Alain. Whilst he sipped his coffee, Alain read through the terms and conditions. Alain felt that they were very good indeed.

"Monsieur Orly," said Alain as he put his empty cup down, "I am prepared to sign such a contract and would be honoured to drive for your team."

The two men stood up and shook hands.

"Alain, welcome to Peugeot, and please call me Charles. I now want to introduce you to Nicholas Bocage."

Charles picked up the telephone and asked that Nicholas come in their meeting. The new car's designer, Nicholas Bocage, entered the office. He was a young man in his early 30's. He had been a top engineering student at the Sorbonne. So he and Alain had something in common. Nicholas said that the car would not be ready for testing until later in the season. Nicholas showed Alain the preliminary designs for the car. It certainly looked much different to either the old Darracq or the Mercedes. With all his experience, Alain was the right man to be in at the birth, so to speak. Charles Orly prepared the contract. The terms were excellent. It gave Alain status as Number One driver. The pay was double the amount he was receiving at Darracq.

There were bonuses for winning and a top three finish. He would have control over innovations that would enhance the car's performance. Now he had signed contracts with Peugeot, he felt much better. Charles said that the contract with Peugeot would commence on January 1st 1909. Alain went back to Darracq and told them that he had signed a contract with Peugeot. Marcel was delighted that Alain's future in Motor Racing was assured.

"Good for you my friend, well done. I wish you success."

Alain then asked for a meeting with Bernard Jutant, with a view to taking some leave as now there was little to do now. Bernard was pleased with the news that Alain had found another team that could use his many talents. At the same time, he was sad that Darracq were not going to continue racing.

"Alain," replied Bernard, "take as much time as you like. Go and see that fiancée of yours and the family. You have worked very hard for us, and brought us some success. You deserve a break."

Bernard got up from his desk and shook Alain by the hand.

"Alain Clement, it has been a privilege to know you. One day, you will be World Champion I am sure."

Then he kissed him on both cheeks and hugged him. Alain left his office, went back to his lodging and caught the train back home. The family was delighted to see him. They asked questions about what had happened to his position at Darracq.

They were sad that he had been made redundant. His new contract, as Number one for Peugeot, now the future looked bright. Now Alain could spend time with Francoise. They spent time together, riding and enjoying life.

Chapter 12

Meanwhile, Catherina had returned for her fitting and collection of her new ball gown. Rudolph came with her. She looked absolutely stunning. Karl's designer and cutters had done a marvellous job. The white fox jacket, together with the jewellery enhanced her beauty. Now she was ready for the Mercedes Ball, to be held in the Ballroom of the largest Hotel in Stuttgart. The event would begin, with a formal introduction to the Managing Director Siegfried Gunther and his wife Greta. Rudolph and Catherina joined the queue of employees waiting to meet the head of the Company. Catherina looked at Greta's gown and realised that she had upstaged the Managing Director's wife in her choice of dress. The introductions made, they went into Ballroom, where a band was playing. Several couples were dancing, while Rudolph and Catherina mingled with some of their friends.

The Master of Ceremonies then called for everyone to go into the Banqueting suite for the formal dinner. It was of course a really splendid meal, after which there would be speeches. The meal having ended the Master of Ceremonies asked for silence for the Managing Director. Herr Gunther got to his feet and gave a short speech of welcome and reviewed their successful year.

"Ladies and Gentlemen, began Herr Gunther, "this is a proud moment for me for as Chairman and Managing Director of Mercedes, it is my pleasure to pick out a special person. This man has done so much this year to enhance the reputation of the Company. I call upon our very distinguished driver Rudolph von Lundenberg. He has become an extremely fast and reliable driver. He pushed his cars almost to the limit. I know he has won many prizes this season. You can see these cups in our trophy room. This year he married the beautiful and intelligent Countess Catherina. It is said that she has a more calming influence on his driving than our team manager. I have a special award for him to keep and remember perhaps when times are perhaps difficult. Please welcome Rudolph von Lundenberg."

There was tumultuous applause for Rudolph was very popular. He had a cheerful disposition. He got to his feet and strode proudly over to the top table collected his prize.

The award was a solid gold scale model of a Model '90'. There cries of 'speech.' Rudolph turned and faced the assembled guests.

"Herr Gunther and friends," began Rudolph, "you all know that I am not one to give long speeches. This award is one, which I will always treasure. Driving a racing car really fast and safely within its limits is the easy part. However, without a dedicated team of mechanics behind me I would not have achieved anything at all. So to all those who have put in those long hours of toil in research and development, I can only say a hearty thank you."

Soon the guests returned to the Ballroom and the merriment continued. The evening came to an end, and Rudolph and Catherina said Merry Christmas to all their friends. The factory would close now until the New Year. It was time for relaxation and time to enjoy the festive season. The strains of racing and long hours were behind them for another year, and no doubt, 1909 would bring it challenges too. Rudolph and Catherina went back to their Hotel to have a good night's sleep, for next day they would travel back to Schloss von Lundenberg.

The next morning they ordered breakfast from room service, for they had very little time, they had to catch the late morning train. It was a very cold day and there was a hint of snow in the air. They quickly dressed, then ordered a cab to take them to their home nearby. Then, packing a suitcase and putting on their warmest furs, they got back into the taxi and headed for the Station. Rudolph had requested a private compartment so he could be alone with his lovely wife. They wanted to re-enact their first meeting on that fateful day. Catherina was wearing the same blue fox coat, boots and bonnet, that she had been wearing on that day when she first met the love of her life. The train steamed in and they climbed aboard and found their reserved apartment. Rudolph pulled down the blinds and locked the door.

"You my darling Catherina," said Rudolph passionately, "are the love of my life. I remember the day we first met as if it were yesterday. That fur coat you are now wearing really got my attention. When I first saw you on the Platform and then you came in my compartment, it seemed as if we were fated to meet."

Catherina snuggled up next to Rudolph and kissed him.

"I have news for you my love," she said, "that day we met on this very station, I first noticed you sitting on a seat reading a newspaper. At first, I wanted to approach you, and sit on the seat beside you. Then, I thought that would perhaps not be the best way to meet a young man. So, I hoped you would help me with my heavy suitcase and may be I could share your compartment. I also hoped that you were not married. At the time, I was very frustrated with my life, as you well know. I was really aching to make love to you there and then and I wanted to give my all to you, but had to control myself and hope that you would not reject me. Then we began to talk and I fell in love with you almost at once. I knew that you too would love me if we could find a way, and since that moment I have never been happier. There is one thing that would make it complete."

Rudolph kissed her passionately.

"My darling," he said as their lips parted, "I am sure that I know the answer to that?"

Catherina kissed him again.

"I am sure that you do," she replied, "I just want to have your children."

"Darling Catherina, you know you always arouse me, especially in those gorgeous furs of yours. The softness against my skin sends tingles through my body. You have given so much sexual pleasure that I could not deny you anything. We must always make love, not in a lustful way, but as man and wife enjoying intercourse together."

Catherina knew that she had a partner for life. She started to arouse him and before long they had sexual union. It was something they wanted when they first met. Now it was a reality. By the time they had finished and freshened up the train had slowed on the outskirts of Heidelberg. Here the Count Josef had arranged for his chauffeur to meet the young couple, so that they could get to the Castle as soon as possible.

On the steps of the Schloss, Rudolph's father greeted his handsome son and beautiful daughter in law. It would be a great Christmas. Count Josef was proud of his son's achievements for the Fatherland. The Schloss was decorated as usual with an array of festive decorations and the traditional Christmas trees. Rudolph was glad to be home among the people he loved. Catherina felt that at last she was part of a family, who loved her. The chambermaid, Eva showed them to their room, unpacked their suitcases, and put their clothes in the boudoir. After she had left the room, closing the door behind her, Rudolph and Catherina were alone at last. Catherina gave Rudolph one of her come hither looks; he knew exactly what she meant, for they had an hour before Dinner would be served. So why waste it? There was a roaring fire burning in the large fireplace. They were both naked; Catherina slipped on her blue fox and beckoned Rudolph with her finger. He did not need a second invitation. He was on the bed with Catherina on top of him, for it was time for pleasures of the flesh.

She rode him until they were both satisfied.

"That was absolute bliss darling," she said getting off from the love of her life, "now we can bath together and join the family for Dinner."

Catherina and Rudolph had a wonderful Christmas together. Count Josef and Margarita could see how happy Rudolph was with his bride. She was intelligent, able to talk on a variety of subjects and an astute businesswoman. She had style, beauty, personality, and a great sense of humour. Josef hoped that in time she would produce an heir. It seemed strange to Josef, that in her previous marriage she had no children. Josef would not be so presumptuous as to ask why. Perhaps her first husband was either not interested or infertile. She was very beautiful, how could someone not want to make love to her. Josef kept these thoughts to himself. Over the Christmas holidays she explained to Rudolph that, in fact her first husband had never consummated their marriage. She had been a virgin when she met him. She also said that in Mid-January they would have to go to see her late husband's junior partner. His name is Joseph Taunus and he had just 10% of the Company shares. He was left in charge of her shipping business, when her husband had died. Catherina did not have a lot to do with her husband's business. She had met Josef only twice and then only briefly. After all as she had explained to Rudolph, she was merely an accessory that Johann took with him on some business trips. When Johann had died she was left to pick up the pieces. Josef Taunus had been a great help. She had passed the reins over to him, but she said that she would visit when she could. Whilst she had been in contact with Josef on a weekly basis, she had not had the time to go to see him. The reports she had from the Hamburg Office were encouraging. There was plenty of business. In fact, they had picked up 3 more Clients in the last week. She felt that the business was in good hands. They would have to travel to Hamburg on the River Elbe, for it was here that he had his office. Rudolph said he would ask the factory to left him take some leave.

On his return to the factory, Rudolph had a meeting with Gustav and asked for a leave of absence on a personal matter. There were plans to redesign the cars for 1909, and with no Grand Prix or international events to compete in, January would be a quiet month. Gustav said that Rudolph could take as much time as he liked to sort out the family affairs.

They had not planned any testing until the weather improved. So please be back before the end of January as there was still some wok to do. Rudolph told Catherina all about this, she was happy that her husband could get involved in something other than Motor Racing. Now there was the trip to Hamburg in the New Year to plan and look forward to. Catherina wanted Rudolph to get involved, with what was after all a family business. They did not know how long Rudolph's career with Mercedes would last. Christmas in the von Lundenberg household involved, periods of indulgence in a variety of pleasures, these being eating, drinking, rejoicing and loving. Catherina and Rudolph could really enjoy themselves. It was truly a fabulous festive season and they made passionate love as the old year ended and the new one began.

January 1909 began; plans were made to go to Hamburg to see Josef Taunus and his wife Eva. Catherina had booked them a private compartment on the train with a double bed. It was Tuesday 5th January when they set out on a journey of over 400 kilometres, and would mean travelling through the night. It would be their mobile love nest. They had business to discuss, but not until they reached Hamburg. They would be staying in the Company house on the outskirts of the City. Catherina gathered together the most recent reports that she had from Josef, for he was her right hand man. The weather was cold, so Catherina wore Rudolph's favourite furs, the Blue fox. She knew it would bring back memories of their first meeting. The journey was uneventful, except of course that from time to time meals would be sent from the Restaurant Car. Catherina joked that they were having courses between intercourses. Rudolph laughed out loud. Rudolph recalled that first time, when they had sexually aroused each other on, their first train journey together. That was just over a year ago, time had certainly flown by. That coat that had started it all was there in front of him.

It was her beautiful furs that had made Rudolph notice her on Stuttgart Station. Now that lovely lady was his wife and the love of his life.

On arrival at Hamburg Station, Josef was on the Platform to greet them together with the Company chauffeur. In the warmth of the rear seats of the Daimler, Josef outlined the problems. It was not something that could be resolved easily in a day or so. Josef suggested that they go to the Company house to freshen up.

It was still early in the day, and later they could meet for lunch in a nearby Restaurant and that evening they could all have dinner. Josef would arrange for the car to collect them. Having had a bath, they got ready, the car arrived at noon and off they went to the Restaurant. Over lunch, Josef explained the dilemma. It seemed that when Catherina's first husband, Johann had been killed, he had been returning from a meeting in Scotland. He had been negotiating with a Company called Macdonald & Co.Ltd, to ship some heavy machinery to India. The Manufacturers were Stuart & Co.Ltd of Glasgow, with offices in Edinburgh. The deal had to be completed by the end of June 1909. Orders had been placed for the machinery; these would be ready for collection from Stuart's by the end of May. The job would take the manufacturers three months to make. The final contracts had not been signed, so a swift decision needed to be made. If the papers were not signed by the end of January the deal, worth millions of marks would be lost. On top of this the Company's reputation would be at stake.

Catherina agreed that the first task was to contact the Companies concerned to tell them all was well. They all agreed that there was no alternative but to travel to Scotland

and sign the papers. There was no time like the present. So, telegrams were sent and the Companies responded. Catherina and Rudolph said that they would set off for Edinburgh, as soon as the necessary arrangements were made. It was a week later January 21st 1909, before they could set out on the trip. Neither Catherina nor Rudolph were good sailors, so they would travel by train to Calais then ferry to Dover. It was a very long journey; at times they thought they would never get there. Catherina looked at Rudolph and smiled.

"Darling," she said, "we can always make love to pass the time can't we?"

Rudolph's smile, answered her question. It was an exhausting journey, both sexually and mentally. They were very relieved, in all senses of the word, when their train finally steamed into Edinburgh Waverley Station. On the platform to greet them was a bearded redheaded Scotsman, he was holding up a sign with Rudolph's name on it. As they approached him he smiled.

"Hello Herr von Lundenberg," said the Scotsman, "may I introduce myself my name is Donald Macdonald. I am the Managing Director of the Company. Welcome to Edinburgh."

He shook Rudolph warmly by the hand.

"It is a pleasure to meet you, sir," Rudolph replied in his best English, "and may I introduce my wife Catherina to you?"

Donald bowed and kissed the back of Catherina's hand.

"It is a pleasure to meet you Catherina," replied Donald, "now would you both please follow me I have a car waiting for us."

The Rolls took them to the Company Offices, where Donald introduced them to Mr. Irvine Stuart, the Managing Director of Stuart & Co. They were delighted, that Catherina and her husband were able to come to Scotland, to discuss matters. They were sorry for her loss; Johann had struck a good deal with them. They hoped that they could conclude the deal, so that manufacture could begin, and shipment could take place on time. It was getting late, they asked could the papers be signed and later, perhaps they could all meet for Dinner. Donald said he had booked them in at the Waverley Hotel. Catherina agreed, and the papers were signed. Everyone breathed a sigh of relief. Catherina and Rudolph were then taken to the Hotel, the Company car would return for them at 8 p.m. This gave the young couple a chance to freshen up again get ready for a night on the town.

The time flew by, and by 8 p.m. they were waiting in reception. Donald and Irvine met them and took them to the best Restaurant in the City. It was a great night, Donald and Irvine said he would not talk shop, and they did not. Neither Catherina nor Rudolph had ever been to Scotland. They were surprised at the hospitality shown to them. Irvine asked them if they planned to spend some time in Edinburgh. Rudolph said that they wanted to spend one day as tourists. Donald said he would make arrangements for a car and chauffeur to be at their disposal.

He would guide them around the City, and that night she invited them back to his home to have Dinner with his family.

Next morning at 9.30 a.m. Jock, the chauffeur was waiting for them in Reception. Rudolph and Catherina had slept really well, for another of their problems had been solved. They had a lovely day touring this beautiful City. The weather was cold and dry. Catherina was glad she was wearing her furs, there was an icy wind blowing. Rudolph too was dressed warmly in his fur-lined overcoat and fur hat. They saw the ancient Castle perched high on the hill, and even had time to visit the Art galleries and Museums, and the house at 11, Rutland Street, the home of the famous Joseph Lister. He was the man who used carbolic acid to purify the air and the dressing of wounds. He had operated on Queen Victoria in 1871 lancing an abscess.

After a great day seeing the sites, their trip ended with a traditional Scottish meal with the MacDonald family. Catherina was not that enthused on the haggis, but was willing to try anything new. In any case, she did not want to upset her host. Catherina and Rudolph bade farewell to their hosts, thanking them for their overwhelming hospitality. They hoped that business between their two companies would expand as time passed. The next morning the von Lundenbergs set off home. They had concluded a very successful deal indeed. Catherina and Rudolph had really enjoyed their trip to Scotland and had made many friends there.

The return journey was long, but at least they could rest and watch the world go by, or shut it out and make love. Finally, they arrived home, absolutely exhausted. The next day Catherina telephoned Josef in Hamburg, told him the good news. He was delighted that everything was back on track and he would speak to her soon. Rudolph started to look through the pile of post that had arrived since they had left home. Amongst them, was a letter from his old friend, and ex-Mercedes driver, Hermann Ritter. He had not seen Catherina or Rudolph since their wedding, and asked if they were well and had started a family yet? Rudolph thought, 'no but it not for the want of trying.' Hermann went on to say that he was enjoying working for Maybach but missed the thrill of motor racing. They had now produced some new, more powerful engines that were to be fitted to a bigger airship to be built by Count Ferdinand von Zeppelin. They hoped to do some test flights later in the year. He hoped that they would come to visit him at his home near Friedricshafen on the shores of Lake Constance. He had become engaged to a local girl called Ingrid; they hoped to marry within a year. Rudolph wrote back saying what they had been doing and would love to visit them in the spring for a week or so, if that would be convenient.

As the weeks passed, Catherina started to miss her periods. The family Doctor was called, and he looked at Catherina and tested her with his stethoscope.

He listened to her stomach and smiled at her.

"Catherina my dear, said the Doctor, "you are pregnant."

Rudolph was delighted. He was going to become a father. Catherina was absolutely thrilled; at last she could be the Mother of Rudolph's children. She was two months into her pregnancy.

Rudolph was now hard at work, developing a new car for the road. The Model '60', and '90' had served the Company well, they now needed replacing. There were no major races now, so Rudolph asked for a week's holiday to visit his friend.

"Why not," replied Gustav, "you have been working hard?"

Catherina and Rudolph made arrangements to see Hermann in his new home. It was their first visit to the town on the shores of Lake Constance. The trip was most enjoyable, again by train of course. Catherina said they could make love on the way, but he must treat her gently. Their journey took them down the valley of the River Rhine, crossing the Swiss border, and on through breathtaking scenery to their final destination. Hermann and Ingrid were waiting for them as their train steamed in. Hermann introduced his friends to his fiancée. Ingrid was an extremely beautiful girl in her late 20's. She had long blonde hair and a superb figure. Catherina saw Rudolph give her a few sideways glances. She gave him a nudge with her elbow.

"Now, now," she would say, "remember me?"

They enjoyed their stay with Hermann and Ingrid. They had the tour of the House and Town plus a trip on a Lake Steamer.

The holiday came to an end far too quickly. Catherina invited Hermann and Ingrid to come and stay for a while when work allowed.

All too soon Rudolph was back at Mercedes, when on Monday 26th July; Rudolph was sitting at his desk sorting out some new drawings, when Gustav rushed in excitingly waving a newspaper.

"Do you see this," he shouted, "do you see this?"

He laid the newspaper on Rudolph's desk. The Newspaper banner headline read: - 'FRENCHMAN BLERIOT FLIES ENGLISH CHANNEL.' On Sunday 25th July 1909 French aviator Louis Bleriot in a machine of his own design had flown from La Baraques in France and landed at Northfall Meadow near Dover Castle in England. The machine was powered by a 23 h.p. Anzani engine. The flight took just over 36 minutes. The flight started at 4.41 a.m.

"After this monumental event," said Gustav excitedly, "Mercedes will no doubt have to start designing aircraft engines."

"That may well be the future," replied Rudolph on a cautionary note, "but everyone will always need car engines."

"That is true, Rudolph but we must look to the future and expand our interests. Aircraft are still in their infancy, but we all know how fast technology moves. We must be in the forefront. We must progress more quickly than our competitors; otherwise we shall be playing catch up."

Rudolph nodded in agreement for he knew Gustav was right.

"Knowledge is power." Gustav continued, "we have the knowledge here at Mercedes. We have to use that to beat all of our rivals. You remember when you were racing. Can you tell me who came second? I bet you cannot, for nobody remembers who comes second do they? The future is now!"

Rudolph pushed his chair back.

"Gustav, my friend," replied Rudolph, "I will do anything to help you and this Company. You have been very good to me since I started here. You have my entire support. For any new project."

Gustav shook Rudolph by the hand.

"I knew I could count on you Rudolph," replied Gustav, "we have an excellent team here, we can do anything and everything. This I believe is the start of great things."

The two men hugged each other. The news of Bleriot's flight had made them realise that they could no longer be complacent; they had to push for more money for research and development.

Gustav knew that the Management would be behind them. They had conquered the Motor Sport world, so far, now they hoped to triumph to the skies, by building the best engines to power the greatest aircraft the world had ever seen. Certainly this would be a tall order.

Chapter 13

For John Ashdown 1908 had been a busy year. The Brewery had done especially well, profits were up and the shareholders were pleased. In late April, Lord John had taken Victoria for a two-week holiday to the Lake District in Northern England. They had gone by train, for he thought that the drive of some 300 miles would be too much for his pregnant wife. They needed to get away for a break. The Hotel was at Bowness-on-Windermere. It was a beautiful place, and the view from their Hotel suite looked across Lake Windermere. They could see the lake steamers cruising, full of happy holidaymakers. John and Victoria would go for walks in the hills, and even enjoy an ice cream and the occasional cream tea.

They made several trips on the lake steamers, visiting Ambleside, and the other picturesque villages along the lake. They had a wonderful time; it was like being on honeymoon all over again. After dinner each evening, Victoria made John keep to his New Year Resolution every night. They were away from the stresses of the Brewery business. They could be themselves and have fun. A word that did not come into their vocabulary that often. It was great not to have the telephone ringing with problems at the Brewery. Early mornings, resolving this and that. It was wonderful to lie in bed, make love and have room service. This break enabled them both to recharge their batteries, so to speak. John promised Victoria that this would be a holiday. He would not contact the Brewery at all. He had left his Manager, James Colgate in charge. Any problems that arose, then he could solve them. Most of the time, the Brewery almost ran itself, well almost.

When John had taken over from his father, he had created a system for each department. He had run classes to instruct each supervisor how to achieve maximum efficiency, using his system. Everything now worked well, with levels of responsibility set down for each area of operation. John kept his word while they were in the Lake District; he did not make one call. Victoria made sure that his thoughts were on pleasure, not work. The holiday did them both the world of good. They travelled back to Horsham feeling totally relaxed. Victoria was now starting to get a recurrence of her morning sickness.

John was soon back at work taking the reins, for he knew with the warmer weather just a week or two away, there would be increasing demand for his products. He had received a letter from Maria di Gigli, explaining that now that her husband's affairs were in order, that she would like to continue negotiations regarding supplying wine to his Brewery. John had made arrangements to meet Maria's husband just prior to his death. However, it all had been put on hold. John did not know whether Maria was interested to carry on her husband's business or not. He hoped that he could do business with her for the terms suggested by Marco were very good indeed. He sent a letter to Maria saying that he would like to meet her to finalise their arrangements, later in the year. John explained to Maria that his wife, Victoria was expecting a baby at the end of September. He could meet her in early December in Italy. This would give her time to set aside supplies for him, and should there be any problems with the birth of his child, he would be there for his wife. Maria wrote back and suggested that they meet in Milan on Tuesday December 1st 1908, at the Grand Hotel. John was looking forward to the trip; it had been some years since he had visited Italy. He had been to Spain where he had been getting supplies from wineries in the Rioja region. The Italian wines would expand his range of fine wines. He could then expand into the retail market and increase his Brewery's profitability.

Summer had arrived, and the Ashdowns went along to speech day at Christ's Hospital. It was a special day of the school year, held on a Saturday about a month before the end of term. This year 1908, it was held on Saturday 13th June. The Lord Mayor of London attended the event as usual. Parents would have special tickets to go into the building known as Big School, to hear the Senior Grecian, Francis Bell give the oratory. He would narrate in detail, without the benefit of notes, the events of the School Year.

Later, in the afternoon there would be tea for all in the Dining Hall. That would give a chance for all the visitors to see the fine ceiling and the wonderful Verrio painting. Nigel had been playing both Rugby and Cricket for his house and the team had won the inter-house competitions. They had played other local schools with a good deal of success. Nigel was now 13 years old and growing into a handsome young man.

He was very popular and had lot of friends and introduced several of them to his parents. They enjoyed the day, for they knew that their son would soon be home for the summer holiday. The days soon passed, and the chauffeur collected Nigel from school, the family was now all together once more. Nigel always enjoyed the summer holidays, he was always out with his friends, but like all boys his stomach knew when it was mealtime. It gave him time to relax, go horse riding, and sometime amuse himself in his hobby of model making.

The warm, lazy summer days enabled Victoria to sit outside on the vast lawn in her favourite wicker chair. To drink cool lemonade, enjoy tea in the bright warm sunshine. She was now very conscious of her diet, so the family Physician, Doctor Vernon made regular visits to check on her health.

It was during the last six weeks of her pregnancy, that Doctor Vernon had advised her that intercourse would have to stop, as it may affect the baby's development. She realised now that she would have to satisfy John, and not herself. John had always been gentle with her during their lovemaking. When he knew that she was pregnant, he was even more careful. They both wanted this child, whatever sex it might be. Victoria wanted a girl, perhaps she would get her wish, for John and Victoria were loving parents and would do nothing to upset each other. Nigel thought they were perfect parents. Although John could get annoyed if pressed, he was always approachable. He had his own business to run, as well as being head of the family. He treated his employees firmly but fairly, and he ran his family the same way, but with tenderness and love. August turned into September; Nigel was now back at Christ's Hospital with another term ahead with more challenges no doubt to his brainpower. Victoria felt her time to give birth was fast approaching. She felt unbalanced, and would be put into a wheelchair if she wanted to go out in the grounds of Ashdown Hall. Any travelling was out of the question. In the last week of September, John took time off to be with his wife. All was going well, Victoria was a strong woman, and all the checks showed that the baby inside her was healthy.

In the early hours of September 30th 1908, the Doctor and Midwife were called.

Victoria had gone into labour that last 8 hours. With the Doctor, Midwife, and John at Victoria's bedside she gave birth to a baby girl. They named her Alexandra Victoria; she came into the world in the early afternoon of the 1st October 1908, weighing in at a healthy 8 lbs. She was a dark haired beauty just like her Mother. When Victoria held the little baby in her arms for the first time, John was by her bedside. Victoria leaned across to her husband.

"My darling John, thank you for keeping our New Year resolution for so long. I have that wonderful Silver fox Coat and a really sexy husband to thank for giving birth to this gorgeous young lady. I do love you so much."

"Dearest Victoria, I love you so much. I know that those furry gifts were the catalyst to our sexual union. I have that coat and you to thank for more pleasures in our lives than I can possibly imagine. I am certain that there are many more to come."

Baby Alexandra started to cry. Victoria looked down at their newborn daughter.

"Darling John, isn't she the most wonderful baby girl? I think I should start feeding her now."

She moved her daughter up to her right breast. The little baby took the nipple in its mouth and began to feed. John was overjoyed at the new arrival. They both thanked God for bringing them closer together. They had a healthy daughter who they would love and cherish. John phoned Nigel at School and told him the good news. He now had a baby sister, both the Alexandra and Mother well doing well. A new era had begun for the Ashdowns.

The next event on John's mind would be the visit to Milan to meet Maria. Victoria's main concern was her daughter. Nigel asked his House Master Mr. Swan for a day's leave so, that he could see his new sister. That weekend, Lamb House did not have a Rugby Match, so Mr. Swan was happy for Nigel to see his family. Apart from seeing Alexandra, he said it was nice to have proper food again. The School had just employed a new Chef, and he had yet to get to grips with mass catering. Some of the dishes, Nigel actually recognised. He said most of the boys, were so hungry that they would have eaten the tables. They had only 20 or so minutes to consume their lunch. He always kept his fingers crossed that the culinary expertise of Mr. Ronald Maxim, the so-called Chef would improve with time and experience.

On Sunday morning, Nigel was back at school in time for Morning Service.

After a day's diversion at home, it was back to normal, sleeping on those hard horsehair mattresses. Mr. Swan called him into his study one morning. He asked him to sit down, because he wanted to ask Nigel about his future, what he intended to do after he left Christ's Hospital. Mr. Swan told him that the school had an excellent academic record, especially foreign languages and with the grades he was getting a place at either Cambridge or Oxford would be well within his grasp.

"Well sir," answered Nigel confidently, "my father wants me to go to University and perhaps follow in his footsteps at the Brewery. He also wants me to obviously get good grades, and a degree in Engineering rather than the Arts. He wants me to perfect my foreign languages such as French, and German. You see the Brewery has business in those countries. I have a feeling he would like me to go to Oxford University and even learn to fly."

Mr. Swan stroked his chin and looked thoughtful for a moment.

"I think young Nigel, that you have very clear idea of your future. French and German will certainly be an asset to you. Learning to fly will be useful in the years to come. I have a feeling that in years to come most people will travel that way. After all it is so much quicker than by boat, or train. Technology seems to be moving so fast these days. Most of you boys here always seem to be in a hurry. May be we have a school full of potential pilots. Any problems at anytime please call on me. Please don't struggle alone"

Nigel got up, and thanked Mr. Swan for his time and advice.

The next few weeks passed quickly. Alexandra seemed to be growing by the day and was becoming what John called - 'a proper little character'. The Brewery was doing very well for retail sales had increased through their off-licences. John hoped that if he had the new range of wines from Italy in his public houses and off-licences then 1909 would be an excellent year. Even if they were half as popular as his Spanish ones.

On Monday 30th November 1908, John was up early and packed for his three-day trip to Milan. He was excited as the prospect of doing a good deal, providing Maria would stick by the terms laid down in a draft agreement by her late husband Marco. The morning was cold with hardly a breath of wind and the sky a clear blue. John was well wrapped up in his fur lined leather coat and fur hat. Victoria hated him in hats. He told her it is going to be cold on this journey I am certain, so I intend to keep warm.

His chauffeur dropped him at Horsham Station, where he caught the train to Victoria. Here he caught the Express to Dover, and then transferred to the ferry to take him to Calais for the next part of the journey. John made his way into the Ship's Lounge and looked out across the English Channel, and the sea was like a millpond. He walked up to the Bar and ordered a drink. The bar steward asked what he would like.

"Just a soft drink please." John replied.

The steward returned with a glass of orange juice. He put the glass down on the bar and John put down three pennies on the Bar.

"No money needed sir," replied the Steward drying a glass, "that drink is with the compliments of the Company. Looks like we shall have a smooth crossing today."

John picked up the glass and taking a sip replied.

"Thank you for the drink steward. I'm pleased that it is going to be a good crossing for I am not that fond of the sea. Although I did sail home with the family from India years ago. Can't think how many times I was seasick."

John moved away from the Bar and found a seat. Soon the ship lifted its anchor and they were off to Calais.

The sea trip was just as the steward had predicted and they docked on schedule at Calais, and he passed through Customs. Those passengers going on to the SNCF train, were escorted to it by a French Railway Inspector. John soon settled down into his reserved compartment as the train steamed out of Calais heading for Paris, which was the first stop. John looked out of the window at the flat French countryside; the train blasted its whistle as it passed through many little stations. Then it slowed as it came into the Gare du Nord, and shuddered to a halt as the engine came against the buffers. Over the station loudspeaker system there was an announcement, in French of course, informing passengers to remain on the train, which would be going on to Milan. The Station announcer then gave out a list of stations where the train would be stopping. John looked at his itinerary, apparently the train would arrive in Milan about 8.30 p.m., that evening, the Grand Hotel was only minutes from the Station and they would serve dinner until 10 p.m. John settled down to read a book he had brought with him, although he was not an avid reader, but he enjoyed a good thriller. The train steward came around to tell him that the Restaurant Car was open. So John made his way down to the Car, which was crowded with early diners. The steward said that he would have to share a table, but John said he did not mind.

His dining companion was English, his name was Martin Jensen. He was a buyer in Ladies fashions and was travelling to Milan for the Spring Collections. He was an interesting man in his 40's and owned his business, with a showroom in Bond Street. He invited John and his wife to visit his showroom when they were in London. He would introduce them to his wife Antionette, who was French of course. The two men got only really well, which was surprising as they were from completely different backgrounds. John had that talent to make anyone in his company feel at ease. The rest of his journey seemed to pass by quickly and soon they were in Milan. When they left the train, John hailed a taxi and said farewell to Martin. They shook hands and hoped that they would meet again. John was now quite weary for it had been a long journey. Having checked in, the bellboy took his case up to the room. The reception clerk informed John that dinner was being served for another hour. By now John was feeling really hungry, and so, he did not bother to unpack, he tipped the bellboy to do that for him. He had a quick wash in the Bathroom and made his way to the Restaurant for a filling meal. The waiter suggested, Minestrone Soup followed by the Steak Diane with Baked Alaska as a dessert. John was ready for this and he cleaned his plate and headed for his room for a good night's sleep. Lying there, it seemed strange not to have Victoria by his side, for this was the first time they had been apart since their marriage. Having slept soundly, showered, it must have been almost 9.30 a.m., by the time he reached the breakfast table. He was now looking forward to meeting the Maria, for he remembered meeting her on one previous occasion. So having finished breakfast he returned to his room, and then he made his way to the reception area to await Maria di Gigli.

On the dot of 11.00, Maria appeared in Reception with Dino by her side. She looked stunning in her furs and finery as she waltzed over to the reception clerk. He directed Maria and Dino to John who was seated in one of the leather armchairs. Maria took Dino's hand and led him across to where John was sitting. Maria looked down at him and smiled.

"Are you Lord Ashdown?" she asked in broken English:

John stood up and kissed her hand.

"Yes I am Lord Ashdown, you must be Signorina Gigli, but please, call me John."

Maria smiled again.

"Yes I am Countess di Gigli John and my first name is Maria, I would like you to meet my partner Dino. He knows all about these agreement things. He was in Banking."

John looked at the dark haired young man by her side.

"Delighted to make your acquaintance Sir," answered Dino.

John returned his gaze to Maria. She was certainly the loveliest lady he had seen in a long time. He hoped that she had a head for business. Her body was very shapely and it was clear how she attracted a handsome young man like Dino.

"Maria," said John, "if we are to discuss business I will ask the reception clerk for a room where we will not be disturbed."

John went over to the desk, where he spoke to the clerk who handed him a key. They were supplied with coffee in the room where they talked about many things. They agreed to the terms originally set out by Maria's late husband. These were fair on both sides. Financial arrangements were made for payment and everyone was happy.

They celebrated over lunch. In the evening Maria took them all to the opera to see Mozart's Magic Flute that was fantastic, in the beautiful Opera House. The evening ended with Dinner and more conversation, and John then said he hoped that he did not appear rude, but he felt tired and wanted to go to bed, for he had a long journey the next day. Maria gave him a draft copy of the contract that they had agreed. John kissed her hand to wish her goodnight and hoped that they would meet again soon.

Maria turned to speak to Dino once John was out of earshot.

"That is what I call a true gentleman. I would love to meet his wife she sounds like a real lady."

Early next morning, John checked out of the Grand Hotel and returned to England. He did not meet anyone interesting on the return trip, so he managed to finish the first book he had read for ages. He had concluded his contract and was delighted with the terms that had been agreed with Maria di Gigli. No doubt when he arrived home Victoria would be interested to find out what sort of woman he was going to do business with. As soon as John arrived home, Victoria wanted to know everything that had transpired since he had left Ashdown Hall. John told her everything and that how Maria di Gigli was very beautiful woman and had been widowed for some time. She was living with a young man Dino Borghese who was separated from his wife; he could tell from their meeting that Maria kept her partner on a very short leash.

She was a good businesswoman and had a reliable source for good quality wine. Victoria asked what he thought about her apart from business. He told Victoria that her personal life was of no concern to him, and in any case he never listened to gossip.

"My darling Victoria," answered John, "all I know is that the quality of her wines are excellent. We shall make a good profit from their sale through our licensed premises."

Nigel had been enjoying his year at Christ's Hospital; he had worked very hard to get good results in the end of term exams. It had brought rewards in the form of school prizes. He was glad to be home for Christmas, to relax and be with his parents. The diet that Nigel had been experiencing at Christ's Hospital was far removed from the fare he was now enjoying at home. He was always hungry and was forever raiding the kitchen. The Cook, Doreen Matthews, asked him one day, whilst she was making bread.

"Have you got hollow legs, young Nigel?"

Nigel was too busy eating a hot scone to reply. During the holiday, John let his Nigel loose driving the Mercedes around the estate. John would spend time with him when he was not busy at the Brewery. Nigel was eager to learn.

The Model '60' was a big car to handle for a 13-year-old. John was surprised how quickly he managed to control the car. John and Victoria held the annual Brewery Party, which as usual was a big success. There were bonuses for those that had helped increase the productivity of the Company. These were presented by Victoria. Nigel was allowed to attend and managed to dance with a few of the ladies present. It was a time of celebration, and of course it was baby Alexandra's first Christmas and everyone made a fuss of her. Lily Green, the Nurse had been given other jobs around Ashdown Hall, once Nigel began as a boarder at Christ's Hospital. She had become a lady's maid to Victoria, but now that there was a new baby in the household, she got her old position back again. Alexandra took to Lily very well and hardly ever cried.

The Family Christmas Eve Party was a roaring success, for all the local gentry were invited, and Nigel met up with his friend, Andrew Crowley, for they had a lot of catching up to do. Andrew had won a scholarship; he was at Marlborough School, so they only managed to meet up at Christmas and sometimes in the summer holidays. Andrew was studying languages, and doing very well and he hoped to be a translator one-day.

It was like old times as the two boys got in a huddle in one corner, until Victoria asked them to mix with the guests. The guests enjoyed a sumptuous feast as always with presents being exchanged. Victoria wondered what her present would be this year. She recalled the silver fox coat she had last year, and she very much doubted if that could be topped. When the party ended and John and Victoria had said farewell to the last of their guests, they both breathed a sigh of relief.

"My darling Victoria," said John, "I know last year I gave you that beautiful coat, bonnet and boots. This year I could not let you think that I had forgotten you."

Victoria was curious, what could it be this time?

"No my love," continued John, "it is not another fur coat, but some real hand made Italian leather boots. I got them on my trip to Milan. Go and try them on?"

John led Victoria up to their bedroom, and produced a large black box tied with a red ribbon. Victoria carefully undid the bow and opened the box, and inside was the most beautiful pair of black leather, slip-on silver fox fur topped boots. Victoria took them out of the box and tried them on and they fitted perfectly. Then she walked up and down the room in them finally returning to John who was standing watching her.

"I feel like Cinderella darling," she said, "except I already have my Prince Charming, who is about to grant me three wishes. I will certainly not leaving one of these behind."

John laughed and looking at her could tell how much she liked his present.

"Those boots look lovely on you darling. By the way, I have another present for you."

He walked over to a cabinet by the side of the bed and got out a red leather case.

"Now open this," he said.

Victoria opened the case and inside was a pearl and emerald necklace. John helped Victoria put it around her neck. She went over to the full-length mirror and admired the workmanship of the jeweller that had made the necklace.

"It is absolutely wonderful, my love. Now it is time to perform our New Year Resolution."

John saw her getting out her silver fox coat, and he knew what pleasure was forthcoming.

"Well," she quipped, "I shall need this coat tomorrow too you know. It is likely to be cold."

John laughed out loud. He was about to express his love for his lovely wife in the best way he knew how, the physical union of their body fluids. They made passionate love all night long.

The next morning, having had a good night's sleep, Victoria and John were feeling wonderful after their night of sexual rapture. Nigel was already downstairs enjoying a hearty breakfast.

Soon, his parents joined him, he noticed that they were smiling, and that was always a good sign that they would be in a good mood for the rest of the day. Christmas Day was always a special day for the family. After breakfast they all got dressed up ready for the short trip in the Limousine down to the village church for the Family Service. Victoria was dressed in her silver fox from head to toe was wearing her new boots. The chauffeur brought the car around, the family climbed aboard and soon they were at the Church. Victoria was feeling wonderful after her night of passion, and sensuous too, wrapped up in her furs, for sitting next to her was the love of her life.

The Vicar Rev. Ward greeted Victoria, John, and Nigel as they walked up the path to the Church porch. The organ was playing as the congregation was getting seated in their pews. The little church was crowded for the Christmas morning service that was no doubt the most popular of the year. To the right of the altar there was a nativity scene, the villagers had made this. The organ struck up a familiar hymn and the service began. Victoria was singing, and glancing at her husband John; he had his mind on other things but still managed to utter the words.

Nigel meanwhile, was singing and thinking, 'I wonder how long the sermon will be today?' Sitting next to Nigel was his friend Andrew Crowley; he too had the same thoughts. They always enjoyed the Christmas morning service, but they both agreed that the sermons of the Rev. Ward were always far too long. Somehow, they thought he had lost the plot, and more often than not they could not figure out what he was getting at. Then the moment the boys were dreading, the Rev. Ward climbed the stairs up to the lectern to give his sermon. Victoria huddled in her furs was still miles away, thinking of the pleasure of giving birth to a lovely, healthy little girl. The church was never kept very warm; the Vicar said it kept his parishioners awake. John thought he was trying to save money on the heating bills. During the year there had been the usual appeals, bring and buy sales, and of course a harvest festival. The congregation knew that their church would be cool and always dressed accordingly. Finally, the sermon came to an end. John gave Victoria a nudge; she shook her head and got ready for the final hymn. As they left, John and Victoria asked the Rev. Ward back to Ashdown Hall for the traditional drink.

This year, the Vicar declined the invitation, as his wife had prepared an early lunch, for he had a baptism in the early afternoon. Victoria said that they must arrange for baby Alexandra to be christened soon, perhaps early in the spring. Victoria said that it would be too cold for her to come out when the weather was so cold. The Ashdown family, wished the Vicar and his wife a very Happy Christmas and then it was back into the Limousine to Ashdown Hall. It was lovely to be back home again, and all the family were looking forward to the Christmas lunch, when the traditional Turkey and all the trimmings would be served.

Nigel, Andrew, and John were deep in conversation in the Morning Room, while Victoria was in her bedroom removing her furs. Her new boots were so comfortable, that she did not want to remove them. Soon, all the family members were around the table in the Dining Room, tucking in to a hearty meal. Nigel particularly enjoyed Christmas dinner, because Cook always came up with a new dessert to tempt the palate. This year it was Chocolate Orange Christmas pudding with Brandy Butter. Nigel thought it was delicious, for he often remarked that he knew little about cooking, but a lot about eating. With dinner over, and having eaten their fill, the men adjourned to the Morning Room. In the nursery, baby Alexandra had been fed, given her bottle and lay now fast asleep in her cot. The nurse, Lily was reading and also keeping an eye on her little companion. This was the kind of Christmas that everyone in Ashdown Hall enjoyed; there was peace and quiet. Everything was in harmony.

Chapter 14

Carla was miserable; she knew the very moment that her marriage to Dino had started to go downhill. She recalled his three-week trip to Rome, and how he had not phoned each evening. This was the first sign that all was not well. Obviously, hindsight is great; you can see things very clearly, after the event. Now she had time to do that. Then she thought about his trip to see Luigi, this was again a lie. She found Luigi's telephone number one afternoon, when she was looking through some of Dino's files, and called him. He told her that he had not heard from Dino for months, and that his finances were in very good shape, and as for his health he never felt better. Things then seemed to go from bad to worse. They had that blazing row, just before Dino walked out on her. She was not surprised that his Father had stuck up for her, for although he loved his son, this was adultery of the worse kind. He was so angry with Dino, that he could leave his wife, child, job, and home for a woman who was a man-eater. Carla thought that she must have some kind of hold over him.

While the weeks passed, Carla became very lonely and angry. She had now moved back to her home and was now living in the villa in Fiesole that she and Dino had bought together. This brought back the kind of memories that left her feeling sad and empty. All the hard work she had put into the marriage was gone. She thought about dispensing with the services of Sophia, the Nanny, to reduce her overheads. Dino had just left, making no financial arrangements to pay household expenses. He held the purse strings; so now, Carla had to draw on the meagre savings in her personal account. Enzo had frozen all Dino's assets; she did not know when she would be able to access them. Her own savings were running low; she had to make a decision soon. Then one day she told Sophia, that she was going into the Bank of Italy to see Signor Borghese, her father-in-law. She telephoned and Enzo as he now liked to be called was delighted to hear from her. He asked her if she had heard anything from that no good husband of hers. She said that she had not. He said he was not surprised. Carla had a favour to ask Enzo and could she come into the Bank.

So on Thursday October 29th 1908, she got dressed in her best winter clothes, and wearing her silver fox furs, that always made her feel special, she headed into the City by taxi. She arrived at the Bank at 11.00 a.m., and knew exactly where to go, for it did not seem that long ago that she was an employee there. Carla knocked on Enzo's door.

"Please come in," a voice called out.

Carla entered Enzo's office, as she did so her father-in-law came across the room to greet her, and invited her to sit down. He picked up the telephone and ordered coffee for them both.

"Carla my dear," began Enzo, "it is a delight to see you again. You are looking a little strained and I can understand that. You know that you are always welcome at the Bank. I see that you have not lost your taste for good clothes and make up. Anyway, enough of small talk. How can I help you?"

At that moment the door opened and Maria, Enzo's secretary, brought in a tray of coffee and biscuits. She looked unamused to say the least, and her body language emphasised this. She left the room without saying a word, and closed the door behind her.

Carla commented that his Secretary did not look too thrilled.

"Oh Maria!" exclaimed Enzo, "it seems from office gossip that her latest man friend has just given her up. I expect it will blow over. It will only be a week or two before she gets another one."

Carla sipped her coffee and began to tell her story about her husband's behaviour. She apologised for being so critical, but that was the way she felt.

Enzo listened intently and sympathetically.

"I agree with you entirely Carla. There is no way that I could ever condone the way you have been treated by my son. It is absolutely disgraceful. I cannot find words to express my distaste for this whole nasty episode. I understand that Dino did not make any financial provisions for either you or Dino Jnr. This is where I can help, I will arrange for some of his funds to be passed to you. In addition, I would love you to come back to the Bank as my Personal Assistant. Sophia could then look after Young Dino. So you see there will be no problem."

Carla's face changed to an expression of surprise.

"That would be marvellous Enzo. It would give me the zest for life once more. I feel at a loss, pinning my hopes on the idea that something will turn up. When can I start?"

Enzo said that she could start on the following Monday. In the meantime, I suggest that we go to lunch, to celebrate your re-employment at the Bank.

Enzo picked up the telephone dialled a number and spoke:

"Hello, is that Franco? It is Enzo Borghese; there will be two for lunch today. OK?"

He put the receiver down turned to Carla.

"Well Carla that is our lunch organised."

They talked for a while about family matters. Carla did not mention her marital troubles again, now she had the answer to some of her problems. At last, she could get her teeth into a proper job once more. Enzo helped Carla on with her coat and then made their way down to Enzo's favourite Restaurant down by the Ponte Vecchio. Enzo's table was by the picture windows, which had a view along the river. Over lunch, Enzo discussed with Carla the terms of her new contract. It gave her a substantial salary and more responsibility. Enzo told her that since Dino had left the Bank, a number of Clients were not very happy. He showed her a list of those that needed an urgent visit. He would call them all before Monday, to prepare them for Carla's visit to each of them during the following week. Carla was over the moon with this new job offer. After lunch, they went back to the Bank where Enzo prepared her new contract, Carla signed it, and Enzo embraced her.

"My dearest daughter-in-law," said Enzo, "may I welcome back to the Bank. I will arrange for an Office, some telephones, and a Secretary for you. I look forward to seeing you on Monday morning."

Carla could not believe her luck. Perhaps things were going to improve and life would return to some sort of normality. On arriving home she gave Sophia the good news, she too was delighted, but Sophia would also have to do the housework as well. Carla enjoyed her weekend and on Monday morning she was back at the Bank. She had still heard nothing from Dino. She was still angry, but after some serious consideration of her position, decided to bury the past. I shall not be able to concentrate on my job, for I have my own future to consider now. Carla's first few weeks at the Bank were very busy. Her Secretary, Juliet was very efficient, and so Carla was able to visit all the Clients on Enzo's list. They were satisfied that at last; they had a reliable contact at the Bank.

Time seemed to pass quickly, and before she knew it November had become December, and the shops in the City began to put up their Christmas decorations. Enzo asked Carla if she had any plans for Christmas. She said that she had not given it much thought. So, Enzo said why not spend the festive holiday with us? Carla said that she would be delighted, for then Sophia would be able to spend Christmas with her family in Florence. Even though Carla had spent a really good Christmas with her in-laws, she could not get Dino out of her mind.

The scars were still fresh and would take time to heal. After the holiday she went into see Enzo to ask his advice. He suggested that she should see a solicitor and file for divorce; he recommended Luciano Arrezo, who is a family friend. Carla telephoned his office, and made an appointment to see him the very next day. Why waste time, she thought? I have to get on with my life. The next morning, Carla arrived at Luciano's office. She decided to wear her fur-trimmed coat and she was now a businesswoman and wanted to look the part rather than be overdressed. Otherwise they may take the view that she had money to burn.

Luciano Arrezo was a tall dark hair gentleman in his late 40's. He welcomed her and invited to sit down and take coffee with him. Carla related the sad tale of her marriage breakdown, and how Dino had behaved after his trip to Rome. She would now be suing for divorce on the grounds of adultery and desertion by her husband Dino and named the other woman simply as Maria. He asked how she knew the name? She told Luciano that she had made love to her husband on the return of one of his trips and when they came to climax Dino had called out the name Maria. Luciano asked, did Carla know where this Maria lived, and was Dino with her? Carla said she thought that Dino must be with her, where else could he be?

"Please leave it with me," replied Luciano, "we will make enquiries through various channels, and we will meet again when I have made progress. I will use a friend of mine who is a Private Investigator."

Carla left Luciano's Office feeling a good deal better; she felt she had at least made a start in putting her life back in order. On arriving back at the Bank, the telephone rang it was Carla's father-in-law.

"Carla," asked Enzo, "how was your meeting this morning?"

"I do not want to talk about it over the telephone," answered Carla, "can I come in to see you?"

"Come now if you are free," said Enzo.

Carla walked back to Enzo's office and gave a short account of her meeting with Luciano. Enzo was pleased that things had started to move, the last thing he needed was his Personal Assistant and daughter-in-law feeling unhappy. Enzo said he had heard from Dino that very day. He said that he was living with a lady called Maria in a villa in Venice and they were not to worry about him.

Carla interrupted Enzo, who was in full flow.

"Excuse me Enzo, but that husband of mine is the least of my worries at the present time. However, I am sorry please continue."

Enzo continued to relate the message by saying that if Carla wanted a divorce, he would be happy to agree terms. Enzo said he would inform Luciano about this; no doubt this would make things easier when it came to the Divorce Court. The telephone rang and Enzo picked up the receiver, it was Luciano and he wanted to speak to Carla. Enzo passed the phone to her. Luciano said that his Partnership dealt with a lawyer named Alfonso Torino, he specialised in divorce and would be briefed well before the case was given a court date. Luciano told her not to worry, for it seemed to be a straightforward case of desertion and adultery.

Carla then threw herself into her work, and would stay late at least three evenings each week to ensure all her paperwork was kept up to date. In the meantime, there was no further word from Dino. Carla worked hard and acquired several new very profitable clients for the bank. At weekends, in early spring she would take Sophia and young Dino for drives into the glorious Italian countryside.

Then in late April 1909, she was summoned to a meeting with Enzo and several other Directors of the Bank in the Boardroom. They had been discussing other matters prior to the moment when Carla came into the room.

"Please sit down Carla," said Enzo, who was sitting at the head of the table.

Carla sat down wondering why she had been called to such an important meeting.

He leaned forward and spoke to Carla directly.

"You have done extremely well, since you have been back at the Bank. We do not want to lose you."

Carla's immediate thoughts were that Dino had written to his father asking for her dismissal from the Bank and her face dropped. "Carla," continued Enzo with a smile on his face, "please do not be unhappy, for you have not heard what we have to offer you yet."

Carla smiled as Enzo opened a file and scanned the page.

"Now my dear let me explain. As I have said we do not want to lose you. We all realise that working in this building will always bring back memories to you that, shall we say are somewhat painful. We want you to work at the Bank for as long as you wish. However, a certain opportunity has arisen and we would like to offer it to you. We hope that you will agree to consider the scheme we have in mind. It will solve certain problems we have at the Bank."

"Enzo," replied Carla looking a little unsettled, "I love working for the Bank, and would do anything I can to help solve any problems."

Enzo nodded his head and he knew then that Carla might accept his proposition.

"Carla, you know that your are a valued employee. You have done an excellent job. Now to the nuts and bolts of the matter we want to put before you."

Enzo took a sip of water from the glass in front of him.

"Carla," continued Enzo, "let me explain the situation to you, and then you can make an informed decision. In the last month we have had some disturbing reports, from one of our best Clients. He has three very large and profitable boutiques; it is fashion house called FORUM. They have one store here in Florence; the others are in Milan and Rome. It has come to our notice, that FORUM has been losing a great deal of money over the past year. There were small sums to begin with, but the situation has become worse and large sums are disappearing every month. I do have the figures here. We, the Bank that is, have guaranteed the owner certain loans against stock he has purchased to produce garments for next season. We think that the owner is competent enough, for we have seen his account books. It is therefore somewhat obvious to us, to put not too fine a point on it, that someone is misappropriating the Company's funds. Their Head Office is at their Rome store. I would like you to go down to Rome, there you can meet the owner, and his name is Ricardo Armari.

See what you can discover from him, and make a few discreet enquiries. Be careful, and please report back to me. Use a public telephone for any confidential information and of course reverse charge all calls to the Bank. How do you feel about this task Carla?"

Carla thought for a moment and then realised the opportunity Enzo was offering.

"Enzo, you know that I will do anything I can to help any of the Clients of the Bank. When do you want me to go to Rome?"

"Carla, I hoped that you would agree. So, I would like you to go to Rome tomorrow morning. I have booked you on the 10 am, train. I have made a reservation for you at the Hotel San Angelo, which is close to the FORUM offices. The account at the Hotel is in the Bank's name, and all expenses are covered. If you manage to solve the problem, I will personally see that you get an extra bonus. On this particular project, you will also learn something about fashion as well. Here are copies of all the relevant correspondence on the case."

He handed Carla a very thick file. Carla again thanked her father-in-law for the challenge ahead. That evening, Carla left the Bank early went home to pack for her trip. Enzo had given no indication as to how long Carla's project would last. So, she guessed it would be a week. She told Sophia about the trip, and said that she would contact her each day to check on young Dino.

The next morning, Carla's taxi arrived to take her to Florence Station. The train came in on time and Carla settled back to watch the Italian countryside flash by as the train steamed south. Her compartment was empty; Carla was pleased, because she did not feel like small talk with a stranger. Up to now she had not had the time to look at the FORUM file, for it had been given to her at the last minute, so this was an excellent opportunity. Opening up the portfolio, she began to read and the more she read the more she was intrigued. Most cases she had been involved with, at the Bank, were usually fairly mundane. However, on the odd occasion the tide of events seemed to be obscure. These were the cases she revelled in, for she liked nothing better than a good mystery.

The series of events as far as FORUM were concerned read like a good novel, but there did not seem to be a happy ever after. That part was up to her, it seemed. She was brought back to the present by a knock on her compartment door, which slid open. Carla looked up and saw an attendant standing there.

"Excuse me Signorina," he said, "lunch is now served in the Restaurant Car five coaches to the left."

Carla thanked him, put her file away in her briefcase, and taking it with her, she locked her compartment, and headed down the train to eat. She enjoyed a light lunch in the Restaurant Car. Then back to the compartment and her heavy reading matter, and the time seemed flashed by, and soon the train steamed into Rome Station.

Now, her task was about to begin. She recalled the times that she had been here with Dino; also this was the place that Dino had started to play around with the 'other' woman. She had now, to put these thoughts out of her head. This was an important project, which had to be completed with a certain amount of secrecy. Her emotions must be kept under control. She hailed a taxi and was soon at her Hotel. The Receptionist greeted her and told her that a 3rd floor suite had been reserved for her. All, meals taken in the Hotel would be covered by the account. The Hall Porter took her bags and they headed for the lift that took them to the 3rd floor. The Porter opened the door, and put her bags into the Bedroom. Carla gave him a tip and he thanked her and bowed.

"Signorina," he said, "dinner is served until 10p.m."

He turned and left. Carla looked at the clock on the mantelpiece that ran across the top of the impressive fireplace.

It was 7.30 p.m., plenty of time to unpack, freshen up and go to the Restaurant. She looked around the room. Along one wall were some large picture windows; she walked over to see the view. Below was the Via Flaminia, the streetlights picking out the cars and people passing by. This was the first time that she had been alone in a strange Hotel. She walked around the rest of the suite thinking. How can I solve these problems that Enzo has given me? How much help can I expect from Ricardo Armari? Other questions went through her head. Then she said to herself. I cannot perform miracles alone; I will enlist all the help I can get. I do not think that this case is quite as simple as Enzo made it appear to be.

Carla started to feel hungry, so after a quick bath she went down to the Restaurant. The headwaiter greeted her; she requested a table for one. He was puzzled as to why this lovely lady was eating alone, but he respected her wishes. Carla enjoyed a Cordon Bleu meal in peace. Then she headed back to her 3rd floor suite. She was tired, and wanted an early night so as to be fresh for the meeting on the next morning. It might be a long day? Carla had undressed and put on her dressing robe, when there was a knock on her door. She wondered who it could be, for very few people knew that she was in Rome. She opened the door.

The Bellboy stood there, holding a sealed envelope.

"A message for you Signorina," he said handing her the envelope.

Carla gave him a tip and he left and she closed and locked the door. Carla went over to her dressing table and opened the envelope. The note read: -

Carla, sorry I missed you at Dinner. Please have breakfast with me in the Hotel Restaurant at 8 a.m. to discuss problem. Signed Franco Luciani.

Carla slept like a log. It was the first good night's sleep she had enjoyed for some time. She was brought out of her deep slumbers by the telephone ringing. It was her early morning call. She looked at the clock on her bedside cabinet. It was 7.15 a.m.; she had a bath, dressed, put on her make up and descended to the Restaurant. Franco was already waiting in the Reception. Franco Luciani was a tall handsome man in his mid

30's. He had dark wavy hair, piercing eyes, an aquiline nose, and a small moustache. He was dressed in a dark grey woollen overcoat, and underneath a blue pinstripe suit.

Franco approached her and as he got close a smile appeared on his face.

"Good morning Carla my dear," said Franco, "how lovely to see you. Let us go and eat breakfast."

Carla was taken aback for moment; she had not expected to see Franco again.

Carla stood up and recovered her composure.

"Good morning Franco. It is lovely to see you and a surprise too. You were our Deputy Bank Manager when I was here with Dino. It must have been almost two years ago."

He kissed her on both cheeks, then took her arm, and escorted her into the Restaurant. The Restaurant Manager showed them to a secluded table tucked away in a quiet corner.

Franco pulled back the chair for Carla and then having sat down looked at the menu.

"Sorry for the cloak and dagger approach Carla," began Franco, "but there is a reason for all this, which will become clear as I explain. Anyway Carla, welcome to Rome."

Carla did not know how much Franco knew, so she decided that he could do the talking. Perhaps, it would fill in some of the blanks. The waiter arrived and they ordered breakfast.

Franco began to tell the story, and Carla listened intently.

"Carla I wanted to meet you before you had your meeting at FORUM. Your father-in-law telephoned yesterday and asked me to assist you in any way I can. Like Enzo, we too have been monitoring the FORUM funds. We cannot make out who is doing the dirty on the Company, for the owner seems straight enough. By the way, I was sorry to hear about Dino, please accept my commiserations. Anyway, to the matter in hand. Incidentally, I am now the Manager here in Rome. You may remember Signor Musselo the Manager here? Well he moved back to Turin when the Manager there retired. He came from Turin and was glad to move back near to his relatives. Now down to the real business."

Slowly eating their way through breakfast, Franco explained in detail the situation to date. They had a very thick file on FORUM. He explained that there were a vast number of problems that Carla had to face. He felt the biggest one was that she was a woman. Not that he was a male chauvinist, but on the other hand they may not suspect her, as she was a woman. It may well be a daunting task; the enquiries they had made seemed to lead nowhere. Carla did not imagine that this task would be so complex.

"Well Carla in conclusion, that is about all I can tell you about this case. You will have to solve it piece by piece as you go along. I will help you as much as I can. I can show you the accounts of FORUM, which we hold, in the Bank. I am certain, that they have another set of books; these will no doubt show everything in the garden is rosy. We shall supply as much confidential information as we have on file. The rest is up to you, for I do not think that this will be a problem that can be solved quickly. Still stay as long as you like. If you get fed up with the Hotel, then please come and stay with my wife Franchesca and I. You would be most welcome."

Having now finished their working breakfast, Carla thanked him for his in-depth briefing of the FORUM case. He said that he would arrange for a taxi to collect them in around 15 minutes from reception, they could then go to the Bank and she could go on to FORUM for her meeting. Carla returned to her room, she adjusted her make-up and put on her coat and gloves, then hurried down to the Reception. Franco was waiting for her and got into the cab, which dropped Franco off at the Bank and Carla off to start her investigations at FORUM. The cab pulled up outside an impressive building, which was in the heart of the City's shopping district. Carla paid the driver; she took a moment to admire the decor of the building, which had an extensive frontage. Opening the glass door she looked around, she observed that no expense had been spared on the interior design. It must have cost a fortune to create this 'Garden of Eden'. She thought I wonder where the snake is?

She stood there for a few moments taking in the atmosphere of the place. There was a distinct perfume that permeated through the entire shop.

A lady assistant sidled up to her.

"Good morning, Signorina, can I show you anything?"

"Yes," replied Carla," can you please show me to Signor Armari's office, I wish to see him."

The Lady assistant responded.

"Please will you follow me Signorina?"

The two ladies wended their way to Signor Armani's office, passing row upon row of expensive dresses, furs, and lingerie. Finally, they came to a large door that was heavily decorated with carvings and painted in gold and silver. The assistant knocked on the door and went in.

In a moment she reappeared.

"Please go in," she said, "Signor Armari will see you now."

Carla pushed the heavy door open, and there, behind one of the biggest desks she had ever seen was Signor Ricardo Armari. He got up from his large, high backed, leather chair and walked around to greet Carla. She noticed he was a short, overweight, balding and probably in his late 40's. He had started to grow a beard; this he hoped would make him appear more of an artist. He greeted Carla by embracing her and kissing her on both cheeks.

"Bon Giorno Carla," said Signor Armari, " I am truly thrilled to meet you, and I know why you are here. Please, do not be embarrassed. I know we have been losing money for some time now. I always wanted to be successful in this business. I started with a little shop in Florence, you know, that was 20 years ago. I have tried very hard to build the business up and quite often there has been a cash-flow problem."

Carla sat and listened. Unfortunately, it was a story only too familiar to Carla. Signor Armari began by saying telling her a story.

Carla wondered what sort of tale her would tell her, but she was there to listen and find the cause of the problem and solve it.

"Carla, let me begin at the beginning. I have always wanted to expand into other cities in Italy, and decided to open a shop in Milan. It had been opened a matter of days, when a local 'so-called' businessman approached me. His name was Benito Antonati. Benito told me that he had a great deal of money to invest in local business, and would I be interested in an investor. He was very cagey about where his money came from. I should not ask any questions, but accept the funds into a 'special' account, which I could use for the business. Time passed and we expanded the premises, it was the finest fashion house in Milan. Our investor kept well away from the shop, the only way I knew he was around was by the funds coming into our 'special' Bank account.

A firm of accountants, which we had used since I started, kept the books. Then one day Benito came into the Office and forcefully suggested that we change accountants. He told me that Colenso & Co. was ripping us off, and that we had to change to his accountants Reggio & Co. I, like a fool, did as he asked and it was not long before I found that they were really evil people. They would pass large amounts of money through the Company accounts. Very large sums both in and out. Then, I was visited by the Revenue, asking about my taxes on the throughput of funds. I referred them to Reggio & Co. Two weeks later they were back again. Reggio & Co. were gone, nobody knew where, and I was in really deep trouble and the scapegoat. I quickly switched back to my old accountants. Then I tried getting in touch with Benito, who of course was nowhere to be found. The Revenue told me that they knew of Benito under various different names, and he had used my Company to launder money. He had tried scams similar to this in the past. He was really crooked, he had been involved in drugs, had narrowly escaped capture in France he was wanted there and in Spain. He returned to Italy, where he had laid low for several years.

Then during the Boer War, he had sold arms to the Boers, and indeed anyone who wanted illegal arms. He decided that the best way to launder his cash was to invest in lots of small companies, like mine for example. Then his money would come out of the other end as clean as a whistle."

Carla was dumbfounded; she sat there amazed. This was new to her. She had heard of money being laundered, but this was the first case she had to deal with. Ricardo at this point stopped talking, picked up the internal telephone and ordered coffee for them both.

"Now Carla, I am sure that you would like coffee, in the meantime may I continue my tale of woe?"

"Certainly a coffee would be very welcome," replied Carla, "and do continue your story as I need all the facts."

"So," continued Ricardo, "this Benito was hiding out in Sicily, and he wanted his money back now. Right away and all of it, plus interest, which incidentally was now considerable. Benito was bleeding the Company dry. For as FORUM expanded Benito claimed 50% of the profits. He still had the papers I had signed, making him a partner. What could I do? I was absolutely desperate.

My plans were the get Benito in front of a Court of Law and charge him with embezzlement. This might prove difficult. So, I called in the Bank to help me in this tricky situation. The books of the Company show that trading is healthy enough. However, over the last 6 months, we have had a number of cheques returned stamped insufficient funds, return to drawer."

Carla had listened intently to this tale of woe, thought for a moment or two about what Ricardo had told her.

"Signor Armari."

Ricardo interrupted Carla.

"Please call me Ricardo."

"Ricardo," Carla continued, "I appreciate all that you have told me. I am here to help you and try to resolve this situation."

She told him that her father-in-law was Vice-President of the Bank and she had full authority to do anything to help one of these most prestigious Clients. It would be less conspicuous, if she made the investigations, for they may not suspect a woman. Ricardo agreed as he looked at his watch.

"Carla," he said, "this might be a good time to go to lunch."

Over lunch, Ricardo told Carla all about his family. He had been married for 22 years to Fiorina, a girl he had met when he was working in a fashion house in Florence. They had two children Alberto who was 21 and a daughter Rosetta and lived in a small villa outside the City.

When they returned to the Ricardo's office, Carla asked if she could call the Bank and her son's Nanny. Carla made the calls. During her call to Enzo he suggested that she take whatever action she thought fit. Carla asked about the possibility of young Dino and Sophia staying at Enzo's house. Enzo said it was a great idea; it would no doubt make Carla feel better. It would also enable the Grandparents to get to know their grandson better.

Carla then phoned Sophia, who was delighted that at last she would have some female company. Carla felt better now, for she did not want to leave Sophia and young Dino for too long. This investigation might take longer than she expected. So, to divert attention away from her scrutiny of the Company business, Ricardo and Carla thought up the idea of making Carla a member of staff. Her title would be trainee manager and administrator. Carla would learn all about the business of fashion, from start to finish. Ricardo would show her how the gowns were designed and manufactured, together with the art of the furrier. She would oversee the accounts, and all cheques coming into and going out of the Company would have to be cleared by Carla. She would also be the Company's contact with the Bank in Rome. Ricardo was determined to get this matter solved once and for all. Carla enjoyed the work; the staff at FORUM were helpful and friendly. Carla thought, surely they must have known something fishy was going on? She also got on well with Ricardo's family especially his wife, who was glad of female company. Their children who were at University were home for some weekends. Most weekends Carla was at FORUM trying to resolve matters. On Sunday's, she would go out with the Armari family, for by now she had more or less forgotten about Dino.

By early summer they had amassed enough evidence to bring Benito Antonati to trial. Carla discovered he had 'stolen' thousands of millions of lira from FORUM, and had laundered billions through the Company funds. On June 3rd 1909, a warrant was issued for his arrest on a wide range of charges. He was seized by the Police, trying to leave Italy from the Port of Genoa. On him they found Bank drafts for 300 million lira, plus a kilo of hashish. It seems he had started his drug dealing again. He was taken to the central Police Station in Milan, where he was formally charged. Carla turned all her documentary evidence over to the Police.

She was asked to appear in the court at Milan as a witness at Antonati's trial later in the year.

Carla had enjoyed her task at FORUM, which had come to a happy conclusion. It looked as if Ricardo might get some of his money back. At least 250 million of the bank drafts were payable to FORUM. Ricardo was now delighted with the outcome.

Carla's job was over, she would be sad to leave and return to Florence, for the next thing on the horizon would be her divorce from Dino. Ricardo was sorry to see her go.

"Carla," said Ricardo, as she was about to leave, "if you ever want to leave the Bank, there is always a job for you here, as my business partner? I cannot express the gratitude for all the good work you have put in here. I know the Bank has paid you. We want to give you a present."

He beckoned to a young lady, who came forward with a large box tied with a big pink bow.

"Please accept this with our sincere thanks."

Carla was overwhelmed; she opened the box and inside was a silver fox jacket.

"Ricardo," said Carla trying the jacket on, "this is the most wonderful present I have ever had from a Client."

She moved towards Ricardo and kissed him on the lips. The staff all cheered.

That night Ricardo and Fiorina took Carla out to dinner; Carla wore her new fur jacket. In the lining was her name - just Carla. Ricardo aware of her forthcoming divorce and so he left out her surname. Fiorina was overjoyed that at last Ricardo had met someone from the Bank that was able to help the Company. They had learned a very hard lesson, in future they would be very careful, who they would accept as investors. That night Carla slept like a log; her problems in Rome were over. Tomorrow back to Florence.

On her arrival back at the Bank, the following afternoon, she went straight up to Enzo's office to report on the Rome trip. Enzo was thrilled that Carla had been able to solve the mystery of the missing millions. It had been a nasty business altogether, but it had ended successfully. She told Enzo that Ricardo had given her a silver fox jacket as a present. That Ricardo Armari was a straight as an arrow, but his knowledge of accounts had left something to be desired. This Benito character had certainly pulled the wool over his eyes. She had learned a great deal about the fashion industry. It was a fascinating business.

"Enzo," said Carla, "on listening to Ricardo it was a very sad story of a man needing money to expand his business and a crook who found a gullible man through whom he could launder his ill-gotten drug money."

"My dearest Carla," replied Enzo, "you deserved that fur jacket. I will be giving you an extra bonus for the work you have done. The Bank could never have worked out that drug money was involved. I look forward to your report on the forthcoming trial. Please take the rest of the week off."

Carla thanked him, and went home. When she arrived there Sophia and young Dino were delighted that Mummy was home again.

The weekend for Carla was soon over, and she was back at her desk, when she was called into Enzo's office. He asked her to sit down he had a letter from Ricardo in Rome.

"Carla, I have this letter from Ricardo it is addressed to me but concerns you. He was so elated with your performance on the Antonati affair, that he has offered you a partnership in FORUM. Are you going to take up his offer?"

Carla thought for a moment before replying.

"Enzo, Ricardo did offer me a partnership when I was with him. At the time I thought he was joking. I must admit that now he has mentioned it in writing. I would seriously consider it."

Enzo scanned the letter further.

"Actually Carla, he has offered you the position of Partner, Manager and Financial Controller of all business transactions in Italy and overseas. What are you going to do Carla, what shall I tell him? I do need to give him a reply?"

Carla sat thoughtfully for a moment, as this would mean moving to Rome, and she realised that this would be a life changing move for her.

"In my view Carla, I think that this could be a great opportunity for you."

He could see Carla's face lit up as she made her mind up.

"I'll take the job, Enzo," she answered confidently; "I'll take it. My decision was not one she had taken on the spur of the moment. With the divorce on the horizon, it may well affect my position at the Bank, particularly with some of the Clients. I love you Enzo and your lady very much. I want us always to be friends. With FORUM I shall need a friend at the Company's Bank. Also the memories of working with your son."

"I fully understand and respect your decision," said Enzo who was now smiling, "I may be your father-in-law, but I will always be your friend whatever the outcome of the divorce. My son's behaviour has been absolutely despicable in the extreme. I cannot find words to express my anger; at the way he has treated you and young Dino. We shall be sorry to see you go, but you will always have my support."

Carla kissed Enzo, who looked slightly embarrassed.

"Thank you Enzo, I really appreciate all the help and support you have given me and my son Dino Jnr."

"Carla," replied Enzo, as Carla was about to leave his office, "any help that the Bank can give you, you only have to ask. You know that you will always be welcome at our home."

Carla left Enzo's office wondering if she had made the right decision. She sat at her desk contemplating her future. After giving the matter due consideration, she knew the only answer was to telephone Ricardo in Rome. Carla picked up the receiver and asked the operator to get her Signor Armari at FORUM. A few minutes later her phone rang.

She picked it up it was a man's voice she heard.

"Hello Carla, it is Ricardo. How are you?"

"Hello Ricardo. I have seen your letter addressed to my father-in-law and the kind offer you have made me."

There was a slight pause on the line.

"Carla, what do you think of my offer?"

Carla thought for a moment.

"Ricardo, I would love to take up the position you have offered me. However, there is a problem with moving to Rome at present."

"Carla I do not expect you to move to Rome. I want you to work out of the Florence store. Would that be OK?"

"That would be excellent Ricardo. I would have to resolve a few problems here at the bank first, however I could start with FORUM in about a month, if that is satisfactory."

"Carla, that is about the timetable I had envisaged. I'll speak to you soon. We will arrange to meet in Florence soon."

Carla was now feeling much better. Here was a new career handed to her on a plate. The future looked brighter now. Only the divorce was the cloud on the horizon. She broke the news to Sofia about her new job and that as far as she was concerned it meant status quo.

Carla worked her notice at the bank, doing the job to the best of her ability. Enzo introduced her to Carmello Franchini the woman that would be tasking over from her. Enzo told her that she would also be looking after the FORUM account. Carmello was a slim, dark haired woman in her late 30s. She had previously worked in their Milan branch. She had recently married and her husband, who was an Engineer, was transferred to Florence. The offer of a position in the Florence branch had come at a fortuitous time. Carmello and Carla got on really well. Carla now knew that she had a reliable contact at the Bank, as well as her father-in-law. She really looked forward to the move to FORUM, as the time with the Bank came to an end. This was indeed a new era for Carla, but at least, she thought, she knew what she was getting herself into. This was a new challenge, and she now had a relative and friend at the Bank of Italy. This had given her new confidence. Now all that lay ahead was the divorce and the drama of a Court appearance no doubt.

It was now late August, and Florence was having a very hot spell of weather, humidity levels were high. Carla had one more week before her work at the Bank was over. On arriving home one evening there were two important letters waiting for her.

She opened them. The first was the papers concerned her forthcoming divorce proceedings. The Court date would be Monday 13th September 1909. Would this be unlucky she thought? The other referred to the trial of Signor Antonati, this was scheduled for Monday 6th December 1909, the Court proceedings to be held in the Central Criminal Court in Rome.

Carla was due to start her new job with FORUM on Monday 27th September; it had all worked out well it seemed. Once her own divorce case was over, she could concentrate on her new position at FORUM. Then she could look through the files concerning the Antonati case. It was certainly going to be a difficult period for her. The last two months had been very hot, and with the strain of her marriage, Carla wondered how she had managed to get through each week. With cooler weather ahead and a change of scene, perhaps her stressful life may get easier. However, with two Court cases, both important to her, on the horizon, it may be some time before her life got back to anything like normal.

Chapter 15

It was Friday January 1ˢᵗ 1909; Alain left home, said goodbye to his parents and his fiancée, Francoise, and headed for Paris. It was a New Year, a new job, and a new apartment. He had a top floor suite of rooms in a block in the Montemarte district of the city. It was certainly an improvement on the last hovel. This time around, there was no landlady to tell him what to do. He settled into his new abode that consisted of a lounge, bathroom, kitchen, and bedroom. In the street below he could hear the rattle of the taxicabs as they went by. Just around the corner was the famous Moulin Rouge, where for a few francs one could see a Floor show with nudes. The place was always packed. Under the trees he would see artists at work painting their masterpieces. After all it was the artist's quarter of this bustling City. His neighbour was one of these struggling artists. His name of Pierre Auguste le Tour. He had the nickname of 'Renoir', a current French impressionist painter born in 1841. His parents obviously had a sense of humour thought Alain.

One evening, Pierre invited Alain in to his very tiny apartment for a glass of wine or two. Pierre showed Alain some of his paintings. Alain thought if he is an impressionist, his paintings make little impression of me. Alain knew something about art, for he had seen the masterpieces on the Count de Longchamps chateau walls. Pierre was fascinated that Alain was a racing driver. Alain suggested that perhaps he could become an artist that might specialise in painting, architectural subjects, racing cars or anything that involved action as well as a landscape. Pierre admitted that he was pretty useless at portraits and he then showed Alain some pictures he had painted at horse races, and Alain said that they were very good. He had a superb painting of the Sacre Coeur Church that was almost as good as a photograph. Pierre took Alain's advice and later visited races from 1911 onwards. He became famous for his paintings of motor races and landscapes.

Alain meanwhile, had his career to think of; here he was giving Pierre advice. His first day at Peugeot went well. He had a meeting with the Managing Director, Charles Orly, and the Chief Designer Nicolas Bocage.

Nicholas had brought to their meeting designs for a revolutionary new car. They agreed that Mercedes were the big threat to their success. The Mercedes was a big car with a very large engine, built under the regulations of 1908. It developed power it was true, but it was not an easy to drive. Alain agreed with that, and he said that his experience with Darracq, a car with an engine of similar capacity, was equally ungainly. They agreed what was needed now was a car that performed, handled and braked far better than anything else on the road. This was a tall order but not impossible, they would have to put their thinking caps on. Alain was given an office next to Nicholas, and they became great friends. They could start with a clean piece of paper.

For the first week or two they struggled to come up with a design that was practical. Then Alain had a bright idea. He told Nicholas that they should develop an engine of smaller capacity say 4 litres. This could have a shorter stroke and a larger cylinder bore.

Each cylinder would have four valves operated by a chain driven camshaft. This would enable the engine to breathe better, and so develop more power per litre. He had played with this design when he was at the Sorbonne. The transmission to the rear wheels would be by a shaft from the gearbox. Alain said that chains had a habit of breaking. They prepared detailed drawings and showed the finished blueprints to Charles Orly. He asked could they use such an engine in a sports car version to sell to enthusiasts.

"Well Charles, replied Alain, "it is my opinion that an engine such as we have suggested would need detuning to make it less stressed. This would give greater reliability."

"That seems a good idea Alain," answered Charles, "we could then match the performance of the Mercedes Sports Cars. It would certainly give us a new market."

Alain agreed.

The next few weeks were hectic, but slowly and surely the engine took shape. They hand made every component, and checked everything.

Meanwhile, they were also designing other parts including bodywork, which they agreed would be minimal, but with some protection for the driver and mechanic. The machine gradually came together. Alain said that they should add four wheel braking. He had experimented with it at Darracq, and it gave the driver a definite advantage. This together with smaller diameter and wider wheels would help the road holding. The beast was finally ready to be tested, on Bastille Day, Wednesday July 14th 1909.

They thought it appropriate if it did not perform that they might be condemned to the Bastille.

They called their new car the L70; L for Lion, for a Blue Lion was the Company trademark. (97 years later of course it is still the same today) The next morning, they could not wait to test it. The engine had been run on the bench and sounded wonderful. They had mated it to a revolutionary five-speed gearbox with reverse. Everyone else was still using three gears.

Early next morning they went down to the garage checked the oil, water and tyres, before heading out on a test run. They had donned their leather coats, boots, and gloves. Alain wore his crash helmet that Rudolph von Lundenberg had given him some years ago. Nicholas cranked up the engine, gave the starting handle a spin and the engine burst into life. They let the engine warm up for a few minutes, then Alain depressed the clutch pedal and put the car into gear, and they sped off into the suburbs of Paris. They took it easy until they were out into the countryside. They found a straight piece of road, and Alain opened up the throttle. The car accelerated very quickly. Alain was taken by surprise. Here was a car with an engine of four litres, with the speed of a much larger machine. The speedometer they had fitted went up to 160 kilometres, and they had already reached that, with a lot more to come. They were running out of road, so Alain applied the brakes carefully, bringing the car under control. The left hand bend they took at around 80 kph, as if the car was on railway lines.

They were both delighted the test had gone so well. They came to a small village and entered the square, where a café was just opening.

"Alain," said Nicholas, "I am really thirsty swallowing all that dust. Let's celebrate with a coffee."

"Good idea Nicholas," replied Alain, "let us have a croissant too."

The two men were sitting at the table by the window, when the waiter, still sleepy eyes wandered over and asked.

"What can I get for you gentlemen?"

Nicholas looked up at the waiter standing with his order pad.

"Two coffees and two croissants please garcon."

The waiter strolled off to the kitchen. Alain looked out of the window into the square. There were a few people about, over the far side one or two stallholders were setting up for market.

There were several locals looking at their car. The waiter arrived with their coffees and croissants, and the two men tucked in. Soon as they were finished, they went outside, started up the L70, and headed back to the factory. The test drive had gone like a dream. Was this the car to beat the rest? As they drove back into the Garage, Charles Orly was waiting for them.

He looked excited and shouted over the noise of the exhaust.

"Well gentlemen, do we have a winner here?"

Alain took off his helmet, and stopped the engine.

"Well sir," answered Alain, "the test drive went very well indeed. We covered about 100 kilometres and had her up to 160 kph. She handled extremely well and the braking is the best I have experienced."

Charles smiled, as he looked the car over.

"Now Alain," said Charles, "can you suggest any improvements?"

"Yes. I can," replied Alain, "in fact, there are several improvements we should make.

Number 1- Improved weather protection for driver and mechanic. What we now have is inadequate to say the least.

Number 2 - Larger diameter and wider brake drums. These should be ribbed to assist cooling and to prevent brake fade.

The braking is insufficient considering the speed this car is capable and the drums overheat following heavy braking

Number 3 - More comfortable seating and a better driving position. If we are to use these cars in future, for long distance races we must consider the comfort and safety of our drivers. It is like sitting on a park bench."

"Alain," replied Charles, "thanks for your expert advice. So go ahead and make the modifications, after all we want to win. By the way, that helmet you wear Alain, where did you get it."

Alain showed him the safety helmet he always wore when racing and testing.

"Monsieur Orly," answered Alain, "I had this helmet presented to me by Rudolph von Lundenberg, the Number One Mercedes driver. He always wears one. I swear by it. It has saved a few lives."

Charles Orly studied the helmet carefully.

"Alain, I want all our drivers to wear these. Safety of our drivers is paramount. Please get some quotes and get some made"

Over the next month, Alain and Nicholas made the modifications, and carried on testing. Alain asked Nicholas, did he think the car was ready for some serious competition? Nicholas agreed the only way was to run the car in some minor races first. So, they entered the car in the Paris Motor Club Autumn Cup, the event would be held on the second Sunday in October. So Nicholas had a meeting with Charles Orly, who agreed that their new car had to be tested against some kind of opposition.

This event would be ideal, particularly as there were to be no International events or Grand Prix during the coming year. So the entry was submitted, and they were given start number seven by the organisers. Alain would carry Nicholas as his mechanic for the event. Alain was looking forward to the event, which would start in the grounds of the Palace of Versailles. Nicholas had never been a participant in a motor race before and was thrilled at the prospect of being with Alain, who he knew was an experienced driver.

Alain had other things on his mind. Every weekend that Alain went home, he would meet up with Francoise. They were very much in love, and had discussed marriage on several occasions. Francoise wanted to wait until the summer was over, because it was quite possible that Alain would be involved in some Motor Sport with his new Company. They decided to get married in September, on the second Sunday. Alain asked Nicholas if he would be his best man. He told Nicholas that, he had lost touch with many of his friends that he had met at the Sorbonne. He had made few friends at Darracq.

"Alain," replied Nicholas, "don't give me excuses that I am the only friend you have. Of course I will be your best man."

The ceremony would take place, in the little village church on the Estate of the Count de Longchamps. Alain told Charles Orly of his wedding plans.

"Alain," answered Charles," you have made great progress with the new car. Get married on the day you have planned Alain, and take a week's holiday and enjoy your honeymoon with your new bride. I will give you a special present when you return to work."

Alain was delighted that his boss was not raising any objections to the time he needed to be with his new bride. He wondered what the present might be.

The day of the wedding drew closer; the bride started to get very nervous, as most brides do. Alain could sense this each time they met. Although she loved Alain dearly, Francoise began to wonder if she had made the right decision. Her parents assured her that, Alain was the right man for her. He was caring, reliable, not flirtatious, and a rare breed in their book. They knew his family background, and although he was not from the landed gentry, the Count de Longchamps treated him like a son. This gradually allayed her doubts.

Soon time passed, and their wedding day dawned. Neither, Alain or Francoise had slept a wink the night before the ceremony. It was a glorious September morning; the sun was shining down out of a clear blue sky. Alain and his best man Nicholas, who incidentally, had slept like a log, after their night out on the tiles. They were ready and down at the church well before 11.00a.m, when the ceremony was due to begin. The little church was full. Pierre Clement and the rest of the family filled the pews to the right, whilst the Count his family and friends of the family filled the pews to the left. Father Canard would perform the service. The congregation sat and waited whilst the organist Michel Pau, played a selection of church music. Francoise was getting dressed and still very nervous.

Her Mother, Justine was fussing around her, and her Father, Henri pacing up and down.

"Hurry up mother," he kept saying, "we are going to be late at the Church."

Francoise looked absolutely perfect in her pure white silk wedding dress, trimmed with Chantilly lace and a long train. Her veil was also of the finest lace. She looked as pretty as a picture. When she was finally satisfied that her appearance could not be improved, she turned to her Mother.

"Well, Mother, I am still nervous, but I am ready go to the Church to marry Alain."

Her parents breathed a sigh of relief. Henri took one more look at his daughter and he had to admit she looked radiant.

"You my darling daughter, "said Henri, "look absolutely lovely. I am proud to give you away today; to the finest young man I have ever met. You never need worry about Alain, I know he loves you dearly and will be true to his vows that he will make to you today, and love you until death do you part."

Francoise smiled and inside she felt that perhaps all her worries about her big day were unfounded. Henri took her arm and together, with Justine following behind went out of the home and into the carriage to head off for the Church. The horses pulling the open carriage were becoming restless, and had been pawing the ground. The coachman had been stroking their noses to calm them down. He was very relieved, when he saw the bridal party coming down the steps from the house. Now they were on their way to the church, there was now turning back.

Inside the church Alain, and Nicholas, Alain's best man was still waiting. They, like the rest of the congregation were wondering what had happened to the bride. Had she changed her mind at the last minute or was it a bad case of nerves. All they could do was sit and wait. The organist had gone through his repertoire once, and had started going through it again. Father Canard was waiting too, looking towards the west door of the little church for any sign of the bridal party. Then, Justine appeared in the doorway and made her way slowly down the aisle, to her pew. She signalled to Father Canard, and the organist struck up "The Wedding March." Francoise and Henri entered the church coming out of the warm sunshine, into the cool, reverend atmosphere of a family wedding ceremony. As the bride passed each pew, everyone admired her fantastic wedding dress. Alain and Nicholas were standing in front of Father Canard, as Francoise came to stand by Alain's side.

Father Canard began the service with a hymn, and then came the part of the service where Francoise and Alain would be joined in holy matrimony. To the bride and groom the whole thing was as they were in a dream. The best man found the rings and finally they were blessed and Father Canard was now coming to the end of the ceremony. Alain was still in a daydream and came out of it as Father Canard concluded the ceremony with the words.

"I now proclaim you Man and Wife. You may kiss the bride."

Alain did as he was asked and gave his new bride the most sensuous kiss he could manage. The bride and groom now walked back up the aisle to sign the marriage register. Then, they stood in the porch of church to greet all their friends and neighbours. Outside the church, several of the well wishers had formed an arch of exhaust pipes, whilst the rest threw rice over the new Mr & Mrs.Clement. The open carriage that had brought the bridal party to the ceremony now took them back to the Chateau for the wedding reception. Alain and Francoise waited in the Entrance Hall to receive their guests.

In the Banqueting Hall, the wedding feast was laid out as if for a banquet. Each guest had their own place with the newlyweds on the top table, together with their parents and the Count and Countess. Everyone was dressed in their finest clothes for this 'wedding of the year'. All around were floral displays; the whole Hall was just a mass of colour. Everything was perfect. The cooks had prepared a feast, fit for a King. As well as some local delicacies, there were meats, fish, and vegetables to suit all tastes. The Count's servants were dressed in their finest livery. Alain was very proud of his new bride for she looked absolutely radiant. After the sumptuous meal, the speeches began; praise was universal about the bride and groom. The Count said how delighted he was, to be able to arrange the wedding breakfast for such a lovely young couple. In the background Alain's parents were feeling so proud of their son and new daughter-in-law, on this their special day. The Count had hired a small group to play for the occasion.

When the speeches were over, the Count invited everyone to go into the Ballroom to dance if they wished. Francoise and Alain started dancing, and soon the floor was full of whirling couples. The wedding presents were in a side room, where guests could view the wonderful array of presents given by relatives and friends. The Count gave the best present of all.

In front of all the guests, the Count mounted the small stage.

"Ladies, Gentlemen and Friends," he began, "Francoise as you know is the daughter of one of my oldest friends, Alain her husband I like to think of as the son I never had. He is the son of another of my oldest friends. I feel that what they need is a home, where they can settle down. May be raising a family there. Marriage is about sharing. So I hope this lovely couple will share the gift I am making to them. I am giving them the keys to a house just outside the village here. It is bought and paid for. I have arranged for you both to choose the furniture, for these are my gifts. I give it with all the love I can give to the finest couple I know."

Francoise and Alain could not believe it. There was a round of applause and cries of speech from the guests. Alain thought it appropriate to say a few words, so he mounted the stage with Francoise and holding hands with his new bride the applause abated.

"Count & Countess de Longchamps, Ladies, Gentlemen and Friends," began Alain, "this is as you can appreciate, is the happiest day of my life, being joined in marriage to my beautiful Francoise. She is the only woman I have ever loved. I have made my vows and will honour and love her always until death do us part. I cannot thank the Count and Countess enough for their generosity to my family and I over the years. I would not be here today and married to this lovely lady without the help and love of our friends, the Count and Countess. To my parents I owe my gratitude for their love and advice. Finally, Francoise and I want to thank you all, for the wonderful presents you have given us. We are very proud to be among the people we love and respect on this special day. We thank you all from the bottom of our hearts."

The assembled guests and gave three hearty cheers for Alain and his new bride. The celebrations went on for hours; everyone was enjoying themselves so much. Young Helene-Marie, was dancing too with the youngest son of one of the Count's neighbours, she was having a great time. Henri de Villeneuve had arranged their honeymoon Hotel for his daughter and son-in-law.

This was to be at the Hotel Grand Plage at seaside resort of Veules les Roses, some 20 kilometres from Dieppe. The Count had insisted that they spend their first night together in the west wing of the Chateau. Here they would not be disturbed. The Count had arranged that the next day his chauffeur would take them in his Limousine to their honeymoon Hotel. Sadly, the merriment came to an end. Pierre and Marie found young Helene fast asleep in the Chateau library. Alain and Francoise said goodbye to their guests and made their way to the west wing.

The suite of rooms had been prepared for them as they entered the bedroom; they saw the large four-poster bed, where they were to spend their first night together. Alain closed the door; at last they were alone together. They both sat on the bed, it felt very comfortable, and then having undressed very slowly, they felt a little embarrassed, but also exhilarated at the thought that they were now husband and wife. The shyness soon left them, as they stood naked in front of each other, still unsure that by joining their bodies together and exchanging body fluids, that they would be committing a mortal sin. Francoise was still a virgin; she had kept herself pure all these years.

She was now 21, and although she had been out with several young men she had kept at a distance sexually. Alain had enjoyed the company of young ladies, but his sexual appetites had been thwarted by many of his conquests, in his students' days. Since he began his motor racing career, a number of women had flung themselves at him, but he had been reluctant to take matters further. In some cases these ladies were married, some just free spirits. Now he had a lady who had all the attributes. She was beautiful, caring, intelligent, loving and now she was his wife. They stood there for several moments, realising at last they were husband and wife. They day had passed as if they were in a kind of dream. Now they could be themselves. Alain made the first move and began to caress Françoise's breasts. These were well formed and firm. This was something neither he nor indeed any other of Françoise's suitors had ever done. She had heard from her girlfriends that making love to a man was an art as well as a pleasure. She had also heard, that it was one of the most pleasurable sensations that a woman could have. As he looked into her eyes, her eyes told him that he was the man that she loved for she was now his wife and lover. Francoise began to enjoy this, she then lowered her hand to touch and play with Alain's male member that stiffened as she rubbed it gently. Alain guided his new bride over to the bed, and she lay on top of him, her sensuous body raising his sexual senses. Alain knew that he must arouse his new bride until she was ready to accept his mating muscle.

So, he gently rubbed her private parts until she sighed with contentment.

"Darling Alain," she whispered, "please, please make love to me. I want you so much it hurts."

Alain did not need a second invitation; he gently slid his erect phallus into her.

She cried out with pleasure as they made love for the first time. Francoise had never known such a feeling, it was both pain and pleasure, but she knew that the second time would be easier. That she hoped would come soon. They moved in unison, until Francoise gave a little cry of pleasure.

"My darling Alain," she gasped, "I have had the most strange feeling inside. It is something I have never felt before. It feels really wonderful."

Alain was still moving inside her and enjoying every moment.

"My dearest Francoise that means we have made love properly for the first time."

Francoise was still in ecstasy as Alain continued to make love to his bride as she moaned in absolute ecstasy.

"If this is lovemaking," she sighed, "I am feeling marvellous doing it with you my love. You know that I am a virgin and this was my first time. I really did not know what to expect. Next time we shall enjoy it more."

As Alain withdrew, he noticed there was a trickle of blood.

Francoise looked down at herself.

"My love," she said looking a little worried, "I'm bleeding."

"Don't worry my darling Francoise. It is nothing to worry about. The doctor at the Sorbonne gave us some sex education and told us that women who make love for the first time always bleed at little. Next time, that will not happen. Just have a bath, and then later we can do it again. If you want to."

Francoise laughed out loud.

"Later, will be after I have had a bath, then we can go to sleep?"

"Not necessarily my love," answered Alain, "let us wait and see."

They went into the bathroom together, where Alain soaped her all over and Francoise did the same to him.

"If I need a bath after making love Alain, why don't we make love in the bath?"

Alain agreed it was a good idea. So, they made love again.

When they had finished Francoise looked down.

"There is no blood my darling," said Alain, "I told you so."

Francoise said that she felt fantastic and ready for more lovemaking. Alain knew that here was a woman, who had never made love before tonight and had taken to it like a duck to water. He had heard stories of friends who had married virgins, and the new brides, had the idea of making love as disgusting. The husbands had found solace in the company of women who were broader minded. Some even paid for sex, and had paid the price in either broken marriages, or had caught sexually transmitted diseases. He had learned about these too from the Doctor at the Sorbonne.

It was now getting late, so they decided that now they had made love and knew that they have the pleasure anytime; sleep would be a good idea.

They both lay on the bed naked; soon they were in the land of dreams. They were disturbed from their slumbers by a knock on the door. Alain woke with a start. He looked across at Francoise who was still sleeping. He quickly covered her over, threw a dressing gown on, and opened the door. A maid stood there with a breakfast tray.

"Bonjour, Monsieur, your breakfast. It is 9.00a.m."

Alain smiled and looked quickly across at Francoise.

"Good Morning, thank you very much. I will take the tray."

Alain carried the tray over to the small table near the bed. The coffee smelt marvellous, and the croissants were warm and freshly baked.

Alain woke up his sleeping bride, and they enjoyed their first breakfast together. Having finished eating, they had their baths and got ready for their journey to the honeymoon destination by the sea. They looked splendid with Francoise in her light blue summer dress and Alain in a light blue striped blazer and white trousers. Georges, the chauffeur had collected their suitcases and packed them into the Limousine. The happy couple said goodbye to their hosts, and they were now setting off on their new life together. They snuggled up to each other as the big Renault cruised through the countryside, hardly noticing what a beautiful day it was outside their little world. Arriving at their Hotel, Georges took their luggage up to their suite. He told them that he would call back for them on Saturday next. Now they were alone once more, and lovemaking would soon be on their agenda. They unpacked their suitcases and hung up their clothes, then went to look at the view.

From their balcony they had a wonderful scene, the beach was wide and sandy, and in the distance, a small harbour with boats riding at anchor. It was just a wonderful day, and a perfect start to their marriage.

"At last we are alone, to enjoy ourselves," said Francoise, "I just love being married especially to you."

"Together my love," answered Alain, "we shall have a marriage that will stand the test of time. We can overcome any obstacle if we are a team, and friends as well as lovers."

Francoise went over and pulled the heavy drapes,

"Husband," said Francoise, "I love that word, it is time to practice our lovemaking again."

This time they undressed each other, and were soon making love, this time with knowledge that they were now past the initial sensation. They now knew the pleasure that was to come. They climaxed until they were exhausted. Francoise was eager to please her husband, but at the same time enjoyed their sexual union.

She more than aware that, sexual gratification was part of a blissful and successful marriage, that their decision not to enjoy sex before marriage was the right one.

They were both now ready to eat. Down in the Restaurant, the diners had already started to arrive, as Alain and Francoise walked through the door, the Maitre d'hôte showed them to a table in a quiet corner. He beckoned to the Headwaiter to leave the menu with the newlyweds. Having made their choice they chatted away. The other diners looked across, to see a very happy pair of young people, who were obviously on their honeymoon. During the days that followed, they swam and did a little sightseeing, whilst at night they made love. The week passed so quickly, and on Saturday morning Georges arrived to take them back to their new home. They soon settled in, for now the furniture had arrived, but on the Monday morning Alain had to return to Peugeot. He was getting ready, when there was a knock on the door. Francoise answered it.

There on the doorstep was a man in a uniform and wearing a cap, which he touched.

"Is Monsieur Clément here?" he asked, "I am his chauffeur to take him to work."

Alain was surprised and having got dressed said farewell to his lovely Francoise. He would arrange for an apartment near the factory, so they could be together. They could then spend their weekends at the house. So it was back to a more normal life now. There was hard work ahead to get the car prepared for the challenges to come. Alain thanked Charles for the ride to work.

"That car is yours Alain," said Charles, "incidentally I have made arrangements for you to have a company furnished apartment near here. Then, you and your new bride can be together."

Alain was astounded; this was more than he could hope for. A new life had now started for Alain and Francoise. They would certainly recall these memories in the future, when their lives would become difficult.

Chapter 16

Whilst one marriage was being consummated, another was about to be dissolved. For Alain and Francoise, the honeymoon was about to begin, but for Carla and Dino the honeymoon was definitely over. The divorce had come to Court. It was Monday 13th September 1909; the marriage had lasted 4 years and 10 months. Carla was deep in thought as she made her way to the Court Room in Florence, where the hearing was to be presided over by Judge Julius Benneto. Carla wondered if her errant husband Dino would be in Court? As she entered the chamber her question was answered. Dino was sitting quietly with his counsel, who was in deep discussion with his Client. Following behind Carla was Dino Jnr. and Sophia the young Dino's Nanny. Carla's counsel had advised her to bring their son into Court, as this might help sway the Court's decision on the question of custody. Then there would be the matter of maintenance allowance for the child's education etc. Dino Jnr. was now a very lively 4-year old and a real chatterbox. Sophia's other task was to keep him quiet whilst the Judge heard the case. They would remain at the back of the Court, until a request from the Judge would be made for the boy and his Nanny to come close for any remarks and questions that might be relevant.

Carla sat in the benches immediately below the Judge to the left-hand side of the Court, whilst Dino and his counsel sat to the right. There was an appropriate space between the two parties. The Judge would be seated on dais above the main body of the Court. Carla looked at the clock that was to the left of the coat of arms of the City, which was immediately above the Judge's chair. There was still five minutes to go before the Judge would walk into the Court. Carla looked around the courtroom. The walls were cream painted plaster, with oak panels going half way up the walls. The minute hand on the clock had at last reached the hour. The Bailiff called for silence and asked for all those present to stand and announced the entry of Judge Benneto.

The Bailiff then asked for them to be seated.

"We are here today," began Judge Benneto addressing the Court, "to determine the case of Borghese versa Borghese. This is a marriage that seemed to begin with good intentions. Now we are here to decide the future of this marriage. Divorce is always a sad occasion. However, I will now hear the submissions from the plaintiff's counsel."

Alfonso Torino stood up and presented the case for his Client.

Alfonso was a short and stocky but with a great presence, for what he lacked in stature he made up with in deliverance of his cases. His opening remarks clearly stated why they were in court today. He told how his Client's husband having an adulterous affair had deceived his Client. The lady concerned, and this was agreed with both parties, that she be known as Countess X. Apart from the adultery, her husband had abandoned his Client and their small son, who incidentally was present in Court, and could be brought forward should the Judge see fit. After about half an hour, Alfonso returned to his seat and conferred with his Client. Carla felt happier now that a real professional had put her case so clearly, concisely and forcefully.

The Judge then called for the Counsel for the defendant to put his side of the case. Dino's counsel was a Frederico Cantello, he was middle aged, slim and a well-known divorce lawyer, and also renowned for his expertise throughout Northern Italy. He knew the only way to win the case for his Client would be by careful manipulation and questioning of the plaintiff. He realised that Countess Maria, whose name must not be mentioned, was paying his fee. His put his case very strongly, using his experience to good effect. Carla listened carefully to his submission, and even started to believe that it was she who had been in the wrong. After about forty minutes Frederico sat down. He turned to Dino, opened a large book in front of him, turned to a page, and pointed to a section in it. He asked Dino to read the marked passage. Dino did so, and then whispered into his Counsel's ear. Frederico nodded. The Judge then asked for further arguments and submissions from both parties. Both counsels knew their divorce law from A to Z. It was like two Titans struggling for the upper hand with words, rather than physical power. The stakes were the lives of two young people. The costs would be their property, pain, and legal fees. Whatever the outcome, someone would have to foot the bills.

As the morning wore on, the two protagonists put forward one argument after another. It was all very fascinating to those witnessing the event, on the other hand painful for the parties involved.

At 12.30 p.m., the Judge said they would recess until 2.30 p.m., when he said that he wanted concluding statements from all parties. Then, both Carla and Dino Borghese would be called to the witness stand. It was a very hectic two hours, as over lunch, in separate Restaurants, both parties conferred with their counsels. Each counsel advising their Client, on how to answer possible questions when confronted by opposite number. Both Carla and Dino had little appetite for their meals; all too soon they were back in Court to resume their confrontation. The testimony given by Carla and Dino pales into insignificance, compared with the arguments put forward by their counsels. The Judge listened carefully, as first Carla made her prepared statement followed by Dino. Both parties were asked a barrage of questions. Carla felt that she was on trial for her life. Finally, the ordeal came to an end, for now all the evidence had been gathered. The Judge said, he was satisfied that a decision could be reached without too much delay. He would see counsels in his chambers.

It was now 4.00 p.m., and he would reconvene the Court at 10 a.m. next day to conclude the proceedings. So for Carla and Dino the nightmare was not yet over. The counsels followed the Judge to his chambers, where they discussed in private the terms and conditions they would expect if they won their case. Carla and Dino went their separate ways, to enjoy another sleepless night. Next morning they were back in Court. On the stroke of 10 a.m., The Bailiff called for silence in Court as Judge Benneto entered the Court. He reviewed the case, congratulated both counsels on their convincing arguments of their cases. However, the fact remained there had to be a winner, and a loser. The truth of the matter was that the Husband, in this case Signor Borghese, had an adulterous affair with another Lady. He had the affair willingly. He had family responsibilities, and this he could not ignore. Signora Borghese now had a young son. There was the question of custody of the boy. Who would have the responsibility of raising him? What were her chances of remarrying, or indeed starting a career?

All these matters had to be taken into consideration, when a verdict had to be given. Judge Benneto liked examining both sides of the argument before giving what he called his Judgement of Solomon.

"Finally," said Judge Benneto, "I have carefully considered all the facts presented in this case. I have spoken separately to counsels, after yesterday afternoon's session. The only verdict I can arrive at is this."

He paused for a few moments. All the parties held their breath. Carla knew in her heart that she had won the case, and would get custody of their son.

Judge Benneto cleared his throat.

"In this case, I find for the plaintiff."

Carla gave a little silent cheer; she would be free of Dino. Dino was not surprised. Maria would be delighted she could now play with him as she pleased. Dino would of course be dancing to Maria's tune. He felt relieved in one way but sad that he was losing his son and the love of a wife he once loved. Perhaps they could work out something, so he could have access.

"Before I clear the court," said the Judge, "I will see both counsels in my chambers."

Terms of the settlement were agreed, and the divorce would be made absolute by 31st December 1909. The Judge could see no reason to prolong the agony for either party. In short it meant that, the house in which they both lived should be sold, Carla would get 60% of the proceeds and Dino 40%. A sum would be set-aside for Dino Jnr as a trust. Dino would pay a set sum each year as maintenance for Carla and Dino Jnr., until Carla felt she no longer needed it. Then it would be reduced so that it applied to Dino Jnr., only. In fact, it was no less than Dino expected. Carla also claimed a sum to be paid to her for expenses for living in the family home until it was sold. Then a further sum until she had a suitable income to cover all her needs. All these terms were agreed and entered into the divorce papers.

Carla and Dino did not hate each other; they felt that they had both gone into the marriage with their eyes wide open. They had loved each other very much; they were both sad to see it end this way. When she first met Dino she knew that he flirted, but had hoped in her heart that marriage would have cured him. Seeming not. A pretty head, the promise of sexual deviation and a clandestine affair, were more than her husband could resist. Carla thought, he has made his bed, he can lie in it. She didn't even know a small fraction of Dino's new behaviour, or indeed what he got up to with the mysterious Countess X.

Now she did not care for she was her own woman at last and free. She felt a little strange, and now had to come to terms with a different way of life, where she was the breadwinner.

In future years, may be she would regret the events of the last few months, or on the other hand may be not. Now only time would tell. If she had met Dino at a different time in her life, would their marriage have gone the same way? It was a rhetorical question. Then you can always be wise in hindsight. She left Court wondering about her future now that she was alone. She knew in her heart, that fate had planned for her something far better, than being married to a philanderer. Dino was full of charm that much was true. She now thought that rather than being faithful to her, Dino was using this talent, leaping on the first sensuous, heavenly body that came along. She knew that if it were not the mysterious Countess X, who no doubt had furs, money, and an enormous sexual appetite, it would have been another rich and beautiful woman. She was glad to be rid of Dino. Now she could put him out of her thoughts, and get on with her life. Dino too thanked his counsel, and walked out of court, but not a free man. He too had the wisdom of hindsight; he was a wiser man in some respects, but unfortunately not in others, as we shall see.

The next day Carla telephoned Enzo at the Bank; he was delighted with the outcome of the trial. She asked if they could meet at his Office to discuss a few things. Enzo agreed that they should meet the following Monday, for he had a free morning. When Carla arrived at his office, Enzo ordered coffee and they sat and went over the Antonati case. For in a week or so Carla would have to familiarise herself with all the facts, as the case was to come to trial. She would be one of the key witnesses, plus the fact that she would be a partner in the FORUM business. Enzo said he would make all his documents available to her. Enzo said, "That crook Antonati deserves all he gets." The coffee arrived and they went over the case carefully. Enzo looked at Carla, and noticed that the strain of the divorce was showing on her face. She had matured quickly from the young lady he had employed only a few short years ago. They wrapped up the discussion concerning FORUM.

"Don't forget Carla," said Enzo, "if I can help in any way with anything with regard to the divorce settlement. Please just ask."

"Enzo that would be marvellous. I may need your help and guidance on many things. This is a New World to me."

As Carla closed the door to his office, Enzo sat back to think about his son, and what a fool he had been to abandon his family, for what exactly? No doubt he was indulging his sexual appetite with this so-called Countess X. He thought back to when Dino was a young boy, who had never had a platonic friendship with a girl in all his life. He had 'touched up' ladies in the street and pinched their bottoms, usually with a gang of his friends. When challenged they would look all innocent. By the time he was 14 years old he had romped in the hay with many a young girl. Enzo had faced many an angry father, whose daughters had come close to Dino's private parts. So it was no surprise to him that he had strayed again. Put temptation in his way and he would submit to it. Even the steadying influence of Carla could not stop his son's hot Italian blood coming to the surface. How long would this affair with the Countess X last? Now the divorce had been splashed all over the papers. Enzo was angry that the family name had been dragged into the mud. Although Enzo loved his son, the recent events had strained his affections to the limit.

Carla then went home to spend time with her son.

Young Dino kept asking the same question time after time.

"Where is my papa Mama? Where is my Papa Mama?"

At first, Carla did not know what to say. Then she decided to tell a white lie and told him that daddy was on a very long trip. Sophia would play with young Dino, and tell him stories to keep him amused. In a week Carla would be at work once more, and this she hoped would take her mind off the recent divorce.

Dino meanwhile, went straight to a Bar, and had a few drinks. The decision of the court was no more than he had expected. He telephoned Maria and told her the result of the divorce.

Her answer was simple and she put on her sexiest voice saying,

"My Darling Dino, you poor little boy, how dreadful this business has been for you. Come back to your naughty Maria in Venice tonight. I'll be waiting for you and we can have a night and day to forget your worries and celebrate. You know how I like to celebrate don't you? You are a extremely naughty boy and you will have to be punished in my very special way."

She rang off. Dino made his way to the station and caught then next train for Venice. Now he could not wait to get back to Maria. On the train he was thinking how relieved he was to be free of Carla at last. He could now fully indulge his sexual fantasies with Maria to the limit. His conscience was clear. He was free to do as he wished. Maria would incite and excite him. He felt like a man who had dropped a heavy load.

On arriving at Venice Station, Dino took a taxi to the Villa. Maria was waiting for him dressed in her favourite furs and with a long lingering kiss, she led him into the bedroom where she set about certain punishments, she had thought up especially for this occasion. First of all she told him to take off his clothes, as he deserved a spanking for being a naughty boy. Then followed the sexual celebrations that were new to Dino. She gave him the full treatment, for the next few days were just one round of lovemaking in every conceivable way. Maria had her man where she wanted him at last, for now he was there to be at her beck and call. Carla now his ex-wife was history.

Over the next few months, apart from his household chores in 'uniform', Maria made Dino think he was on one long honeymoon. However, Maria had other ideas but really Maria was just training Dino. He was enjoying life so much that he did not realise what was happening.

Carla meanwhile, enjoyed her last weekend before going to work for FORUM in their Florence store. This was situated about 300 metres from the Bank. She was happy to be staying in Florence, but ultimately she knew that she would have to move to Rome. This store was the hub of the FORUM Fashion Empire. She would stay in Florence until her house was sold. When she arrived for her first day at FORUM, Ricardo Armari greeted her. He had travelled up from Rome to show her the ropes. The Manager was Arturo Toscetti, and well built man in his early 40's. He loved his food, and his figure showed it. His wife was Lucretia, a lovely lady, who had been a model for the business when Arturo had become Manager some 10 years earlier. They had feared that their business would go under because of the Antonati case.

They were delighted that Carla had come to join them; after all it was she that had unveiled the guilty party. They hoped the money stolen would be retrieved if only in part.

Her first day was spent meeting the staff, and the models. Carla quickly realised that she would have to update her wardrobe, if she were to keep up with the latest fashions, in her position at FORUM.

During the last few months she had become much closer to Sophia, who was more like a friend than a nanny. It was a relationship that the two women would enjoy for many years to come.

Dino Jnr. loved her like a big sister, and as the weeks passed he no longer asked the question.

"Where is Papa, Mama?"

Carla thought it was sad, and she could not understand why Dino had not asked for access to his son.

Carla was now spending long hours with Ricardo as the days passed, getting ready for the Antonati trial. Ricardo's wife Franchesca had her suspicions, that her husband was having an affair with Carla. However, as she grew to know Carla better, she realised that Carla had been brought in, to make FORUM a fashion force to be reckoned with. She had her doubts about Carla when she started at FORUM, for Franchesca was a jealous woman, and insisted that she accompany her husband whilst he was at the Florence store. Antonati had left them with a vast number of problems, which gave Franchesca and several other Managers the feeling that bringing in outside people would bring nothing but trouble. With all the help Carla had been in bringing Signor Antonati to justice, Franchesca slowly realised that there were people outside of the business that cared what happened to FORUM. The Bank of Italy had appointed an investigator, Carla. She had virtually saved the Company from ruin. Carla was now well into the swing of things and now the winter fashions were in the store. Carla could now afford to buy designer fashions. Although she had her full-length silver fox coat, she decided that she would have a full-length blue fox coat as well, and contacted their Furrier, Enrico Laurenzetti. He came into the Office and had a meeting with Carla. Enrico's label was just an elegant EL, and he had been FORUM's top furrier for the past five years.

He had produced some stunning designs, so he asked which of the pelts from his sample file she preferred.

Carla chose a very beautiful Blue fox. He then showed her, his top designs, she made her selection. Enrico then took some measurements. After two fittings the coat was finished, and it was absolutely fabulous, she also had boots and bonnet to match. She felt she could now attend functions laid on by the fashion houses, with the feeling that she was a partner rather than just an employee. She always paid for her clothes, for until the time came when FORUM were in a strong financial position, she would not accept 'presents' from her own company. Although, Ricardo had often told her to help herself to any coat or dress she wanted.

One day, about a week after she had her first fitting for her blue fox coat, Carla found that she had some spare time, this was indeed a luxury. She had already ordered her blue fox, but just for fun, she decided to become a fashion model for a couple of hours.

She wanted to become a customer in her own shop, rather than a partner, just to see how it felt. She took about 30 gowns of all styles from the racks, and moved them into her own office. Next came a whole rack of furs, boots, and shoes. Then she pulled down the blinds of her office windows and put a sign on the door that read - IN CONFERENCE DO NOT DISTURB. She locked the door, told the receptionist that she wanted no calls, and please would she take messages.

Then Carla had the time of her life, she felt that she was in a clothes shop, and could have simply anything her heart desired, regardless of cost. Finally, after trying on 23 different outfits, she found the ideal evening gown. Next came the search for the day ensemble. This too took a time to choose, plus she needed the boots and shoes to accompany it. Finally, came the fur coat, hat and gloves and there was so much to choose from. Often she had looked at a full-length sable coat in the Fur section at FORUM; she looked at the price and nearly had a fit. Now she had the chance to wear it for FREE. When she tried it on, she was upset to see herself in the mirror. It did not suit her at all. DAMN she thought, I always wanted that coat ever since I started here. Let's try something else. She removed a beautiful full-length silver fox coat, her second favourite. She slipped it on; it had a shawl collar. The fine soft fur complimented her slim face and dark hair and complexion and it felt superb and made her feel sensual.

Then she selected the full-length red fox coat, and matching fur accessories. It blended well, and she felt this could be her third choice. This combination made her look vibrant and ready to party.

"Look!" she felt it said to her, "here I am, notice me!"

After due consideration however, she decided that she looked her best in the silver fox of course, that was a different design to her own, and in it she felt the true lady. The blue fox fur that she had chosen had to be made especially for her. This coat was one she could wear to any occasion, without feeling overdressed. Still the world was her oyster now, and Carla intended to be the pearl in it. She would have to work hard to achieve her aim. Her errant husband had abandoned her. Now, she was a single mother, with double responsibilities.

Firstly to her son and secondly to her business and now she needed the second to take care of the first. Her two hours of daydreaming in expensive clothes were quickly coming to an end. The time spent was like a little dream of luxury, that ladies often have. As she dressed herself in her working clothes once more, she sighed. In her mind was the forthcoming trial of Antonati, as she put all the beautiful clothes back on their racks. She picked up the telephone and asked one of her staff to replace the racks. Sitting back at her desk, she knew that the world of fashion was a fickle one, even in the early part of the 20th Century. Most fashion guru's looked to Paris as the fulcrum of European fashion. Designers were hard put to keep up with the fads of the public. Carla felt that she was ready to face this new challenge; she had a good team at FORUM, who wanted to put Italian fashion well and truly on the map.

On the Tuesday of the following week, Enrico and his assistant Carmel arrived with three suitcases with the initials EL on them. He arrived at Reception and asked for Carla. She welcomed him and asked him to come to the office. Carla was excited this was her first dream as a business lady to own a custom made fur. She put the notice on her door - IN CONFERENCE and pulled the blinds down. The last thing she wanted was an audience.

Enrico opened the largest case.

"Carla, my dear, behold your coat."

Carla looked at it in astonishment. It was the finest example of his expert furrier's craft. The coat was simply stunning. Carla knew that he was good, but this was perfection. She put it on, and it made her feel wonderful. The bonnet and boots were in the other suitcases, and in a few moments she outfit was complete. She looked at herself in the mirror. It made her look like a Queen; she felt that it was the image she needed to portray now as a partner in the business. Enrico told her that, the coat and accessories would be present for her, as he too had lost a great deal of money to Signor Antonati, in his scam. Without her help he would have been made bankrupt. If all the money was returned to him, it amounted to several billion lire. Then the he would not make any charge. Carla was speechless. Carla asked Enrico how long his contract to supply furs to FORUM had to run. Enrico said that it ended, at the end of the year.

"Enrico would you work, exclusively for FORUM on a long term contract?" asked Carla.

"Yes Carla," answered Enrico, "I will sign up with FORUM once the Antonati trial is over."

They shook hands, and the deal was done.

"One more question Enrico, when the trial is over, I want you to teach me all about fur. How to recognise the good from the not so good. As you know I was in Banking. Now I want to know all about fashion, furs and materials."

"Of course I will," Enrico replied, "it will be my pleasure Carla."

He handed a bill to Carla; it showed no charge for the coat, bonnet and boots.

"After the trial Carla, I hope we can tear this up."

Soon the weeks passed, and the start of the Antonati trial was now just days away. Their Law firm of Musso and Musso were appointed as Forum's team to prosecute the case. Carla and Ricardo felt that it could be and open and shut case, and should only last a few days. Carla travelled down to Rome on the Thursday before the Trial to stay with Ricardo and Franchesca in their villa. This would be interesting, for like her divorce case, Carla had a personal interest in the outcome.

Musso & Musso had already a thick file on Signor Benito Antonati. Since Carla's investigation, Ricardo had been compiling evidence. Musso's solicitor, Gino Solsi, had been brought in to prepare the brief for the chief prosecutor, a terror of the financial world when it came to embezzlement, a certain Fabio Otti. The two days prior to the trial, Carla spent almost all day with Gino and Fabio. They were honing up their evidence to ensure a short trial. At last the day arrived, Carla put on her business dress, plain black with a white frilly blouse and her fur-trimmed coat and hat. As she left for court, by car, she felt confident that her first task with FORUM was to seek justice, and put away this slimy, creature, Antonati, who had robbed them of billions of lire. In addition it had dragged the Company reputation down into the mud, with money laundering. The whole affair would give the press a field day. She would then have the unenviable task of rebuilding the Company standing in the business community.

It was Monday 6th December 1909 and the case was being held in the Central Criminal Court in Rome. The Judge Enrico Titian had a reputation for dealing out very heavy prison sentences to those who broke the law. The Court was packed with people who Antonati had 'conned' over the years.

Carla sat there with Ricardo by her side. Just behind her sat Enrico Laurenzetti. The whole courtroom was a hubbub of conversation. All became hushed, as the Solicitors, Barristers, and other parties involved filed into the courtroom. On the stroke of 10.00 a.m. the Clerk of the Court announced they all should rise and the Judge took his place. A door opened on the wall to the right of the judge's dais, and two uniformed prison guards brought in the prisoner. The defence had asked for trial by jury, so the twelve good men and true sat ready on benches ready to listen to the evidence. Carla looked hard at the man in front of her that was standing in the dock. There was the man who deserved a long prison sentence for almost bankrupting a wonderful business. She hoped and prayed he would get a very long prison sentence.

The Judge asked the prosecuting Barrister to start his opening statements. Fabio got to his feet, and told the Court the long story that how Antonati had a long history of criminal activities going back to 1890. He starting work for an arms dealer, importing guns from the German Company Krups. He had sold guns to the Boers in South Africa. When the Boer War ended, he switched his interests into investing his capital into local businesses. He had started with Forum, when he had met Ricardo and Franchesca Armari, at a business convention in Rome, when they were just starting out back in 1902. At first he seemed genuine, for his Client needed funds to expand and buy top quality merchandise. FORUM had benefited from the billions of lira that; the defendant had poured in. Suddenly, their profits soared, Antonati took his cut. His lifestyle had now really taken off. The highlife beckoned. In the next three years that followed he got involved with some local drug dealers, who were bringing in cocaine and hashish from Morocco.

This was a good sideline, and soon his bank balance got too hot to handle. So he laundered money through FORUM. When the drug dealers were arrested, Antonati began to embezzle money from FORUM, to maintain his lifestyle. He persuaded his Client to change accountants, and subsequently siphoned off funds to a Swiss Bank Account. All the evidence was there. Fabio called for Antonati to be punished to the full extent of the law, and the money returned to his Client. The Judge thanked Signor Otti, for his eloquent delivery of his Client's case. As it was 12.30 p.m. the Court would recess until 2.00p.m.

Carla now felt happier that at least the evidence had been presented in a forceful way. Ricardo, sat next to Carla, both of them had listened intently to the evidence for the prosecution. Over lunch, Ricardo wondered what stories the defence, were going to come up with. They did not have long to wait.

At 2.00 p.m., on the dot, The Clerk of the Court asked everyone to rise as the Judge entered the courtroom, and the case continued. The defence barrister was Franco Ordini; he was short, fat and stuttered. He said his Client had a poor childhood in the streets of Rome. His father had abandoned him, as Franco went on with his tale of woe, obviously looking for sympathy from the Judge and Jury.

After about fifteen minutes as Franco Ordini told what sounded like the Sermon on the Mount, the Judge was getting decidedly irritated.

"If it is not too much to ask Signor Ordini," interrupted the Judge in a laconic tone "can we get to the point of all of this? I do not want the life story of your Client."

Now Franco started playing to the gallery with some dramatic inflections in his voice and exaggerated hand movements.

The Judge pulled him up again.

"Signor Ordini, I love watching an actor in full flow, but not in my Court. Try to conduct your defence in a manner more appropriate to a Court of Law, and not as theatrical performance."

Ordini started feeling embarrassed and started to stutter. This was a ploy he used when backed into a corner. As the afternoon wore on, he gave the best defence for his Client that he could. He painted a picture of his Client, how he had fallen in with bad company and was forced into a life of crime. He was the victim of trickery. The Judge started to smile, as if he had heard it all before. Franco Ordini knew in his heart that his Client was guilty, the evidence was overwhelming. He had tried every trick in his book.

During the whole day, Antonati just sat there staring in disbelief that his case had actually come to court. When Signor Ordini he sat down at the end of his presentation, the clock had moved around to 4.15p.m, and the Judge ended the day's proceedings. The Court would reconvene the following morning at 10 a.m., and asked for the Court to be cleared. He sent the Jury off to a Hotel for the night. Carla and Ricardo went back to the Villa, where Franchesca asked how the day had gone. Both Carla and Ricardo told her that they were confident of a guilty decision. The trick of the light would be getting the money back. They had a fairly sleepless night. At 10 a.m., they were back in Court. The Judge asked the prosecution to present a list of creditors to him. The Judge looked down the list that was extensive.

"Gentlemen of the Jury," began the Judge, "this is the worst case I have seen for years. I cannot ask all these people to take to the witness stand. I shall take the evidence in the form of all their statements into consideration when I instruct the jury. Thank you Signor Ordini."

Fabio began by summarising the evidence for the prosecution and again demanded full retribution, and the reclamation of all funds, embezzled and profits from money laundered by the accused. He sat down.

Then, it was the turn of Franco Ordini; he was going to try a last ditch stand. He called his Client to the stand, and began to cross-question him. Antonati broke down, and Ordini had a difficult job, getting him to go over his statement. Franco then took his turn with Antonati, and tore him to pieces. By the time the prosecutor had finished, Antonati was a shivering, nervous wreck. The Judge then summed up the case, and gave instructions to the Jury then asked them to leave the Court and consider their verdict. The court was cleared would reconvene at 2.00 p.m., and he hoped that in the 2 hour recess, that the Jury would be able to come to a verdict. Antonati was led back to the cells. Carla and Ricardo went off to a local Restaurant for lunch. They felt confident that the jury would find Antonati guilty.

At 2.00p.m, the Court rose on the entrance of Judge Titian. The Jury filed in and sat down.

The Judge called to the Foreman of the Jury.

"Signor Foreman, have you reached a verdict on which you all agree?"

There was a moment of hushed silence, and a tall, greying man stood up. In his hand he held a piece of paper. The silence in Court you could have cut with a knife.

"Your honour," he began, "we have considered carefully all the facts in this case. The decision we are all agreed upon is that the prisoner in the dock is guilty. He is guilty of all the crimes on which he has been accused."

He sat down.

The Judge turned to the jury.

"Thank you Gentlemen for doing your duty here today."

The Judge then turned to Antonati, who was now a broken man, and broke down in the Dock.

"You sir," said the Judge in a dominant tone, "are a man who knew exactly what he was doing. You have led a charmed life as a criminal, who felt that crimes, not against the person were legal. Here we have seen the kind of person you really are. You used your position as an investor in FORUM, to bring the Company almost to its knees. Without the fine work of Signor Armari's new business partner, your life of crime would have gone undetected no doubt.

I sentence you to 20 years imprisonment without parole. This is the sentence for your crime according to present Italian law. Your Bank accounts will all be seized, and the funds will be returned to FORUM, together with any interest they may have accrued. Your Swiss account will also be involved, for we have ways of accessing this. Guards take him down."

Antonati shouted out as the Guards took hold of him.

"You have all made a mistake. I am innocent. I will appeal."

"This is a clear cut case of fraud and deceit," said Titian, "the law has spoken. The law only allows an appeal in the case of murder and other areas as defined in the statue books. Case closed. Please clear the court."

Enrico walked up to Carla, hugged and kissed her on both cheeks.

"Thank you Carla. You have made me a very happy man. That deal we had, let us now confirm it. Have you got that piece of paper?"

Carla pulled out the note from her handbag and handed it to Enrico. He tore it into little pieces.

"Well Carla," said Enrico smiling, "that is that bill paid."

"We will do good business together Enrico."

She hugged him again.

"How can I ever thank you?" Enrico replied,

"The result of this trial is enough for me Carla. Remember our conversation in your Office? What more can I ask? I shall be able to restructure my business. Now with FORUM as a Client, I am the happiest furrier in Italy. I will see you soon; in that work of art I have made you. I will also show you the art of the furrier."

Carla was over the moon; she had been paid in kind for her work, by a very grateful business contact, and a friend.

Carla and Ricardo breathed a sigh of relief, for they could now get on with their lives. When they arrived back at the Villa, Franchesca could not believe their good fortune. If it had not been for Carla, they would be well and truly bankrupt. Franchesca apologised to Carla, forever doubting her. Carla said that she should be getting back to the Florence store. All this business with Antonati in Rome, with the court case etc., meant that her work in Florence had suffered. So, that night, Carla packed her suitcase, and caught the early morning train back to Florence. With all those old problems out of the way, she sat down to enjoy the train journey back to Florence. She arrived at the store to see that all the decorations had been put up for Christmas.

The store windows were full of festive displays, with even a small nativity scene in one corner. Trade had been good over the past few months and Carla soon got down to work.

Now she could look forward to Christmas and a new career. By December 31st she would at last be a free woman, but still a single working mother.

As Christmas approached, Enzo phoned to ask how things were going. Carla told him about the Court case with Antonati. Enzo was delighted that they had got a good result. He told her that some of the money had filtered through to their account, which was no longer in the red. He would be delighted if she would bring Sophia, Dino Jnr., with her to stay with him over Christmas. Carla said she would be delighted. Enzo promised her and his Grandson a Christmas to remember after all she had been through during the year. He was true to his word. Carla, Dino Jnr. and Sophia had a wonderful time with Enzo with presents for everyone. Even with plenty of food, friends and good cheer around him, Enzo still missed his son, but was still very angry that he could have been so stupid, as to have abandoned his family. Now, in a few days his son and his daughter in law's marriage would be over. A very sad end indeed to what could have been a happy life for them all. Enzo had never met this Countess X., and did not even know her identity. Her picture never appeared in the paper during the trial. He felt that Carla and Dino Jnr. were still part of his family. He did not know whether to ask Carla, whether she would keep her married name or not. It was too early yet. In time she would tell him, no doubt. They enjoyed Christmas and New Year. Carla enjoyed the rest, for she felt very much under duress during the last few months. Now she could enjoy herself before getting down to work after the Yuletide holiday.

Chapter 17

The highlight of the early winter months in the lives of Catherina and Rudolph von Lundenberg, was the birth of their son Manfred Rudolph. Catherina was well into her pregnancy, by the time Rudolph had gone to Brooklands, in England, for the last event of the racing calendar. She loved going with her husband to the races, and enjoyed the smells and the excitement of the racetracks. The colourful characters and the clothes people wore to these events showing a side of society, that differed from anything she had seen before she had met Rudolph. However, with only some two weeks to go before the birth, even with all the best will in the world, travelling would not be an option. She was fond of England, and the beautiful countryside, with its quaint little houses. Now she was about to have a baby, and this was something she had longed for all her married life. Her first husband, who had never really loved her, had denied her the delight of having children. He had shown this very clearly; simply by the way he had treated her ever since their marriage. Now she found true love with Rudolph, she wanted his baby more than anything else, apart from the love of her husband. They both hoped for a son to carry on the family name, for Rudolph was his father's only son. The baby it seems was very co-operative, being very lively within the womb, giving the usual kicks to make its presence felt.

Whilst Rudolph was away in England with the Mercedes team, Catherina stayed at the Schloss Lundenberg with a nurse from the local hospital. She rested during the day in a bright, warm, airy room, which looked across the gardens. The trees were now stripped of their leaves, except for a few Fir Trees, that swayed in the winter winds. Count Josef and Margarita insisted that Catherina stay at the Schloss until the baby was born.

Rudolph did not enjoy his trip to England, even though he won the main race at Brooklands. He could not help thinking about Catherina and the child within her womb. He could not wait to get back home to be with her. Gustav gave him time off to be with Catherina until after the baby was born. Then at midnight on November 1st 1909, Catherina went into labour.

The nurse was in attendance. Catherina was in labour for over twelve hours. At 2.30 p.m. on November 2nd 1909, young Manfred greeted the world, weighing in at a healthy three kilos. The crying of their new-born son heralded a new era for all the von Lundenbergs. The nurse washed and clothed the baby, then gave him back to his Mother. Catherina offered up to her right breast and he began to suckle. Everyone gathered round, it was a grand day for them all. What would the future hold for Manfred Rudolph? Certainly, he would be protected against life's many tribulations, until he could stand on his own two feet.

Young Manfred was a good baby, although he always craved attention, like most babies do, and so Rudolph and Catherina decided to engage a Nanny. Catherina said that she would wait until Christmas was over, when they would move back to their own home. Count Josef suggested to Rudolph that his grandson should be christened at the little church on the estate. Catherina and Rudolph agreed. The ceremony would be arranged for the 19th December 1909, the Sunday before Christmas. Invitations were sent out, these included Rudolph's team-mates at Mercedes and Alain Clement, together with their wives or partners. Everyone replied, although Alain and Francoise said they could not make it, but sent a present. With the present was a note saying that they hoped to meet again soon, when racing resumed. He sent hearty congratulations on the birth of a son. Herman Ritter and Fritz Lang were chosen as Godparents. The day was sunny but very cold. All the guests had stayed overnight. Hermann had brought his latest lady friend and Fritz Lang had invited a dazzling blonde called Helga Strayger. It was a happy occasion for Catherina and Rudolph. Young Manfred was behaving himself, as they got ready to go to church. The ladies were all dressed in their furs and finery, whilst the men were dressed in suits and leather coats. The car cavalcade made its way to the Church. Outside stood the Priest Heinz Kirk, who greeted them as they all alighted from the Cars and made their way in and sat in the pews. Catherina held the little baby close to her bosom, keeping her son warm against the soft warm fur of her coat. The ceremony began with a hymn, then the blessing and finally the godfathers were asked to come forward to give their solemn promise to look after the child, should anything happen to its parents. The service ended and everyone went back to the Schloss, to celebrate. Christmas 1909 was special for the von Lundenbergs, now that they had another addition to the family. This year it was more reason to celebrate than ever.

It was the 8th January 1910, before the new parents finally left to return home. The servants had prepared a Nursery, for Manfred and Catherina had interviewed several prospective nurses before hiring Ursula Graf. She was a lady of 26 years, and had been a Nanny to several of the landed gentry in the area. She loved boys, and Manfred was easy to love and well behaved. Rudolph was now back at work, for there was plenty to do. Since he had been away, Gustav and the team had been making enquiries, as to when the next series of races would take place, and would there be a change in the regulations. The authorities informed them, that there would be no Grand Prix Racing in Europe during 1910 or 1911. The only races anywhere in the world would be in the United States of America. The 1910 race would be held in Savannah, Georgia on November 12th, there would also be another race on the same course in 1911. Gustav had received a request from a Ralph de Palma, an American driver for a car for the 1910 event. Gustav said that they could not get a car built and tested in time, but would be happy to supply a car for the 1911. Ralph de Palma wrote to Gustav, he enclosed a copy of the regulations for the 1911 and 1912 races. The maximum engine capacity allowed was a massive 9800 c.c, the engine could have as many cylinders as the manufacturers wished, and there was no weight limit. Gustav scratched his head when the letter arrived with all the regulations. He called Rudolph into his office and showed him the correspondence. "This request," said Rudolph scanning the letter from Mr. de Palma, "would give us good publicity in America. In his letter he tells of a Championship in America called the AAA National Championship, that runs from February through to November on nine different circuits. The only problem as I see it, is that we need to manufacture an engine almost twice the size of our present race car."

Gustav went into a think mode. Then he looked at another sheet of paper attached to the regulations. Mr.de Palma had listed out the circuits, winners, and speeds of events that had taken place in the AAA National Championships for 1909. The average speeds ranged from 38m.p.h. to 76 m.p.h.; therefore, they needed a car with speed and stamina. A tall order indeed. Gustav wrote back saying they would supply a car suitable for the races, and invited him to come over during the year to see the car being built and tested.

During 1909, Rudolph had spent time away from his beloved Catherina, now with this new challenge they would be at the factory developing a car that they would not see racing. This was a new departure for the factory. Catherina was pleased to have her husband home at night. The designers were hard at work designing this monster. Various configurations of cylinder layout were tried. In the end they decided on a 'V8' this would make the engine shorter, it would help the weight distribution too. The designs were slowly coming together. The engine would be literally two of their current engine blocks, placed on a common crankcase. Rudolph went down to the engine shop and watched the castings of the new engine taking place. They had decided to reduce the stroke length giving the engine a capacity of 9 litres. In another part of the factory the chassis was being constructed. Due to the increase in power, that the engine would no doubt produce they went for four-wheel brakes with cooling fins. It took several months for the car to take shape and be ready for testing. Rudolph would oversee this, and he looked forward to getting into the driving seat.

Alain had enjoyed his honeymoon, more than he could ever express. His lovely and charming new wife, Francoise, realised that it was not an anti-climax saving herself all these years. She loved having intercourse with her husband; she wanted it at times more than he did. They were very much in love and it was a happy balanced marriage, for they were both interested in each other's pursuits and they were sure it would last.

Alain got back to work at Peugeot in those last months of 1909, even with all the hard work, a car which had first seemed to have great potential, had an 'Achilles heel' it seemed. The test drive had gone like a dream, with no problems. On later tests, gearbox problems began to occur. The gearbox was stripped down, and it was found that metal fatigue had set in at an early stage and several teeth were broken. They had burnt the midnight oil for almost a month, before the fault was cured. They decided that the only way was the ultimate test.

They entered the car in the last International race of the 1909 season at Brooklands. Alain and the team, always enjoyed their trips to England, they were treated like heroes. He met up with Rudolph, who admired the new lighter Peugeot L70.When the race began, Rudolph shot into the lead with Alain close on his heels, as the passed the start and finish line on lap 3, Alain overtook Rudolph to take the lead. He was pulling away nicely and had a healthy lead. Then the car started to loose power. Alain and his mechanic could not make out what the problem could be. Was it fuel starvation, a blockage perhaps? The big Mercedes thundered past, as did several other cars. Alain was feeling very frustrated. He was now almost last. Then, the engine gave a cough, and the power returned. Alain started passing cars as if they had stopped. Now he was in 4th place, then 3rd. He thought he might have a chance of at least 2nd place. Then the car lost power again. Something was wrong somewhere, even dirt in the petrol. Cars started to pass him again. Then the Peugeot engine coughed again and his speed picked up. Rudolph was well ahead of the field and Alain could just see him passing the checked flag. Alain eventually crossed the line in 5ᵗʰ place. The disappointment showed on his face as he collected his prize.

Rudolph came over to him and looked concerned.

"Alain," he asked, "whatever was wrong with your car? You passed me as if I was out on a Sunday drive."

Alain shook his head for he was still mystified.

"No idea my friend, I think I must have gremlins in my engine."

Rudolph shook his hand and consoled him.

"By the way Alain," replied Rudolph changing the subject, "Catherina is pregnant. I hope you will be able to come to the christening. I will write to you."

"Congratulations to you both," replied Alain, "that is great news. I will come if I can."

The two men hugged and parted.

Alain returned to the factory at Peugeot, where they stripped down the engine. The cause was indeed a blocked fuel line. Alain was not happy that a simple thing had caused the failure at Brooklands. A new type of filter was fitted, and in future all fuel would be filtered before it went into the fuel tank. They found pieces of rust, which had no doubt, come from a steel fuel container. In future tests the car ran like clockwork. By and large Alain was very happy at Peugeot; he had seen the chance of victory escape. He wanted to win and the glory that went with it; he was a very patriotic young man. He asked for a meeting with the Managing Director, Charles Orly. Alain asked point blank if there would be more money for developing the L70 design?

After all Alain explained the car had a great deal of potential.

Charles sat back in his chair, for he had some sad news to impart to Alain.

"Alain," began Charles, "I do realise that you have worked very hard on this new car. However, the problem is that we do not have any International Races in France or indeed in Europe during 1910 or 1911, they are all in America. We cannot afford to send cars and drivers to these races. It is not practical. So my friend, we cannot have extra money spent on a car that will not be raced. We want to improve our road cars, and the lessons learned on the race cars will mean we can build better road cars and improve sales. We shall be doing a big advertising campaign, and you will be featured in this. I am sorry that we do not have money for modifications and redesigning."

Alain left the Office feeling a bit unhappy. He was in a no win situation. Even if he applied to drive for another factory, there would still be no racing for the next two years. May be some small local events.

Like Rudolph, Alain was feeling the strain of lack of competition, it showed on his face. His lovely bride of just four months had already noticed a change in him. As newlyweds, she wanted to be loved, and seduced by her husband. Her body was there for the asking, she longed for his manly organ to give her pleasure when he came home after a day's work. Much as she tried to help him relax and enjoy life's many pleasures; she felt that he had the world's troubles on his shoulders.

One evening, Alain came home from work, after a hard day, it had been a frustrating one when nothing seemed to be going right. Francoise tried to stimulate him, but he seemed to have little interest in lovemaking.

"My dearest," asked Francoise, "what is the matter? You seem so wound up and drawn these days. You do not seem to be able to raise a smile, let alone anything else?"

Alain's face moved towards making a grin, and nearly made it.

"Francoise, my dearest love," he began," I love you more than anything else in the world. Some days I think that in my work, I have jumped out of the frying pan into the fire. I had great hopes of this new car the L70; it has great potential that could be exploited. I had hopes of beating the Mercedes team with all the new ideas. Try as I might, there always seemed to be something that went wrong to thwart our efforts at the last minute. Success seems just that further bit away. Every time you think you have it in your hand it slips out. It is very frustrating. Believe me; I am sorry that I am behaving the way I am to you. I must conquer this one way or another.

The other problem is that there are no International Races in Europe this year or next. So no factories are spending money on new developments. I am sorry to bring my troubles home to you. In future I will leave them at the factory gates. Unless I can win a big race soon, my days at Peugeot may be over."

Francoise went over to her husband, and wrapped her arms around him, kissed him.

"Darling," she whispered, "I understand I really do. Now please come to bed and make love to me? We can work this out."

Francoise took Alain by the hand, and led him to their bed. They made love for hours. After they had exhausted themselves, enjoying each other, they knew that things would work out somehow. They had to be patient. That night they both slept well. Next morning, Alain felt a good deal better as he eat his breakfast. The post had arrived; there was a letter with a German postmark. The writing was not familiar; the town in which the letter had been posted was Mosbach. Francoise wondered who had written it. Alain opened the envelope, and saw the crest on the top of the headed notepaper. It was from his rival in nearly every race he had driven in.

He was surprised and turning to Francoise exclaimed: "This is a letter from Rudolph von Lundenberg. I will read it to you: -

(It was dated November 12th 1909)

Dear Alain and Francoise,

I was extremely sorry that I could not come to your wedding, and I hope that the gift I sent arrived safely. My wife Catherina had a son on November 2nd, so he is keeping her very busy. We are hoping to have the christening before Christmas, hope you can both come. I have a proposition to put to you and hope you can respond quickly. You may know that my team-mate, Fritz Lang has left Mercedes and gone to drive for the Austrian team Austro-Daimler. I have no need to tell you that we not amused at that. I was sorry to hear that you were not driving for Peugeot in that race; we could have given them a run for their money. I am holding up the honour of the team alone. The trainee drivers have not come up to scratch. I have spoken to Herr Gunther, about asking you to join us at Mercedes. I have told him you are the best driver I know. You have the right temperament for this business. We have some headstrong drivers to race against you and I. I realise you are under contract with Peugeot, but may be an arrangement can be made.

You can write or send me a telegram care of the Mercedes Factory. We never did get together for that home visit. Please get in touch as soon as you can, and come and spend a weekend with Catherina and I. We can talk over old times, and about the future.

Your friend   (signed Rudolph.)

Having finished reading the letter, he passed it to Francoise, who read again very quickly.

"Well my love," she said putting the letter down, "let us not delay in replying to Rudolph. He thinks very highly of you. That is strange considering he has always been your greatest rival in Motor Racing. He must be a true gentleman and now a friend as well. The offer seems like manna from Heaven. After all things seems to be stagnating at Peugeot. I think we should take the opportunity while it is there."

The next morning, Alain sent a telegram to Rudolph, expressing his thanks for Rudolph's efforts to secure him a drive with Mercedes. Alain also told him that he and Francoise would like to visit over the weekend 10th & 11th December 1909, but would have to pass on the Christening, as they would be spending Christmas with the family.

So it was arranged, and Francoise was really looking forward to the journey. Alain wanted to know more about the drive with Mercedes, before seeing his Managing Director about leaving Peugeot. As the days passed Francoise got quite excited about the forthcoming trip. It would be the longest train journey she had ever done, and it would be her first visit to Germany. They knew the heating in the trains was most unreliable. Francoise searched through her wardrobe for her warmest clothes.

On a visit to the Chateau one weekend, Francoise told the Countess de Longchamps about the trip, who said it would be very exciting, but a very cold journey. Francoise casually mentioned to the Countess that she did not have a really warm winter coat. Immediately, the Countess Claudine stopped talking and thought for a moment. This young lady needs to keep warm and then an idea came to her.

"Francoise," said the Countess, "please come with me to my boudoir and choose a full-length fur coat to wear, with matching gloves and bonnet of course."

She took Francoise up to her bedchamber and there in another room were all the Countess's clothes.

She opened an oak-panelled door and inside was a rack full of furs. Francoise stood there for a moment, dazzled by the array of furs. The Countess looked at Francoise who was standing there open mouthed.

"My dearest Francoise," said the Countess breaking the silence, "please choose any Fur that you would adore to wear, my love. I am sure you would look marvellous in any of them."

Francoise felt like a little girl in a sweet shop. She did not know which one to pick. Claudine watched her for a few moments. Then selecting a beautiful silver fox she turned to Claudine.

"Go on now Francoise," said Claudine "why not try this one to start with?"

Claudine helped Francoise put on with the exquisite coat. To Francoise, who had never owned her own fur coat in her life, it felt wonderful. She looked at herself in the mirror. She looked like a Princess. Claudine handed her the bonnet and gloves that went with it. Again Francoise admired the result.

"Do you like it?" asked Claudine.

"Do I like it? It feels fantastic," replied Francoise.

"Now, Francoise, just for fun, try this full-length blue fox fur complete with all matching accessories?"

Claudine was now helping Francoise take off the silver fox and on with the blue fox. Now dressed almost from head to toe in blue fox fur. Francoise was now admiring her image in the full-length mirror. She could not believe how wonderful she looked and felt.

"Claudine," she gasped, "those silver fox furs are gorgeous, but it is a very expensive coat indeed. If I may I would like the Blue fox furs please. I promise I will look after them."

The Countess Claudine smiled for she could see how happy Francoise was at that moment. She was radiant.

"That is a wise choice, my dear," replied Claudine, "you look absolutely stunning. Alain will adore you dressed in those gorgeous furs, I am certain."

Francoise was turning this way and that, admiring herself.

Claudine was watching her and smiling.

"By the way Francoise, I think you take the same size boots as I do. So try these blue fur lined boots on as they match the coat."

Francoise removed her shoes and put on the boots. She had never worn anything so sensual. The other wardrobe was full of boots, and shoes of all designs. Claudine knew exactly where to find the boots. Francoise walked around the room as if she was a modelling for one of the fashion houses of Paris. Claudine watched her, and could see how thrilled Francoise appeared.

"My darling Francoise, you obviously love that ensemble. I think I have worn it twice. Now it is my pleasure to make a present of it to you. Call it a pre-Christmas gift. Look after that man of yours, I always feel that he is the son that Guy and I never had."

Francoise was absolutely dumbfounded.

"Thank you, thank you so very much," was all she could say, "I am extremely happy Claudine. It is such a wonderful present."

Claudine was delighted at giving these furs to Francoise and kissed her on both cheeks.

"Just enjoy the present and the trip Francoise. We are so happy that you and Alain have such a strong marriage. You Francoise are the daughter of my best friend. I will always be there for you and Alain, in the good times and bad. Please take the bonnet, boots, gloves and coat with you with my love. Keep those furs on and we will surprise both your Alain and my husband."

Francoise was over the Moon, for she really felt like a Fairy Princess. Elsewhere in the Chateau, Alain was talking to Count Guy about his offer from Mercedes and the trip to Germany. The Count said more or less the same as Claudine that the trip would be exciting for Francoise and a chance to get to know Rudolph Von Lundenberg. It seems that as well as being an adversary on the track; and obviously wants to be your friend, for he must be an honourable man. Alain told him that they were going by train. At that moment, into the room came Francoise and Claudine. The Count looked round and saw the two ladies; Francoise was all dressed in her new blue fox furs.

Claudine was first to speak.

"Hello Alain," she said, "you two must be discussing your trip to Germany. Francoise too has been telling me all about it. What do you think of her new travelling clothes?"

Alain was speechless for a moment.

"She looks absolute gorgeous!" Alain exclaimed, "just like a Princess."

Claudine smiled with contentment.

"I agree," replied Claudine, "she looks wonderful. So wonderful in fact, that I have given her the fur coat, bonnet, gloves and boots as pre-Christmas presents. I had already spoken with Guy, that for Christmas we should give you both practical presents."

Guy left the room and returned with a large parcel, which he presented to Alain.

"This present is for you Alain," said Guy, "with our love."

Alain opened the parcel and then gasped as he removed the wrapping. Inside was a full length Racoon Coat and Hat.

"Do try it on Alain, and let us see how you look beside Francoise."

Alain put the coat on and he felt wonderful as he stood next to the lovely Francoise. Both Guy and Claudine could see how happy the young couple looked.

"Now you two" said Claudine, "look like you could face the cold of the North Pole. Now no more talk of the cold, let us go and have something to eat. I am starving."

The visit to the Chateau that day and the gifts from the Count and Countess of their new winter clothes, set the seal on what would be a change of fortune for Alain and Francoise.

The next few days were very busy; Francoise had to get a passport. Alain already had one, as he had been racing around Europe and the pages had been stamped many times. There were tickets to buy, and train timetables to be checked. They found an express that would take them as far as Heidelberg, where Rudolph would meet them. There seemed little time to spare, plus the fact that Alain was still working at Peugeot. Alain had a few days leave owing to him, and so did not have to return until the following Tuesday. At last, there was time for the young couple to enjoy their lovemaking at leisure. Enjoy it they did. Francoise finally had her husband all to herself, she could arouse him and they could be joined as only man and woman can. This was the pleasure than they had begun on honeymoon, and now it was theirs to indulge in as they pleased. Life seemed to have now dealt them a fresh hand of cards.

How they played their game remained to be seen. They were a team, a love team, and a team for life. So, the day dawned for the start of their journey. It was Friday, and they knew that they would not arrive at Mosbach until late that night. The taxi called early. It was a very cold day, with the threat of snow in the air. The clouds were grey overhead. Francoise was now dressed her Blue fox furs, and the first time she had worn it since that day at the Chateau. Alain too, now had his Racoon Coat; they needed to be wrapped up well against the strong wind blowing across the fields of Northern France. Enveloped in their furs, they snuggled together as the taxi chugged its way to Rouen Station, where they arrived in good time to catch their train to Paris and on to Germany. Alain paid the taxi driver, who in turn handed Alain his suitcase containing their clothes for the weekend trip. This was indeed an adventure for Francoise, now she would meet the famous Rudolph. She wondered what he would be like. Now having purchased their tickets; they strolled to the Station Platform to await the arrival of the Paris Express.

They certainly looked a very handsome couple, cuddling up to each other in the waiting room. The fire in the fireplace was not throwing out much heat. It was at least warmer than outside, where the wind was gathering strength. Alain looked up at the clock over the fireplace. They had just ten more minutes to wait before the train arrived.

The journey was almost ready to begin, for they had booked a private compartment all the way. They could shut the world out, and have whatever pleasure they desired, as they sat there kissing, and cuddling, they we brought back to reality by the whistle of the approaching train. They got up quickly and went outside on to the platform, as the Express train steamed into the station and came to a grinding halt. The guard called out 'All aboard'. Alain helped Francoise up the few steps to the carriage, then went back to collect the small suitcases. The Carriage attendant welcomed them on board and showed them to their compartment. He informed then that breakfast would be served in the Restaurant Car in 15 minutes. Now they were alone, time to talk, and then after breakfast make love. Alain stored the suitcases and locked the door. They hung up their coats and talked about the future. Alain hoped that his meeting with Rudolph would mean that the offer from Mercedes was real and a contract was in the offing. This would mean security for them both.

The attendant came along announcing breakfast was now being served. Having had only a cup of coffee before they left, Alain and Francoise were now really hungry. They made their way down to the Restaurant Car, and ordered a hearty breakfast. The other diners looked at the young couple in envy, for the seemed so happy, probably wishing their marriages were as good.

Whilst they were eating, the train slowed as it came into the outskirts of Paris. The train then pulled into the Gare du Nord. Looking out of the window, they could see the workers hurrying off the train to go to their Offices. Soon the train jolted, as it started on the next leg of the journey to Germany. Breakfast over; Francoise and Alain made their way back to their compartment. After closing, and locking the door, Francoise was feeling decided broody.

"Darling Alain," she whispered, "I have never made love under furs and on a moving train. So my love, I would love to try."

"Dearest Francoise," sighed Alain, "neither have I my darling. I want to make love to express my love to you."

They pulled down the blinds and now the world outside now held no interest to them, and now having undressed put on their furs. They were in a world of love of their own. Francoise was feeling very sensuous in her new blue fox; and she massaged Alain with her furs until she was ready to perform. Once they had begun, it was like their honeymoon, only far better. Under the furs they were now joined together, and so much in love. Now they could express their love for each other physically without disturbance. They continued until they were exhausted. They lay there on the bed in each other's arms. Whilst they were enjoying each other, the time passed quickly. There was a knock on the door, and a voice called out that lunch was being served. Alain and Francoise did not realise that they had made love under the furs all the morning, and it was truly a wonderful sensation.

"My darling," gasped Francoise as she came up for air, "that was the most fantastic morning of my life. I love you so much it hurts. I hope we can make much more love under those furs after lunch?"

"Francoise, you are the love of my life. I can deny you nothing. Now we have got the hang of this lovemaking on the train. I do think we need more practice after lunch, especially under those furs."

They had lunch, taken at their ease, and then returned to their compartment to continue their lovemaking where they had left off.

The train rattled on with the usual rhythm of the rails, whilst Francoise was top of Alain, making love to her own rhythm. This was wonderful; she felt that all her worries had left her. Alain too was in his element. He did not realise that lovemaking could lead him into a state of ecstasy, but it had. Time passed and the train slowed. They were coming to the border between France and Germany. The train ground to a halt. Alain could hear the border guards and immigration police climbing aboard the train. He withdrew from Francoise; she had been well satisfied with their afternoon of sexual activity. Soon there was a knock on the door.

A man's voice called out.

"Your papers or passports please".

Alain picked up their passports and opened the door slowly. A short fat man in uniform stood there, next to him was a much taller man in a soldier's uniform of the German Army. They looked at Alain in his bare feet and racoon Coat, then a swift glance at Francoise who had her blue fox coat wrapped around her.

The short man took a second glance at the loving couple.

"Ah!" he exclaimed, "you are honeymooners yah?"

"Yes we are," replied Alain, "it is our first train trip together."

The man smiled, stamped the passports, and returned them.

"Enjoy your stay in the Fatherland," he said as he slid the door shut.

The train started again, and soon gathered speed. Alain looked at his watch, and turned to Francoise.

"We had better get dressed soon, darling as we shall be in Mosbach in about an hour."

Francoise opened the front of her furs and smiled sexily.

"Just once more darling Alain."

Alain could not resist her and so he performed on her until they both came to climax.

Then, they really did have to get washed and dressed, for now the train was slowing again as it approached Heidelberg Station. They were now fully dressed and ready to meet the von Lundenbergs.

The afternoon light had faded into near darkness, as they alighted from the train. The Station lighting was not that good. Alain and Francoise noticed how cold it was. They were glad of their furs to keep them warm and cosy.

In the distance, they could see a tall figure dressed in a black leather coat waiting on the platform. This thought Alain must be Rudolph. As they got closer, the man walked forward into the light. It was Rudolph with a broad grin on his face. Alain had never seen Rudolph this happy, perhaps once when he had won a big race. He greeted Alain warmly, shaking his hand firmly,

"Hello Alain," said Rudolph still smiling, "welcome to Heidelberg. This lovely lady must be Francoise."

He bowed, and kissed her gloved hand.

"I hope you had a good journey," he continued, "we have some interesting things to talk about. My wife Catherina is waiting for us in the car. We have a drive of some 60 kilometres to my home."

"Rudolph," replied Alain, "I am delighted to see you again, not as an adversary, but as a friend. Our journey was very tiring."

At this point he winked at Francoise, who caught his meaning. Rudolph turned to Francoise.

"Francoise, it is a great pleasure to meet you at last. Alain did mention you several times when we last met. He did not however tell me that you were such a beautiful lady. This husband of yours is one of the nicest men I have ever met. That is not flattery, that is the truth."

By now they had reached the Mercedes Limousine, and Rudolph opened the rear door.

"Catherina my love, this lovely lady is Francoise Clement and this young man is my friend Alain."

Catherina was wrapped in her silver fox coat, but she leaned forward and embraced Francoise:

"I am delighted to meet you at last," said Catherina, "Rudolph has told me that you had married Alain. You must be Alain."

She put out her hand, and Alain kissed it.

"It is a great pleasure to meet you at last," replied Alain, "may I call you Catherina?"

Catherina peered out from under her fur bonnet.

"Of course you may Alain," she answered, "any friend of Rudy's is a friend of mine."

Alain had never heard Rudolph called Rudy before. This was something he would get used to.

They all sat in the back of the big car, for Rudolph had a chauffeur, called Hans for this occasion. He wanted to spend as much time as possible with the Francoise and Alain. The big car pulled out of the station. The interior of the car was not that warm. Alain and Francoise were glad of their furs to keep them warm. As they drove along, the ladies got talking about, all sorts of things. Alain remarked to Rudolph, that car interiors were always cold. Pity nobody had come up with a form of heating. Rudolph agreed and said he would mention it to his Managing Director. The journey would take just over an hour, and there had been a snow shower early in the day. It had left a light dusting over the trees and fields, as left Heidelberg and headed out into the countryside. Rudolph was delighted that both Alain and Francoise could come to visit; it was a chance to get to know them properly. Francoise spoken fairly fluently in German and likewise Catherina spoke French very well indeed. So, in deference to their guests, Catherina spoke to Francoise in French and Rudolph did likewise.

The time passed quickly, and soon they were at the home of Rudolph and Catherina. The door was opened by one of Catherina's staff, and the four friends, went inside to a warm reception by the von Lundenbergs. Rudolph and Catherina showed Alain and Francoise up to the guestroom, and told them dinner would be served in about an hour. Time then to bath and freshen up thought Francoise. Alain was already undressed and trying the bed for comfort. Francoise was now naked and gave a sly look at her husband and pointing to the bed asked the question.

"Later my love?"

Alain knew what she meant and smiled. He ran a bath for them both. It was certainly a big enough bath for two. So they scrubbed each other's backs, and got ready for dinner. Dinner was laid out in the large oak panelled Dining room.

Over Dinner, Catherina said how much she enjoyed woman's talk with Francoise; she hoped that they could visit her and Alain at Rouen, in the spring. Francoise described how lovely it was where they lived. Francoise enjoyed the countryside, and riding on horseback. Catherina said that she had never visited the area of France where Francoise lived. She had read about it in books, but that was all. Rudolph began talking to Alain about his present contract with Peugeot, and could he be released from it, and what notice he had to give. They talked of the races won and lost, and about their lives. After dinner, Rudolph took Alain into the library.

He wanted to talk business with Alain and go into greater detail. Rudolph said that he had the authority, and he gave Alain a letter from the new Mercedes Managing Director, and signed by Siegfried Gunther, formally asking Alain to join them for the next season. The position was Number 2 driver. His salary was mentioned; this was more than double his present one at Peugeot. They would pay for accommodation and moving expenses. The contract to start on March 1st 1910. Alain related to Rudolph his doubts about Peugeot spending the required money on research and development. There was a lot of development needed to improve the car to a winning formula.

"Alain," said Rudolph, "you are a very good driver, in a car of the same quality and performance, we would dead heat. This is a good deal for you. Think about it and telephone me within a week."

Alain said he would and they talked on for what seemed like hours. Then Catherina knocked on the door.

"Rudy, my love," she cooed, "Francoise has fallen asleep in the Morning Room. I think it would be a good idea. If we all went to bed don't you?"

Rudolph agreed, and that they would continue their conversation on the following day. Alain carried Francoise up to bed. 'No lovemaking tonight' he said to himself. He undressed Francoise and put her to bed. She did not even open one eye, she was dead tired. Once Alain lay down he was asleep in no time.

The next morning, there was a knock on the door. Alain got up and opened it. There stood a maid with breakfast in bed for two.

"Thank you" said Alain.

Francoise was still asleep, whilst Alain poured coffee. Then the aroma reached Françoise's senses and she woke up. After breakfast they made their way down stairs. Alain could hear Rudolph talking to someone, he was already in the Library, whilst Catherina was organising her staff for the day's chores. Rudolph was on the telephone to the Managing Director at his home. Rudolph told him that; he had given the letter to Alain, who would no doubt have to discuss it with his Managing Director on Tuesday. Siegfried said that they had to sign Alain up before another team did. Rudolph said that Alain was a friend, and he was certain that they could sign him up. Rudolph put the phone down.

Catherina went up to the Nursery and brought down their son Manfred, he was a bonny little boy. Alain and Francoise said how lucky Catherina was to have such a beautiful, healthy son. Francoise asked Catherina did she ride, on horseback that is.

Catherina said it had been some time since she had been out riding. So it was agreed that they should all go out, as it was such a lovely day for a ride in the wooded countryside, and also see some of the estate. There were out for a couple of hours, and had soon worked up a thirst. Rudolph took them to a small beer house he knew in a village not far away. They all sank a few steins, well the men did, and the ladies had wine of course. Then back for lunch. That afternoon both couples sat in the library around a roaring fire just talking about this and that. It was a change not to be talking about racing. Rudolph was quite a conversationalist. He started to talk about aeroplanes. Now, this was a subject dear to Alain's heart. He always wanted to learn to fly, ever since that Frenchman flew the English Channel. Soon the afternoon passed away, and before they knew it, dinner was only an hour away. They had enjoyed a really great day together.

The two couples had started to become really firm friends, being in the same crazy business they could relate to one and other. They felt that they could discuss all manner of things, without upsetting the other. Now they would all be part of the same team. The weekend seemed to be flashing by; they were all enjoying each other's company so much. Over dinner, Rudolph said how much he appreciated the friendship they had established. They made a vow that whatever happened in the future; they would always remain friends in the true sense of the word. That night Francoise and Alain made love; to celebrate Alain's new appointment. They both felt relieved both physically and mentally, that things had taken a turn for the better. Francoise now had her man, her furs, and a future. Alain had his woman, and his future. Next morning, Catherina had arranged that Francoise and Alain have breakfast in bed.

On Sunday morning, Catherina always went to church, dressed in her finest clothes and furs. Rudolph asked Alain and Francoise to join them, as they were the same religion. Francoise was interested to see how the service in a German church differed to their own church back in France. It was a clear, but a very cold day, and as the Church was so close by, Catherina suggested that they walk to the church. It was now Francoise and Alain were grateful for their furs to keep the cold at bay. Catherina told Francoise and Alain, that the Church was the one where they had been married, and young Manfred would be christened. The four young people sat in the front row of pews, whilst the Priest a Father Reinhardt, took the service. The church was not very crowded; only about 40 parishioners were there. Francoise and Alain were able to follow most of the service. At the end of it, Rudolph introduced his new friends. Father Reinhardt shook Alain's hand and spoke in perfect French.

"Monsieur Clement, it is a pleasure to meet you and your lady. I do hope that we meet again soon."

He then kissed Francoise's hand.

Walking back to the house, they worked up quite an appetite for lunch. It would be a day of rest for there would be a long day ahead of Francoise and Alain on their return trip to Rouen. So after lunch, they all sat in the Library to enjoy a conversation on a wide range of uncontroversial matters. Rudolph said he could not remember, a more pleasant afternoon. Catherina loved a good old-fashioned discussion; it was something that she missed. Most of her friends, were partners or wives of Rudolph's associates from the Mercedes factory.

Some of whom were extremely boring and either had too much money or too little. Many of them had not done too much with their lives, and some belonged to what Catherina called "women's groups."

So time spent with Francoise and Alain, was a refreshing change. They found that they had a lot in common with each other. The day passed quickly, it was dinner, more conversation then bed. For the Clements, it would be an early start to return home to France.

First of all, they had the task of packing their suitcases, for they had to catch the train from Heidelberg by noon. Francoise was sad to leave the von Lundenbergs, but they had things to organise now. They would move to Germany to be close to the factory by the end of February 1910. Now, unfortunately it was time to go. Francoise dressed in her blue fox furs felt absolutely regal, Alain too in his Racoon hat and coat felt like a prince next to his princess. Rudolph too was in his favourite coat and Catherina in silver fox of course. The car was ready for them with Hans behind the wheel. The two couples climbed into the rear of the Limousine.

Hans swung the starting handle and the big car was brought to life. They were so busy talking that they hardly felt the car slow down as it drew into Heidelberg Station. They had made it with 15 minutes to spare. Catherina and Rudolph said au revoir to their guests, they knew that they would meet again in the New Year. Francoise was absolutely delighted to finally spend time with Catherina. The French by and large, never did like the Germans, so they had been told, but here was a German lady with charm and breeding. One of the old school.

As they stood waiting for the train, Catherina gave Francoise a big hug. Rudolph shook Alain firmly by the hand.

"Alain," he said, "this is the first weekend for years that Catherina and I have really enjoyed ourselves. I value your friendship and that Francoise very much indeed."

Alain went up to Catherina, who was peering out from under her silver fox fur bonnet, for it was really a very cold day.

"Au revoir, Catherina," said Alain, "this has been a really wonderful weekend. We have really loved visiting you both."

Catherina put her arm around Alain's neck and kissed him passionately on the lips.

"I have always wanted to kiss one of you sexy Frenchmen," she whispered as their lips parted.

Francoise looked across to see her husband kissing Catherina. She thought well if Catherina can, then so can I. Rudolph was about to kiss Françoise's hand, but like Catherina she moved her arm around Rudolph's neck.

"This is to thank you and Catherina for everything. I want this kiss to seal the friendship between our two families."

Francoise kissed Rudolph full on the lips too. Rudolph, being a gentleman to the last, was a little embarrassed.

"That kiss Francoise," replied Rudolph as he regain his composure, "apart from those that my wife gives me, was the sweetest kiss I have ever had. I now have also kissed my first French lady."

The two couples embraced once more. In the distance the train appeared, blowing its whistle as it approached the station. Finally, they waved goodbye as the Francoise and Alain mounted the steps to climb aboard their carriage. A final wave and the train started off, as Francoise and Alain made their way to their private compartment. Alone at last, and time for lovemaking. They celebrated by enjoying the fur covered physical contact, of two young people hopelessly in love. The future that looked rosy, now with their new friends, they could both relax for a while.

Alain knew that once he got into the swing of things at Mercedes, there would be a lot of hard work ahead. However, he did know that he would be getting well paid for his expertise at last. On arriving home, the Count wanted to meet Alain and find out all about his protégé. Alain told him about the offer from Mercedes, and how Peugeot had told him, that they did not want to spend lots of money developing a car when there were no International Races to compete in. Mercedes had a different attitude. However, they had to move to Germany. The Count would be sorry to see them go, but Alain had to look to his career as a racing driver.

The train pulled out of the Station, Catherina and Rudolph gave a final wave and made their way back to the Limousine.

"My darling," said Catherina sitting in the warmth of the Limousine and pulling her furs around her, "Francoise and Alain are absolutely lovely people. I can honestly say that I have never enjoyed a conversation so much with another lady. She is so knowledgeable about so many things."

"My love," answered Rudolph, "you are correct. I have only known Alain as a very strong adversary. Now as a friend we can build not only an excellent racing team but also a friendship that will stand the test of time."

Then they kissed and hugged each other until the car then drew up at their home. Catherina and Rudolph went up to their bedroom to undress, where Catherina looked at Rudolph's naked body.

"Let's relax darling," she said, "and enjoy the horizontal exercise we love so much."

Rudolph did not need a second invitation. She slipped on her silver fox furs and began to make love to her husband and lover. Catherina wanted another child, hopefully a girl. Soon they were in sexual unison and enjoying pure ecstasy. .

"This time let us make a little Catherina."

"Darling wife, I'll do all I can."

"I will make sure you do just that my love," answered Catherina.

She was determined to get pregnant again and wanted Rudolph to make love to her at every opportunity. The weekend was gone and it was almost Monday. In a few hours Rudolph would be back at work. As soon as he arrived at the Factory, he was called to a meeting with the Managing Director Siegfried Gunther, and also the Team Manager Gustav Schumann. Rudolph sat down, and was asked the question, by the Managing Director.

"Rudolph, did you manage to persuade Monsieur Alain Clement to join our team?"

"Herr Director," answered Rudolph confidently, "I had a along meeting with Monsieur Clement at the weekend. He will be joining us with effect from 1st March, on the terms agreed."

Gustav got up with a big grin on his face and walked around to shake Rudolph by the hand.

"That is excellent Rudolph. Now we have a team that will beat everyone. There is still the testing to do for the new 9-litre car. You can both be responsible for that."

Rudolph was pleased to have a friend driving with him for 1910. It looked like it was going to be a busy year for the Mercedes boys.

Meanwhile back in Rouen, Alain had the prospect of telling Peugeot, that he would be leaving at the end of January 1910, to drive for Mercedes. It was a meeting with Charles Orly, which he was not looking forward to, but it had to be done. His future was at stake.

On the Monday night, he slept restlessly; Francoise asked him what was the problem. He told her. She said do not worry. After all they told you that they did not intend to race in 1910 or 1911.

Alain's meeting with Charles Orly took place in the Paris office of Peugeot on Friday on that week. Alain told him that he had been offered a drive with Mercedes and that the salary and bonus payments were very generous. Alain told Charles that his new contract would start on 1st March 1910, but he would like to terminate his contract with Peugeot on 31st January 1910. He appreciated all the Company had done for him and was sorry to leave. He also said that it would mean moving to Germany, to be close to the factory. He had a good friend Rudolph von Lundenberg, who would be his guide and would help him. Charles was sad that he was losing the best driver Peugeot had had up to that time. However, if Alain had made up his mind, then Charles could only wish him good fortune. The two men shook hands, and the meeting ended.

Christmas was extra special that year for Francoise and Alain. The Count had one of his lavish parties, and he made Alain, a kind of guest of honour. This could be the last Christmas that 'his adopted son and daughter in law would have in their beloved France and he called for a speech from Alain. Alain took hold of Françoise's hand and led her on to the stage.

"My friends," he began, "the Count has been like a father to me. He has given me opportunities that otherwise I would not have had. He let me have an education at the Sorbonne, and introduced me to the most beautiful lady in the world. I cannot thank him enough. Now a window of opportunity has opened, it will mean moving to another Country to pursue my chosen career. I have a good friend there a Rudolph von Lundenberg. For many years I raced against him. Although he is German, he is a gentleman of the highest order and his wife is a true lady. We have a bond between us, for Motor Racing is a dangerous sport. So on this festive occasion I would like you all to stand, and raise your glasses to toast, the Count and Countess de Longchamps."

The assembled guests stood up, raised their glasses and said in one voice, "The Count and Countess de Longchamps."

The Count and Countess were slightly embarrassed but felt extremely proud of both Francoise and Alain.

Christmas and New Year seem to fly by, now Alain had to think about moving to Germany. They decided that they would still keep their home in Rouen. However, the small rented flat on the outskirts of Paris, was to go. They would move their goods and chattels, to their new home in Germany. Rudolph and Catherina had found an ideal house of 3 Bedrooms close their home.

The month of January was cold, and there was very little to do at the Peugeot factory. Alain was starting to get bored. He was anxious to move now. At least he had more time to spend with Francoise, for this she was grateful. The month came towards its end, and the day for moving was almost here. On his last full day at Peugeot, Charles Orly organised a farewell party in the Main Office. Alain was presented with a large carriage clock; on the plinth below the dial was a model in silver of their last racing car. Alain thanked Charles and his colleagues for their generous gift. As he left the factory for the last time, he felt a tinge of sadness.

This has been a step up from his last job at Darracq, now for more challenges no doubt. Francoise welcomed him home, and was delighted with his leaving present.

The next morning the lorry arrived and the removal men started loading all their worldly possessions from the Paris flat. Finally, the last stick of furniture was packed, and the lorry set off for their new home in Germany.

Chapter 18

The Christmas break had given Carla time to clear her brain. The stress of the Antonati court case was far behind. The culprit, that had cause so much financial damage to the FORUM Fashion Empire was now, settling down to a long jail sentence. Then she received a letter of resignation from Arturo Toscetti; he felt that the whole Antonati affair had undermined his authority at FORUM. She felt that perhaps there might be more to it than a simply case of naivety. Although Arturo was a good Manager, there was really no way without a great deal of financial experience that he could have every figured out what Antonati was up to. If he had informed the Bank much earlier perhaps they could have prevented some of the damage. So Carla accepted his resignation and now had to take over the position as Manager as well, subject to Ricardo's agreement. She contacted Ricardo, who agreed that it was the obvious solution to the problem. She mentioned their designer Umberto – real name Gino Verdi. He was middle aged but enthusiastic, and would often come up with some refreshing new designs. He and Carla became friends; he had lived in Florence for several years with his wife Fernanda. He had often asked Arturo asked if it were possible at some time to move to Rome, but Arturo would not listen to him. Now that Arturo had resigned and Carla was his new boss, perhaps he could ask her when the time was right.

Over the next few weeks, Ricardo, and Carla spent long hours together, burning the midnight oil. She only ever saw young Dino at weekends. This was sad but necessary, there were a lot of bridges to build, and mend with Clients, plus new investors to be found.

Ricardo's wife Franchesca even had her suspicions that Ricardo was having an affair with Carla. She had had these notions before when Carla was investigating the Antonati case. Carla called on her one evening and they had a long discussion.

"Franchesca," said Carla in a serious vein, "we have been through this all before. I am not having an affair with your husband. In fact, I would like you to get more involved in the business. Then you will see that as a team we can make FORUM a force to be reckoned with in the fashion world."

From that evening onward, Franchesca came into the Office every day; she became interested in a range of matters that Ricardo and Carla had little time for. It had taken Francesca a while to get over the fact that outsiders were trouble. The Antonati case had left a nasty taste in her mouth. They had all trusted him, and look where it had got them, into serious financial trouble. Now they had Carla to thank them for jailing the culprit. She had to change her belief that there was outsider who cared for the Company. As time passed she realised what a gem they had found in Carla. She was a wizard with figures, and handled business contacts with an expertise not previous seen at FORUM. Her doubts disappeared, and now she had a friend in Carla. The Bank of Italy had stood by them when many other so-called friends had deserted them. Initially, Franchesca had been totally surprised when Ricardo had asked Carla to be a partner in the business. As things turned out, she realised that it was the best thing Ricardo had ever done. One day Gino asked Carla if there might be an opening in the Rome store for his talents. Carla said she would keep it in mind, because she was looking for another designer for the Florence store, as she heard that he had been unhappy since Arturo had refused to listen to him about moving to Rome. This made Gino much happier and the quality of his designs improved.

Young Dino was a regular visitor to the Armari house, especially in the summer months, the staff and models dressed him up, and he loved it. Carla previous experience at negotiation became paramount in the months to come. Finding investors to put money into a Company, which had tottered on the brink of bankruptcy, would be difficult. So at a board meeting they decided that would contact some local businessmen who wanted to make money long term. Carla had meetings with several well-known entrepreneurs, and managed to raise several hundred million lire. Several drove very hard bargains; once cheeky fellow asked a question nobody had ever asked Carla before.

"Signorina Carla," he said, "if I put money into your Company. Can you make clothes under my own label?"

Carla soon put him in his place. Gradually FORUM found its feet and business got back to normal and their old customers returned. The fact that the Company's had survived after the Antonati case soon boosted their reputation. This had always been for high quality goods, after sales service plus excellent customer and Client relations.

Now a new advertising agency had come up with a first class campaign, the Company sales boomed. With autumn now blowing its cool breezes up the Arno Valley, the customers were flocking in to buy their winter fashions. Enrico now had a part of the Florence showroom to himself. Orders were flooding in for his 'designer' furs. He had a book of stunning styles; he could make a coat for a customer that was unique, for a price. Carla was busy doing administration and keeping a close eye on the financial aspect of FORUM's Florence store. Pressure was building and she knew that it would not be long before she had to move to the eternal city of Rome. The store there was ten times the size of the Florence store.

Ricardo and Franchesca had now left Carla in charge, but the store needed to expand. There was not really enough room for a fashion show. Carla had to use local dance halls and exhibition halls to have her fashion shows. With a limited budget, she knew that she needed to expand. The premises across the road came up for sale. Carla decided that this would not really serve the purpose, as it would split the store in two. Just before Christmas the Company that owned the shop next door contacted Carla. The lease had come up for renewal. The leaseholder had decided to retire; he sold leather handbags, luggage, and footwear. The store was four times the size of the FORUM store. The lease was a good price and for 25 years. Carla had a meeting with the Freeholder - Rossina & Partners. Carla drove a hard bargain, and managed to get the lease at the same figure as the departing leaseholder. She also got a renewable clause entered into her Lease. In a few days, the deal was done. Now they could expand. Carla called in her shop designer and it was decided that the shop would open for the spring collections.

Carla spent Christmas with Enzo, again. He did not even ask about his son. For Carla after all the excitement of the previous months and the expansion plans, she was only too pleased to have a quiet Christmas. Young Dino enjoyed, seeing his Grandfather dress up as Father Christmas and of course get some good presents. Now that Carla was being well paid at FORUM, she was able to give her son some good gifts too. However, there was not one word from Dino.

Carla's parents invited her and young Dino to spend New Year with them in their Villa. Since her divorce Carla had spent little time with her parents. They were under the impression that their daughter had thrown up a promising career with the Bank of Italy to go and work in a shop. Carla would tell them the true story. She would dress up in her new blue fox outfit and finest clothes. Young Dino had new winter clothes too. She wanted her parents to know that she was running a high class Fashion House. She was a partner not simply just a woman who worked in a shop. Carla's parents, Florina, and Guillermo had moved to a little town called Lastra, only a few kilometres away from Florence. When Carla arrived, Florina was really astounded to see her daughter in her beautiful furs, and young Dino looking like a young man in his fashionable suit and overcoat. All obviously designer made. Carla's parents were at last able, to know the truth why Carla had left the Bank, and all about her problems, and Court case with Antonati. They were amazed that their daughter had fallen on her feet, after the way her ex-husband had treated her.

There were more presents for him to play with. Florina and Guillermo, had always supported their daughter and brought her up to be honest, loving and above all to be focussed on her career. They were devastated when they heard about Dino's sexual exploits, and were delighted that at last Carla was rid of him. They said any help they could give, and support, she only had to ask. They asked if Dino had ever been in touch.

"No, not even once," she replied angrily, "I am sorry for my attitude over this matter, but the last time I saw him was at the Divorce Court, and even then he ignored me."

They asked if they could come to FORUM's new premises to see what kind of empire that their daughter presided over. Three days after her stay, Carla's parents called in to see her. They were amazed at her fashion house, after a good look around; Carla took them to lunch.

During the months that followed, Carla still had heard nothing from her now ex-husband. He did not even remember to even send a card or present on his son's birthday. Maria's attitude was now that you are with me; you must forget your past life.

The trouble was that Dino was now so much in love with Maria, and with their pleasures of their sexual perversions, he had completely forgotten his old family ties. He had never written to or communicated with his Father. His driving exploits were few and far between.

The year 1909, had been a bit of a disaster for Dino Borghese, he had 'lost' his family, gained an avaricious lover, and the low light of the year was the acrimonious divorce. This had split the family asunder. Maria had encouraged him to use his driving talents, but the disappointing results with FIAT, soon led to his contract being slowly but surely being eroded away. Maria decided that his talents would be better used in the financial world, and particularly in her bedroom too.

So with the arrival of the winter social season, Maria threw one of her fantastic parties. Dino of course, was instructed to dress up in his Santa Claus costume that Maria had bought the year previous. She had kept him on a very tight rein all year, and was she delighted that he was at last 'rid of' that wife of his, Carla. Now she had him all to herself, and if he had strayed just the once, she would have him hung, drawn, and quartered, metaphorically speaking. Dino still did not as yet realise that he was Maria's puppet on a string, and had to dance to her tune, for he was so happy with his new relationship.

On Thursday 23rd December Maria instructed Dino to start dressing up as Santa Claus and he knew that it would bring its own sexual rewards from Maria, and he was right, for she could not get enough of him. She of course dressed as Mistress Christmas. She had been reading her erotic books and had found new ways to arouse Dino, so that he could fulfil all her fantasies. The Christmas Party on Christmas Eve was a masked ball; naturally Dino was the masked Father Christmas. Maria allowed him to dance with other female guests, all of whom had very large sexual appetites. The bedrooms were full of mating couples, none of whom were related to each other. It was a Roman Orgy, but as the Hostess, Maria, who was wearing her Mistress Christmas costume, with nothing underneath, kept disappearing and returning to her guests with a satisfied smile on her face. Dino was approached by several of the lady guests, but all he got was a quick squeeze of his crotch, plus a few hot kisses.

However, he had to be certain Maria was not around. Otherwise he knew he would be in trouble.

Maria then began to talk to an old friend; she took him by the hand and led him off to her bedroom, where she thought it would be exciting to be serviced by another man in her own bed. His name was Alfonso who it seems was very well endowed, and not afraid to show it. She would of course, describe this in great detail to Dino. Alfonso's wife, Lucretia had the same liberal attitude, and was in another part of the villa, being sexually entertained by Alfonso's cousin, a Mario Sureto a party going regular.

When the party ended, Maria rewarded Dino for being celibate, whilst everyone at the party seemed to be otherwise. Later on Christmas Day, having told Dino all about Alfonso's session with her, Maria then showered Dino with presents. She led him into his bedroom to show him presents she had added to Dina's wardrobe. There were now even more frilly blouses, dresses, a fabulous full-length blue fox fur coat, bonnet, gloves and leather lace up boots with blue fox trimmings. Maria always got so sexually excited watching her man cross-dress and become her Dina. Now that he no longer needed to dress up in 'her' clothes. She told him that he had his own large wardrobe of ladies clothes to choose from. Maria knew that she had to completely domineer him; after all he had left his wife for her. Dino now belonged to her body and soul. She would never let him leave her, and would ensure that he never strayed.

Maria had read an article in one of her erotic books about how to further humiliate the male. This gave Maria her next idea of mortifying Dino, which delighted her so much, that she could not wait to try it on her Dino. She asked herself a question. Why does Dina have all these lovely clothes, when all he does is wear them around the villa? I will take her out and show her off as Dina, my new 'sister'.

One evening she instructed Dino dress up exactly as she directed, and with his make up and wig the transformation to Dina was complete. She looked at him and smiled.

"You look absolutely lovely Dina," remarked Maria, "so ladylike that from now on I am going to call you Dina in public. Tonight we are going out for dinner and dancing, with you dressed as Dina of course, you will really love it my darling. So you must put on your best frilly dress, your new erotic lingerie and blue fox furs for tonight we really going out to enjoy ourselves."

Dino could not wait to dress up as Dina the Party girl. He looked at himself in the full-length mirror as he first of all he put on his new erotic lingerie, applied make up. Then came the black long curly wig, frilly Party dress and finally those gorgeous blue fox furs. Then he gazed longingly in the mirror, as he pulled the furs around him. Now as Dina was now getting sexually aroused. Maria arrived, and having inspected him, nodded her approval before they set off by taxi. Maria smiled with pleasure when the driver made a 'pass' at Dina.

Maria was certain her plans were going to work well. She was very amused, when they were both sitting at their table in all their finery, when a man asked Dina to dance and suggested that he take her home with him for the night. Dino didn't know what to say. To play along he answered in a high voice that he did not dance. The man muttered and walked away.

"If he had tried something," Maria quipped, "he would have had a big surprise."

This little episode, really sexually excited Maria, for at last she felt that she had started to reduce Dino to the humiliation level she really wanted. She had many more tricks up her sleeve, and she would return to her erotic books to see what she could do next.

Meanwhile, Dino was always getting very excited playing the part of Dina and did not feel the way Maria had expected him to be. In any case, Maria was a long way from completing her plans for her Dina. She loved the way things were working out, although she did understand how much Dino enjoyed playing his she/male role. In turn Dino felt that now his sexual activities could now be widened. Every time Maria was out, which was very often, at home dressed as Dina, 'she' could thoroughly enjoy playing the she-male. Maria just did not care, for she knew exactly where he was all the time, for she was sure that he would not go out alone dressed as Dina. To Dino this felt all rather strange at first, but he soon started to indulge himself when alone. Dressed in his furs as Dina, he had now got into the spirit of it all so to speak. He was seeing the female side of his own character that may have been hidden for years.

One day when he was alone, he recalled the time when he was just a youth when he had tried on his Mother's underwear and her fur coat for the very first time. He felt really 'naughty' and strutted around her bedroom and noticed that he had got very sexually aroused. He knew then really that he would love to dress like this whenever he could. However, the opportunity never arose again until he met Maria.

His Mother, who was very strict, would have no doubt punished him severed for his behaviour. Luckily for Dino she was not at home and so she never discovered what he had done.

Now he was with Maria and with her approval he could be 'naughty' any time he liked, and it felt absolutely wonderful. Maria always left strict instructions that before she came home that Dina had to be in her best dress and furs. Maria knew exactly what she wanted from she-male. Dino really wanted to marry Maria, now that he was free, he asked her several times but she would have none of it.

One day when he asked her she waved her index finger at him.

"Dina," she told him in no uncertain terms, "what difference would marriage make to us? We make love and enjoy all the sexual deviations that we can possibly imagine. I know when I am out; you enjoy yourself in your furs and erotic lingerie. What would be the point of being tied down with a marriage contract? So as long as you are a good 'girl' the sexual sweet shop will remain open. If you stray then better prepared for some dire consequences."

So life continued as it always had for Maria and Dino. Maria always full of surprises, life for Dino was never sexually dull when she was around. He wondered where she got all these ideas? However, whilst she continued to please him, even though some of the things were a somewhat bizarre, he was happy to go along with everything that she desired. His love for Maria had grown even stronger now. She let her Dino do whatever 'she' wanted to do, and long as Dina dressed as Maria ordered 'her' to whilst at home. He knew that if he did stray then it would be very easy for Maria to found out, for unless Maria was with him he was not permitted to leave the grounds of the villa.

Carla met the New Year with her usual enthusiasm. The Shop next door was taking shape, but the pressure was still on for her to move to Rome. She knew this would be inevitable, but who would look after the administration in Florence. The days flashed past, the shop next door was now almost ready. The shop fitters were there, completing the décor. Carla was absolutely delighted with the final result. It was the exact mirror image of the original store. The builders had knocked through and put in an R.S.J. to ensure that the archway between the shops would be absolutely safe from collapse. Carla had heard disturbing rumours of so called professional builders, who had cut costs so much that the structures had literally fallen down, days after completion.

Carla now threw herself into her work, she sometimes craved sexual satisfaction, but this she knew had to be on hold.

Her life with Dino was well into the past now. She no longer thought of him, although with young Dino, she would always be reminded of the past. She was now a looking to the future.

A relationship with another man at this stage would be a bit of a disaster. It would deflect her focus from making FORUM, a force to be reckoned with in the Italian fashion scene. She knew in her heart that it would only be a matter of time before she would have to move to Rome. The year of 1910, would be a testing time for Carla, now she had more staff, and had employed an assistant to help with the administration. Young Juliet Cappelo, who had family in Turin, was simply a whiz with figures. She had graduated with honours from the University of Pisa. She was 22 and full of vitality and she had long dark brown hair and dressed in the latest fashions. One day Carla knew that she would end up being the kingpin in the FORUM store in Florence. Pressure was mounting for Carla to go to Rome, she wondered when the call would come from Ricardo.

It was late March when Carla received her phone call from Ricardo.

"Carla my dear," he said, "I must ask you have to move to Rome within the next month. We have opened two more stores in the City and we need your expertise."

Carla thought very hard and long before answering. Moving to Rome would mean she would be further away from her family. Juliet gradually took over the reins, but Carla knew she would have to take on another person to assist Juliet. Carla was loath to let go, but she was aware that she had to delegate. She interviewed five prospective candidates. She chose young man Marco Sintani. He had been at the Bank of Florence for three years. He was 22 and a bit of a ladies man. He got on well with Juliet in those first few days. Carla instilled into him, that any sexual involvement with any of her staff, and he would be looking for another job.

Four weeks passed by, and FORUM was doing well. Carla called Ricardo and told him she would be moving to Rome at the end of May. Could he find her a house?

Within two days Ricardo called back.

"Carla," said Ricardo, "you will be pleased to know that I have found you a delightful villa just 5 kilometres from our store. It has a mature garden, with a fountain, four bedrooms, plus the Company will pick up the rent. If after three months, you still love it the owners will sell it to you."

The next few days were very hectic, as Carla made her arrangements to move to Rome. The move went well, and she soon settled into this wonderful house. Young Dino had plenty of space, and her nanny Sophia had decided that she would come with her. Sophia had her own rooms, and felt quite the lady of the house. Carla decided that she should have a gardener and a cleaner three times per week. It was a big garden that needed plenty of tender loving care. The gardener Pietro was a wizard with plants. That summer the garden bloomed as never before. Carla felt at home. The business was going well; she had good feedback from Juliet and Marco. She was really happy for once in her life, and her team at the Rome store had welcomed her with open arms. They had heard that it was Carla that had saved them from bankruptcy and redundancy. Carla felt this was the place she wanted to live in. She made an offer for the villa that was accepted, and she was a property owner at last, in her own right.

Meanwhile, Dino was still being led around on Maria's sexual string. She had been in contact with Lord John Ashdown on a regular basis, as shipments of her wine over the past year had gone down very well in the Ashdown family's hostelries. Maria had sent John a big Christmas Card, and said that she would like to visit him early in the New Year. She had never been to the home of an English Lord. She would like to bring her friend Dino with her. John replied that he would be delighted to see her after Christmas. John suggested mid-January before the business started getting busy after the festive season.

The year 1910 had been a good one for Maria's wine business, for John Ashdown was now taking 25% of her output. She also supplied many Hotels, Restaurants, and shops in Florence, Milan, Turin, and Venice. Her wealth had increased considerably, thanks to Dino considerable talent for figures. Maria used him when she felt like it.

One day Maria made another decision. She informed Dina that 'she' should come into the office and do some work there, and instructed Dina to be dressed as her Personal Assistant. Dino was so obsessed with Maria that he would do absolutely anything, and got excited about going to the Office.

When they arrived in the general office Maria made an announcement to all the Office staff.

"Ladies," began Maria, "I have a statement to make to you all. As you know I have a man friend. He loves cross-dressing as a lady, wearing ladies lingerie, dresses, high heels and furs. Especially furs he has a fur fetish. This not only at home but also in public. I wanted to introduce you to him and so I have brought him to the office. You must call him Dina, for that is his name from now on. Remember to call 'her' by that name always. Come forward Dina and be seen and curtsy."

Dino came forward and tried to stem his blushes under the heavy make up and curtsied.

"Remember everyone," continued Maria, "Dina has to do as 'she' is told. I may ask you to inspect 'her' from time to time."

The staff were all taken aback for a moment, but then they were fairly used to Maria's strange ideas.

She treated Dina like the Office Junior especially when she thought 'she' had misbehaved, under her rules. She enjoyed giving Dina a daily dressing down in front of the staff. At first this amused both Bernardetta and Elsa and especially her new Sales Assistant Emilo.

One day whilst they were in the Office, Maria informed Dina (as she called him out loud when 'she' was in the Office), that they were going to England in mid-January, for about 10 days. They would be staying with Lord John Ashdown.

Dino of course would travel as Dina, so 'she' would be taking some dresses and blue fox furs for 'her' to wear on the journey. This would prevent men making passes at her, for Dina would be her chaperone. However, for the meetings he would have to wear a man's suit, which she had recently bought, but underneath he would wear Dina's frilly bloomers.

Over Christmas Maria and her 'man' wore their Santa suits. She especially enjoyed giving her Dina more 'girlie' presents, and 'she' had to make love to her on command. The usual band of partygoers dragged themselves along to her New Year Party. Alfonso 'the Stud' as he was known, took Maria aside, and gave her what she wanted several times, behind locked doors. Dino meanwhile, was walking around feeling a bit 'rigid'. One of the more liberal ladies, looked at the mound in his trousers, took him to another part of the villa, and took her pleasure from him. Dino was a bit surprised, and embarrassed, but very happy to 'do it' with another willing female. This lady a Constanta Mugello was a distant cousin of Maria's, and like her cousin was sex mad. She loved having her wicked way with husbands, particularly when the man's partner was around, especially at Maria's kind of party, it heightened her excitement levels. She promised faithfully not to tell Maria, as long as Dino did not tell her husband. They agreed, and Maria never did find out about Dino's hour of utter pleasure with her cousin.

Once Christmas and New Year were over, Maria made plans to go to see John Ashdown. She carefully selected the clothes, that Dina would be taking with 'her', packing them carefully herself into a small trunk. Travelling as Dina, this way if he saw an attractive lady on the train; she would not realise he was a man, and would ignore him.

Maria was a jealous, cunning woman, and any sign of a flirtation would result in a 'punishment' for Dino. Then the day dawned, and Dina was very excited as they set out together from Venice Station on the Paris Express.

Dino really looked and felt very ladylike in his blue silk and lace trimmed bloomers, blue velvet dress, blue fox fur coat, high-heeled fur topped boots, gloves and bonnet. Maria had even bought him a dark brown wig to complete the effect. She even attended to his makeup to make sure that he was perfect lady.

Maria had reserved a private compartment all the way. To ensure that her 'little lady' did not even make one pass at another lady passenger, and she had all meals sent to their suite. She kept him occupied by reading her erotic books to him, and letting him playact with her to their mutual delight.

They changed trains in Paris to get the London Express into Victoria Station. On this leg of the journey she allowed him to change into his gentleman's clothes, but reminded him that this was only temporary until they had concluded their visit with Lord Ashdown. Then it would be back to the dresses as usual. Dino was just happy to be with Maria on a business trip, where he would perhaps add a little to the negotiations. John was delighted to meet up again with the vivacious Maria di Gigli and her friend Dino.

John met them with his chauffeur at Horsham Station. On the drive back to Ashdown Hall, John chatted to them both, asked about their journey, and said that he was pleased with the way sales of Maria's wines had gone over the last year. On the steps of Ashdown Hall, Victoria greeted her guests, whilst the John's chauffeur, carried the trunks in from the car. John's new housemaid Dorothy led them up to their room. Maria and Dino 'freshened up' and went downstairs to meet John and Victoria in the Library. "Lord John," asked Maria, "how is your son Nigel? I understand he is at a famous school nearby."

Now John was very proud of his son, who had being doing so well at Christ's Hospital, and was well on course to go to Oxford University. John knew the history of Christ's Hospital, and Maria was fascinated by it all. Maria was an intelligent woman. She said that if she had a son like Nigel, she would have loved him to go to such a famous school. Dino was quiet; John and Victoria noticed this. Victoria tried to open up the conversation. Dino knew that he had to guard his tongue, one slip and Maria would think up some other form of retribution to play on him. This might be either pain or pleasure, you could not tell with Maria. She had a very inventive mind. Dino decided to talk about his very short motor racing career and how much Maria had helped him, how he had assisted Maria with her wine business after they had met. He kept his private life, very much out of the conversation. Only to say that they were both career minded.

"Maria," asked Lady Victoria inquisitively, "have you any plans to marry Dino?"

There was a deadly silence for a few moments. Dino looked at Maria who smiled sweetly.

"Lady Victoria," answered Maria, "we are partners in business, and perhaps we might have plans to marry in the future. We shall have to wait and see."

Maria gave a quick look at Dino, who seemed relieved at the answer to Maria's question. The Butler, Yeats announced that lunch was served.

The conversation over lunch turned to other things. In the afternoon they relaxed. Maria asked John what it was like being a Lord. John told her how he had inherited the title from his Father, and how he hoped his son Nigel would carry on the tradition. He gave her a brief history of the House of Lords, and Ashdown Hall. Maria was fascinated. She asked about the King and Queen of England. John explained it all including his attendance at the late King's Funeral. It seemed he had died on May 6th 1910. His Brother George and his wife Queen Mary would succeed him. The Coronation would be on the 23rd June 1911.

"Can I come?" asked Maria cheekily.

John explained that only special guests could go, even he was not certain that he and Victoria would be invited. Victoria glanced at Maria and Dino several times, they seem engrossed in all the facts that John laid before them. Victoria sensed there was something different in the relationship between Maria and Dino. It was a good job she didn't know; otherwise she would have had a pink fit.

The next day, Tuesday, it was back to business; John took them down to his Office at the Brewery. They were amazed at the workings of the fermentation plant and the organisation John had built up. They met some of the staff, and Maria complimented John on having such a happy team working for him. That night, after dinner, Maria said that she and Dino were tired after their long day, so wanted to have an early night. Maria of course wanted to have Dino for herself, she had decided he had worn his 'male' clothes for long enough. He might get used to wearing them again, and that she could not allow. The room in which they were spending a few nights had a four poster bed. This was the first time either Maria or Dino had slept in a bed in a mansion like this. Maria locked the door, and then told Dino to take off his suit and into Dina's nightdress. Maria now rewarded Dino for his excellent script, and so neither of them would get much sleep, but plenty of pleasure. Then Maria remarked to Dino how much fun it would be to make passionate love in this ancestral home. She sighed and said how lovely he looked in the lingerie she had chosen for him, and made him model it for her. Then he had to model the blue fox furs. This aroused her and she could see how much he loved being Dina and finally, she made sure that she satisfied him completely.

"Now be a good girl Dina," she told 'her', "and put on your lovely night-dress and negligee and go to sleep."

She looked at him lying next to her, smiled and then fell asleep herself. Maria wondered how much longer Dina would keep up his good behaviour. Either way she would either give a reward or a forfeit. Maria felt now that had to make plans to return to Italy. Before they left Maria had signed a ten-year agreement to supply Lord John's Company with wine. Victoria was delighted that they had to come over to see them.

The next morning Maria made Dina pack her trunk, making sure not to leave anything behind, which could cause any suspicions about her sexual deviations. Dino was carrying two furs coats and Victoria wanted to pose the question as to why she had two fur coats with her, and so much luggage for such a short visit. Then she thought, really it was none of her business. John's chauffeur took them to Horsham Station, where Victoria and John said farewell to their guests. Maria gave John a kiss full on the lips.

"Lord John," replied Maria, "our visit here has been fantastic, you must bring your wife for a visit to my home in Venice."

Victoria hugged her two guests.

"My dear Maria, we would love to come when we have time."

The midday train for London steamed in, and Dino struggled to get the cases on to the train, whilst Maria just held the furs. As the train pulled out Victoria said to John:

"I do not know what to make of those two? That Maria seems a bit over the top?"

"That my love," answered John, "is an understatement."

The Sussex countryside soon gave way to the London suburbs. Maria could not wait get her 'man' to change clothes and get back to being Dina wearing 'her favourite female' clothes. They boarded the London - Paris - Venice Express. Dino pulled down the blinds and locked the door of the private compartment. Maria's fun was about to begin. First of all she made Dino remove his suit, which Maria then packed away. Soon he was dressed as Dina in a dress and furs. Maria now played with her she/male, until she was ready for 'her' to perform. It was that way all the way home. Maria would play act and then later ask for forgiveness, as she knew that Dino was such a willing participant in her grand plan. Life for Maria and Dino would be one big party for two. But for how long? We shall see.

When they arrived home, there was a letter from FIAT, which said that FIAT would not need his services as they had now employed a new professional driver. They sent a cheque for 350,000 lira, as a severance and goodwill payment. Maria smiled when she heard this. Now she thought he could concentrate on my business and pleasure. Life now was back to Maria's liking; she now had her Dino in an even tighter rein. He would be under her gaze now, with no more little trips to play racing driver.

Chapter 19

Francoise and Alain's first few days in Germany felt a little strange. Their furniture fitted in well, more by luck than judgement. On the first morning that Alain was due to start at Mercedes, Rudolph called for him and together they went in for a meeting with Gustav Schumann.

"Good morning Gentlemen," said Gustav, "and a special welcome to Mercedes, Monsieur Clement. May I call you Alain?"

"Please do sir," answered Alain.

The two men shook hands.

"Alain," continued Gustav, "I believe you know Rudolph fairly well as a worthy adversary. Now you are in the same team he will show you the ropes. I know this might seem mundane, but I ask all my drivers to familiarise themselves with the car, as we cannot ask drivers in races to hang about for the mechanics to come and fix their cars. I am sure you were taught this at Peugeot and Darracq. Have you anything to say to me? Any Questions, anything at all?"

Alain thought for a moment.

"First of all can I call you Gustav?"

"Of course" replied the Team Manager,

"I am sure Gustav, that I will have lots of questions for you, once I get down to testing etc."

"Alain," answered Gustav, "as Rudolph knows only too well, my door is always open. We are a team here. Together with will succeed, alone - no. Thank you gentlemen I shall see you soon."

Now it was time for both Alain and Rudolph to get down to some really hard at work in the competitive world of motor racing, Catherina decided to call upon Francoise. The curtains and coverings, had been left by the last owners a Luther and Stephanie Beckstein. Catherina suggested that they go shopping for new curtains etc. The two ladies dressed in their furs, called a taxi, and headed into town. Catherina and Francoise both had excellent taste. They spent the whole day shopping and lunching. They chose really stylish materials, and managed to get them at a good price. Catherina was very houseproud, and Francoise too wanted the better things in life.

Over the next few weeks, Rudolph and Alain were developing the 'monster' Mercedes for Ralph de Palma, who would race it in the American Grand Prix at Savannah, Georgia on November 30th 1911. The race would be 24 laps of a 17-mile course, total distance 411.36 miles. The car had to be driven almost flat out for a period of some 6 hours. A tall order, for a car still being designed. By early summer the engine emerged, it was massive.

In the months that preceded this, another project reared its ugly head. A number of smaller companies had abandoned the idea of large engined Grand Prix cars and had started their own form of racing. This was called Voiturette racing. This was for cars up to 3 litres in engine capacity. It was one of the classes that Alain hoped that Peugeot would enter, but they wanted the glory and acclaim of the Grand Prix, not some minor event. The races had started back in 1908, but the big factories were not interested. The first car to have success was a French car, of course, called a Sizaire-Naudine. A name now long forgotten. It was the first car to have independent front suspension. In 1910, along came a car made by Hispano-Suiza that too swept all before it. It had a 4-cylinder 2.6 litre engine, with side valves and twin camshafts. A man called Birkigt designed it. Also in 1910, there was a big report in the Motoring Press about Ettore Bugatti's new car. This had shaft driven overhead valves and shaft drive to the rear wheels. This made Gustav and his Managing Director Siegfried Gunther, sit up and take notice. The car was light, the engine was 1327 c.c, and developed 22 h.p, it was capable of 60 mph. Sigfried said that if a small engine like that could produce that much power then our engines must be able to produce much more power for their size, and he called a meeting with Gustav to include his drivers, mechanics and the development and research team in the boardroom.

When they were all assembled, Siegfried called for silence and introduced Gustav who would begin the meeting.

"Gentlemen," began Gustav, "now that you are all sitting comfortably I shall get to the point of this meeting. Frankly, we are getting left behind in the race for engine power. These small cars are producing more power per c.c, than ours, are a good deal lighter and even as fast. So with the prospect of no Grand Prix racing until June 1912, the only project we have is the 'Monster' for Mr de Palma for next November. Benz is producing cars for the American Grand Prix this year. We must look to getting our name before the public. We must produce a 3-litre car this year and grab the honours. I will now open the meeting for the discussion of general points. Gentlemen I am looking for real input and not flights of fancy. We have to have both reliability and performance."

There was some head scratching and even some muttering. Finally after a few minutes Rudolph got to his feet.

"Gentlemen," he began, "we the drivers and mechanics who ride on the cars really appreciate all the work you all have done on the cars. However, we must remember that over the past 4 years the governing body of our sport has changed the rules for competing cars no less than three times. Personally, I cannot see it changing its policy, when every year they come up with something different, and for us it is back to the drawing board. If we can produce a 3-litre car with a good performance, why not sell it to the public as well; this will enable enthusiasts to purchase a racing replica. In my conversations with our new driver Alain here, he tells me that Peugeot have this idea in mind too. A while ago a British Company Vauxhall, a car designed by a Mr. L.H. Pomeroy won a race it was a severe test over 2,000 miles run by the British Royal Automobile Club. I have heard that another British Company, Sunbeam are producing a 3 litre to race in the Coupe de L'Auto in Dieppe in the near future."

There was a round of applause as Rudolph sat down.

Siegfried got to his feet as the murmur of conversation following Rudolph's comments died down.

"Thank you Rudolph for your observations, and this is something I think we should pursue. Well Gentlemen, the gauntlet has been thrown down, now it is for us to pick up."

As they left the meeting, Rudolph and Alain started talking for they knew that their Managing Director was right. Now they had another task to perform. The engine design teams were told the good news. So it was back to the drawing board. It would be a busy summer. Francoise saw little of Alain during the week, but weekends they would relax and would spend time gardening. In the evenings sometimes they would get together with Catherina and Rudolph, and gradually they began to enlarge their circle of friends. By the end of their first summer they began to feel at home in the new Country. At last the engine drawings were finished and the castings were made. The final design was a 6 cylinder short stroke engine, two valves per cylinder with a carburettors that had leanings towards the one used by the Aero engine division, only smaller. The first time the engine was started it ran like a dream. The chassis too, was taking shape, elsewhere in the factory. The cars would be custom built, for speed, comfort, and reliability. They would have 4 wheel brakes, and some streamlining of the bodywork to cut down wind resistance. Alain had tried this out with Darracq and Peugeot. Both he and Rudolph were looking forward to the first road test. Meanwhile in another part of the vast Mercedes factory the 'Monster' was taking shape. This machine would be a different 'kettle of fish' so to speak. It was absolutely massive. Gustav had even now set up an experiment department to test new ideas. Some inventor had come up with hydraulic brakes, with a fluid in tubes forcing the brake linings on to the drums. The hot summer was with them now; the atmosphere in the factory was stifling.

The teams working on both the new cars were burning the midnight oil to meet their deadlines. The 3-litre car was almost ready. The 'Monster' was still taking shape. It had to be right; after all if it failed the sports writers in the U.S.A. would report that German cars are not good enough to beat the American cars. The factory wanted to win, and the glory and fame that went with it. It would be the first time that Mercedes had raced in the New World, and this was a very big chance for them to make a name for themselves. Gustav told his teams that their rivals, Benz had finished 2nd and 4th in the 1908 event. The gentlemen driving their car in the 1911 race had completed the fastest lap in a Fiat at over 65 mph. Mr. De Palma would it seems be visiting the factory in September to see how work was progressing and also if the car was ready, take a test drive. The factory then hoped to ship the car to America by mid-October. So the challenge was on. Alain and Rudolph could not wait to get out and give the new cars a good run. By mid July the 3-litre car was ready to test.

Early on a Sunday morning Alain and Rudolph arrived at the factory; the last thing they wanted at this stage was a crowd on onlookers, and photographers. Inside the experimental department, the white painted machine was ready. Mechanics had been there half of the night, checking everything and giving the new car a final polish. The chief mechanic gave one swing of the starting handle; the engine burst into life. The open exhaust resounding around the almost empty building. Sitting lower down than on their old Grand Prix cars, they had the luxury of a small windscreen. The seats were shaped to support the drivers. Rudolph felt comfortable behind the smaller steering wheel. The lock-to-lock gearing had been lowered to make handling easier. Rudolph engaged first gear, and the engine burbled happily as the car made its way to the factory gates. Alain lowered his goggles as the car picked up speed. They had the new four-speed gearbox and shaft drive. Soon they were out of the town and on to the open road. With the engine oil now nicely warmer up, Rudolph opened up the throttle. He was astounded by the amount of power available. They were soon doing over 120 kph. Then into top gear and finding themselves on a beautiful piece of straight road, Rudolph gave it full throttle. He wanted to drive it to the limit. They were now doing almost 160 kph, and the car was steering straight as an arrow.

After about 15 minutes and full throttle, Rudolph began to brake and change down. Everything was working well. He handed the controls over to Alain, and they returned at high speed back to the factory. They sat down over a coffee and discussed the test drive. Apart from a little adjustment to the brake balance all seemed OK. The 3 litre car had great potential, for further development. On returning home Catherina and Francoise wanted to know how the test had gone. Their husbands gave the new car definite thumbs up'.

On Monday morning, Alain and Rudolph had a meeting with Gustav, who was thrilled that the test had gone well. He told them that the 'Monster' had to be tested this week. Should there be any modifications to be made, they would have time to do it. By Wednesday, the new 9-litre car was ready. This machine had so many different new ideas on it, which Alain wondered if it would all come together. The first time the complete car was started up the exhaust noise was just deafening. The whole building seemed to shake. This car was a different animal indeed. It was more like their old Grand Prix cars. Just brute power. Unlike the 3-litre car, this vehicle had a slower revving engine at 2,500 rpm, it was calculated to churn out some 220 h.p; again a four-speed gearbox was fitted. It had a massive amount of torque, so they ratios chosen were fairly wide apart. Early on Thursday morning, Alain, and Rudolph were again off on a test run. The V-8 had a different feel amount it. As Rudolph sat behind the wheel with Alain beside him, they knew that this would be no picnic. This was a long distance racing car. It was designed to travel at speeds up to and beyond 170 kph, for periods of over one hour at a time. The brake drums were the biggest ever produced by the factory, and on all four wheels. The car was very light weighing in at just over 1000 kilos. This vehicle would be a handful.

Rudolph was used to cars with brute power; some of the early Mercedes had been almost impossible to control at times. Would this one be the same? As they drove out of the factory gates, Rudolph found that this car had a character not dissimilar, to the 3 litre. The engine was very docile, until he stirred it up. The power was massive, and he spun the rear wheels more than once as he accelerated through the gears, as they got on to the open road.

The factory had got the balance right. On the return trip Alain found, that considering the bulk of the machine, it handled far better than they had expected. When they arrived back at the factory, both Manfred and Gustav were there to greet them. Their first question posed by Manfred was: "Gentlemen, have we got a winner here?" The drivers both said a definite yes. Then both Manfred and Gustav insisted on being taken for a ride in their new car. Back in the boardroom, Siegfried suggested that they open a bottle of Champagne to toast the successful first test of the 'Monster', and of course the new 3 litre car.

Rudolph suggested that on both cars they increase the size of the fuel tank by about 10 litres and reposition it lower down on the car. This would give a better centre of gravity. It was agreed and the modifications were incorporated into the final version of the car.

In Mid October Mr.Ralph de Palma came to the factory. He drove both of the new cars, and was delighted with the 'Monster'. That evening Siegfried, Gustav, Alain, and Rudolph together with their wives took their honoured guest to dinner. Ralph told them all that he knew he would have stiff competition in the 1911 event. In the 1910 race, there were entries from Europe, include the famous Felice Nazzaro in his famous big Fiat, plus two very quick drivers, a David Bruce-Brown and a Victor Hemery, in two big Benz cars. It would be a tough race. The 1908 event had been a real struggle, he had retired with engine trouble, and Felice had gone on to finish third, whilst the other FIAT driver Louis Wagner had won the race. It was interesting for the Mercedes men to hear from an American who had taken part in a similar kind of race to the European Grand Prix. They could relate to him, and after dinner the conversation went on until the early hours. Ralph thought that the car was ready to ship back to the USA. Siegfried said that they had a couple of minor adjustments to make. This would include a larger fuel tank etc. When this had been done they would arrange for one of their mechanics to accompany the car on its journey. He would stay with Ralph's team until he was happy that they could manage without factory help. Ralph was driven back to his Hotel, and he thanked them for their hospitality. He looked forward to receiving the car soon. They shook hands and the deal was done.

At home Francoise, was always busy, her garden as spring turned to summer was a blaze of colour. She had a small gazebo at the bottom of the garden, where she spent many happy hours with her friend Catherina. With the onset of autumn, the leaves turned brown, and she knew that the cold German winter was not far away. The House had a very large fireplace in the main Lounge, and she looked forward to spending winter evenings with Alain by the fireside.

It was now mid-November, and Rudolph wanted to know how the American Grand Prix had finished, it was held on the same circuit as the 1908 event.
The winner and a complete surprise to Rudolph was not old adversary Felice Nazzaro, who had put up the fastest lap at almost 71 mph. but David Bruce-Brown in a Benz, who Ralph de Palma had mentioned. In fact Benz had taken the first two places. This made Gustav even more determined that their new 9-litre car should win in 1911. The race was along one 24 laps of a 17-mile circuit a total of 411 miles. Only time would tell if they would succeed.

Then Rudolph had a call from his old friend Hermann Ritter; he had recently had promotion at the Maybach Aero Engine Division, and asked if he could come to stay for the weekend. Catherina and Rudolph said that they would be delighted to see him. Hermann said that he had a lady friend was it OK if she came as well. Francoise said that as they had not had a house warming party, that as Hermann, and his lady were coming for the weekend, why not make it a party on the Saturday. Hermann arrived at

Rudolph's home just before midday on the Saturday with his lady. Her name was Greta Wolff; she came from a good family. She was very well dressed, and well spoken. She had an air of sophistication. Hermann introduced her to Catherina and Rudolph. Hermann removed her expensive Silver fox Coat, and underneath she had a stunning dress in claret velvet with a very low neckline. Rudolph noticed she had a very good figure and a deep cleavage. As he was looking at her, Catherina gave her husband a little nudge. After a quick coffee they headed across to Alain's home. The party had got underway, and the conversation flowed. In mid-afternoon Gustav and his wife arrived. It was a great party. Hermann was happy, for he had an attractive lady on his arm, and Rudolph was pleased to see his friend. All the guests bought little housewarming presents. Francoise felt quite embarrassed by it all.

When the Christmas holidays arrived, the factory closed for 2 weeks. Francoise said she would like to go back to see her parents, and Alain thought it would be a great opportunity to visit the Count de Longchamps. Catherina and Rudolph also took the chance to go home and visit parents. After all Christmas is a family thing.

So both households packed their suitcases and made their travel arrangements.

Rudolph had but a short journey to make, so they went by car. Francoise and Alain had to make a long train journey. They booked a private compartment all the way from Heidelberg. Francoise, now she was settled into her new home and wanted to have children. They both had been so busy; that sex had taken a back seat. Now they were together on a long train journey. Francoise knew exactly how to arouse her man. This time she would make sure that she became pregnant. The train began to pull out of Heidelberg Station, and Francoise and Alain now settled into their seats.

"My love," whispered Francoise, "I am feeling very broody? I want to be sexually satisfied as never before. I so really want to have your baby. It would make my life complete."

"My princess," replied Alain, "your wish will be granted."

He removed her fur coat, dress, and underwear. She then started to sexually excite her man, until her was ready to perform for her pleasure; they were soon under the furs, making love. She kept on riding on top of her Alain until she was certain that he had given her all she needed to become pregnant. Francoise was determined that she would continue to make love to her husband until she knew in her heart that she would become a Mother. Their journey passed on their bed of love, interrupted only with breaks for meals. Lovers get hungry too you know. They were more in love than ever.

When they arrived at the Clement home, they were treated like the prodigal couple. Pierre could not believe that he had such a lovely daughter in law. Even young Helene embraced her new sister in law. Marie, Pierre wife was just thrilled to have her 'children' home.

Germany seemed a long way away from their French farm. The next day they all drove up to the Chateau, where the Count Guy and Countess Claudine invited them all in for lunch. Guy took Alain into the Library, for he wanted to know all that Alain was doing in Germany. He was sorry that he had to go to Mercedes, but the French car industry seemed to be going through some growing pains. Alain told him about their new cars and the Count was fascinated. Whilst this was going on in the Morning Room, the ladies wanted to know all the gossip and the latest fashions from Germany. They also wanted to know was Francoise pregnant.

She almost replied, "we are trying our hardest," but resisted the temptation and thought of a more modest response.

"Well Ladies," answered Françoise, "we are planning to have a family soon. It is that Alain has been so busy at work."

Then she decided to change the subject.

"In our new house we do have a lovely garden. The flower beds are just ablaze with colour."

She had cleverly steered the conversation away from the subject of babies. Francoise knew when the time came, and she began to 'show' then that she would break the news. Francoise was planning a lot more horizontal jogging with Alain, to make absolutely certain. She loved to make love. It relaxed them both. They were expressing their intense feelings for each other in the most physical way that they could. Christmas and New Year was just one round of parties.

Across at the Schloss Lundenberg, the festivities were also underway. It was a time to celebrate; not that 1910 had much to offer them, except for the successful completion of the two new cars. One of which was now safely in America with Mr. de Palma.

Christmas melted into New Year, and Alain and Rudolph were back at the factory developing the new 3-litre car. To give the car a really good test, they decided to pitch it up against their last Grand Prix car driven by Alain, whilst Rudolph would be in the new car. They both carried mechanics, which of course was in the rules of the day. They took both cars to a circuit of about 8 kilometres that they often used. In previous tests the Grand Prix Car had averaged about 125 kph, and it had a top speed of some 160 kph. So this was the standard the car would be judged by. Alain had to follow Rudolph at a safe distance, due to the dusty roads. A timekeeper would be at the start and finish to time the cars over 2 laps. Rudolph went off first, and then one minute later Alain set off in pursuit. Rudolph was trying hard as he could.

They were hitting speeds in excess of 155 kph, and whizzed pass the start and finish line. Exactly one minute later Alain steamed by, going almost flat out in the GP car. On the second lap, Alain made up 15 seconds on Rudolph, as the test finished. It was a resounding 'thumbs up' for the new car. The newer technology had paid off, over brute force. The two friends shook hands, and made their way back to the factory where Gustav was waiting for them. He was thrilled that their new 'baby' had performed so well, now they could show their competitors in the Voiturette class, that Mercedes could come up with something new.

The next race for this new car was to be held on a circuit last used in 1907, when the Kaiserpreis race had been won by the English Lord Brabazon of Tara, in a Minerva at an average speed of 60 mph. The course was 73.4 miles, and the 3 litre cars would cover 4 laps a distance of some 293 racing miles.

The circuit at Bastogne was in the Ardennes Forest in Belgium. Mercedes decided to enter just the one car for Rudolph to drive and Alain to act as mechanic. The race would be held on the last weekend in August. No full practice was allowed, but most teams went around it in road cars. Alain suggested that he took pace notes to help them keep up speeds. They drove around the course on the Wednesday before the race, and Alain made notes of braking points, how long the straight sections were, and the severity of bends etc. On the day of the race, these notes would make a mile of difference. The night before the race, Alain and Rudolph checked the car over once more. They had set up their pit area, for refuelling and fresh tyres if required. The factory had designed a new form of wheel removal. This mean removing just one large nut and the wheel was off. Tyres were already on the wheels. This would cut down time spent changing wheels. The mechanic carried a spare wheel and a big spanner. Other teams had small nuts and bolts around the wheel in order to remove any damaged tyre.

On the day of the race the crowds had gathered early to witness the spectacle. Gustav had told his drivers, that if the new car was successful, then they would produce three more, and enter more races. The drivers paraded with their cars in front of the hastily erected grandstand. The Belgian flag flew on a tall pole by the start and finish. The large silver cups stood on a counter in front of the VIP enclosure. The race would be on a timed basis, the roads being narrow; it was decided to start the cars at 30-second intervals. In all, there were 30 entries, 20 from professional teams, plus the top 10 amateur drivers. There were entries from Sizaire-Naudine, Renault, Fiat, and some other small factories.

Now that race time was drawing near, speculation on the new car from Mercedes grew; photographers wanted pictures for the newspapers. So Rudolph and Alain posed for the cameras, hoping that the photographers had got their shots of the winners. The signal was given for the first ten competitors to start their engines. Competitors had been issued with numbers according to the professionalism of the drivers, which gave Alain and Rudolph Number 1; this suited our men down to the ground. They would not be following a dust cloud, and the difficulty in trying to overtake others as if in a thick fog.

The starter mounted the rostrum, Rudolph raised the engine revs, and as the flag dropped he engaged first gear and the white car shot up the road, then it was second, third and fourth gear. The road had some long sweeping bends so they were able to keep up a pretty good pace. The first place they reached was Vaux-les-Rozieres. Thundering through the narrow streets, the exhaust note bounced off the walls of the shops and houses. In less time than it takes to tell, they had left this sleepy town behind, for the competitors that followed in their wake. The road led on to Longlier, where there was a series of tricky bends to negotiate. The car was running like clockwork, but there was still a long way to go anything could happen. Next it was Anglier, and on at breakneck speed to Habay-la-Neuve, where there was a tight left hand bend. A tricky section of twisting bends took them to Heinstert. At the next village of Martelange, the road straightened out all the way to the end of the first lap that ended with a really sharp left hairpin bend at Bastogne. They flashed by the start line, knowing that had to do it three more times. On lap two by the time they had got to Legalise, they had already passed three cars that had expired. By the end of their second lap, Rudolph and Alain pulled in for fresh tyres and fuel. Their pit stop took about 2 minutes, and still there was no sign of the crew in second place. So they set off once more, at the same pace. Rudolph was driving well within the capabilities of their car. As they pressed on, to what appeared to be their victorious way, they passed crashed cars, others with wheels missing, and several that had gone off course. They passed the finish line, and the chequered flag fell. They had won easily. The next car to complete the course was Number 4, a Renault driven by Gaston Le Blanc.

Only 8 cars completed the event. Rudolph and Alain went up to collect their prize. It was the first time Alain had helped win an event for Mercedes. The photographers massed around our two heroes. Everyone wanted an interview for their papers. This was supposed to be a minor race, but without any international races during 1911, the motoring press wanted something to fill their pages. The first Belgian to finish the race, was Claude Boussen in an Opel, he finished 6th. He got praise as the local ace, supported only by his local garage. He had made a monumental effort to finish, after going off the road twice, luckily without damage to himself or his car.

When they got back to the factory, Gustav was over the moon. It was not just that Alain and Rudolph had won the event, he knew that their new 3 litre could be a real force to be reckoned with. He directed that three more cars are built, next time they would not just win; they would wipe the floor with the opposition.

The remainder of the year was spent perfecting the 3-litre cars. Rudolph and Alain took it in turns to win, their cars being far in advance of the opposition. Gustav's words were true; they did wipe the floor with the opposition. Towards the end of the racing season, Gustav called a meeting one Monday morning to introduce a new recruit to his Grand Prix team. Gustav had always wanted three drivers. The problem always seemed to be the same one, and that was where do we find these Champions? Gustav introduced Hans Lang as their Number 3 driver. Hans Lang had been doing some excellent work in the Aero Engine Division, but he had expressed the desire to become a Racing Driver. Alain had the task of training him, and at the same time testing the new 3-litre car. Hans was a willing student, and took to driving the new machine like a duck to water.

Francoise meanwhile was watching her garden mature. When he arrived home after a hard day, Alain would relax in the garden with a glass of wine to evaporate the stress that built up during the day. For despite the fact that there were few competitive events, the constant striving for excellence was wearing on our three heroes. Hans was doing very well and enjoyed the longer distances. Gustav decided in his wisdom to enter one of their 3-litre cars to race in Sicily. It was the TARGA FLORIO, it was run over public roads and had since the first race back in 1906, had always been won by an Italian car and driver. Gustav knew that with average speeds between 30 & 35 mph, this would be no flat out race. He decided to get Hans Lang to drive the only entry, as he wanted his two star men to remain in Germany to participate in events closer to home. He had big plans for them. Meanwhile, Hans and the team of mechanics headed off to Sicily with two cars, the race car and a car to recce the route. It was a long journey; Hans and his mechanic spent many hours touring around the course. The advice given by both Alain and Rudolph was to make some course notes. Hans had to contact Gustav at the end of each day by telephone from his Hotel. Apparently the roads were awful, and the car he was using to check the route out, kept getting punctures. So he asked for more tyres to be sent out to him.

On the day of the race Hans and his mechanic Ludwig Schmit, covered themselves in glory by finishing 2nd to Ernesto Ceirano in a car called a SCAT. The winner had averaged about 50 kph, with Hans just 4 minutes behind the winner. On his return Hans gave a vivid report of this race, which he called organised suicide.

"Gustav," he continued, "the crowds that were supposed to be controlled were all over the roads, and it was nothing short of a miracle that nobody was killed. The other drivers went absolutely crazy driving far too fast, and there so were many crashes Ludwig and I really lost count. Frankly we were relieved to cross the finish line in one piece. That was an event that we shall remember for some time."

"Great work Hans," replied Gustav, "were are delighted that both you two and the car are back safely. You certainly have earned your spurs this time."

The Cup presented to them would be a real coup, and the only time that Mercedes figured in the results until 1922.

The year 1911 drew to a close, winter began to set in over Europe, and over in Savannah, Georgia, the United States Grand Prix was taking place on November 30th. Gustav was wondering how the 9-litre monster would perform in the hands of Mr. Ralph de Palma. On the 1st December Gustav received a telegram from the USA, from Mr.de Palma.

It read: *DELIGHTED WITH CAR, FINISHED 3RD. ONLY 3 MINUTES BEHIND WINNER. WILL CONTACT YOU AGAIN SOON. REGARDS. RALPH DE PALMA.*

Gustav had the telegram framed and put up in his office. He was proud that they had built a car that had performed well. Maybe they would win in 1912. Gustav had just received the new regulations for racing in 1912.

There would be a minimum width of 1750 mm; this would mean that their 3-litre cars would be eligible.

Gustav wiped his brow and muttered to himself:

"At least we have got something right for next year."

The round of Christmas parties began, with Alain and Rudolph spending time at the Schloss Lundenberg. Count Josef considered Alain and Francoise as part of his extended family. They were always welcome, this gave both the young Clements a feeling of belonging, and they no longer felt like strangers.

Francoise still wanted children, and always was a little envious of Catherina and her son.

"Francoise," Catherina said to her one evening, "one day you will have a son and you will adore him. You and Alain will make the perfect parents. Rudolph and I made love many times before we had Manfred. I want more children, perhaps a girl."

"You are right Catherina, I am impatient. I do love my husband so much. We enjoy making love and I look forward to the day that I can give birth to a son."

That night Francoise told Alain of the conversation with Catherina. Alain agreed that they should make love at every opportunity, life was good to them now and it was a very good climate in which to raise children.

So that night and every night Alain and Francoise enjoyed their sexual pleasures. The holiday was time for the friends to just relax prior no doubt to a hectic season, testing, making improvements to the cars and coping with the new regulations. The snow lay heavy around the Lundenberg family home. They decided one day to go for a sleigh ride. This was something new to Alain and Francoise. So they all dressed in their warmest furs and Rudolph took the reins of the two horses, and they headed off to a local Inn, where they sat around a roaring fire and drank their fill of the local mulled wine. Francoise could not believe the amount of snow that had fallen over the last two days that they had spent in the Schloss. Everywhere looked like fairyland. She had seen pictures on Christmas Cards of snow-clad hills and trees, but had never experienced it at first hand. On the way home she snuggled up to Alain, and he could see that look of love in her eyes. These were happy days for both the Clements and the von Lundenbergs. They enjoyed making love to their wives, drinking, eating and making merry with very good friends. For sure when they returned to Mercedes in the New Year it would be back to Canstatt and reality. There would be a hard season ahead, but now it was Christmas and they looked to ringing out the old year and running in the new.

The calendar of events for the 1912 season would mean only one Grand Prix in Europe, this to be held at Dieppe on 25th & 26th June, over the all too demanding 47.840-mile course, to be covered 20 times. This would be a staggering distance of almost 957 miles (some 1531.0 kilometres).

This was exactly twice the distance of the previous race held in 1908. Gustav had just received entry forms and the Regulations, so he called in Rudolph and Alain to a meeting to discuss the event.

"Gentlemen," began Rudolph, "I have here in front of me the Rules, Regulation and Entry Form documents for the French Grand Prix. I leave you to read them for yourselves. I can assure you that this would be the greatest test yet for our cars. In fact, almost like the old City-to-City races. I doubt that even the French have resurfaced the roads. I jokingly suggested that Mercedes enter a team of fast lorries rather than fragile grand prix cars, an idea with which our Managing Director actually agreed. Back in 1908, the winner's average speed was over 110 kph, and I expect the average speeds to be about the same. So gentlemen, we have work to do modifying that 3-litre car. It is quick enough, but it needs beefing up to cope with the rugged conditions that we will encounter. Oh! Incidentally the M.D. said that our lorries could not average 120 kph, so you will have to drive the cars. Suggest you get out there to win."

Alain and Rudolph spent the next hour or so reading the regulations; the race it seems was more of an endurance test. They wondered at times what sort of person would think up a race of this distance, especially as they did not have to drive in it.

Rudolph thought back to the 1908 race, which was bad enough, this one would be race of attrition. Alain calculated that they could be racing for 14 hours, possibly over 2 days. It would need of lot of practice and planning to win this one. They knew through the grapevine that Peugeot had decided to enter, plus a team of 3 cars from the English Sunbeam Company. This would be no Mercedes benefit. The challenge for glory was on once more.

Chapter 20

In Italy meanwhile, Carla was making plans to visit her parents once again. It would be a quiet time, she would be thankful for a well-earned rest from FORUM. It had been a very successful year with sales of all her designer clothes giving the best profits the Company had seen in years. The move to Rome in May had been a success, for now FORUM was one of the foremost fashion houses in Italy. Now that young Dino was 5 years old, Carla decided that he should start to have some kind of private tuition, his nanny Sophia, had been doing an excellent job and had taught young Dino to read a few words and made sure that he pronounced his words clearly. She would play with him around the house, and often he would have some young friends into play. Carla advertised in the local newspaper for a tutor. After interviewing about a dozen applicants she settled for Dario Zorro. He was a teacher, in a private nursery school. Then one day the owner decided to sell off the school, and Dario lost his job. Carla thought he had the right attitude, and he got on really well with Sophia, who had a soft spot for him. Now that she had Dino's immediate educational needs sorted out she could get on with the business of running FORUM.

She had regular reports from Marco Santini and Juliette Cappelo in Florence that sales were booming, and this was confirmed by the accounts for the branch. Now she had to decide the Company strategy for 1912. The winter season had started back in the heat of August, when the models had sweated on the Catwalks in heavy dresses and furs designed for winter. Enrico's designer furs were selling like the proverbial hot cakes. He visited FORUM's Rome store regularly, and took on a partner Carmel Pirro. Carmel was very talented; she had worked with Angelo Versanti, the famous Milan furrier. She had joined him 4 years previous, and wanted to branch out on her own. She had spoken about this to Angelo who said that his friend Enrico was looking to expand his business, and just maybe he would take her on. Carmel had a meeting with Enrico, who was amazed at her talent for designing top quality furs. Now with his exclusive contract with FORUM, Enrico wanted someone to look after the stores in Milan, whilst he took care of stores in Florence and Rome. Carmel was from Milan, and had a large flat just outside the City Centre. He told Carla of his plans; she said if he recommended someone as a partner, then that fine with her. She did tell Enrico that before Carmel did any work for FORUM; she wanted to meet Carmel at the Florence store. So it was arranged. Carla decided to give Carmel a test to satisfy herself that Carmel could work alone, without supervision from Enrico.

The meeting was scheduled for Thursday November 30th at 10.00am. Both Enrico and Carmel had stayed overnight and the meeting began on time.

Carla welcomed her to the store.

"Carmel," began Carla, "I understand you are going to be working with Enrico our furrier here in the store? I can tell you he is a hard act to follow. Providing you can satisfy me that you are as good as Enrico says you are, and then I will give you a joint contract with Enrico. Now what have you to say?"

Carmel who was rather a short young lady of some 5ft 2ins with bright red hair sat and listened to Carla, taking in every word.

When Carla had finished Carmel sat quiet for a moment before answering.

"Signorina Carla," replied Carmel, "I understand that taking on someone new is always a bit of a gamble. You have my C.V. there in front of you. As you can see I worked with Angelo Versanti in Milan and here is his letter of recommendation. I have prepared some designs for you plus two fur coats; so that you can see that I am a professional furrier, not just somebody that wants a job with FORUM."

Carla read the letter from Versanti; she certainly knew his designs. Carmel gave Carla a folder that contained several full length and jacket designs, and Carla's eyes just lit up. These new designs looked really special. Carmel then opened a large suitcase and revealed two superb furs. The full-length coat was mink in white and black with a heart shaped pattern on the back. There was a number of small buttons on the bottom hem, so that the coat could be lengthened or shortened. Carla thought this was a great innovation. The Jacket in sable had Silver fox collar and cuffs. This was the first time that Carla had ever seen a mixture of furs on one garment. She was so impressed with Carmel that she agreed that she take-over the area of the Milan store in partnership with Enrico. Carla took them to lunch to seal the contract.

She was hoping that once Carmel Pirro had established herself in Milan that Enrico could move to Rome.

Carla knew that she had a rich clientele in the Eternal City, and Enrico talents would then come into great demand.

Just before the Christmas break; Enzo Borghese telephoned Carla to tell her that if she was interested, there was a premises available in Turin that would be ideal as a new showroom for FORUM. The lease, held by the Bank, was due to expire at the end of February, and he gave Carla a contact telephone number saying that she had a make a quick decision. Carla said that she had been thinking of opening a store in Turin, and would phone the number he had given her straight away. Carla put the phone down and went into Ricardo's Office. She told him about the opportunity, and he agreed they should go to Turin as soon as possible. Ricardo then asked the operator to get him the Turin number.

Three minutes later the phone rang.

"Your Turin number Sir," said the operator.

"Hello," answered a man's voice, "this is Luciano Gelazi, can I help you?"

Ricardo explained the reason for the call, and the two men chatted for a while. Then Ricardo passed over the receiver to Carla, who explained who she was and the business they were involved in. They made arrangements to meet on the following Tuesday morning, December 12th, just 2 weeks before the Festive Holiday, but did not give a time for a meeting with Luciano. Ricardo and Carla would travel together and stay overnight in a Hotel in the centre of Turin; young Dino would stay with his nanny. Carla dressed in her business clothes and furs met Ricardo at Rome Station, and made their way to their adjoining compartments. The Bank had supplied details of the property in Turin, which looked a good deal by any standards. The business had started to lose money over the past twelve months and Carla smelt another Antonati in the woodwork.

Although, she could be wrong. The journey passed pleasantly enough, and the Hotel was very comfortable.

At 9.00am, the next morning they made their way to Signor Gelazi's store. They decided to try and find out how Gelazi treated his customers, so arm in arm Ricardo and Carla walked towards the store. They noticed that the outside had not been painted for years, and the window displays were badly in need of expert attention. Ricardo opened the door and Carla dressed in her blue fox coat and accessories walked in. There were several assistants at the back of the shop chatting, several were drinking coffee and one young lady was reading the newspaper. The premises inside were somewhat dowdy, but there was a good floor area and Carla and Ricardo reckoned that with some redecoration and planning the store could be ideal for their purpose. Carla and Ricardo browsed around, looking at dresses, fur coats and shoes, comparing the prices with those of FORUM. The stock seemed to have been around for some time, for some of the shoes had a layer of dust on them. Some of the dresses were styles from a year or two back. Carla started looking at the Furs; she was getting a bit bored to say the least. It seemed that the staff could not care less whether they served or not.

Then after what seemed an eternity a young lady approached, her body language was one of indifference.

"Good morning Madam," she said in a monotonous tine, "can I be of some assistance to you?"

Carla looked her up and down.

"I thought no one would ever ask," replied Carla who was feeling a little annoyed having had to wait to be served.

"I am sorry you have had to wait," answered the young lady, "my name is Paula and I am new here and have had little training."

Carla thought for a moment and decided that rather than reveal her true reason for the visit to the store, she would adopt the attitude of a customer.

"Now Paula," said Carla, "let me see I should like to try on this red fox coat, that silver fox jacket and several of those blouses in all the colours over there, and a dress from that rack."

Paula smiled and was now thinking of the commission that would be coming her way if she sold Carla all these garments.

"Thank you Madam, I will get them for you," she replied enthusiastically, "would you like to go over to the Changing room? I will bring those you have selected over to you. "

Carla decided to be a difficult customer; after all she had experienced enough of them in her time at the Bank and FORUM.

First she removed her coat, as Paula brought the garments into the changing room. First she tried on the blouses, they were well made, and obviously stock that had been around some time, and on close inspection Carla could see that they were looking a little tired. Next came the dresses and finally the red fox and silver fox furs. Carla admired herself in the various outfits, but even though she liked them, she put them back on the hangers. Paula returned after another 10 minutes, and Carla who had tried on all the clothes as well as the furs was wearing the red fox fur coat.

Having knocked on the changing room door Paula entered the room and smiled.

"May I say," said Paula, "that red fox coat really suits you Madam."

Carla rolled her eyes; FORUM forbade any shop assistant to pass comment on a customer's attire. No doubt this young lady would learn by experience. Carla removed the Fur and placed it with the other garments that she had tried on.

"I am sorry my dear," replied Carla keeping a straight face, "I just really cannot make my mind up at present as to what to buy. May be I will call back again soon."

With that Paula's face dropped she could see her commission going out of the window. Meanwhile Ricardo was looking around making mental notes, he liked the potential of the store, but the present staff was a nightmare. Carla must have been about 30 minutes or more in the changing room, Ricardo was wondering if she would be found out as the possible buyer of this place. While Ricardo wandered around no one came near him; neither did any customers come into the shop.

The street outside was crowded with people going to work and shoppers who gave a quick look into the Gelazi shop window then walked on. Carla reappeared from the changing room, and Paula started taking all the clothes that Carla had tried on, and replacing them from whence they came. Whilst Carla had been trying on all these clothes, Rudolph had been looking around the store. Seeing Carla appear from the changing room he walked over to her. By now Paula was well out of earshot.

"Well Carla," asked Ricardo, "what is your verdict?"

"Ricardo, let us go and find a Café and think about our strategy for this deal. Obviously the owner could not care less, and the staff seem to have the same attitude. No wonder they do not have any customers. The attitude of the staff is dreadful and they are badly in need of training."

They found a nearby café and sat down that was quite busy. They found a table in a quiet corner and within a few seconds a waiter appeared.

"Would you like to order Signor?" he asked in a cheery voice.

Ricardo looked up turned his face to the waiter.

"That's what I call service," he answered, "waiter we would like two coffees please."

The waiter walked back to the counter and starting making the coffee behind the counter.

"Well Ricardo," she began, "with the experience we have just had it is no wonder that Gelazi's business is going downhill. The attitude of the staff has to be seen and heard to be believed. If we had staff that acted that way towards customers, then I would have sacked them long ago."

Ricardo shook his head.

"Carla I totally agree with you," he replied, "we shall have to modify our approach to Signor Gelazi; they may well be a reason as to why this situation has occurred. I had a look at the stock; whilst you were trying on the garments, although there is quite a lot we could use. We might have to sell it off at a discount, but we would still make money, providing we could get it all at a good price. As for the premises they need completely refurbishing to bring it up to our high standard. The other thing of course, is that the location is good being within the main shopping area."

Carla nodded in agreement.

So, after a second cup of coffee, they got up from the table, and Ricardo paid the bill.

"Before we start negotiations, Ricardo," said Carla as they emerged into the street, "I think that we will go along to the Bank of Italy. I want to appraise my father-in-law of the situation facing us here and ask his advice on how we should proceed."

They strolled along to the Turin branch and met with the Manager. He put a call through to Enzo, and then handed the phone back to Carla. Carla explained the situation, and asked who owned the freehold. Enzo said the Bank held the freehold, but Gelazi only had a short 10 year lease and this was due to expire at the end of February. This could be made available to a new purchaser.

"Thank you Enzo," replied Carla, "can you please give me first option on the freehold? I will negotiate with you, rather than go through it all with Signor Gelazi."

"Carla my dear," answered Enzo, "once you have had a meeting with Gelazi, and agree a price for the stock, then we can make financial arrangements for you to take on the freehold rather than a lease. This will give you far more security."

"Thank you Enzo," replied Carla, "I will call you once things are resolved here."

Carla felt relieved as she put the receiver down.

"Ricardo," she said cheerfully, "we can have the freehold, rather than just the lease. So all we have to do is do a deal on the stock we want, and listen to a long tale from Gelazi."

So Carla and Ricardo, walked back to Gelazi store, and re-entered the showroom. There was still a 5 minutes wait before a rather laconic older lady wandered over to them.

"Can I help you Madam?" she said in a whining kind of voice.

She sounded if she was actually doing Carla a favour by trying to serve her.

Carla looked her up and down.

"Thank you," replied Carla feeling rather annoyed, "for actually taking time out of your busy day, to actually do your job of serving a customer."

The lady in her late 40's dressed in a white blouse and black skirt seemed to ignore Carla's sarcastic comment.

"Well Signorina," responded the assistant, "do you want help or are you just browsing?"

Carla could not believe this saleslady's reply.

"If it is not too much trouble for you," answered Carla feeling very displeased, "I want to see Signor Gelazi. I have an appointment my name is Carla Navarrio."

(Since the divorce she had reverted to her maiden name for business).

The lady's expression did not change one bit.

"Please follow me," she replied as she turned on her heels.

Ricardo and Carla followed the lady, who seemed to walk very slowly as if she had all day. Finally they reached Signor Gelazi's office. The lady knocked on the door. Luciano was seated behind his desk wearing a worried frown on his face. He beckoned his guests to come in and sit down. The lady assistant then left Signor Gelazi's office to return to the showroom.

"Bon Giorno Signorina," said Signor Gelazi, "can I be of some assistance to you?"

"Signor Gelazi," replied Carla, "I am Carla Navarrio and this is my business partner Ricardo Armari. You may recall a telephone conversation concerning the lease on this property, which I understand expires at the end of next February?"

Luciano's face lit up and he smiled.

"Ah yes Signorina Carla. I remember! Yes. Let me see I have some notes here. What would you like to know? But first let me order coffee."

Five minutes later the refreshment arrived.

Carla started by explaining that she had information from the Bank of Italy that the store was available for lease, but she wanted the freehold. All FORUM stores were freehold. She had made enquiries and found that the Bank held these documents. She was interested in purchasing the stock, but as for the staff, well their attitude left a lot to be desired. They were so laid back as to be horizontal. Customer relations must be at an all time low. She also mentioned the state of the premises and could she see the accounts. Luciano handed her a large ledger that contained the last two years figures. With her Banking background, a quick glance through this told her that his business was on the brink of bankruptcy. She asked who his main creditors were. Luciano passed her a list; this totalled to about the same amount of money that Carla was prepared to pay for the stock. She passed the ledger and the list to Ricardo, who studied it for several minutes, nodded and passed them back to Luciano. Carla then broke the silence, for she could see Luciano was looking very apprehensive.

"Signor Gelazi," said Carla, "is there something you want to tell me, or do I try to guess?"

"I think it is best, Signorina Carla, to tell you my story from the very beginning."

Carla and Ricardo had a good idea of the story that was about to unfold.

"Signor Gelazi," answered Carla, "we want to know everything. Leave nothing out for we are prepared to listen."

Luciano started to tell a tale of woe. Carla and Ricardo thought this is it, get out the handkerchiefs, and have a good weep. Luciano told them that he was originally from Palermo in Sicily; the family had a farm there that was very run down. It couldn't support the family; so his father Pauli gave him a few thousand lira and said go find a business in Italy. He took a train to Turin and got lodgings. The landlady told him that a friend of hers had a dress shop and was looking for a salesperson. Luciano applied for the job and got it. Later he became Manager, then the owner died leaving him the business. He married a local girl called Romana and they had a son, Julius. Things went well for several years the boy grew up and after he left school, he went into the fashion business, and three years ago he joined my business. Two years ago my wife died from influenza, I left the business in the hands of my son. He liked the high life and gambled. Soon he was taking money out, about twice as fast as it was coming in. I went to the Bank and borrowed lots of money to keep the business afloat. Then one night about a year ago, he was coming out of a Gambling Club, after a big win, when he was shot dead and robbed of his winnings. This has meant I have had to run the business alone. During this three-act play, which Carla guessed had only reached Act Two, she wondered what other drama would rear its ugly head. She wasn't wrong either. Luciano continued, and then letters came in from suppliers demanding payment of overdue invoices. Julius had not paid them; instead he had used the money set aside for gambling. Now that the lease is ending soon, I have to quit and try to sort my life out.

Carla and Ricardo having listened patiently to Luciano's tale of woe and they both felt that perhaps all was not lost.

"Thank you Luciano for sharing your story with us" replied Carla, "our purpose here today is to make you an offer on certain terms and conditions."

Luciano's face lit up once more.

"Signorina Carla," he responded quickly, "what actually had you in mind?"

Carla looked at Ricardo and they both nodded in agreement.

"Ricardo," asked Carla, "would you like to put our outline proposal to Luciano for his consideration?"

"Luciano," began Ricardo, "we know that you have a lot of problems, and from these accounts these are mostly financial. We are prepared to buy all your existing stocks of clothing, footwear, furs, hats and shop-fittings. The deal is we pay the amount of money for the stock that you owe to your creditors. That way you will walk away free. The staff here, have they been paid?"

"I owe them two months money," replied Luciano.

"Fair enough," continued Ricardo, "we will add that sum to our offer. I want you to make all of the staff redundant except Paula. They will be paid off. Paula is the only one who seemed interested in serving customers. In the meantime, I want you to stay on as Manager here. We shall completely refurbish the place and then decide. Do we have a deal Luciano?"

Really for Luciano it was a case of Hobson's choice. Luciano smiled for the first time since Carla and Ricardo had come into his Office. He stood up and embraced Carla and shook Ricardo's hand.

"Thank you Ricardo and Carla, thank you so very much, you have saved my life and business what else can I say."

Ricardo and Carla took Luciano to lunch to seal the arrangement. Now it was left to Luciano to give the good news to his staff. Later that day Carla and Ricardo caught the train back to Milan, it had been a good day's work. The store there under the Manager was running like clockwork, so after a brief visit they got the late train back to Rome.

The days running up to Christmas passed quickly for Carla, and before she knew it was time to go to Florence to visit her parents. The news about the store in Turin was good, and Enzo was delighted that Carla had done the deal, and got the freehold at a good price. Enzo felt sorry for his Client Luciano, but the bank was not a charity. Carla picked up the phone and made reservations on the Florence express for herself and young Dino.

Two days later, she had packed her suitcase and got her son ready for the journey. The morning of her departure was very cold, so Carla dressed in her full-length silver fox coat and accessories, whilst young Dino had new winter clothes too. Carla was particularly pleased with herself, business was booming, and she was delighted with the Turin deal.

Carla had left Sophia behind, as Sophia's parents were coming to visit her for the first time. Early in the morning of Thursday 21st December, the taxi arrived at the Carla's villa, wrapped in her furs she and young Dino set out for Rome Station. When she arrived there the station was very crowded with passengers travelling in and out of the capital city. Carla eventually found a porter with a barrow to take her two suitcases to Platform 1, whilst young Dino held on to his Mother's hand for dear life, he certainly did not want to get separated in the crowds. Finally the trio fought its way to the Florence express, and the Porter helped Carla get her suitcases into her reserved compartment. Closing the door, they settled down in their seats, Carla breathed a sigh of relief; she could now have some peace. Young Dino meanwhile, was staring out of the window watching the crowds hurrying by, as another express steamed in. Just at that the compartment door slid open, and a man stood there.

"Excuse me Signora, but we seem to have the same compartment reserved?"

Carla looked up from her magazine, having loosened her coat.

"Let me see your ticket Signor?"

The tall stranger showed his reservation slip, and sure enough it was the same as Carla's. Carla thought this is all I need a man in my compartment. She looked him up and down. He was in his 30's very handsome, and dressed in the latest style.

The stranger broke the silence as Carla inspected his ticket.

"I'll try to find another compartment," said the stranger, "if there is a problem. This train is very crowded. Can I introduce myself my name is Francisco Puccini, I am a fashion designer?"

Carla was now resigned to the fact that she would have to share her journey with a fashion designer.

"Very well Signor Puccini," replied Carla, "if you have no alternative but to join me, then perhaps I should introduce myself and my son to you. My name is Carla Borghese (she decided to use her married name to begin with), and this is my son Dino."

"I am delighted to make your acquaintance," answered Francisco, "are you travelling far Signora Carla?"

"Signor Puccini," replied Carla, "my son and I are going to Florence to stay with my parents for the Christmas Holidays."

Francisco sat down, putting his suitcase on the overhead rack and his briefcase on the seat beside him. The train started with a jolt, then gathered speed and had soon left the eternal city behind. Francisco asked Carla if he could get refreshment for her and her son, Carl agreed and Francisco disappeared.

Carla opened her magazine and began to scan the pages; young Dino was looking out of the window watching the scenery pass by very quickly.

The door opened once more and there was Francisco with coffee for Carla and himself and a soft drink for Dino.

"I see," said Francisco putting down the refreshments, "that you are reading a fashion magazine, are you in that business?"

Carla was not in the mood to talk shop, but on the other hand she could not be rude.

"Yes I am," she replied, "may I enquire what you do?"

A long conversation at this stage she did not need. It had been a hard season with fashion shows to see and run; now all she wanted was a quiet journey.

"Carla, I am travelling to Florence I have submitted designs to a company called FORUM, I hear that they are the best fashion house in Italy."

Carla looked at him and thought I have not heard from Marco about this. Carla's interest was aroused.

"Excuse me Francisco could you help me remove my furs? I have at last warmed up."

"With pleasure Carla. That is certainly a beautiful fur coat, and those boots and hat must have been made for you. If I may say so, you are a very attractive lady, and you have a very handsome son. You must be proud of him. I hope you will not be offended by my compliments."

Carla blushed a little, for it had been a long time since she had been flattered in such a way. Then she thought shall I come clean, he is bound to find out anyway. By now young Dino had got his head into a comic book, and was paying little attention.

"Actually Francisco, I am involved with FORUM, a partner in the Company and based in Rome. Could I possibly see your designs?"

Francisco smiled and felt just a little embarrassed.

"Certainly Signora Carla, that would be my pleasure."

He opened the briefcase and inside were some really wonderful creations, the two of them sat down and the hours seem to pass so quickly that it was now time for lunch.

They all went down to Restaurant Car and enjoyed a superb lunch including young Dino, who always seemed hungry. When the bill arrived Carla had already opened her wallet.

"No argument Francisco, lunch is my treat."

Francisco wanted to pay, but Carla insisted on paying.

"This will be your only free lunch Francisco."

Carla wanted to find out more about Francisco, before making any decision about offering him any kind of contract to design for FORUM. Having finished lunch, the trio made their way back to the compartment. Young Dino was tired and fell asleep on the seat. This was Carla's chance to get some background on his handsome stranger. So she began the conversation again.

"So Francisco having seen your designs why don't you tell me about yourself?"

Francisco told Carla that he was born in Naples had studied fashion in Paris, where after five years at the Sorbonne he was apprenticed to 'Lucienne', the fashion house. After two years the Company went into receivership and he was out of work. So he went back home to Naples. His father had a small clothing factory, so he helped him with some designs and the business flourished. Then his Mother was killed in a road accident and his father lost interest in the business, so he sold it before the creditors could move in, earlier this year. Since then he had submitted designs to several Italian fashion houses, hoping for work.

Carla felt that he was genuine case, and deserved a chance with FORUM. After all she thought that his designs were pretty good.

"Francisco," she replied, "here is my business card. I think that we have something to talk about. Now I shall be in the Florence store on Saturday from 9am until noon, please call and see me."

Francisco thanked Carla for the opportunity to meet her in her office. The train slowed as in came into Florence Station; Carla woke young Dino as the train ground to a halt. Francisco helped Carla on with her fur coat and took hold of her suitcases placing them on the Platform and called a Porter. Carla felt the time on the train had just flown, and had been particularly fruitful. As they parted Francisco said he would look forward to seeing her on Saturday morning. Carla hailed a taxi outside the Station and headed for her parents' house. It was a delightful homecoming. The villa was full of Christmas decorations and a great big tree covered in baubles, Christmas lights and there were presents around the foot of the tree. Carla made her way up to her room and flopped on the bed without taking her coat off, she felt shattered, now for at least the rest of today and tomorrow she could relax. Finally, she got up took of her Furs, unpacked her suitcase and went to see what young Dino was doing. He had already taken his coat off and had run downstairs, to see and greet his Grandparents.

When she finally made it downstairs Guillermo her parent's butler gave her a glass of red wine and she sat down in front of a roaring fire. It was great just to relax, and be waited on. Young Dino meanwhile, was playing with his Grandfather in the Study. Luckily, young Dino was a happy child and no longer asked after 'daddy'.

Early on Saturday morning, the taxi Carla had booked arrived at the front door. Carla in all her sumptuous furs climbed aboard and set off for her Florence store. At the main entrance she paid off the taxi, and the doorman saluted her by touching his hat.

"Bon Giorno, Signorina," he said cheerily.

He opened the door for her, and Carla made her up to Marco's office, where Marco greeted her:

"Good morning Signorina," he said, "it is a pleasure to see you. Would you like a coffee?"

"Good morning Marco. Yes I would love a coffee."

Marco helped her off with her fur coat and hung it up.

"Incidentally," continued Carla, "I am expecting a young man named Francisco Puccini. He is a fashion designer."

Marco thought for a moment.

"Oh yes Carla! I have some designs sent in by a gentleman of that name. I am sorry I forgot to mention this to you."

Marco produced the sketches and Carla glanced over them. The coffee arrived and Carla sipped it slowly. The sketches were very good indeed, obviously done by Francisco.

Carlo looked up and posed two questions:

"What do you think of them Marco? Have you shown them to Juliette?"

"Carla, I thought they were very good and so did Juliette. True some of the designs are a bit way out, but they could be a future trend. Fashion never stands still."

"I agree Marco," replied Carla with a smile, "if he shows up and shapes up, then we may have a new designer on our staff. Incidentally, and this is between the three of us, I am in the process of acquiring a new premises in Turin. I'll keep you posted on progress. By the way, how is Juliette, have not seen her around when I arrived. Is she not in the store today?"

"Juliette has gone to see a couple of our suppliers who are having a few problems Carla. It is nothing she that cannot handle. She should be back soon, at least I hope so."

At that moment Juliette Cappelo came up the stairs and knocked on the door, Carla waved her in.

"Good morning Juliette," said Marco, "is everything O.K.?"

Juliette was a little flustered and sat down in the chair opposite Marco, she glanced across at Carla, and when she had got herself together she was ready to answer Marco.

"Good morning Marco and Signorina Carla. There is no problem at all. I have been to see the suppliers, as one of their lines has sold so well, I have ordered another two dozen."

Carla smiled for whatever problems there had been had now been resolved. Something less to worry about she thought.

"That is good news Juliet," replied Carla, "now this affects both of you. I have a project that will take place in the New Year, and I shall need you to think about it. I have acquired premises in Turin; this will come into our little empire on March 1st. Juliette, you have family in Turin. Is it too late to go to stay with them over Christmas? If not, then take the late train, then after the holiday I want you to go to this address and see Luciano Gelazi. He at present owns the store we have acquired. Tell him I sent you. Take Ivan Benuchi; from the Bank of Italy, his is Deputy Manager at the Turin Branch. Go through the accounts with a fine toothcomb, and then report back to me. Look through the stock, I have already valued it. When we open there we will have a sale to move most of the stock. I will also send Enrico, our furrier to meet you. He can value the fur collection, to see if we can sell the coats as they are, or restyle them. Anything not worth restyling we can sell at a discount. I have calculated that should not take more than a week, two at most."

Juliette was amazed; at last she was actually going to be able to do a job without someone staring over her shoulder.

"Carla," replied Juliette, "it will be terrific to go to see my parents; I have seen them for months. Thank you Signorina Carla for the opportunity you have given me. I shall carry out your instructions to the letter."

There was a knock at the door. It was Francisco.

"Sorry I am a bit late Carla, I do not know Florence very well, and I got lost."

Carla got up and shook hands with Francisco.

"Good morning Francisco," said Carla, "Florence can be a bit of a maze. Never mind you are here now. Let me introduce, Marco Sintani and Juliette Cappelo."

Francisco shook hands with them.

"Please Francisco," continued Carla, "do please have a seat, we are all informal here. Now we have had a good look at your designs, and they are very good. Although I did see some copies when we met on the train. What we would like you to do is to work under our present designer Umberto, for a couple of months, just to get the hang of the way we work here at FORUM. Then if all is satisfactory we can take you on permanently, for I have something in mind, which at present I cannot reveal. I'll have a contract ready for you after Christmas. Have you money to live on for the time being?"

"Thank you Carla," replied Francisco who was now smiling, "you can rely on me; I will not let you down. As for money, I do have a few thousand lira, but if you could arrange to pay for some accommodation, I will have enough money to last over the holiday period. Thank you for the offer."

"Francisco, we have an account at a local Hotel, I will tell them to expect you," answered Carla, "on Wednesday next week when we reopen and go and see Umberto."

Francisco was absolutely thrilled; he almost kissed both Juliette and Carla, but managed to restrain himself. He thanked Carla for the opportunity she had given him, he would see Umberto on Wednesday morning as arranged, and took his leave of them.

"I would now," began Carla, "like to wind up the meeting. First of all like to thank you Marco and Juliette for your excellent work this year. I have arranged for you both to have an extra bonus apart from the usual staff bonus. I have also arranged to have your salaries increased, and there will be promotion for both of you in the New Year I am sure. Now have a very Merry Christmas and I will see you soon. I am off to spend Christmas and New Year with the family, which I so seldom see. Now Juliette, do keep in touch over the Turin business. I am expecting great things of you. Marco you have not been forgotten, I have plans for you too."

Marco helped Carla on with her silver fox furs and she left the Office to spend her Christmas in the warmth of her family. All over the Holiday Carla could not get Francisco out of her mind; the last thing she wanted was love at first sight. Now this man had come into her life and she was in turmoil. She would be frightened to approach him direct in case he rejected her. She was a rich and successful businesswoman, and now she was seriously thinking about falling in love with a man she had only just met. True he was a very good designer, but her marriage with Dino had put her on guard. She had become angry that her ex-husband had cuckolded her, and the subsequent divorce had made her bitter towards men. Rich handsome men often had approached her since her break-up with Dino, but she had always resisted the temptation. However, her emotions got the better of her, and so she decided to go to the meeting on the following Wednesday when Francisco would meet Umberto.

Over in Venice, Maria was already getting excited about the forthcoming party season. She was always longing try out her new sexual deviations on her 'Dina', who was always a very willing participant. Dino knowing that he would be dressed as Santa Claus, really longed for the time when he would wear that red velvet fur-lined suit. As soon as he saw Maria as Mistress Christmas, it stimulated his sexual urges even further.

In the days leading up the Christmas holiday, it was very cold indeed and Maria insisted that Dina went into the Office dressed as her very Personal Assistant. Every day Maria personally selected Dina's costume, especially the erotic lingerie and furs, which 'she' had to wear. Dina was now working with the other ladies, for her only male sales assistant had given in his notice. She now had Dina making telephone calls to suppliers, all the secretarial work and of course checking the account books.

One evening Maria took Dina to the Theatre dressed in an evening gown, full make up, a long black wig and 'her' new silver fox furs that Maria had 'bought' her own she/male. Dina looked lovely as 'she' got in the taxi. The driver made a pass at Dina and called 'her' Signorina, and so did the usher taking them to Maria's Box. They sat and watched Mozart's opera the 'Magic Flute', whilst Maria smiled to herself and gave occasional adoring glances at her Dina. The Magic Flute was Maria's favourite and very apt because Maria called the tune and Dino's flute rose to the occasion. After the show they went to dinner, where there was a quartet playing for dancing. A handsome young man came over and asked Maria if she could dance with her friend?

Maria thought this very episode very amusing.

"Of course my sister Dina would love to dance with you," said Maria to the handsome young man, "however, please do not take liberties with her, and she cannot go home with you."

Dina got to 'her' feet, adjusted 'her' dress and the young man led 'her' on to the dance floor. He held 'her' very tight as they whirled around, and kept making suggestive remarks in Dina's ear. Little did his partner realise that he was dancing with a man cross dressed as a lady. Maria always made sure that her Dina always looked like an attractive young woman. Maria thought this was great entertainment, as she watched them waltz around together. When Dina came back to their table, she was quite breathless but did not say anything to Maria. The evening as far as Maria was concerned was just perfect. When they got home Maria rewarded Dina for being a 'good girl' by letting her make love to her as her she-male plaything.

The following evening Maria decided to play another prank on Dina. They started drinking early, and Maria ensured that Dina was well and truly drunk. Then she pulled down 'her' sensuous frilly pink bloomers, lifted his dress over his head and put some sticky fluid on his legs. Dina could not remember if 'she' had entered Maria or not. Dina finally surfaced the following morning.

"Don't fret darling Dina," quipped Maria, "last night you had a wonderful time just look at your legs."

Dino could be sure of one thing; his life as Dina with Maria was certainly never dull, for she was always full of sexual surprises.

Soon it was Christmas Eve and time to dress up as their personal Santas, for Maria was having one of her Christmas orgies, and Dino was to play his traditional role in the proceedings.

"Dina my love, apart from being my sexy Santa," said Maria waving her index finger, "my cousin Mariella Salani will be at my party. You will like her for she has, the most beautiful red hair, green eyes and an insatiable sexual appetite, a superb figure and loves you know what. However, if I catch you with her and having your way with her, you know what retribution I can come up with? So be warned."

Dino nodded that he understood. So now he was really looking forward to meeting this Mariella, who must be really exciting sexually. After Maria description here was a chance for extra sexual adventures. Then he thought, if I do not get found out that would be a real bonus.

On the evening of the Party guests began to arrive, with Dino as Santa welcoming them all with and handshake or a kiss, and of course that traditional Santa Greeting.

"Yo ho ho, and a Merry Christmas to you. Enjoy the Party."

When Mariella arrived alone, Dino knew his luck was in. Mariella had just been through a very messy divorce, when her husband Franco was found in his own bed with her best friend's daughter, giving her the business. Mariella had not taken too kindly to this and started putting herself about. Dino thought that at last I have met her at the right time.

Maria introduced her to Dino, who seeing her beautiful breasts beneath her silver fox coat, thought – 'yes I really want to give her what she really wants.' Mariella kissed him, her tongue searching inside his mouth. Their lips parted, her hand reached down to squeeze his crotch.

"Santa," she whispered in his ear, "I have heard a lot about you and I want some of that later."

Luckily for Dino, Maria was out of earshot.

Soon, the party got underway and the drink started to flow, as one by one the guests, including Maria disappeared into various bedrooms to sexually entertain their new partners. Poor old Dino was just sitting there in his Santa costume, with the usual mound in his fur-lined trousers. He was wondering what to do with himself, apart from the obvious. Then help arrived in the shape of Mariella, still wearing her silver fox furs. She sat beside him and reached down inside Dino's trousers and felt something stiff.

Mariella came straight to the point.

"Darling Santa," she said, "forget the foreplay, and let us just do it. If you know what I mean, and I am sure you do."

Dino was absolutely delighted; here was a beautiful woman who wanted to play with his magic wand, as Maria always called it. Mariella knew all the places where one could be alone in Maria's villa; she had been there before. She led Dino upstairs and through a trapdoor into the loft, locking the door behind them. There was a mattress covered with sheets and blankets. She soon had Dino's trousers down around his ankles. Then she climbed on top of him and sucked him dry, and then she wanted even more and more. Dino was happy to oblige; they were up there for hours.

She sighed and moaned with pleasure as she performed on Dino with gusto, and they were both in furry seventh heaven. He had wanted her from the moment he had first seen her.

"Santa," she whispered, "that is a great present you have there. I saw you several times with my cousin, she doesn't deserve you, and I do. I will always be grateful. If you know what I mean."

Dino certainly knew what she meant, and was thrilled to know that another woman wanted him purely for furry sex. Mariella continued to ride Dino until they were both absolutely exhausted.

"My darling Santa," she said pulling up her erotic silk bloomers, "that was really wonderful journey on your sleigh. We must do it again very soon. I will never tell Maria about this, so don't worry."

Mariella gave Dino's crotch one last squeeze, and then helped Dino pull up his trousers. The couple finally made their way down to the main area of the Villa. When they passed the room where Maria and Alfonso were still going strong, and they could hear their sexual groaning quite clearly. Mariella asked Dino if he was coming to her Party on New Year's Eve. Dino said that he would be coming with Maria.

"Wonderful my darling," Mariella replied, "will you take my booking now? I need another trip with you on your sexy sleigh."

"Yes, Mariella," said Dino smiling, "I have made a special note in my diary. I am looking forward to that."

Mariella took him by the hand into a corner, for the room was still deserted. She pulled him towards her, ran her hand inside his trousers and began to massage him again. Dino began to get sexually aroused once more, and wondered what was coming next.

"Darling Santa," whispered Mariella, "I know there is plenty more in there, and I want a lot more on New Year's Eve. I have already made my Resolution, how about you?"

Dino could not wait for his second session with Mariella.

"I must go now my lover," she cooed, "remember I will be anxiously waiting for you. You naughty Santa."

Dino blew her a kiss. Then he lay down on a nearby sofa and fell asleep still in his Santa Claus costume and dreamt of Mariella.

When he woke up the winter sun was streaming in through the windows. He looked down and there was no mound in his trousers. Still wearing his Santa Claus costume he went into the kitchen and made himself some coffee; about three hours later a very bedraggled Maria appeared.

"That Dina," she gasped, "was the greatest sex I have ever had in my life. I have got to judge who is the best you or Alfonso. I do not choose you. You are a very poor second."

Dino didn't care he had given his all to Mariella, and knew that he was on a promise for New Years Eve.

For her cousin's party Maria had another trick up her sleeve, and this would mean Dino's secret cross-dressing would be out in the open once more, this time amongst Maria's friends.

The days passed with Maria teasing her Dina for all she was worth. She made him do the accounts at home dressed as Dina her Secretary. She told him he had to wear a striped blouse with leg of mutton sleeves, a frilled skirt and silk and lacy bloomers. She would wait for the right moment when he was concentrating on the account sheet in front of him, and then pass by opening her skirt up so he could see everything she had. She made him stand up and show her that he was wearing the 'correct' lingerie. When it got colder, she would wear her furs with nothing underneath and play all sorts of tricks on him. She made him add up figures in the account books that she brought home, whilst she aroused him sexually with her furs.

Then the day of the New Year party arrived, Dino started to get really excited at prospect of giving Mariella another injection of what she had had from him at Christmas. Maria too was aroused at the thought that Mariella may have invited another young man to give her even greater satisfaction. After all she could have Alfonso and Dina any time she liked. Her plans for her Dina were a complete cross-dressing makeover. Maria told Dina to wear her best evening dress, with padding in the right places, a superb curly black wig, and of course 'her' new silver fox furs. By the time Maria had finished dressing Dina and attending to her make up, she was sexually aroused herself.

"Now Dina," Maria told 'her', "you must be a good girl and don't get into trouble, otherwise I will have to punish you. You know what that means don't you."

Dino had some idea of what she meant and now was at his limit of sexual containment. He needed relief right now, but Maria told her Dina not to be 'naughty' as they were off to the Party, and there was no time for that sort of thing.

Maria telephoned for a taxi to go to Mariella's villa, which was some 8 kilometres away. The taxi driver started making advances towards both Maria and Dina.

Mariella greeted them at the door in all her furs and finery "Maria darling," said Mariella, "how lovely to see you again. Who is this lovely lady wearing such wonderful furs?"

Maria smiled sweetly and kissed Mariella on the lips.

"This my darling," answered Maria with a sexy smile, "is my new friend Dina, you will really love her for she is so amusing and different from all my other friends."

Mariella did not recognise Dino at first in his party dress and silver fox furs. She hugged and kissed him on the cheeks.

"Darling Dina," said Mariella, "do enjoy the party I will definitely get around to you a little later."

Maria then introduced Dina to all the people at the Party, which soon started to swing and couples, started to disappear. Maria, had now left Dina, and had been taken in tow by a new partygoer, known simply as Luigi. Luigi was a playboy whose family was in the Olive Oil business. No doubt Dino thought he would be very well endowed. Another of Mariella's male guests, a fellow who Dino did not know from Adam, came over to chat and tried to kiss him. Just as their lips were about to meet, Dino reached down between this man's legs, took a handful and squeezed very hard. The man went very red and stifled a scream. Dino thought serves you right. I adore being Dina but no way am I going to get involved with a man. The room emptied slowly, and then Mariella came waltzing across.

"Darling Dina," she said kissing Dina on the lips, "I see you dealt with our lecherous friend? He tries it on with all the women. He is a friend of that Alfonso; the one they call 'the stud.' His name is Luigi; I cannot remember his other name. He is bisexual and he is always turning up and these parties. Sometimes I wish he wouldn't. Anyway you look absolutely stunning, your dress is absolutely beautiful, and those furs are simply gorgeous. However, I do not think we have met before have we?"

Dino was now in a dilemma and felt that he had to explain to Mariella that his crossdressing was Maria's idea, and not the fact that he utterly adored it too. Then he changed his mind.

"Mariella darling, I'm Dino. Maria told me it was fancy dress. So here I am."

Mariella laughed and took another look at him.

"Dino I really did not recognise you. You make a really lovely and convincing woman. Anyway it is time for my second booking with you. Remember? Now follow me."

Mariella took Dino's hand and led him to her secret place, where she lifted up Dina's dress and seeing the gorgeous erotic lingerie began to fully arouse him.

"Dino my darling," she remarked, "I just love your adorable lingerie. I bet you love wearing it?

"Mariella, I love wearing it, it makes me feel special."

"You naughty boy," quipped Mariella, pulling down Dina's erotic bloomers.

Then Dino asked the question he had to ask.

"Won't Maria find out what we are doing?"

Mariella was now climbing on top of him.

"Don't be concerned about Maria," she said, "she will get her fill with Luigi and no mistake. He will keep her occupied for hours. Now that's enough conversation let have some action."

That was all encouragement Dino needed; he was longing to give Mariella all the satisfaction she desired. They began their sexual union until they were finally sexually exhausted. Mariella got up and went over to a cabinet on the wall, poured two drinks and brought them back to Dino.

"Even lovers deserve refreshment Dino," she said.

Having refreshed themselves continued their lovemaking; oblivious to everyone. Mariella said that Maria would never uncover their affair, and she never did.

When they finally finished their lovemaking, Dino decided to tell Mariella the whole story about his cross-dressing and fur fetishes and that Maria called him Dina all the time. As Dino began to tell his story, Mariella listened enthralled and amazed. When he had finished she kissed him and began to arouse him once again.

"Darling," she replied, "I will keep both of your secrets, but I must say that your cross-dressing does sexually excite me intensely too. There will always be a warm part of me for you if you ever need it. If you know what I mean, and I am sure you do. So from now on may I call you Dina whenever we are alone?"

Dino was still very sexily excited, and had certainly enjoyed making passionate love to Mariella.

"Of course Mariella my love! Please call me Dina I'll love that. I will always dress as Dina for you whenever you ask me."

"Hello Dina," said Mariella, "you naughty little girl."

They kissed once more and made their way back to where the main room where the party had begun.

By now all the guests, except for Maria and Luigi had left. Dino tidied himself up, put his furs back on, and then telephoned a taxi. He was home in bed wearing his negligee and bloomers when Maria finally arrived home around midday.

She looked absolutely shattered and flopped on to the sofa.

"Dina that was the most terrific party," she muttered, "I am sexually exhausted, that Luigi was really terrific. Luigi had me so many times and he makes me feel like a real woman, and he is a real man. Much better than Alfonso, and far better than you."

Finally, she wandered into her bedroom, where she collapsed on the bed in her party clothes and fell asleep. Dino strolled into his bedroom, where he sat in an armchair now wearing his silver fox furs over his negligee and was now wondering what the future would hold for him? At the moment, Luigi looked as if he might be a permanent fixture? He would just be 'the House Girl', never the husband? He absolutely adored playing 'Dina', that he had already decided, and he would never change that side of his character. It was Maria who held his future in her pretty little hand, which had a tight grip on him. He dozed off, and decided that he had to accept the inevitable. Whatever the future had in store only time would tell.

With Christmas over, Carla had decided that she would get to the Florence store around 9.30 am, so that she could talk to Umberto and Marco before Francisco arrived.

She looked pretty as a picture in her full-length silver fox coat and accessories. As she alighted from the taxi outside FORUM, the commissionaire tipped his hat.

"Welcome Miss Carla," he said, "it is a delight to see you and a Happy New Year."

"Thank you Carlo," she replied with a smile, "and a Happy New Year to you too."

Carla made her way to Umberto's desk, as Carla approached he got up.

"Carla," said Umberto, "it is lovely to see you. How was your Christmas?"

"Most enjoyable Umberto," replied Carla, "I have decided to come in to the showroom today, as I want to formally introduce Francisco to you and Marco."

"Umberto," said Carla, "can we have the meeting in Marco's Office. It will be more private there. I want to see him first of all."

Carla walked up to Marco's office, and he stood up and helped Carla off with her fur coat, which he hung up on a hanger on the coat stand in the corner of the room.

Carla sat down and began to speak.

"Marco I have been delighted with the way you and Juliette have handled the business here. I have seen your figures over the last six months and sales have gone really well. Today as you know I have Francisco Puccini coming and I think that if he can work well with Umberto then we shall have another excellent designer on our staff. By the way I am promoting you to General Manager here from February 1st, and increasing your salary by 20%, you certainly deserve it."

Marco was astounded at the news.

"Carla," he replied, "I have enjoyed every minute of my time here at FORUM. Thank you for the opportunity you gave to me when I first applied for a job here at your magnificent fashion house. Running the fashion shows here every week has at times been frustrating, but we have pulled the crowds in and the customers. The local papers and the fashion magazines have had nothing but praise for our designs and the quality of our goods. The number of new customers that we are getting, are in the main those who have been recommended to us."

"That Marco," answered Carla, "is due to our training programme for new staff and of course customer relations and service, plus the quality of our goods, which you have already mentioned."

Carla looked at the clock it was 9.55a.m, so Carla got up and went downstairs to rejoin Umberto. On the stroke of 10, Francisco walked through the doors and having removed his hat went straight up to Carla.

"Good morning Carla," he said, "it is an honour to meet you once again."

"Francisco, good to see you. Hope you had a good Christmas, and may I introduce you formally to our chief designer Umberto. I will leave you two to talk and will come back later. I will order coffee for you."

Carla called over one of the shop assistants who was not busy with a customer and asked that she take two coffees over to Umberto. Carla meanwhile went back to speak to Marco. They talked about the business, and then Carla asked Marco to help her on with her furs.

"Keep up the good work Marco," she said, "I do not know whether I have told you, but I have moved Juliette to the new Turin Store. That needs so much work done on it; she is taking a member of the Bank of Italy staff with her to sort things out. There are big problems that we are resolving slowly but surely. The owner Signor Gelazi has got himself into a rather bad state of affairs. The shop has potential, but I fear he does not have the expertise to turn the shop around. In addition to that he has neither the funds nor the will. I shall be going there myself soon, once the lease has expired and we can get down to the redecoration. I shall need to recruit staff there too, the existing staff are pitiful, and could sell ice cream in the summer. I will see you soon Marco".

"Carla" he answered, "it is always a pleasure to welcome our lovely lady boss to the store where she made it all happen for us".

Carla blushed slightly.

"You always were a charmer Marco. Happy New Year."

Carla made here way downstairs and returned to Umberto, who was still talking to Francisco.

"Excuse me gentlemen," said Carla, "I have to go now. Are you two going to be able to work together?"

"We shall be a great team Francisco and I," Umberto replied. Carla smiled and kissed Umberto on the cheek.

"That's what I like about FORUM," answered Carla, "we are one big happy team. Happy New Year gentlemen."

With that Carla walked through the showroom, passing crowds of customers. Carla was content she knew she had picked the right man to work with Umberto. Carla hailed a taxi and returned to her parent's villa, where she would spend New Year. Now she could relax for a few days for she knew that when the holidays were over the hard work in FORUM would begin once more.

She wondered as the taxi took her on her way, what challenges would be coming away. She could not predict the future but she knew she would give her FORUM business 100% effort and she expected nothing less from her staff. Success was in her own hands, and taking on the Turin store that too might bring its own problems too.

Chapter 21

The holiday for both Alain and Rudolph was now over, and the hard work would begin to get the three cars ready for the French Grand Prix at Dieppe on the 25th and 26th June. On January 4th Gustav held a meeting with his three drivers, and their chosen mechanics. Rudolph would have Wolfgang Benz; Alain was partnered with Heinz Schlesser, and Hans with Ludwig Schmit, who had done so well as a team in the Targo Florio. Gustav was going to back his horses both ways.

 "Gentlemen," began Gustav, "this forthcoming Grand Prix, is yet another chance to grab the glory from the French. I know I have said this before, and forgive me for it. The French write the Rules and Regulations, then they organise the event and run it in France. This way they expect to win."

He turned to Alain with an apologetic look on his face.

"Alain my friend," Gustav continued, "this does not reflect on you one bit. It is aimed at those who write the Rules. To you as a Frenchman I can only apologise for these remarks, but I am sure you would agree."

Alain, who had always been patriotic in the past when driving for a French team, now, saw the other side of the coin.

"Gustav," answered Alain, "no need to apologise to me. Even when I drove for Darracq and Peugeot, I felt that we should have Grand Prix races in other countries apart from France. As for the regulations there should be a proper discussion by all parties on how the events should be run and the rules governing the cars themselves. I totally agree with your remarks"

"Thank you Alain, so Gentlemen," continued Gustav, "I have decided to enter three cars for this marathon event. There will be two 3-litre cars with the new 4- speed gearbox will be driven by Rudolph and Alain, and the 5.7 litre by Hans, this too has the new 4-speed gearbox but strengthened to cope with the extra power. This way we can hedge our bets. I have given instructions for the improvements to be made in all areas, including better seats, with much more padding. We shall also tailor the driving positions on the cars to ensure that comfort and control are as the drivers' desire. So let go and get the show on the road, so to speak."

Over the next few weeks, the Development Department burnt the midnight oil. There was a great deal of work to be done. Catherina and Francoise hardly saw their husbands, except at weekends. By early March the two 3-litre models were ready for testing. Rudolph would take the Number 1 Car, to be followed by Alain in the 5.7 Litre.

Early one Monday morning they fired the engine up, and let it run for a few minutes to warm up the oil, whilst Alain did the same with the 5.7 litre machine.

The cars even though they were out in the large courtyard in front of the workshops, made a tremendous sound. It was music to both Alain's and Rudolph's ears. It was great to be back testing and getting their machines ready for the ultimate test in Dieppe. The cars looked good enough, but would they stand up to the battering they would get? Rudolph and his mechanic Wolfgang, climbed aboard the new car, engaged first gear and shot out of the factory gates, closely followed by Alain and Heinz. They had the route planned; it would be a 30-kilometre route, well known to the test drivers. It incorporated all the hazards that they would encounter during the actual race. They estimated that it should take them approximately 20 minutes, giving an average speed of some 90 kph, well within the capabilities of the machines. The first lap went well, Alain keeping a safe distance from Rudolph, there had been some rain overnight, so the wooded sections were a bit slippery, and so both drivers took care and drove well within their limits. By the end of the second lap, they had cut the time down to 15 minutes, which was truly amazing. The cars handled perfectly, with the new wider wheels and four wheel braking, this had made a vast difference to the performance, as they could now brake later, and corner much faster. The cars had been lowered by five centimetres; this had helped no doubt. Rudolph had suggested that add two small thick glass windscreens in front of the driver and mechanic, these would deflect any stones or debris, thrown up from other cars. Gustav incorporated all these little improvements to all three cars. With driver comfort improved, the testing distances increased.

One morning at the beginning of April, Gustav called his two best drivers, Alain and Rudolph into the office for a meeting.

He ordered coffee for them all and when they were all seated he called for silence.

"Gentlemen," began Gustav, "I understand from the reports I have had so far that from you two drivers, that the tests are going very well. I am also delighted with the technical information that I am getting from the Development Department. Now I am going to offer you a break. No not a holiday, we do not have time for that. How would you like to spend some time down at the Aero Engine Division, just down the road?"

Rudolph and Alain nodded their approval then wondered what he was up to. They kept quiet, as they were sure Gustav had a reason, he always had.

"Gentlemen," said Gustav, "I should like you to take a look at our factory there. Have you seen it yet?"

Alain and Rudolph replied to the effect that hadn't.

"I know you have not had time," continued Gustav, "in the circumstances I suggest that you go now, and see the Director Harald Alzen. Have a nice day gentlemen."

Alain and Rudolph borrowed one of the factory cars and drove down to Herr Alzen's office, about 10 kilometres away. The Aero Engine Division was situated in a small complex of buildings; beside which was a large grassy field used an airfield.

Rudolph knocked on the Director's door. A tall, slim man in his early 40's with a clipped moustache, got up from behind his desk and opened the door and greeted them.

"Good morning Gentlemen, my name is Harald Alzen, I am Director here. Would you like refreshment, a glass of wine perhaps?"

"Pleasure to meet you Herr Alzen," answered Rudolph, "thank you we would enjoy a glass of wine."

Harald Alzen opened a large glass fronted cabinet nearby and poured out three glasses. Having handed his guests their wine glasses he returned to his leather-backed chair behind his large desk. Harold and Rudolph thanked Harald and took a sip from their glasses.

"Gentlemen," Harald began taking a sip of his wine, "let me explain a few things to you. Just a few short years ago, the Company set up this new division. It was clear that aircraft would be the transport of the future, although the Motor Car would always be the form of transport for those who did not care to fly. We were very disappointed not to get the contract with Zeppelin, as you know this went to Maybach. I would like to take you around our small factory here and answer any questions you may have. After that I will make you an offer, which I hope you will not refuse. Then we shall have lunch."

Harald showed Alain and Rudolph all around the factory, they were fascinated to see the new developments taking place as far as engine design was concerned, and asked lots of questions. Harald obviously knew his stuff. Finally, having seen everything, they arrived back at Harald's office.

Harald sat down again at his desk.

"Now, gentlemen," asked Harald, "have either of you ever flown?"

"I have left the ground a couple of times," Rudolph jokingly replied, "and that was going too quick over a humped back bridge. Didn't fly far the car was too heavy."

The three men laughed out loud at Rudolph's joke.

"Yes I have done that too gentlemen. No I mean really flying?"

Both of the drivers shook their heads.

"Then Gentlemen," Harald continued, "my offer to you today is for a flight in our little plane. Are you willing to be a passenger with our very experienced Pilot Uwe Danner?"

Alain and Rudolph became very excited and decided to jump at the chance, for here was something completely different.

"Yes please", they said enthusiastically in one voice.

Harald picked up the telephone and spoke to Uwe, who within a minute or so entered Harald's Office. Uwe Danner was a small, slim man in his late 20's. Harald introduced his guests, and they all left the office and made their way to a hanger outside of which stood a small monoplane.

"This little aeroplane," Uwe explained, "is a Bleriot Type XI, which we have modified to take two people, a pilot who sits in front and the passenger behind him. We have replaced the original engine a 25 hp Anzani, with one of our own design that is rated at 45 hp. The original engine suffered badly from overheating, and was not powerful enough for our purposes. We actually bought the plane from the Bleriot factory, some 9 months ago, and it seems very reliable. Having said that, there only remains for you to put on a helmet and goggles and climb aboard."

Uwe handed goggles and helmets to both Alain and Rudolph.

"Right Gentlemen!" Harald shouted, "who wants to be first?"

"I would like to be first," said Alain, "that's if Rudolph does not mind?"

Rudolph nodded his approval. Uwe helped Alain climb into the passenger's seat, and then climbed in himself. The Chief mechanic then appeared and turned the two bladed wooden propeller. Uwe explained to Alain that this was part of the starting procedure. Uwe pushed down a couple of switches and moved the throttle control. After a couple of swings of the propeller the engine coughed into life, and then settled down to a healthy tick-over. Uwe let the engine run for a couple of minutes, so that the oil would warm up. Then he opened the throttle and the little plane gathered speed, and before Alain knew it, the tail had come up and in a few seconds they were airborne. Alain had felt some misgivings as he had climbed into the frail little aircraft. Now as they climbed into the clear blue sky he was enjoying the unique thrill of being aloft. Uwe climbed the plane higher, they were now at almost 1,000 metres, and Alain could now see the main Mercedes factory quite clearly. The houses and animals in the patchwork of fields below, looked like tiny models. Alain felt wonderful and was disappointed that after only about 20 minutes they returned to the field and made a perfect landing. Rudolph meanwhile had watched whole thing, and was a little apprehensive, as he watched the little aircraft take off and disappear into the distance. He was subsequently relieved when the plane reappeared and landed. Uwe climbed down first, and then helped Alain climb down.

"Did you enjoy the flight, Alain?"

"Yes Uwe, that was absolutely wonderful. Thank you."

That made Rudolph feel better, by the time he was in the passenger's seat any fear had left him. Alain watched as the plane took off once more and disappeared in the blue. By the time he had returned Rudolph like Alain, was really hooked on flying. They both asked Harald if there was any chance of them learning to fly?

"I dearly hoped that you would ask that," replied Harald, "I have arranged for Uwe to give you flying lessons starting tomorrow. It will be theory in the classroom to begin with, followed by practice in the aircraft. Flying is like learning to drive; only it is much more dangerous as you will find out. On land when you are driving your racing car, you can change gear and brake to a standstill.

In the air any problems and there is simply no such control. Crash in a car, you will get away with it probably. In a plane crash and you may not survive. If you are taught correctly then problems can be eliminated to a certain degree. After all you would not expect anyone to drive one of your racing machines without proper tuition would you?"

Rudolph and Alain agreed with Harald and were pleased that Uwe would teach them all they needed to be safe in the air. After a short discussion they adjourned for lunch.

In the afternoon back at the airfield office, Uwe gave them some instruction books to read on the theory of flight.

"Take them home and study them," he said most emphatically, "they may well save your life. Everything that must be learned, must be remembered and become second nature if you are to be good pilots. You have succeeded in the world of Motor Racing, now you must apply the same professional approach to your flying.

So go home now and study those manuals carefully. I will see you at 8 a.m, sharp tomorrow for your first lesson in the Classroom. Welcome to the world of flight Gentlemen."

That afternoon, both Alain and Rudolph arrived home early. Francoise and Catherina thought something was wrong. Alain explained to Francoise, how they had been invited along to the Aero Engine Division of the Company and had been given a flight in an aeroplane. Francoise thought this was even more dangerous that Motor Racing. She had read about aircraft crashing and the pilots being killed. Alain told her that they had been given the chance to learn to fly from one of the Company's top pilots. He did not dare tell her that Uwe was probably the only one. He after a while convinced Francoise that it was safe, they would have excellent tuition. Catherina asked the same questions of Rudolph when he broke the news to her. So there was an uneasy peace in the Clement and von Lundenberg household over this flying thing. Somehow, both Alain and Rudolph had to convince their wives that it was safe.

The next morning at 8 a.m. sharp, our two would be pilots turned up at Harald's office. Uwe arrived and led them to a room nearby that was used as a lecture hut. There was a blackboard, a table and two chairs.

"Good morning Gentleman" said Uwe, "now have you read the books that I gave you yesterday?"

"Yes Uwe," replied Alain and Rudolph, "we read them from cover to cover, very interesting and informative."

Excellent," answered Uwe, "then I shall begin, and please make notes in the books in front of you. Keep them safe."

Over the next hour or so Uwe explained how planes could fly even though they were heavier than air. Then, how the planes were controlled, and the need to take off into wind. Next came dangers from the elements, the importance of navigation, knowing where you are, plus a host of other things. Alain and Rudolph, both of who were very meticulous, so they wrote everything down, to study later. Uwe then took them out to the aircraft to explain how the controls worked etc.

During the course of the next few days they learned a great deal about flying, and by Thursday they had each taken the controls and were flying under instruction from Uwe. Harald called them into the Office on Friday afternoon to assess their progress.

"You two are my star pupils," he told them, "nobody has ever learnt to fly as quickly as you. This weekend why not bring your wives down to the field and let them see how safe it is for themselves. They may even like a short flight with Uwe, who knows?"

Alain and Rudolph said they would invite their ladies, as for a flight, well they would ask.

On arriving home Alain and Rudolph gave their wives the invitation, Francoise said she would love to have a flight in a plane. Rudolph made out to Catherine that he knew that Francoise had agreed to a flight.

"Rudolph," said Catherina, "if Francoise has agreed then so will I if young Manfred can come too."

So on Saturday morning with both Ladies dressed in their warmest furs, they all set off for the airfield. They assembled at Harald's office and all the introductions were made. First Rudolph went off for his flight with Uwe instructing, followed by Alain. The ladies thought how peaceful it was after all the noise and excitement of Motor Racing. When Alain returned, Francoise put on the helmet tucking her hair inside it as best she could, and then goggles. Uwe helped her climb aboard and settled into the passenger's seat and soon the little plane was airborne. Francoise had no fear at all; she loved being aloft in the clear blue sky, looking down on the fields and houses below.

When she returned she was very excited.

"Thank you Uwe," she gasped, "that experience was simply breathtaking. Catherina you will love it."

At that moment Catherina was putting on the helmet and goggles and she smiled at Francoise. Uwe then helped Catherina climb into the aeroplane; she was not so sure that this was a good idea as she settled in the passenger's seat. However, she could not lose face, after all Francoise said she had loved it. Uwe shouted a few words of encouragement, but her heart was still pounding as the engine revved up and the little plane gathered speed. So she closed her eyes tightly, then all of a sudden they were flying. Catherina felt that now she could open her eyes, and she looked down to see the landscape laid out before her like a map. Her heart rate got back to normal and she started to really enjoy the flight, with the wind whistling past her head. By the time they returned to the field, with yet another perfect landing, she was really excited.

"Francoise." said Catherina, "you are right. I loved it."

The practical demonstration had worked, and now it was time for a slap up lunch. Over lunch, the conversation turned to the great sensation of flying. Both Catherina and Francoise said that they would like to do it again sometime.

The weekend passed very quickly as they had a habit of doing. On Monday morning Gustav asked Alain and Rudolph, how they had enjoyed their week. They all agreed it was great. Gustav said that now they had learned to fly he wanted them both to get a Pilot's licence, this could be very useful. So each Friday, weather permitting they should spend the morning with Uwe, to put in the required number of flying hours. Then take the necessary written examinations that were just coming into force. During the rest of the week they must test, test and test again to make sure the cars entered for the French Grand Prix were the best they could be. So it was back to the grindstone.

By the end of April the two 3-litre cars were ready, so Alain, Rudolph with their mechanics on board led Hans in the 5.7 litre model out on a final test. They did 4 laps of the 30-kilometer course and got the time down to under 15 minutes, this was an unofficial course record. Now they were looked forward to the ultimate test, which of course was the race itself. This would take place over two days, Tuesday and Wednesday the 25th & 26th June 1912.

The race was being held in Dieppe, a town on the English Channel, Gustav thought it would be a nice gesture to invite all the Driver's family members to the race. After all Alain's family did not live that far away. Alain asked if he could invite Rudolph and his family to stay with him in his parent's home near Rouen. They could then motor to the circuit. Gustav agreed, and it was arranged. The cars would be sent by special train, and be loaded on to wagons designed especially for the purpose. Whilst the mechanics, support staff and Hans would travel in luxury carriages owned by the Company.

Alain, Francoise, Rudolph and Catherina set off by early express train from Stuttgart to Paris on Wednesday 20th June 1912, the train carrying the cars, spares, tyres and the rest of the support staff plus Hans would leave the next day.

For the two families and especially young Manfred, it was an enjoyable ride, despite the fact that it was a long one.

The border crossing went smoothly, the officials even having a joke with young Manfred. They saw little of the French Capital, for all it was a quick change of trains at the Gare du Nord.

Finally, late on Wednesday night so tired and not quite exhausted they were pleased to have arrived at their destination Rouen. Mind you, Manfred had slept on and off for most of the journey. The taxi from the Station dropped them off at the Clement farmhouse, where they all got an extremely warm welcome indeed. Marie had laid on a splendid meal for them all. Even though they were tired, they enjoyed Marie's home cooking and during the meal the conversation really flowed. Manfred was put to bed and slept the clock round. Alain, Francoise, Rudolph and Catherina having finished their meal were shown to their rooms. Here they undressed and fell asleep almost at once. It had certainly been a long day.

The morning had already started by the time everyone was awake. The rooster in the farmyard had been making his calls for some time; everyone was so tired that they did not even hear him. Marie had made breakfast; Pierre said that he had received a telephone call from Count Guy, who had invited them all for dinner that evening at the Chateau. Catherina was looking forward to that she had never been in a Chateau before.

When her late husband, was doing business, he never took her out of Germany. The day wore on, and they all sat out in the garden, enjoying the warm summer sunshine, whilst Pierre made sure that there was plenty of refreshment on hand.

That evening they dressed up in their finery, the Count's car arrived; they all climbed aboard and headed for the Chateau. On the steps the Count and Countess greeted their guests. He was delighted that at last Alain was driving for a winning team. Over dinner the Count and Countess wanted to hear all the news plus of course all the gossip. He was intrigued that both Alain and Rudolph had learned to fly; this was something that Guy had planned, but never achieved. He asked about the forthcoming race as well.

"Guy," Alain explained, "if I may call you by your first name. I have an invitation from Mercedes for all of us to go to see the race in Dieppe. You will all be in the VIP enclosure. There will be plenty of refreshments of course. The event lasts two days, and the day prior to that, will be for practice. It will be a very long and tiring race indeed. The Company has booked you all into a Hotel from Sunday night until Thursday morning. Do you all accept this invitation?"

He laid the letter of invitation on headed paper upon the table in front of the Count. The Count picked the letter up and read it, and a smile beamed across his face.

"This is wonderful!" he exclaimed, "I will arrange transport us for all to Dieppe. It will be a great event to watch. I remember Alain, that very first motor race we saw together back in July '94. Goodness me how things have changed. I have not had a chance to see another race for years."

So, it was all arranged. After a couple of day's rest the fray would begin. They set off early on Sunday morning and arrived in Dieppe by lunchtime. The small seaside town was filling up with race fans; all the Hotels and Boarding Houses were crowded, as a very large number of spectators were expected. The Count's Party had checked in at the Grand Hotel du Plage and was soon settled into their suites of rooms.

Alain and Rudolph had their course notes from the previous race back in 1908, they were certain that no improvements had been made to the roads. It would a very tortuous circuit full of hazards, and fraught with danger no doubt. The recalled the 1908 event, which had certainly been no Sunday drive. When they had finally unpacked Rudolph had a telephone call, it was Gustav making sure that they had all arrived OK. He told them he would be having a briefing at 5 pm, in the Hotel's meeting room, all the team and the mechanics would be expected to attend. He would outline the problems that he envisaged and inform them of the race plan and strategy.

The meeting started exactly on time, Gustav had always been a stickler for timekeeping and hated lateness, which he considered being disrespectful. The small room was crowded everyone eager to hear what Gustav had to say. Behind him was a blackboard; on the table in front was a pile of papers.

Alain, Rudolph and Hans knew that when Gustav held a meeting, he really had something to say. Sometimes he was a man of few words, and at other times he would lay things out chapter and verse. They all felt that in view of the importance of the Practice that would start early the following morning, plus two race days, it was most likely to be a chapter and verse job. They were not wrong. There was a buzz of conversation in the room before the meeting began. Gustav got to his feet and opened the meeting, and called for silence.

"Gentlemen," he began, "can I start by reminding everyone that this is a team effort. Everything is to be checked and double-checked. The cars have left the factory in pristine condition, before any practice takes place, drivers should check their own cars with their mechanics. Do forget check oil and water levels, clutch adjustment, brakes you know the drill. No pit stops. Refuelling, check that you had the right fuel. Do not wait until you are very low on fuel. Remember the lap length. There is no excuse for running out of fuel, and that goes for oil too. Someone could always 'spike our guns'. Remember that we are in France. Sorry Alain. They do not like us much anyway. They run the races and write the Rules, so be prepared. Rudolph, will you say a few words, as a very experienced driver you know a few tricks."

Rudolph cleared his throat and got to his feet.

"I can Gentlemen," he began, "only to echo the excellent information that Gustav has shared with us today. Above all the Rules and Regulations for this event must be adhered to. Some competitors try to cheat and run you off the road. When I took part in the 1908 race, I made course notes, and these I found absolutely invaluable. I doubt whether the course has changed and the French have repaired the surface. I recall that the road surfaces were terrible. So I have passed copies of my pace notes to the mechanics of the other two cars in the race. This gives both speed and hazard information. The mechanics should shout these out to the driver. I know this may be difficult due to the noise. Try your best. I hope this will give us the edge we need. Official practice starts tomorrow; they have only allowed us three hours to learn this 76-kilometre course. That is almost impossible in the time allowed. I suggest that you need to cover at least 4 laps. One standing start and one flying lap then come in check everything, and then go out again. The fastest lap in 1908 was just over 36 minutes. You should be looking at a lap time of about 36 minutes or less. Have a good race gentleman. Let's win in style."

Rudolph now resumed his seat.

"Gentlemen," Gustav continued, "Rudolph is absolutely correct. His words and notes are worth their weight in gold. He completed this race in 1908, but this year it will be doubly difficult because the race is twice the distance. Keep your course notes safe and use them. See you in the garage at 6.00 a.m., practice starts at 7 o'clock sharp. So don't be late. Sleep well everyone, you will need it to be on your mettle tomorrow."

Alain and Rudolph rejoined Count Guy and his party who were sunning themselves in the Hotel grounds. Rudolph poured a drink for Alain and himself.

"By gosh!" he exclaimed, "I really need this drink. The race will be a gruelling one and no mistake. Alain I know we can win."

The conversation then got underway once more, and the Count was really intrigued and wanted to know all about the race.

"Guy," replied Alain, "if you really want to know what it will be like, then be at the start line at 7 a.m. The atmosphere there will be unbelievable. I shall look for you in the VIP enclosure."

The next morning to Alain's surprise, the Count appeared for breakfast just as Alain, Rudolph and Hans were leaving the Hotel and making their way to their garage at the back of the Grandstand.

"See you fellows later," he shouted as they passed him.

The garage was a hive of activity as the three drivers arrived. The mechanics had been there about an hour already, tightening up this and checking that. Rudolph asked his mechanic if he had made the following checks, and handed him a list. Wolfgang said everything had been double-checked including tyre pressures. The team was now satisfied that all that could be done had been done. Now they were ready to go to the start line, there was 15 minutes to go. There was 30 entries altogether, after practice only the top 20 would be allowed to compete. The laps would be timed, both from a standing start and the flying lap. In the case of a tie, they would add the 4 laps together and divide the result by 4. Rudolph carried Number 1, Alain Number 2, and Hans 3.

As they made their way passed the various garages, Alain was surprised to see an entry from the Peugeot factory; it was an L76, and a development of the car he had driven a while ago. He had a quick look at it. Peugeot had made several improvements suggested by Alain. He wondered if they could be a threat to Mercedes. The driver was Georges Boillot, and then there was the three-car Sunbeam team of Victor Rigal, Dario Resta and Emil Medinger. The only other top drivers were David Bruce Brown, who had won the American Grand Prix in 1910 and 1911 and Louis Wagner both in FIAT S74s. The rest of the field was made up with some private entries, some of the cars looked as if they would have a problem completing one lap let alone 20.

All the cars were lined up in a long line, as the starter flagged them away; each driver was allotted a start time that would be 30 seconds after the vehicle in front of them. Each competitor being allotted the three hours of practice. Being Number 1, Rudolph's engine had already been running for a few minutes, now as the flag dropped for the start of practice, the engine note rose to a crescendo as he engaged first gear and disappeared down the start and finish straight in a cloud of dust.

Alain now drove gently up to the line, out of the corner of his eye he saw the Count waving at him, Alain waved back. Then his eyes were on the starter who raised his flag as the engine revs mounted, Alain engaged first gear, flag fell and Alain felt the power of his machine shoot him forward. The car quickly gathered speed, with the mechanic holding on for dear life and clutching his course notes. They approached the first corner,

Alain slowed down, changed gear and in a flash they were back to speed again. In the distance Alain could see Rudolph's dust cloud; he knew that by keeping it in view he would be able to match Rudolph's lap time.

Meanwhile Rudolph was having a great run, for with nobody in front of him; he could really get a move on. He realised that he must drive within safe limits of his car; an accident now would be a disaster. He tore on through small towns and villages, with his mechanic shouting in his ear and giving hand signals concerning future hazards ahead. Alain too was keeping up a hot pace. Behind the two 3 litre cars, Hans was doing well; he had caught up with Alain, but maintained a safe distance behind Alain's dust cloud. Count Guy was straining his eyes to get a glimpse of Rudolph and Alain steaming by the start and finish line.

He reckoned that now 30 minutes had passed that they would be coming soon. Then he heard the sound of a racing car engine coming from over a rise in the ground some distance away. The sound got louder and louder, then it became deafening as Rudolph and Wolfgang's car hurled by on their flying lap. He did not have long to wait before Alain sped into view; he was only 20 seconds behind Rudolph, and going like the wind. The third car in the team with Hans at the wheel came into view, and roared its defiance at the half-empty grandstand as Hans roared in pursuit of his team mates.

Then cars starting going by thick and fast, everyone hell bent on putting up the fastest time. By the time Rudolph had reached the wooded section, he noticed several competitors had already crashed into trees; one car further round the lap had gone through a fence into a field. Whilst another had gone off the road and rolled down an embankment into a river. At the end of the lap all the Mercedes team whizzed past the finish line and made for the pits. The mechanics swarmed over the cars like ants. The drivers were asking them to check this and that, so that they could get out again to complete the practice session. It seemed even to the layman, that the trio of cars from Mercedes was streets ahead of the opposition.

Gustav was fussing around the garage like a Mother hen.

"Don't count your chickens," he shouted at the top of his voice, "there is a long way to go yet. Do not forget to check, check and check again. Get out on the track only when you are ready."

Alain was first away this time and really got the hammer down, the car was running like oiled clockwork, the roadholding was superb, and he completed his two laps well within the time allowed. Rudolph too was happy with the set up and put in a very good time. Hans struggled a bit but finished only 30 seconds behind Rudolph.

When the results were announced Alain had put up the best time and would start in pole position, Rudolph was second, Hans third, behind them came Boillot in the Peugeot, Wagner, Bruce Brown followed by the three Sunbeams. The race would be interesting, for Alain now had the distinct advantage of being on the first row with Rudolph; they would have a clear road in front of them.

The cars were now in the garage and again the mechanics were checking everything. They had the fuel supplies under lock and key, and locks had been placed on the fuel fillers on the cars themselves. The organisers of the event to prevent sabotage had posted Security Guards.

That night not one of the Mercedes drivers had a good night's sleep, for to win the French Grand Prix would be a prize above all. They had worked very hard to get their cars to perfection. The test would be 1500 kilometres of French roads that had not been resurfaced for years. The practice had shown that to be true. They were pleased with their times, the best lap by Alain was made at an average speed of 120 kph, Rudolph had managed 119 and Hans came in at 118. The best of the rest was Georges Boillot in the Peugeot L76 at 115 kph. Still this was just 4 laps of practice, now there would be 10 laps tomorrow and another 10 the following day of very hard racing.

At the end of the first day the cars would be locked away until the start of the second day's racing. Then only 20 minutes would be allowed for any maintenance, plus a check for tyres and fuel etc. All these things were on their mind as they tried to sleep.

Early next morning, they all eat a hearty breakfast. The Count and his party made their way to the VIP enclosure for the start of the race scheduled for 10.00 a.m. The team garage had been extremely busy for about 3 hours before Alain, Hans and Rudolph arrived at 8.30. The mechanics assured their drivers that everything was perfect, Alain looked over his car, and all seemed well enough.

So he left the garage along with Rudolph to go and see the Count and their family, all of who were very excited at seeing an International Motor Race. At 9.15, Alain and Rudolph made their way back to the garage, for at 9.30 the cars had to be in their prescribed places for the start of the race. Engines were started and the one by one the cars made their way to the starting grid. This gave a chance for the VIPs to take a close look at the cars.

Count Guy and Claudine were fascinated by the size of some of the cars. Young Manfred wanted to sit in his daddy's car and Francoise, just wanted to give her husband a big kiss before the race began.

At 10 minutes to go, an official cleared the grid of all parties not taking part in the race; this left just the drivers and mechanics. The time seem to pass slowly to Alain and Rudolph, until they noticed an official hold up a sign that stated there was 5 minutes to go, and a request to start engines. The mechanics dismounted from the cars, and as if in a rehearsed ballet. Then they swung the starting handles and 20 engines burst into life, sending up a wall of sound that ricocheted off the tiers in the Grandstand.

Then it was 2 minutes to go. Finally, with just 30 seconds to go starter slowed mounted the rostrum carrying the tricolour. He consulted his watch, and as he raised the flag the sound increased to deafening proportions. The Tricolour seemed to be frozen in space for a few seconds before it swept down. Alain had his eyes glued to the flag as he held the clutch down and put the car into gear. As the flag finished its downward path, he was gone in a cloud of dust with Rudolph was following in his wheel tracks. Hans meanwhile had a good start and was tucked in behind Rudolph. Both Alain and Rudolph knew there were only a few places that cars were able to pass on this sinuous circuit. So if they could keep the competition at bay, then they had a chance to finish in the top three places on the first day. Alain was keeping up a furious pace, but at the same time was driving well within the capabilities of himself and his car. They thundered through small towns and villages, the locals staring in awe as the cars flashed by at breakneck speed. Ahead, Alain saw the start and finish straight; he gave a 'thumbs up' as he passed the Grandstand travelling in excess of 140 kph, the engine sounding absolutely on song.

Close behind him was Rudolph and then just 10 seconds later was the third Mercedes of Hans Lang. The rest of the field was barking at his heels. After the professional teams had started their second lap, there was a gap of some 5 minutes until the first of the amateur drivers a Claude Moreau went by in his Renault, followed closely by several others, who were the best of the rest. Count Guy counted 17 cars that had completed the first lap. He wondered what had happened to those that had fallen by the wayside?

Alain was now well into lap 2, he passed two cars that had hit each other trying to pass on a corner; they had gone straight on up a slip road and hit a tree. The other car to fail on the first lap had got a puncture and the crew was struggling to remove the wheel. They waved at Alain and he continued on his way. Rudolph was slowly but surely catching Alain, even Hans had made up time, and was close behind Rudolph. Lap 2 ended without incident. Then lap 3 and Alain, Rudolph and Hans were lapping at speeds in excess of 110 kph, they were leaving the competition in their dust. Alain, by the time he had completed lap 4, was some 30 seconds ahead of Rudolph and Hans Lang. Alain came into his pit, to refuel and change tyres, that were looking decidedly second hand, and would definitely not have survived another lap. Just as he completed his stop and was about to leave, Rudolph came into his pit; he had a slight oil leak, luckily it was just a loose connection. The mechanic fixed this and having refuelled and changed wheels he set off in hot pursuit of Alain. Next in was Hans for the same service; his car was running well, on the tyres that were threadbare. Then he too was swiftly away. Now all the cars were coming in for their routine stops, now only 12 were now left of the 20 that started. The Count wondered how many would finish? After all this was only the first day. Alain carried on reeling off the last laps, passing more cars that had cried enough, or the drivers had misjudged the corners and crashed. At last the chequered flag fell, and Alain breathed a sigh of relief, close behind only 15 seconds back was Rudolph, and another 10 seconds back was Hans Lang. He had driven a splendid race. Now tomorrow they had to do it all over again.

Some of the other drivers were absolutely exhausted, their cars looked tired too. Before the cars were locked away for the night, the team was allowed to check to ensure that their cars were fit to participate in Part 2 of this marathon. The Mercedes mechanics went over every nut, bolt and clip on their cars, for nothing would be left to chance. They had a golden opportunity to win this event now they lay in the first three places. They had been racing for almost 7 hours, to Alain, Rudolph and Hans; it felt more like 7 days. True the improved seating had helped, but with fairly stiff suspension, driving over the rough French roads was like riding a bicycle over a cobbled street.

The Drivers all retired to the Hotel where they refreshed themselves and soaked in a lovely hot bath to take away their aches and pains of a very torrid and exhausting first day of this Grand Prix. They all said that they ached in places they never knew they had, and eventually they joined the rest of the Count's party

"Alain," asked Guy, "how do you feel?"

"Guy, I feel like I have been run over by a truck. That race is an absolute nightmare. However thought it up, should try driving in it, 1500 kilometres at those speeds is a real killer. To think we have got to do it all again tomorrow. The only consolation if there is one is that Rudolph's pace notes are a godsend."

The party continued with the competing drivers staying sober.

That night the drivers slept like the proverbial logs, they agreed having a sleepless night, would only make them more tired when it came to the race on the morrow.

The next day was rather a case of déjà vu, for not only the Count and his party but also the Mercedes team and no doubt the other competitors as well. Overnight 3 more privately entered cars had been withdrawn; the field was now down to 12, the three Mercedes, three Sunbeams, three Peugeots, two FIATS and one private entry an Excelsior. At the appointed hour the cars were released from the Parc Ferme, where they had been left overnight. The weary mechanics in the garages now had 30 minutes to check their cars before drivers were asked to bring their cars to the start line.

The Mercedes team had checked everything as usual, with Gustav still fussing around.

He insisted that they be washed, before the race began again, so that any slight oil leak might be detected.

The race began as it had started the previous day, with Alain in the lead, Rudolph second and Hans third, the three Peugeots snapping at their heels. The race strategy that had been successful on Day 1 was now adopted for Day 2. The problem was how to prevent the three cars pitting on the same lap. It was decided that Alain would pit on Lap 5, with Rudolph and Hans on Lap 4. So they filled Alain's car fuel tank almost to the brim, whilst Rudolph's would have a slightly lighter fuel load. Would it make a difference, only time would tell? Alain was now thundering along, with the car running as well as ever, going around the corners as if one rails. He had already passed two Peugeots that had given up the ghost; the third one must be behind him somewhere.

He knew that he had the best drivers in Europe behind him and that he where he wanted to keep them. Rudolph was chasing after Alain as hard as he could but could not catch up with him try as he might. He could not understand this, for the cars were identical. Hans was catching Rudolph, but he knew that passing him would not endear him to the management. So he kept his distance, whilst his mechanic kept an eye on the opposition that was getting ever closer. Their nearest rival at this stage was David Bruce-Brown in the FIAT, he was driving flat out and would soon fall by the wayside as the car would not stand the pace being set by the leading trio. Alain went by the Grandstand in a cloud of dust, swiftly followed by Rudolph and Hans, and then 10 seconds later came the FIAT of David Bruce-Brown, with its engine sounding a bit rough. Then the three Sunbeams in line astern, finally the second FIAT; there was no sign of the Excelsior, or the third Peugeot that had seemly expired out of sight of the crowds in the Grandstand. The trio of Mercedes reeled off Laps 2 and 3, and then Rudolph pulled in to the pits, had his service and resumed the race, with new tyres and a full tank of fuel, that should be enough to last the remaining six laps. Then Hans came in and had the same treatment and was away again. He had lost over 3 minutes to Rudolph, the car sounded fairly healthy, but he complained that it would not run at full throttle for long. He thought it sounded like fuel starvation. Gustav told him not to worry; he had time in hand over the next competitor who was over 8 minutes down the road.

Hans pulled away from his pit in the fruitless chase of Rudolph. On the next lap Alain streaked into the pits, the mechanics were ready and waiting for him.

They checked his tyres; they still had some rubber on them. Gustav knew he would only last the race if new tyres were fitted. The mechanics set to work and in just over 2 minutes he was away again with new wheels and rubber. Alain now felt confident that may be victory in this race could be his, for he was still in first place with 5 minutes now in hand over Rudolph. Hans meanwhile was having problems, and on the next lap as he passed the Grandstand the car ground to a halt. They pushed the car into the pits, pulled open the bonnet, and there was the problem staring them in the face. It seems a stone had been thrown up by the front wheels and severed the fuel line. Hans's race was over; there was nothing they could do. Now it was up to Alain and Rudolph to uphold the reputation of the Company.

The fantastic thing was that there were now no French cars in the race; they had been hoisted by their own petard. Either way it would be a victory for Germany, Italy or England now.   Alain was now on his way to victory, thought Count Guy and crossed his fingers for luck. Rudolph was driving very hard trying to make a race of it, for he knew that providing Alain's car kept going, and there was no doubt it would, then the best he could hope for would be second place. Still it would be a team effort and no time for sour grapes. Alain knocked off the final laps with clockwork like regularity. Rudolph was on his last lap, when he felt a strange feeling in the steering, the mechanic pointed to one of the back wheels, the tyre was going down and there was nothing they could do apart from change the wheel. If they did this they could well not finish second. Rudolph had changed wheels out on the road before it took a good deal longer than the pit crew. They had just two miles to go to the finish. Alain had already received the chequered flag as the winner. Rudolph pushed his car to the limit, as he struggled to keep control, for he knew the 3rd place car was not that far behind. With a final thrust he crossed the line to the cheers of the crowd, he only just made it as Louis Wagner in the FIAT crossed the line just one minute behind him, followed by the three Sunbeams some 10,11, and 20 minutes later. They were the only finishers. The Sunbeam team won the team prize whilst Alain went up to collect the biggest cup he had ever won.

The first person to congratulate Alain was Rudolph. It had been a Herculean effort by them all. Alain congratulated Rudolph for his courage in getting his car across the finish line in second place, especially after his puncture not far from the finish.

Now they could celebrate in style back at the Hotel. Gustav was delighted, although it was a shame about Hans not finishing; he could have been third. Next time we shall redesign that fuel line so that problem does not arise again. Then Gustav bought drinks all round at the Hotel, this was very rare, for neither Alain nor Rudolph have ever seen Gustav so elated. Whilst the celebrations were taking place, a gentleman in a suit and a waxed moustache approached Alain.

"Are you Alain Clement?" he asked.

Alain nodded, for he wondered who this fellow could be? He did not recognise him at all.

"You must excuse me Monsieur," the stranger continued, " for this intrusion on your celebrations. May I introduce myself to you? My name is Gaston Le Strange, and I am in business here in Dieppe. I wonder if we can talk somewhere private for a few minutes. I hope that you do not mind?"

Alain still had a puzzled look on his face as the stranger held out his hand and Alain grasped it firmly and shook it.

"Monsieur Le Strange," replied Alain, "I can just spare a few minutes. For as you can see we are celebrating our victory in the Grand Prix here today."

The two men then walked off to a side room. Once they were inside Le Strange closed the door behind them.

"Monsieur Clement," said Le Strange, "my reason for wanting to speak to you is this."

Le Strange paused for a moment and suggested that they sat down in the two armchairs by the picture windows.

"Some friends and I," continued Le Strange, "are very interested in getting an entry into this new competition for seaplanes. It is called the Schneider Trophy. Maybe you have heard of it. The French newspapers have had several articles about it. It is a very prestigious international event."

"Yes," answered Alain, "I must confess I have read something about the event. Why do you want to talk to me?"

Alain was still wondering what Le Strange was going to ask him, although he had a pretty good idea.

"We know you are a good pilot," Le Strange continued, "and we would like you to pilot our plane in this event. It would mean doing some practising here in Dieppe. I know you have responsibilities to Mercedes. When do you think you can give me an answer? We are quite short of time on this."

Alain thought for a moment, now this was something he really did not want to get involved in. He could fly that was true, but this really was a specialised form of flying. There was a moment or two of silence, before Alain answered.

"Monsieur Le Strange, I will let you know in a week or so if that is satisfactory with you? I want to speak to my Team Manager, I am sure that you understand that?"

"Certainly Monsieur Clement," answered Le Strange, "and thank you for your time; can I say that it has been an honour to meet you. I shall await your response."

With that Gaston Le Strange shook Alain's hand and bade him au revoir. Alain returned to the Count's party, by now Rudolph and Hans had washed and were feeling almost human once more after a really gruelling race.

When Alain finally made it back to Françoise's side she was listening to a conversation that Count Guy was having with an Englishman. Alain wondered who this Englishman could be, for the Count was talking to him in English. The Count stopped talking for a moment and said to the Englishman.

"Lord John, may I introduce my good friend, Alain Clement? Alain, this gentleman is Lord John Ashdown, and the Lady talking to the Countess is his wife Lady Victoria. They came over here for the race. They were in the VIP enclosure, as my guests, my winery sells to Lord John who is in the Wine Trade and owns what the 'English' call 'pubs'. Like our wine bars."

"Monsieur Clement, said Lord John in perfect French shaking Alain firmly by the hand, "it is a great pleasure to meet you at last. I think that your performance today in that gruelling race was nothing short of magnificent. Your colleagues too certainly showed the opposition what a really professional team can achieve."

"It is an honour to meet you too sir," replied Alain in English, "thank you for your praise. We all try to do our best for the team. I must confess it is the longest and most tiring race I have ever competed in. We were extremely lucky to win."

"Alain, I hope you do not mind that I call you by your Christian name?"

"Not at all Lord John."

"Alain, I have just had the pleasure to meet your wife Francoise, she is certainly a beautiful young woman."

"Lord John, she is the love of my life."

"Then Alain, I would like to introduce you to the love of my life, my wife Victoria."

By now Francoise and Victoria who had been in conversation made their way back to their husbands. John took Victoria by the hand and led her over to meet Alain.

"My darling, this young man is Alain Clement. He won the race today."

Alain bowed and kissed the back of Victoria's hand.

"Lady Victoria," replied Alain in English, "it is a great pleasure to meet such a lovely lady. I hope you enjoyed the race. I understand you have a son and a daughter, I hope that they are well?"

Victoria was surprised that Alain spoke such good English as she had met very few Frenchmen who managed to speak English.

"They are both well thank you Alain. My son is still at School and hopes to go to University soon. Do you have children Alain?"

"Not at the moment. Perhaps soon Madam, who can tell?"

The Party began to break up, for everyone was tired, but as the room emptied Count Guy and Alain were standing on the balcony looking at the sun setting over the sea.

"Pardon me for asking Alain," began the Count, "but who was that strange Gentleman you were talking to earlier. He was certainly not one of our Party was he?"

Alain thought for a moment and realised that he had nothing to hide, after all the race for the Schneider Trophy was not a secret.

"Well sir," replied Alain, "that man was a Gaston Le Strange his is a local businessman. He and a group of wealthy friends want to make an entry in a seaplane race; it is called the Schneider Trophy. They want me to be the pilot. They know that I can fly, where they have found that out from is a mystery too. Anyway, I do not feel qualified to take part in a race which needs specialised flying skills. The race is to take place next April 16th in Monaco.

The winner will receive a large bronze sculpture, and Monsieur Jacques Schneider will donate this prize. It seems that the organisers are the Aero Club de France, who have also published the Rules. Quite honestly I have enough on my plate with Mercedes, but I have already given the matter some thought. He wants me to test fly this plane. My flying instruction at Mercedes had told me all about the dangers of flying. So I will tell him – **No**. I consider it far too dangerous."

The Count listened intently to what Alain had said.

"I agree Alain that you have made the right decision. The flight could be a disaster. You could crash and may be lose your life."

The two men now returned to their wives, who were now talking to Lord John and Victoria. Lord John was in a small group with Rudolph and Catherina, whom he knew through his business dealings. Lord John then asked the group.

"Are you all going to be at Brooklands for the September meeting?"

"Lord John," answered Rudolph, "it has been agreed that if we all survived this French Grand Prix, then we would race at Brooklands. We are all looking forward to that event."

Lord John smiled, and was delighted that they would all meet again at Brooklands. It would certainly be a spectacle.

"In that case Gentlemen," said Lord John, "I want you all to be my personal house guests at Ashdown Hall, and that includes your wives and of course the most important man in your team, Gustav Schumann."

Gustav who had been fairly quiet up to this moment went over and shook Lord John's hand firmly.

"Lord John," said Gustav, "I know we have not said much to each other. I am Gustav Schumann and I shall be taking my team to Brooklands. I would like to thank you for your very kind invitation. My wife will be so thrilled to meet a real Lord and Lady and staying at your wonderful home."

The Party began to break up as the guests made their way to their rooms for a rest. Francoise and Alain, Catherina and Rudolph just collapsed on their beds.

"That was a great race," said Rudolph to Catherina, "and a great party. Alain deserved to win, ironic though, a Frenchman in a German Car won the race. Not a French Car finished."

"Never mind all that give me a kiss, darling Rudolph, I deserve it."

Rudolph smiled and he came close to her.

"You deserve more than that."

So they made love, and then fell fast asleep.

Alain in the next suite gave Francoise a big kiss too.

"You will always be a winner with me," Francoise whispered, "now it is time to make love."

Alain nodded his approval. So both couples now celebrated by making passionate love.

The French Grand Prix was now over for another year; they awaited the next challenge.

Early the next morning the team cars were already loaded on the special train that would take them back to Canstatt. Later that morning after a hearty breakfast in the Hotel, Alain, Francoise, Rudolph and Catherina caught the train from Dieppe to Paris, then the express to Stuttgart. For Alain the nightmare of an event, had turned into a dream result.

By the time they arrived home Alain and Francoise, were ready for bed, it had been another long day.

Just as they were about to get into bed Francoise was still intrigued about Alain's conversation with a stranger at the Hotel.

"Darling at the Hotel who was that man with the moustache, who asked to speak to you privately?"

Alain was puzzled for a moment, as he did not realise that Francoise had such good hearing.

"Well my love, that man was a Monsieur Le Strange, a Dieppe businessman. He and a group of wealthy friends have a plane, a seaplane with floats. They want me to fly it in the Schneider Trophy Race next April in Monaco."

Francoise looked puzzled, as she wanted to know more.

"What is the Schneider Trophy darling?"

"My love," began Alain, "it is a new competition for aircraft that have floats and can land on water. Each competitor has to fly so many times round a course of some 30 kilometres, at low level and the plane making the fastest time, wins a big trophy."

Francoise patted her stomach; she was just beginning to show.

"You will be careful," she replied, "remember I have a future Clement in here."

Alain smiled and kissed her passionately.

"Of course my love, it is my life too."

In another house not far away Rudolph and Catherina were fast asleep, having already made love.

The next day Alain and Rudolph arrived at Gustav's office for it was time for the race post mortem. After a general discussion between Management and Drivers, the consensus of opinion was that everyone had done their job to the best of their ability, especially Alain who had won such a magnificent trophy. This was displayed on a side table. The new car had performed really well, and the 5.7 litre car was unlucky to have retired due to the fuel line being severed by a stone. Modifications would be made to stop this reoccurring. However, the big problem was tyres. Better braking, more power and better roadholding, the tyres had been wearing out at an alarming rate. This was due partly to the atrocious state of the French roads. They must somehow get better quality, harder wearing tyres. Gustav said he would speak to the Managing Director, and arrange a meeting with the tyre suppliers.

"Well done gentlemen," said Gustav closing the meeting, "we could not have asked more from you. That was one hell of a race."

The drivers went back to the routine of testing, testing, and more testing. The event at Brooklands they hoped would be more light-hearted, but even so they intended to give 100% effort.

Alain told Rudolph about the offer he had received from Le Strange to test fly the plane for the Schneider Trophy.

Rudolph thought for a moment.

"Alain," replied Rudolph, "if you want my advice, leave it alone. If you fly it, well let's say it could be a big mistake; I have a funny feeling about it. It could be a disaster and you could lose you life. You have a lovely wife and a future with Mercedes."

"I agree," answered Alain, "I'll send Le Strange a telegram." The telegram read:

LE STRANGE STOP SORRY UNABLE TO FLY YOUR AEROPLANE IN RACE STOP COMMITMENTS TOO GREAT WITH MERCEDES STOP WISH YOUR PILOT AND YOU GOOD LUCK STOP REGARDS ALAIN CLEMENT

At the time he sent that telegram Alain didn't know that it was one of the best decisions he had ever made in his life so far.

He then forgot about the affair until he read two weeks later in a French newspaper that Monsieur Le Strange and his friends had indeed tested a potential entry for the

Schneider Trophy Race. The machine was a small biplane designed and built in Dieppe; a new and powerful Anzani engine powered it. It had taken off and built up a speed of over 160kph, when the propeller fractured tore through wing struts, hit the pilot on the head and then crashed into the sea. The pilot did not survive. Alain knew that fate had taken a hand in his life. Alain showed Rudolph the article who read the report and turned to Alain.

"My friend, I knew you had made the right decision."

A few days later Rudolph told Alain that Catherina was expecting a baby. Alain was overjoyed at this news.

"Congratulations Rudolph," he said, "looks as if you and I will be Fathers together."

Rudolph was delighted to hear Alain's news.

"You too? That's wonderful," he answered, "when is the baby due Alain?"

"Around the 25th September Rudolph."

Then both of them exclaimed in unison.

"That must have been Christmas that caused that!"

They both laughed at their own joke.

The tests with the Hanseatic Tyre Company were still being carried out, with a variety of rubber compounds. The also tried a mixture of tread patterns, even tyres without treads, but they still kept coming back with the same problem. The tyres just wore out very quickly. Now they had the quick release wheels on all their racecars, it would mean that they would have to study tyre wear whenever the cars came in for refuelling. If necessary then they would have to be changed. The new tyres averaged about 200 miles before they were threadbare. Gustav thought well if that is the best we can do, we shall have to learn live with it. Now Brooklands had a good concrete surface that was smooth. So for the September event they went for smooth tyres, and hoped that it would not rain, they would take some treaded tyres as well just in case.

Francoise's pregnancy was proceeding well, apart from morning sickness.

"Darling Alain," said Francoise to Alain one morning, "I know that the Doctor has said the baby is due on the 25th September. The baby will come when it is ready. That is what making love to me for Christmas has done. Now to change the subject."

"Yes my love," replied Alain.

"Now I understand that the team are going to England to race at Brooklands in September on the 14th and 15th, this will be pretty close to the day when the baby might be born. This was not really what I wanted, as I might be giving birth when you are away in England. Can you see Gustav as he might have a suggestion to make?"

"That is a good idea darling," answered Alain, "Rudolph and I will see him this morning, for Catherina is pregnant too with the baby due about the same time as ours."

Alain and Rudolph at Francoise's suggestion decided to go and see their 'father confessor' as they called Gustav.

That morning they asked to see Gustav who called them into his office.

"Gentlemen," said Gustav, "please sit down and tell me what is on your mind?"

Alain and Rudolph explained their situation to Gustav.

"First of all my friends," began Gustav, "my congratulations on the forthcoming birth of your babies. Give my compliments to both of your lovely ladies. As it is likely that your wives might give birth around the same day, that is some 10 days after the Brooklands meeting. So may I put this suggestion to you? If Alain's parents will agree, to take your wives and young Manfred, a few days before we leave for England, and maybe they can stay with Alain's parents at Rouen. The journey will not be so tiring. However, if the babies are not born by the time you are ready to return, then go from Calais to Rouen and stay with your wives until your children are born and ready to travel home."

Alain and Rudolph were astounded at Gustav's wisdom.

"That is absolutely brilliant Gustav," remarked Alain, "we would be very happy with that providing that is both Catherina and Rudolph agree?"

"Look we need to make arrangements soon anyway," replied Gustav. "Rudolph would you please telephone Catherina and see if she will agree to this?"

Rudolph picked up the telephone and called Catherina and explained the plan. Rudolph put the receiver down.

"Well Rudolph," asked Gustav, "what did she say?"

"Gustav, Catherina thought it was a really great idea, and she will stay with Alain's parents."

Alain thought I have not asked my parents yet. So he phoned Pierre who said that they would be overjoyed to see the birth of their first grandchild and also the birth of another child to their son's best friend Rudolph.

So the plans were set in motion, and all they needed to do now was to get the cars ready for the event and shipped to England in time, and the preparation got underway.

The next few weeks were very hectic for the team, they wanted to put up a good show at Brooklands, and after all no doubt the Sunbeam team would be there. As the 'home' team they would be favourites to win the Grand Prize. The Sunbeam 3 car team were the only team to finishing the gruelling French Grand Prix earlier in the year to finish. Although they had not won the race, they had show excellent reliability claiming the team prize. Their tyres had lasted much better than the Mercedes team. In order to achieve success in future events Gustav knew this problem must be solved.

The rest of the summer seemed to just disappear. There was only the occasional weekend break when Rudolph, Catherina, Alain and Francoise were able to get away to an idyllic spot to relax and watch the world go by. Both ladies were now well and truly showing that they were pregnant. Young Manfred could not understand why his Mother had got a swelling in her stomach? She had the sensitive job of explaining what was happening. He was delighted that he might have a Brother or Sister soon, and was excited to be travelling to Rouen to meet Uncle Alain's family.

The day dawned for the start of the trip to Rouen, although it was a long trip, both Alain and Rudolph knew that their wives would be in good hands in the Clement farmhouse. When they eventually arrived at the Clement home, Pierre, Marie and Helene were thrilled to see them and welcomed them with open arms. Manfred soon made friends with Helene who insisted on showing him around the farm, and meeting all their animals including her pony. Alain and Rudolph made sure that Pierre, Marie and Helene would be able to contact them at their Hotel in Weybridge, if either Catherina or Francoise showed any signs of giving birth.

The next morning after a good night's sleep, Alain and Rudolph said goodbyes to their loved ones. Pierre drove them to Rouen Station where they caught the train to Dieppe. There they boarded the Boat Train to Calais, a short sea trip on the Channel Ferry and another train to Weybridge; finally they arrived at their Hotel. Gustav was already there, fussing around as usual. He told them that tomorrow, Friday 13th September 1912, the day before the event began they would be allowed to practice on the banked circuit. He hoped none of his drivers were superstitious. They all shook their heads. After all they were all professionals, no time for silly superstitions.

"Right then gentlemen," said Gustav, "you must be at the track at 8 am, sharp, we have work to do."

That night all the drivers tried to get a good night's sleep, however, Alain and Rudolph could not help thinking about their wives well and truly pregnant over there in the Clement farmhouse.

The next morning bright and early, after a hearty full English breakfast, this was the first time either Alain or Rudolph had attempted such a meal. It was certainly different from their usual fare. They got ready and at 7.30 that morning the official car called for them and whisked Alain, Rudolph, Hans and Gustav to the famous circuit. As they approached it, Rudolph recalled the last time he was here. He remembered meeting the King and Queen of England. King Edward VII had died some 3 years ago, and Rudolph wondered if he would meet the new monarch King George V and his lovely Queen Mary. The car pulled in through the gates of the circuit, where a security guard checked their passes. Alain and Hans looked in wonder at this marvellous circuit. The concrete surface was beautifully smooth, and in the centre was a large grassed area, parked around this were a number of small aircraft. Finally, they pulled up at their garage; Alain was amazed to see the difference between this and the garage they had occupied in Dieppe for the French Grand Prix. The three cars that had performed so well in Dieppe were here again to try to show the crowds, and the other competitors, why Mercedes were so good, and how they had won at the French Grand Prix. Now they looked pristine, all the dents and dust had been removed, and the engines stripped and parts renewed. The 5.7 litre Mercedes car driven by Hans was started up and driven out on to the circuit of almost 2.8 miles. He took it easy for the first lap, for he knew the reputation of the Byfleet Banking; Rudolph had already acquainted him with the technique required. After a few laps his confidence grew and soon he was lapping quickly in the region of 120 kph, and then drove into the garage.

"Rudolph my friend," remarked Hans, "this is a great circuit, such a lovely smooth surface after the French roads. Our decision to use smooth tyres seems to be the right one. We should do well today. Let's hope it does not rain."

Alain climbed aboard the 3-litre car, which started up with a throaty roar. Putting it into gear he left the garage to begin his first practice. He decided to take Rudolph's advice to take it easy; as more experienced local drivers who had been racing here regularly passed him. Alain wanted to get things correct before opening the throttle widely, for he knew he had the power and speed to pass all the other competitors quite easily. Soon, he was simply whizzing past those that had previous overtaken him; and was now matching the times that Hans had achieved. Last of the team to practice was

Rudolph, and even he took it easy to begin with. He used the same tactics as Alain and quickly got up to speed and put in a really fast lap at 145 kph. Gustav was delighted, as he watched his three drivers put in some really determined practice. Standing on a small balcony he watched the three car Sunbeam team practising, and they too were going very fast. All three Mercedes drivers came back to the pits to make few minor adjustments, before returning to the circuit for further practice.

Finally, all three drivers were happy with the morning's work, and spent time watching the rest of the entry hurtling around the historic circuit. Gustav had been to see the organisers and returned with the Programme. He was delighted to see that King George V and Queen Mary were going to be there, an officially start the event.

There would also be a display of flying from the Englishman Claude Graham-White in his biplane, Maurice Farman in a plane of his own design and Alliott Verdon Roe flying one of his triplanes.

In all a full day of excitement, according to the programme the racing would take place on both Saturday and Sunday afternoon, as the tickets for this event had been sold out for both days. After lunch, the Mercedes team watched the aviators having their practice. Alain and Rudolph, both being qualified pilots managed to talk to Mr. Graham-White and Mr.A.V.Roe.

The Englishmen were amazed that they had learned to fly. "Flying is the future," said Mr.A.V.Roe. Roe, "and we shall need many good men to be trained as professional flying instructors."

These words would mean more to Alain and Rudolph as the years rolled by.

That evening Alain and Rudolph telephoned their wives; they said that everything was going to plan, and not to worry.

"Rudolph," Catherina commented, "I am really enjoying all this wonderful French cooking. However, if I eat like this all the time my figure would be in the same shape as it is now all the time. Alain's parents are wonderful cooks and such sumptuous food. I must get some recipes from them."

Rudolph laughed when he heard this, for he knew how hospitable Pierre and Marie could be. He put the phone down and felt relieved, that both ladies were fit and well, despite their condition. They could now concentrate on the racing, and get a good night's sleep.

Very early next day they were all back at the circuit, and even at 7 am, the crowds had started to arrive. They wanted to get a good spot to watch the day's events.

All competitors were being allowed a one-hour practice session before 9.00 a.m, and then the circuit would close. At 11.00 a.m, the Royal Party would arrive and meet both drivers and aviators. At midday the flying would begin and last for an hour and a half. Then lunch until 2.30 pm. When the racing would commence. It was going to be a tight schedule. The trio of Mercedes drivers went out and did a few laps passing many of the variety of cars entered for different races during the afternoon session. Alain reckoned it was like trying to drive through Paris, but at least all the traffic was going in the same direction.

At 10.45, the Royal Party drove the gates and made their way to the VIP enclosure, and on the dot of 11.00 King George V in his Admiral of the Fleet uniform, together with Queen Mary in her favourite blue dress, greeted the drivers and aviators.

When it was Rudolph's turn he bowed and then shook hands with the King.

"Good morning Herr von Lundenberg," said the Monarch, "it is a pleasure to see you, I remember you racing here in 1907. I was just the Prince in the Royal Party."

"Your Majesty has an excellent memory," answered Rudolph, "I did race here in 1907, at the first meeting. I had the honour to meet the late King Edward and his most lovely Queen Alexandra. May I say that it is a great honour to meet you and your beautiful Queen? I do hope that you will enjoy the day and that I may have the pleasure of meeting you again."

"Sir, may I wish you good luck here today," the King replied, "the Queen and I are really looking forward to an exciting time here at Brooklands. I do hope that we shall meet again."

Thank you your Majesty," replied Rudolph.

The Royal Couple moved on to shake hands and say a few words to both Alain and Hans. They were thrilled, for neither of them had ever been this close to Royalty, let alone spoken to them. The day's events finally got underway, as the King and Queen of England officially started the event, and the aviators took to the air in their frail machines. They gave a wonderful display of flying, swooping low over the huge crowd that he packed into the circuit.

Alain and Rudolph watched as the tiny aeroplanes danced like mayflies in the bright blue cloudless sky. Soon the time had come for lunch, after which, it was the turn of the racing cars to thrill the crowd. In the VIP enclosure was Lord John and Victoria Ashdown together with their son Nigel, who had been given special weekend leave to attend this prestigious meeting. Lord John and Victoria, were delighted to meet Rudolph once again, and asked after Catherina.

"I am sorry Lord John," answered Rudolph, "that neither Catherina nor Francoise could be here this weekend, as they are both expecting babies."

"That is wonderful," replied Victoria with a smile, "I do hope that the births will not be too painful for those lovely ladies. I am certain that you and Alain are very excited?"

"We certainly are Lady Victoria," answered Rudolph.

"Rudolph," said Lord John, "I wonder if you remember my son Nigel? He sat in your car when you were here back in 1907."

Rudolph shook Nigel by the hand.

"Goodness me Nigel," replied Rudolph, "I do remember you. You certainly have grown into a very handsome young man. When I met you five years ago, you wanted to be a racing driver I think? What are your plans now?"

Nigel thought for a moment.

"Well sir," answered Nigel confidently, "I am still studying hard at Christ's Hospital School at Horsham in Sussex. I am hoping to go to Oxford University next year. I want to study Engineering and Foreign Languages, particular French and German. One day I want to be a racing driver like you, but at the moment I am concentrating on my studies."

"That is excellent Nigel, I have told my young son Manfred that he must get a good education, without that you will not get anywhere in life. However, I am impolite, you remember my best friend, Alain Clement. May I introduce him to you?"

Nigel shook Alain's hand.

"Nigel," said Alain, "it is a pleasure to meet you at last. I met your father at the French Grand Prix. Did he tell you about it?

"Yes," answered Nigel, "he told me it was a gruelling race, and how well both you and Rudolph had performed. I also read the race report. My congratulations. I hope that you do well today."

"Thank you Nigel," replied Alain, "I hope you enjoy your day too. This Brooklands is a superb circuit."

Then with their conversations over Nigel and John made their way to the VIP refreshment tent for lunch.

The first event was for amateur drivers; this was seen by many as the spawning ground for those who aspired to drive cars such as The Sunbeam, Napier and Mercedes. It was a close run race over some 20 laps of the Brooklands circuit. Robert Sawyer in a Napier won it; he had lapped at almost 70 mph. Then it was the turn of the professionals; there were some formidable opponents in the shape of Selwyn Edge in his Napier, and the Sunbeam team to name but a few. Gustav and his team of mechanics had done all they could to prepare the cars to ensure victory.

The trio of white cars were started up and made their way to the start line. They would do one parade lap before returning to take up their positions. Now that all the entrants were back in position, the starter with his Union Jack mounted the rostrum. The noise from the cars was now deafening as the engine revolutions mounted. Then with a flourish, the starter dropped the flag and the cars hurtled towards the first gentle bend and then on to the daunting Byfleet Banking. Lord John, Lady Victoria and Nigel had a perfect view of the circuit as they watched the cars streak away and head the dangerous banked section. It was clear that the Mercedes team had done their homework for already the occupied the first three places, with Rudolph leading.

The pack of cars following were in hot pursuit as they left the banking and came on to the Railway Straight, and at the end of which was a sharp right hand corner that brought them back past the start and finish line. By lap three the pace was hotting up even more, with Alain now just a few yards behind Rudolph who was going like the proverbial 'bat out of hell'. By lap 6, several of the lesser names had fallen by the wayside. Lord John told Nigel it would a close thing between the Napier, the three Sunbeams and of course the Mercedes boys. Rudolph with Alain reeled off the laps in clockwork regularity with Alain in Rudolph's slipstream. Alain hoped on the final lap to pip his friend at the post. Hans was holding a solid third place, whilst the Napier had now been passed by one of the Sunbeams. On the last lap, Alain made one last final effort and they crossed the line virtually side by side with Rudolph only inches ahead it seemed.

His Majesty the King presented the Trophy, congratulating both Rudolph and Alain for their display of courage and speed.

Lord John and Victoria invited the whole Mercedes team back to Ashdown Hall. Alain and Rudolph asked John if they could telephone the Clement home in Rouen to speak to their wives? John said of course they could. Francoise and Catherina told their husbands that they were no fathers yet. Victoria asked if the babies were born? Alain and Rudolph said they had not. John declared the merriment should begin and this continued well into the night. They decided that rather than return to their Hotel, they would stay the night at the Hall, then return to the circuit in the morning for day two. The only difference between the Saturday programme and the Sunday one was that there was no Royal Party present. The Main Event this time was won by Alain, with Rudolph in second place. In all it had been a very successful weekend for Mercedes. Now both Alain and Rudolph said goodbye to Lord John and Victoria thanking them for their great hospitality, and hoped that they would meet again soon.

"I hope Alain," said Lord John, "to come to France again soon, probably before Christmas to see Count Guy about a new contract for wine. I would be honoured if I may call on your parents. I really enjoyed meeting them all too briefly at Dieppe."

"My parents Lord John," replied Alain, "would be very pleased for you to call on them, and you can enjoy some real French hospitality. May I also say what a pleasure it has been to meet you again sir?"

Alain then shook Lord John's hand as they finally parted.

Later that afternoon, having packed their suitcases, Alain and Rudolph caught the London train from Weybridge Station, then the Boat Train, and by late evening they were at the Clement farmhouse. They received a rapturous welcome from the Clement family, and their wives. Francoise was particularly concerned about her pregnancy, as this was her first child. On the other hand Catherina was more confident that all would be well with her. The Doctor had been called several times to monitor the progress of the unborn children. Now the husbands had arrived the ladies felt more confident. Gustav had told them before they left England do not return to Germany until the ladies and the babies are fit to travel.

The days passed and the waiting seemed endless, then in the early morning of September 21st, Francoise went into labour and the Doctor and Midwife were called. After a further 6 hours, Francoise gave birth to a dark haired baby boy; they called him Jean Alain after his great-grandfather. Then 4 hours after Jean was born, Catherina went into labour, and 7 hours later she gave birth to a blonde baby girl, they named her Henrietta Marie.

There was now great joy in the Clement household, for Pierre and Marie had a grandson, and Manfred had a baby sister. They contacted Gustav who was thrilled that both babies were healthy. Later Alain and Rudolph would ask him to be Godfather to their children.

Before leaving for Germany, Helene showed Alain a letter she had received, telling her that she had been chosen for the French Equestrian team to take part in an International Show Jumping Event in Frankfurt. She asked if would Alain be able to support her.

"Helene," replied Alain, "I do not see why not. Of course I will come to cheer you on to victory I hope."

They were all sorry to leave Rouen and the Clement family, who had been so good to them before and after the birth of their children. They said that they would see them again soon. The taxi arrived, and they said their goodbyes. All too soon they were on the train back to Germany. It was along tiring journey, and the new babies certainly kept them busy.

When they arrived back home there were nappies to change and it was a little while before Francoise finally settled down to Motherhood. Alain and Rudolph did their share with the new babies. All the parents spending many sleepless nights.

On October 9th, Gustav got a telegram from Ralph de Palma, which read: - *GUSTAV. RACED IN AMERCIAN GRAND PRIX AT SAVANNAH GEORGIA STOP MANAGED 51 OF 52 LAPS HAD ACCIDENT STOP FINISHED 5TH CAR A BIT BENT STOP NO PERSONAL INJURIES STOP BEST REGARDS RALPH*

Gustav was sorry that they had not won, but at least the car performed well, for the accident seemed to be Driver error. They now had to look to the future, whatever it held for them.

The Story continues in the next book – The Learning Curves

Printed in the United Kingdom
by Lightning Source UK Ltd.
134175UK00001BA/154-159/A